OLD BOYS

CHARLES MCCARRY

OLD
BOYS

THE OVERLOOK PRESS
Woodstock & New York

First published in the United States in 2004 by
The Overlook Press, Peter Mayer Publishers, Inc.
Woodstock & New York

WOODSTOCK:
One Overlook Drive
Woodstock, NY 12498
www.overlookpress.com
[for individual orders, bulk and special sales, contact our Woodstock office]

NEW YORK:
141 Wooster Street
New York, NY 10012

∞ The paper used in this book meets the requirements for paper
permanence as described in the ANSI Z39.48-1992 standard.

Cataloging-in-Publication Data is available from the Library of Congress

Type formatting by Bernard Schleifer Company
Manufactured in the United States of America
FIRST EDITION
ISBN 1-58567-545-8
3 5 7 9 8 6 4 2

For E. F. L. and N. C. S.

PROLOGUE

On the night that Paul Christopher vanished, he and I dined together at his house on O Street: cold watercress soup, very rare cold roast beef, undercooked asparagus, pears and cheese, a respectable bottle of Oregonian pinot noir. It was a fine evening in May. The windows were open. We smelled azaleas in the garden and saw reflected in mirrors and window glass the last bruised colors of the sunset. There was nothing special about the occasion. Paul and I are cousins who lived around the corner from each other, and before he went away we used to join up for dinner a couple of times a month. My name is Horace Christopher Hubbard. His middle name is Hubbard.

The dinner was the usual one: small portions, small noises of cutlery on china, small talk. Paul's stomach had been shrunk by the decade he spent in a Chinese prison, and his appetite for deep conversation, never large, was extinguished altogether by Maoist interrogators. This reluctance to waste words drove away his much younger second wife, a woman who never found a bone she did not want to worry. He lived alone now, visited from time to time by his two daughters, whom he loved, and a few friends who were not interested in asking questions. Paul is fifteen years older than me—too large a difference to make equality possible. Since childhood I have admired him greatly—his intelligence, his courage, his adeptness above all; seldom a wrong move or word from Paul. As a youngster I tried to be like him in as many ways as possible.

Of course this was hopeless. Nevertheless, there are many connections besides blood between us. We both served for many years in the Outfit, as we Old Boys call the U.S. intelligence service, never among ourselves referring to it by the three vulgar initials employed by headline writers and other outsiders. I doubt that I would have become a spy if Paul had not led the way. And unless you count a remote ancestor who was captured by the Mohawk Indians, Paul and I are the only members of our families to have gone to jail—even though he was innocent of the charges the Chinese laid against him, whereas I was as guilty as sin. I broke not only the law but also all the rules by confessing, as a witness in a presidential impeachment trial in the United States Senate, that I had used a supercomputer belonging to the Outfit to steal a presidential election. After pleading guilty I was sentenced to five years behind bars and served every day of my term in a federal prison for gentlemen in Pennsylvania. I was deprived by the court of my government pension, frog-marched through the media, and taken to the cleaners by lawyers—just deserts in all cases. I was able to pay the legal bills because Paul loaned me the money. He visited me in prison twice a month, bringing books, magazines, and gourmet snacks from fancy grocers. Underneath all that self-control, Paul is a bit of a sybarite.

The Paul Christopher who disappeared was in his seventies but still in excellent condition—not a gray hair in his dark blond thatch, not an extra pound on his body. He looked not at all like my side of the family, but like pictures of his mother. She looked like someone Dürer would have drawn. Paul had always been good at games and he still looked and in fact was athletic, playing tennis with younger opponents, running every morning in the park, and in summer digging and then refilling ditches in the stony soil of the family's summer place in Massachusetts. In China, as part of the hard labor to which he had been sentenced, he had single-handedly dug a perfectly straight ditch several miles long in the flinty earth near his prison. It has since been covered over, but if you know what to look for you can see it in old spy satellite photos. I suppose he developed a liking for this kind of solitary hard labor, or a need to be reminded of it. His mind remained as it had always been, contemplative yet swirling with neatly filed arcane facts, haunted by memories that I myself could not have borne, and against all odds, utterly sane.

It was dark by the time we finished our meal. As the light failed the many pictures in the long room suddenly were illuminated by little frame lights switched on by automatic timers. In Paul's paintings, mostly inherited and mostly romantic, honeyed shafts of sunlight fell through windows, revealing a beautiful face or a perfect pear or some other trick of pigment—images the two of us had known all our lives. In an Edward Hicks painting I had never liked, vacant-eyed cows and sheep grazed among lamblike wolves and lions in the Peaceable Kingdom. Though not present in these pictures, our childhood also became in some way present: spectral cats of my boyhood, long ago gone to cat heaven, curled up beneath the paintings on sofas and chairs. Ghostly old dogs snored on old familiar rugs.

Finishing the wine, sitting in the dark surrounded by these pools of light and color, Paul and I talked for a while about the Christophers and the Hubbards, who have married one another for generations, sowing confusion at baptisms. Paul's father and mine, born on the same day of boy-girl Christopher twins who married Hubbards, looked so much alike—tall bony horse-faced men like me—that strangers mistook *them* for twins even though one was dark and the other blond.

Around nine o'clock we ran out of things to say. Paul suggested that he walk me home. This was unusual; I supposed he had some errand to run after dropping me off, a bottle of milk, a newspaper. On the front steps, after twisting the key in the lock, he handed it to me. "New key," he said. New alarm code, too." He told me the code, a familiar name easy to remember, easy to enter on the alphanumeric pad. "Got it?"

"Yes."

Paul nodded, as if something important had been settled. We

walked on narrow frost-heaved pavement through quiet streets, sniffed by small dogs whose leashes were held by lofty government servants and two-hundred-dollar-an-hour lawyers. It was a Friday night. Once or twice we were crowded off the sidewalk by half-naked, lovely teenage girls from the suburbs who had driven into the city to make the Georgetown scene.

In front of my house, a very small wooden one, Paul said, "Horace, I have a favor to ask."

He spoke in an unusually strong voice. I was apprehensive. First the key and the alarm code. Now this.

I said, "Go on."

"I want you to be the executor of my will."

I felt a certain relief. "Gladly," I said. "But I'm a convicted felon."

"That makes no difference; I've checked. I've already paid Stephanie her share and set up trusts for Zarah and Lori. All that's left is remnants from the past. Things the girls shouldn't be bothered with."

"All right. What are your instructions?"

"I've put them in writing," Paul replied. "You'll find a notarized letter addressed to yourself and my will in a safe under the desk in my study." He smiled."You'll have to use all your old secret powers to find the safe. It's hidden."

"I don't doubt it. And to open it?"

He handed me half a notebook page with the combination written across the top in his spidery foreign handwriting, learned as a child in German schools.

"Do you expect I may have to open the safe any time soon?" I asked.

Paul said,"I'm healthy as a horse. The combination is a date."

I looked. So it was—a year from tomorrow.

"Open it on that day." Paul said, "or before, if circumstances seem to warrant it."

"What circumstances?"

"You'll know, Cousin," said Paul. He shook my hand, gave a little salute that turned into a wave, and walked away.

Dramatic gestures were not Paul Christopher's style. His behavior worried me. What on earth was he up to? I knew that it was impossible to follow Paul without being detected, so I went inside my house, switched on the television set, and sat down in the dark to watch *Key Largo*. Half an hour later, about the time Lauren Bacall spits in Edward G. Robinson's face, I left by the back door, got into my car, and working to strict rules of tradecraft as I might have done in Beijing thirty years before, drove by a circuitous route to Paul's house.

There was no more light inside the house than there had been when I left, but through the window I could see that Paul was talking to a slender black man, not an American. They were standing. The man was very tall, he towered over Paul, with a handsome Arab face and a beautifully barbered white beard. The suit he wore fit his whiplike body perfectly, and could only have been cut in London.

The man inside handed Paul a large yellow envelope. Paul opened it and withdrew a piece of paper. No, a photograph. I focused the glasses. I thought I saw a face in the photograph. No, a hand. Holding something. A book? A letter?

Inside, Paul carried the photograph to one of the picture lamps and studied it for a long moment. He looked away, studied it again. And when he lifted his impassive face it seemed to me, impossible though such a thing might be, that tears glistened in his eyes.

A trick of the light and the mind, I thought. What right had I to see him so? I went away. When I came back in the morning, Paul was gone, like the cats that were no more.

ONE

1

Just before Thanksgiving, Paul Christopher's ashes were delivered by a Chinese official to the American consulate in Beijing. According to the Chinese, Christopher had died a few weeks before in Ulugqat, a remote mountain village near the border with Tajikistan and Afghanistan in the extreme northwest corner of the Xinjiang Uygur Autonomous Region. No information about the circumstances or cause of Christopher's death was provided. Evidently the Chinese regarded Christopher's age, as recorded on his passport, as reason enough for his demise. Not that they returned his passport or any personal effects. Regrettably, all these items had been burned along with his corpse at the people's crematorium in Ürümqui, a large city not far from Ulugqat.

This news came to me by telephone. The caller, an old China hand named David Wong, half Chinese, half Ashkenazi, just happened to be in Beijing with a satellite phone at his disposal. I did not ask him the source of his information; David knew all the right people in China. He was a walking history of U.S. covert action in East Asia, a fomenter of revolutions and uprisings. He had worked for me when I was chief of station in what was then called Peking. Now he eked out his Outfit pension as a consultant to American corporations doing business in the new China. He looked, gestured, and sounded like a full-blooded Han in Mandarin,

Cantonese and several tribal dialects, but resembled Groucho
Marx when speaking English.

In Grouchoesque tones, he apologized for being the bearer of
sad tidings.

"No apology necessary," I said."I'm grateful. Just ashes, you
say?"

"That's right," he said. "In a nice red-and-gilt urn."

"Any idea what Paul was doing in Xinjiang?"

"No. The country around Ulugqat is still a forbidden zone."

It is a forbidden zone because it contains forced labor camps
for enemies of the regime, mostly intellectuals who, because of
their education and exceptional intelligence, are useful as workers
in prison factories producing high-quality goods for export to the
United States. And because it is not far from the places where
China manufactures and tests nuclear warheads and missiles.

"And then," David said, "there's the curious fact that Christopher
served his time in a prison not far from Ulugqat."

"Did the Chinese delivery boys seem aware of that?"

"Not just aware. Fascinated. As I understand it, they suggested
to our people that it explains everything. Nostalgic American,
grateful to his wise captors, revisits scene of his self-discovery and
redemption."

"They actually said that?"

"Yes. They think, or say they do, that Christopher found peace
and laid him down to sleep in the great Chinese desert, which raises
a question: Why didn't they bury him in his chosen soil instead
of cremating him and shipping what purport to be his ashes to
Washington?"

Interesting thought, David Wong's specialty. In the heyday of
Maoism, Christopher had been held prisoner in an abandoned
Buddhist temple in the middle of a bleak desert—waterless, fea-
tureless, unpeopled. He was the only inmate. His sentence
expressed a certain Maoist-Confucian ingenuity: "Death with ten
years' observation of the results." This meant that Paul could have
been executed at any moment if he was deemed to lack remorse

for his counterrevolutionary crimes. Or, just as capriciously, could have had his sentence commuted if he showed the right spirit and confessed. At a press conference, of course.

Because he actually was innocent of spying on China (almost alone of all the countries in the Communist world), Paul refused to confess to the crime of espionage. He was interrogated for ten years, himself on his knees on a stone floor, his interrogator asking the same maddeningly stupid questions day after day after day. In the end, after being furnished by sources I shall not name with certain incentives to release him, his interrogators believed him. Or said they did, which was quite enough. They let him go—into my custody because I was then posted to Beijing. Immediately thereafter the Chinese intelligence service noticed a warmer and more fraternal attitude on the part of the Outfit. They received bushels of intercepts of communications of the Soviet high command among other goodies, such as a shipment of not-quite-American tanks, along with not exactly American advisers who told them how to deploy those tanks to kill the latest Russian armor.

2

I don't know how they do it nowadays, but during the Cold War the Outfit evaluated intelligence reports as follows: A, B, C, D for the reliability of the source and 1, 2, 3, 4 for the accuracy of the information. A-1 meant that the source was unimpeachable and the information unquestionably true, while D-4 indicated that the source was totally unreliable and the information demonstrably false. Every day, a hive of analysts graded the homework of thousands of sources by comparing raw reports from the field with every other report in the files, plus scholarly knowledge, in order to guess its value. In my long career I never saw an A-1 and only a handful of D-4s. In nine out of ten cases, the designation was C-3, source usually reliable, information possibly true. Logically, this meant that the usually reliable source was sometimes unreliable and that the information described as possibly true could just as possibly be false. It follows that U.S. intelligence spent hundreds of billions of dollars over a period of forty years ferreting out vital information that we did not, as a matter of principle, choose to believe—or for that matter, disbelieve.

Every morning bright and early, we delivered this iffy data to the president of the United States in the form of the Daily Intelligence Briefing. It was up to him to decide for himself what might be true and what might not be, and on occasion, whether to blow up the world on a hunch. No president ever chose to do that, so I guess you could argue that the perverse ambiguity of the system saved civilization by making certitude impossible for the most powerful man in the world.

To David Wong's report on Paul's ashes I assigned a B-3: source reliable, information possibly true. But just as possibly false. Ashes had certainly been delivered, but were they Paul's? I had received bad news about my cousin many times before, but he had always turned up alive in the end. I am told that I cried bitterly when told, as a child, that he had been wounded on Okinawa, but a few months later he came home in his Marine Corps uniform and gave me a captured Japanese pistol (firing pin removed) as a present. A quarter of a century later, I was the first person in the Saigon station to receive the news that he had been kidnapped into China. As we know, he survived that. The list is long, and the point is that Paul always survived, more or less unchanged physically though always quieter, as if his melancholy fate was gradually turning him to stone.

This time, during the months he had been gone, I naturally assumed that he would come back. One afternoon, the telephone would ring and I would hear his murmuring voice inviting me to dinner, as if there had been no interruption of our habit of dining together once a fortnight. The problem now was to establish whether Paul Christopher was or was not a dry quart of ashes inside a gaudy Chinese urn and, far more difficult than that, to accept that this Prince Valiant of my childhood had at last encountered an ordeal he could not survive. Above all, if I wanted peace of mind, David Wong's report meant that I had to figure out what Paul had been up to. Whatever drove him to Ulugqat must have been a matter of great significance, at least in his own mind—something he felt he absolutely had to do, had to know, had to find in order to make sense of existence.

Now there was a thought: Paul seated on some dusty rock in the barrens of Xinjiang, waiting for his ancient soul to escape from a body that had served its purpose. In my prosaic way, I had hoped that he would die with a book in his lap, seated in a leather chair after a light dinner and the aftertaste of, say, a 1973 Château Pétrus lingering on his palate. No last words, no explanations. Everything complete and at peace, picturesque and tidy. I imagined for him a gentle, well-earned and entirely harmonious end to a tumultuous life. And if despite his very strong doubts on the question, there happened to be a heaven, he would be greeted when he opened his eyes by the smiling, ever-young love of his life. Her name was Molly.

As this picture formed in my mind, ten minutes or so after my talk with David, I smiled at Paul in this vision of eternal happiness. And then suddenly I found myself weeping. Such a thing had not happened to me for a long time, apart from sentimental tears shed in a movie house. My emotional shadow, a creature that usually follows tamely behind me, picked me up without warning and shook me—shook a sob out of me, then another. I was astonished, even a little angry. I had been taught from earliest life to keep emotion at bay. As a child, after a tantrum, my father sat me down and played me a game of rummy. He let me win, then said, "Think of feelings as cards, Horace. They're nothing on their own. It's how you play them that makes a fellow happy, wealthy, and wise—putting the ones that are alike together, making runs of consecutive numbers, discarding the ones that are no good to you and keeping the ones that are."

Although, as the Old Man had suggested, life turned out to be a lot like rummy, I had never been dealt a hand of cards quite like this one. Paul, dead or alive, had left unanswered a question on which he had bet his life.

But what was the question? And why did I feel that I had inherited Paul's quest? I didn't want the cursed thing.

3

In darkness, by sense of touch, I put the key that Paul had given me into the front-door lock of the house on O Street. It didn't fit. Someone had changed the lock. I briefly considered picking it, then reflected that the alarm code probably had been changed as well. Breaking and entering in the nighttime was an unwise course of action for an ex-con when the only person who would go to the trouble of getting him out of jail, Paul Christopher, was either dead or otherwise unreachable by telephone.

It was about five o'clock on a brisk fall morning, a lovely time of day and year. The city, projecting misty streetlight onto low cloud cover, was all but silent. Up and down the block, a few bedroom windows showed yellow lamplight—workaholics getting an early start for the office. Out of the corner of my eye I caught an incandescent flash and saw that a light had come on upstairs in Paul's house—not the master bedroom but a smaller bedroom across the hall. I knew the floor plan well, having lived in the house during one of Paul's protracted absences. I walked around the block to kill time. When I came back the kitchen light was on. I rang the bell.

The doorbell is not a sound one expects to hear in the hour before dawn, but as soon as it chimed footsteps approached, quick and confident. The light above the door came on. Paul's house was equipped with surveillance cameras installed by myself. I was dressed like a ninja in navy blue sweats and sneakers and a watch cap. I took off the cap, scrooched down, and looked directly at the tiny lens imbedded in the door knocker. A brief pause, then the click of deadbolts. The door opened a crack, chain lock still in place.

"Horace?"

It was Paul's ex-wife Stephanie, also dressed in running clothes, battered Nikes on her small feet, a cell phone in her hand, her thumb on the SEND button, 911 already dialed, no doubt. Stephanie was a well-organized woman.

She said nothing. Stephanie had never liked me; I was too close to Paul, knew too many things about him that she imagined she had not been told. But she let me in, after first stepping out to look up and down the street to make sure I hadn't brought along a squad of street people. She wore a faded red varsity baseball cap, vintage 1950, embroidered with the Harvard *H*, an odd affectation in this day and age for someone who had actually gone to Harvard (Ph.D. in psychology). It was a man's cap, one of Paul's no doubt (he played second base in college), too large for her small round head, the beak too long for her face. She had made it smaller with a safety pin at the back.

Neither smiling nor cold, she looked me full in the face. Stephanie was not a pretty woman, but she was an interesting one, determinedly unfeminine for political reasons in manner, dress and conviction, but intensely female just the same.

"I gather you've heard the news," she said.

"I've heard what they're saying in Beijing."

"And?" Stephanie was looking at me as if I were a Jehovah's Witness who had knocked on her door at the crack of dawn— harmless, perhaps, but having nothing sensible to say and far from welcome.

I said, "I find it troubling."

"Troubling in what sense?"

"I'm not sure I believe he's dead."

"So you came over to commune with the family spirits by the light of the moon?"

"No, I came over to open Paul's safe and get whatever he left in it addressed to me."

"His *safe?*" Stephanie said, genuinely surprised. "Paul doesn't have a safe."

"Then he misinformed me."

"Paul told you he had a safe?" Her tone suggested that I must be lying. She continued to stare, expressionless, annoyed by my every word but in perfect control. "Why come at this hour?"

What to say at this stage of the conversation that would not lead to misunderstanding, quite possibly to the end of what was left of our brittle friendship? With a kidder's grin I said, "Frankly, Stephanie, I came at this hour because I hoped to avoid bumping into you."

She did not see the joke, or refused to see it. "Why?" she said. "I don't live here. How did you plan to get in?"

"Paul gave me a key. It didn't fit."

"No, I changed the locks. One of the paintings was missing and I didn't know if Paul had taken it with him or what."

"Which painting?"

"The Hicks. The one with the dopey cows."

Not a picture that would be missed, I thought, though it must be worth a lot of money.

"I heard you fiddling with the key," Stephanie said. "That's why I got up. . . ."

Her voice broke slightly—a tightening of the throat, nothing so spontaneous as a sob. But something changed in her eyes; she looked away. Had she thought, climbing out of sleep, that it was Paul at the door?

She said, "This really is something Paul asked you to do?"

I said, "Yes, Stephanie, it is. I have no idea why."

"I do," she said. "He trusted you." She was holding herself together with what was becoming visible effort. Her next words, unspoken, could be read in her eyes, in her lip that quivered ever so slightly: Why did he trust *you?* Why not me?

Gathering herself, Stephanie said, "How much time do you need?"

"I don't know. I have to find the safe first."

"Do what?" she said.

I said, "Find the safe. Paul just gave me just a general idea of its whereabouts. You really don't know where it is?"

Her hand was on the latch. She said, "No, I don't. I didn't even know it existed."

"He was quite specific."

Now there were tears in her eyes. I had put them there and, male that I am, I felt a twinge of guilt.

Stephanie said, "Make yourself at home." She shook her head, wiped her tears with the back of her hand. "Who but Paul could hide a safe from his wife in a house where they lived together for fifteen years?"

Who indeed?

Recovered, Stephanie said, "I'm going running. After that I'll go home and get dressed and go to the office. Do what you have to do, but please be out of here by evening. I want to sleep here again tonight, God knows why."

I thought I knew why, but for once I held my tongue.

4

Apart from the film of dust that had accumulated during his absence, Paul's office was in apple-pie order. He was tidy by nature. The furnishings were spartan: an antique leather-top writing table with sturdy legs that he used as a desk, a rolling chair, bookshelves with volumes arranged in alphabetical order according to author and subject, an unlocked cabinet containing his correspondence (meager) and the manuscripts of many poems. As a young man Paul had published a couple of books of verse, and it looked as though he had continued to write poetry. I read a few lines of the unpublished stuff and thought it slow and far too sad. His early poems had been melancholy, too, but with a lilt, something like *A Shropshire Lad*. All this was not much, taken as the record of a lifetime. Had I been searching an enemy's house I would have suspected that the suspect had left these harmless documents out in the open as bait while hiding the incriminating stuff somewhere else. But this was Paul, who knew that there was no such thing as a safe hidey-hole, so what I found was probably all there was.

He had said that the safe was under his desk. I sat down in the chair and, rolling myself around the desk very slowly, examined the floor from every angle. It seemed to be nothing but what it was, a well-waxed oak parquet, very likely the original nineteenth-century flooring, with a black geometric inlay, somewhat warped by time and usage. I saw no sign of new boards or inlay or variation in color, but of course there would be none if the secret compartment had been properly installed. I got down on hands and knees and felt the floor, inch by square inch, with my hands and fingertips, searching for irregularities in the surface or differences in tension. Wood, even oak nailed to floor beams, is flexible because, between beams, it is a bridge over empty space. A steel floor safe placed under the flooring between two beams will create a numb space that the fingers will feel, like a kneecap at the end of a pliant thigh.

No luck. The art of searching is as ancient as the impulse to conceal and like any other art, it has its rules. The first of these is that an object can be hidden in a limited number of places, all of them obvious. Inside a book or between two books, under the rug or the mattress, between a picture or a mirror and its backing, in a plant or buried in the backyard, taped to the back of a drawer or in a secret compartment, in the refrigerator, in the garbage, in milady's intimate effects, even in plain sight. Finding what you are looking for is usually a simple matter of looking in the places where such things have been hidden since the dawn of time, or at least since the invention of furniture. But not always. One of my old Outfit teams found a strip of microfilm inside a turd floating in a toilet bowl; they extracted the film with tweezers, copied it, and put it back where they had found it.

By now the morning had advanced to the point where I could feel the sun on my legs. I felt sleepy; reluctance has that effect on me, always has had, and I was reluctant to find whatever Paul had left for me. Paul had never before asked me for a favor. Now that he had done so, how could doing it be anything but the first step toward some far larger obligation and who knew what beyond that? I rolled over onto my back. My mood darkening by the moment, I stared upward at the bottom of Paul's writing table. It was a partner's desk, with four large drawers, two in front and two in back. It exuded the faint sour smell of very old, unpainted wood. I tapped a table leg and heard solid mahogany, tapped another and heard the same, then tapped the third and heard and felt metal beneath the surface.

I cleared the desk top and turned the table over onto a rug. The leg in question unscrewed quite easily. I turned it upside down and a heavy-gauge steel cylinder about twice the diameter of a standard mailing tube slid out. At one end of the tube was a safe dial. I entered the combination that Paul had provided and the cap came off.

Inside the cylinder I found Paul's handwritten will, a letter addressed to me, a photograph of a woman's hand holding a holograph manuscript written in an alphabet I did not even try to read, and the Hicks painting, dismounted from its frame and stretcher and rolled into a tight sausage.

5

Dear Horace,

It's a temptation to begin this letter, "If you are reading this . . ." But the reason you hold it in your hands will be obvious. I am either dead or have failed to do what I set out to do a year ago. I want to make it clear that I am not asking you to finish what I started, and that you are under no obligation of blood, friendship, or previous employment to do anything that you do not wish to do. However, as you will see, you are an interested party.

These seem to be the facts:

1. Your old friend Ibn Awad, whose assassination you thought you had arranged ten years ago, is alive.

2. It is possible that my mother, who would now be ninety-four years old, is also still alive and may have in her possession a first-century manuscript, written in classical Greek, that is coveted by Ibn Awad. The manuscript is said to be the report of a Roman official sent on a secret mission to Judea around the time of the Crucifixion to investigate a Roman covert action operation that went wrong. Apparently this failed operation bears a close resemblance to certain events described in the New Testament. The report could therefore be interpreted as evidence that Jesus Christ was an unwitting asset of Roman intelligence. And that, of course, is what interests Ibn Awad. If the manuscript is authentic,

he can argue (and might sincerely believe) that Christianity is a false religion.

3. Awad has obtained and concealed—no one knows exactly where—at least twelve compact nuclear warheads of the type designed by the Soviets to be backpacked into combat by their special forces. These are said to be one- or two-kiloton fission devices. You will find attached a document that is said to be a photocopy of the report of an official Russian investigation into their disappearance.

I was made aware of these matters by a man named Kalash el Khatar, a Sudanese I knew in Geneva in the fifties. We had not seen or heard from each other in forty years until he came to see me in Washington last May. You may know about Kalash from your days in the Middle East. He's a descendant of Muhammad, and is the hereditary ruler and religious leader of a sect of Muslims in Sudan. He is Ibn Awad's first cousin. The latter, of course, is also a descendant of the Prophet. Like nearly everybody else on earth, Kalash had believed his cousin to be dead. But then, at the wedding of one of Kalash's grandsons to a member of Awad's family, he saw Ibn Awad himself.

"He was being pushed in a wheelchair by one huge beetling thug while others stood guard in a ring around him, so it was very difficult to catch a glimpse," Kalash said. "Nevertheless, because I was taller than the thugs, I saw at once that it was him."

Kalash being Kalash, he simply walked over to the wheelchair, brushed aside the bodyguards, and greeted his cousin.

"He may have got the impression from my greeting that I had always known that he was alive, but whatever he thought, he was delighted to see me," Kalash said. "We were chums when we were boys because I got him Somali girls when he came to visit and could find my way in the desert. I taught him the stars."

That evening the two cousins had a long chat. Ibn Awad told Kalash that he had survived the attack on his life, though barely, and because he was afraid the Outfit might try to finish him off, he had decided to let the world think him dead until the moment to strike back at America came. Though still in danger of death from his wounds, Ibn Awad commanded that he be carried into the desert, taking with him doctors and nurses and a complete U.S. Army field hospital that the Outfit had given him in happier times. He had always preferred desert to town, and apparently believed that he would be healed by the wilderness.

Eventually he did recover. Protected by his palace guard, Ibn Awad has lived the life of a bedouin for all these years while one of his brothers ostensibly ruled the country and he laid his plans for revenge against the United States of America. And, presumably, against you personally.

Obviously there is good reason to doubt Kalash's truthfulness or question his motives. You may wish to talk to him if you decide to look into this matter for yourself. He lives mostly in Paris, at 8-bis, avenue Wagram.

What aroused my own interest was the news of my mother. It is the first clue we have had that she might be alive since she was arrested by the Gestapo in 1940. In the photograph of the Amphora Scroll, the scroll is held in a woman's left hand. The ring on the woman's third finger, a ruby set in diamonds, is the ring that my father gave my mother when I was born. And of course I remember the hand, and know that it can be no one's but hers. This is hardly conclusive evidence that the hand belonged to my mother or that she is still alive. But the moment I saw this photograph, I was overcome with the hope that she still lived, that I would see her again, that I would find her. The evidence suggests—to me, at least—the probability that the manuscript she was holding was in Reinhard Heydrich's possession. As you know, my father believed that Heydrich kidnapped my mother in 1940; it is certainly true that he was obsessed by her. If the hand in the photograph is my mother's, as I know it must be, then she was, in fact, with him in Czechoslovakia. This photo is the only proof we have ever had that my mother was alive, a prisoner of Heydrich, long after she was arrested. If she lives, would by now be a very old woman. It is my conviction that she does live. I know that this is not rational. But if there is one chance in millions that she is the one who has the Amphora Scroll, I've got to know.

In case you decide to pursue the Ibn Awad matter, I hereby make you a gift of the Hicks painting you have always despised. Kalash quite liked it and made me a handsome offer for it. I am sure he would pay a million in cash—more than enough to cover your expenses as you look for, and find, Ibn Awad and his bombs. Or simply pass your remaining years in peace. Your choice. I enclose a letter of introduction to Kalash.

Watch your back, Cousin.

As ever,
Paul

6

Did I believe what Paul had written?

I certainly believed that he would go to the ends of the earth to find his lost mother, for whom he had been searching ever since Heydrich's men took her off a train at the French frontier a few days before Germany invaded France in 1940. Paul, then about fourteen, was a witness to this, and to the beating the Gestapo gave his father. Heydrich had been fascinated by Lori Christopher, and what at the time appeared to be an arrest may well have been a kidnapping. I believed that Paul wanted to believe that his long-lost mother was miraculously alive. I believed that if she did live, it was entirely possible that he might find her on the basis of a single clue. Paul was capable of remarkable leaps of intuition. It was his trademark.

Was the emir and holy man Ibn Awad alive despite my best efforts to kill him? Was he thirsting for revenge as only a wronged Arab can thirst for it? I believed—the world believed—that I had killed him years ago, but I had not done the deed with my own hands and there was no reason why he might not have survived, whatever I and the world had believed. The irony was delicious, but frankly I did not *want* to believe Paul's information, at least the part about Ibn Awad. After all, I was the responsible party. As the Outfit's man for covert action in the Middle East, I had planned his murder, recruited the assassin, and (as I had thought) destroyed the target. If in fact I had failed, the world was in trouble. I knew this man well. The pilgrimage into the desert, the slow preparation for cold-blooded mass murder were entirely in character. His immense wealth—he owned a small country that had vast oil deposits—and the impenetrable secrecy of his household made such a charade plausible. As to the bombs, he had acquired nuclear weapons before; that, and his madness, were the reasons we assassinated him in the first place, or thought we did.

Now it appeared that I had fumbled the ball and then made a fool of myself before the world by publicly defending the action as justifiable homicide. It was a wonder to me, the current age of terror being what it is, that I was not dead already. On the other hand, had I been Ibn Awad, I would not have been satisfied with a mere bullet in the head for Horace Hubbard. No, I would have demanded a more lingering death. It was quite obvious that I had not only made a fool of myself in the signature moment of my life but that I had always been a fool.

For years now, imagining that I was forgotten, that I had no enemies, I had lived without tradecraft. Nothing to conceal, nothing to fear. But now, commencing the moment I left Paul's house, I began once again to be systematically careful. As a practical matter this did me about as much good as not stepping on the cracks in the sidewalk. No matter how much of a professional you may be, there is no defense except luck against a stranger who wants to kill you and knows where you are. The Georgetown street with its row of grotesquely overpriced, cavelike houses was all but empty. It was too late for the women and children who lived in the houses to be outside, too early for the career folk to be coming home; it was the wrong night, Monday, for cocktail parties. I was the lone pedestrian, a puzzled old party wandering through the gloaming with a shopping bag full of secrets in my hand and a rolled-up million-dollar painting stuck under my arm like a baguette.

Inside the houses, figures moved in muted light. I remembered the tears in Paul Christopher's eyes on the night he met with his friend from the Sudan. Spying on him from this same sidewalk, I must have caught him at the very moment he recognized his mother's ring, remembered her hand. As I walked along O Street in the deepening shadows, knowing today what I had not even imagined yesterday, I glimpsed what was in store for me now that Paul, bless his soul, had made me curious enough and rich enough and, let's face it, nervous enough, to go back to a life of folly. Because that was what I was going to do, what I "had" to do unless I wanted to wait for the knife, the bullet, the bomb that would cut me off from the answers to the last questions I considered worth asking. Where had Paul Christopher gone? What had he learned? What trail had he left for me?

Already I was through the looking glass. Yesterday I would have thought that I was alone as I walked along this genteel street. Now, with darting eyes, I saw figures in the shadows, heard them mutter into cell phones, saw them vanish, and wondered if I was being passed along a chain of enemies and what awaited me at the last link.

7

It was seven o'clock in the morning when, in theory, Paul was laid to rest. The troops, the riderless horse, the caisson bearing the coffin moved among tombstones through sunshot mist. A funeral at Arlington is the closest thing to pure patriotic pageantry that survives in twenty-first-century America. Troops in dress blues and white gloves, martial music, the nervous black horse with boots reversed in the stirrups, the curiously muffled sound of what General MacArthur called the mournful mutter of musketry, "Taps," the endless muster of tombstones—all this stirs the memory and moves the heart. Dying for one's country *is*, after all, a noble thing. Paul Christopher had not done that, exactly, but it was not for want of trying. The urn containing Paul's ashes had been placed inside a gunmetal coffin. I wondered as the box was lowered into his grave whether Stephanie had transferred the ashes into a more appropriate container. If not, archeologists of the future would have something to wonder about when they unearthed a vermilion-and-gilt porcelain Chinese urn from the grave of an American hero. Christopher's last mystery.

Stephanie had made the arrangements. Everyone present was an Outfit person; she knew them all because she was an Outfit brat—her late father had been Paul's case officer and she claimed that she had fallen in love with Paul when she was still a child.

Yet there was no mention of the Outfit. Paul was not being buried in hallowed ground because of any secret derring-do. The Outfit had never publicly acknowledged his existence or his decorations or his time in prison. His gravestone read *Paul H. Christopher, First Lieutenant USMCR, Silver Star, Purple Heart*, and the dates. The graveside ceremony had been preceded by a funeral service in the Navy chapel, conducted by a hearty Episcopalian chaplain who hadn't the foggiest notion who or what Paul had been. That would have suited Paul just fine, but as the purpose of a eulogy is to praise the deceased and list his accomplishments, I'm not so sure he would have liked what came afterward in the Fort Myer officers' club. I made my speech as short and matter-of-fact as possible, but the Old Boys present had known Paul—many of them by reputation only, because his work had been so compartmented that he had operated in a kind of bureaucratic quarantine from Headquarters. As I spoke about his life, which could have been described (though I refrained) as a death of a thousand cuts, I could practically feel the audience responding in one weepy collective thought: *They don't make men like this any longer.* Actually, with rare exceptions, they never had. But these were old men to whom a past that never really existed was more real than the lives they had actually led. A death in the family made them remember the old days, and if the deceased was someone like Paul, it made them proud of having touched such a hero. The fact that he seemed to have died an unnatural death in the field added to the poignancy of the loss. Most Outfit alumni his age were keeling over with heart attacks or liver failure.

Stephanie provided an open bar, which did a lot to lift the mood of the mourners. I worked my way through the crowd, saying hello to codgers with the faces of men who had been my senior officers when they were in their prime. Owing to my long vacation in Pennsylvania, and also because that's just the way things are, I had not seen most of these people for years. I liked them all in the way you go on liking the members of your college fraternity, for the boys they used to be no matter how much they change. But few had been the stars they'd hoped to be.

Out of a crowd of sixty, I invited four white-haired old cut-throats to join David Wong and me for lunch that day. Taken as a group, they could be regarded as the all-time backfield of the old Outfit. Besides David, who had escorted the ashes from Beijing, they were Jack Philindros, who had been director of the Outfit during difficult times and before that a nerveless operative in Europe and elsewhere; Ben Childress, who knew Arabs and Arabia in the way a baseball fanatic knows batting averages; Harley Waters, who during the Cold War had recruited more Russians and other Soviet bloc types than there were snowflakes in Siberia; and Charley Hornblower, who knew a lot about codes and arcane languages and the mind of man.

In movies, master spies meet by dark of night in spooky aban-doned factories or under elevated highways in a dangerous part of town. In real life they are far more likely to hold clandestine meet-ings in crowded restaurants. This is true not only of decadent Americans but also of everybody else, including the Russians and the Chinese and even terrorists, though the latter usually choose places run by their cousins, who are also terrorists. Desirable tables in fashionable restaurants are routinely bugged by counterespi-onage people in every country in the world, but even knowing this, operatives otherwise famed for their cunning are flattered to be escorted to the same high-visibility table every time they dine.

The Old Boys and I went to a very expensive steak house on K Street. As the rules of tradecraft dictated, I made the reservation in a false name and we arrived one by one as if we were honest citi-zens. The maître d' recognized us for the nonentities we were and seated us at a table near the kitchen that no one had ever bugged. After martinis and oysters and rib steak on the bone and several bottles of pricey but mediocre wine, I told them all I knew about Paul's disappearance and the reasons behind it. They soaked it all up like the blotters they were. Jack Philindros in particular was attentive. He had a personal interest in the matter. It was Jack who had passed me the presidential order to kill Ibn Awad, Jack who had taken the political fall when the operation came to light. He was the consummate bureaucrat and it must be said that he had good reason to think that I was a loose cannon. Everybody else at the table was a loose cannon too except him, and even Jack had his moments. One of the reasons I had chosen them was that each had a burning reason to resent hypocrisy? Philindros had been kicked out of the directorship for his sins and all the rest had been busted or humiliated over operations for which they should have been decorated or promoted. All these fellows had too much imagination to stay out of trouble, and in the bad old days when men were men and spies were spies, they had all been disciplined for it. In Helsinki, Harley Waters had run a profitable call-girl ring, mostly Scandinavian blondes specializing in visiting Soviet luminaries. The girls were inventive, and more than one Soviet bigwig became cooperative when he saw the talkies of their encounters. Long before it was popular, David Wong had given the Chinese and the Russians fits by organizing a self-financing secret network of Muslim zealots along the Sino-Soviet frontier. The others had been similarly off the wall, with comparably embarrassing results.

Jack is the only person I have ever known who has a softer voice than Paul Christopher. On this day somebody else had had to order his lunch for him because the waiter couldn't hear him over the background chatter. In former times he was, of course, in a position that made people want to listen closely.

"What confirmation is there?" he murmured.

"None," I replied, "apart from Kalash el Khatar's report."

"Which is worth what?" Jack asked.

"Finding that out is the point of the exercise."

"And if you establish that Kalash is right about Paul and this Jesus scroll and Ibn Awad's bombs?"

"Then we find Christopher, if he's alive, and maybe save the world from Ibn Awad if *he's* alive."

"And if they're both dead and there are no bombs?"

"Then the five of us will have had some fun."

Ben Childress said, "This is a recruitment pitch?"

"Yes, if any of you are interested," I said.

"You want us to act in this movie on the basis of what some Arab told Paul Christopher?"

I said, "Yes."

"Why?"

"Because the five of us, taken together, used to know most of the people in the world worth knowing. The generation of assets you fellows recruited and worked with still live in all the right places. They still know all the right people and all the right buttons to push."

"If they're still speaking to us," Jack said.

It was true that Americans were even less beloved by the righteous than they had been when we were young. Back then anti-Americanism had usually been skin-deep; everyone but the stomach-acid Left had liked us well enough in private, and even some of them had had a little bit of kindness for us. Nowadays it was a pathology, like anti-Semitism. The people who now ran the Outfit were crashing into stone walls all over the world in their attempts to penetrate Islamist terrorist cells composed of two brothers and a cousin. We knew the terrorists' fathers, uncles, and grandfathers, and in theory at least we had the capability of making an end run because these elders knew they could trust us. Once in, never out, as the old saw has it. Believe it or not, the truth of that saying has nothing to do with fear, but is based on the peculiar and deep friendships that exist between handler and agent. Friendships of that kind are very durable.

"There are a lot of Ifs," I said. "I'd like to take a vote. Is anyone at the table absolutely sure in his mind that Christopher is dead?"

In every case the answer was No.

"Does anyone think it's impossible that Ibn Awad survived and is up to his old tricks?"

No one demurred.

"Does anyone think that the five of us can possibly do worse than the Outfit if we decide to go after the facts?"

Modesty prevailed. There were no shakes of the head, just secret smiles all around. Glances were exchanged. The deal was made. It was unnecessary to say so. We all knew it.

Harley Waters asked an old warhorse's question: "Would we be traveling?"

"I should hope so. The world being what it is, it wouldn't be enough to call up your old friends. You'd have to show yourself, show them the cards we hold."

"Show them the cards?" asked Harley, who had spent his life dealing with Russians on Russian territory.

"If you want them to trust you, you have to trust them. This is not a USA versus USSR or a Great Satan versus Islam situation. It's a matter of old friends trying to prevent a sad ending. That's essentially what we were trying to do in the Cold War, and we did it, so why would anybody who was involved with us then think that we have an ulterior motive this time?"

By now the expense account lunch crowd had departed. We were the last people in the restaurant. The last waiter was becoming intensely interested in our conversation—not because he cared what a gaggle of senior citizens were saying to one another, but because he wanted his tip, meager as he expected it to be. I called him over and we all chipped in and paid the check in cash, again in obedience to the rules of clandestine behavior.

Before we rose from the table, I asked the question. "Who's in and who's out?"

Everybody was in.

"Let's meet again tomorrow to task this thing in a little more detail," I said. "My house at seventeen hundred hours."

8

The next morning, I was making myself a toasted cheese sandwich for lunch when Zarah tapped on the kitchen window.

"How did you know I was in the kitchen?" I asked after letting her in.

"I smelled the toasted cheese sandwich," she replied. "Have you got an extra one?"

I had made two. I gave her the extra sandwich along with a dill pickle and a glass of iced tea. We ate while seated at my tiny kitchen table. Zarah and I knew little of each other and we hardly talked as we ate, but the meal was companionable. She was a beautiful woman, maybe thirty years old—about the same age now as her grandmother had been when Reinhard Heydrich first fell for her. One could see the monster's point.

I felt a certain awkwardness, but that had nothing to do with her looks. Zarah had not attended her father's funeral. Needless to say this had done nothing to intensify Stephanie's love for her stepdaughter, and I had been hauled off into a corner to make sure I was fully aware of just how outrageous Zarah's conduct was. I tended to agree, but what did I know about Zarah or her reasons?

I said, "You were missed yesterday."

"So Stephanie has told me."

She was impassive, controlled. It was remarkable how many glimpses of Paul one saw in Zarah, considering that she had known her father personally for only five or six years. Although I don't know the details, arithmetic suggests that she was conceived sometime around the last day of her parents' marriage. Her late mother, who was as neurotic as she was gorgeous—had she been born a rung or two further down the Kentucky social ladder, she might well have become Miss America—took revenge on Paul by concealing their child's existence from him. He knew nothing about Zarah until, as Stephanie put it, Helen of Troy knocked on the door one day and identified herself as his child. DNA tests confirmed this, but looking at her and remembering her father were enough of a paternity test.

"That's why I've come to see you," Zarah said. "I didn't go to the funeral because I think it was a sham. If my father is dead—and there is no evidence that he is—those were not his ashes that were buried at Arlington."

"You know that for a fact?"

"No. But if he were dead, I would know it and believe it."

"But you don't."

She shook her head.

I said, "Neither do I. I'm no soothsayer, but I don't believe that Paul's death has been proved."

"Why?"

"Because the man I know is too adroit to let himself be killed before he had the answer he was looking for."

I paused for a moment to give her a chance to reply or ask a question, but she seemed to sense that I had more to say and she waited for me to say it.

"However," I said, since the floor seemed to be mine, "I think you should be careful. Your father has spent his life in pursuit of a mother whom the rest of the world has believed to be dead for almost sixty years."

"But who may be alive after all."

"So your father believed, and for all we know he was right. But there's no more evidence that Lori Christopher is living at ninety-four or whatever than that Paul is dead."

Zarah changed the subject. "May I ask you something?"

"Certainly."

"If Ibn Awad is alive and is threatening the same kind of action for which you were ordered to kill him before, how does that make you feel?"

"Incompetent."

"You want to correct the mistake."

"I suppose so."

"Why?"

"I made this mess. I should clean it up."

"Alone? Without help?"

"Your father has helped me. He gave me information and something I can sell to finance the operation."

"Yes, the Hicks. He told me."

"He told you?"

"He left a letter for me."

She handed me a sheet of paper, one page from a longer letter. There it was, in Paul's handwriting.

What to say to all this? What did she want?

She said, "I'd like to help you. I speak Arabic. I know you do, too, but not the way I do. I grew up with Arabs. I don't always understand them, but I know them, and I have a lot of friends among them. And I know things that you might not know about my father."

I doubted this. This must have shown on my face, because after an icy moment she decided to explain herself. "My father made a project of telling me everything he remembers about his life."

This amazed me. Paul opening his emotional files, even to his own daughter? "Paul never seemed the oral history type to me," I said.

"He's not," Zarah replied. "But for whatever reason, he wanted to make this transfer of knowledge to me, and he did. In theory, at least, I know everything and everyone my father ever knew."

"Everything?"

"Wouldn't it be out of character for him to leave anything out after he said he wasn't going to do that?"

"Yes."

They must have spent days locked up together. No wonder Stephanie hated this young woman.

I said, "You took notes?"

"That wasn't necessary. The material is impossible to forget."

"And you'd share all this with me?"

"All of it? No. The parts you need to know, yes. For example, I know the name of a man who worked in the Vatican in the thirties and forties. He was a friend of my father's. This man's assignment was to deal with Nazi officials during World War II."

"And?"

"He's still alive," Zarah said. "At least he was three days ago, when I checked. Very old, but lucid. He's in Salvator Mundi hospital in Rome."

"Okay. But how does he fit in?"

"He saw my grandmother in Prague in 1942," Zarah said.

9

The Old Boys arrived at my house precisely at five in the afternoon. This may sound like an insecure meeting place, but the fact is we were pretty much alone on my block. This was a street on which the near-mighty lived, and at five in the afternoon our privacy was protected by the triage of Washington existence. As twilight fell, my neighbors were all in meetings or having a drink with somebody or stuck in traffic, and my guests would melt into the darkness before they got home. Jack Philindros, dressed like the secretary of state, resembled the time-warp Hellene that he was—olive skin, dense hair slicked back, thick eyebrows that grew together. Charley Hornblower, hearty and long-boned and in need of a shave, was a Falstaff who for many years had been working on his red nose and his connections to people who knew things. Ben Childress and Harley Waters might have been cousins—Yankee faces, Yankee economy; both wore frayed blazers, faded polo shirts and rumpled khakis and drugstore watches. David Wong was his usual self, oldest of the Marx Brothers—bodhisattva smile, quick tongue, quicker brain. He was the only one among us who showed no sign of being the worse for wear. Philindros, a teetotaler, refused the Laphroaig I was offering, but the others did it justice. It was a treat to hear the voices of men and to smell whisky in the house where I had been all by myself for such a long time.

That afternoon I had bought five satellite phones at $498 each, including one year's access for each to communications satellites in 130 different countries. I distributed the phones. Everybody got an index card listing the others' satellite phone numbers. No code names necessary; we would recognize one another's voices.

Philindros, always the security nut, said, "Do you think these phones are secure?"

"No, but they're the best way to keep in touch."

"You don't mind having half the world on the party line with us?"

"What difference does it make?" I asked. "This operation will either succeed within the month or fail miserably in less time than that. If it succeeds we go off the air forever. If it fails and Ibn Awad's bombs go off, our little group will be the least of the world's worries."

"If we're found out by the wrong people, they'll roll us up."

"Not in this time frame they won't," I said. "Our advantage is that we can move fast because nobody can say no to us."

Jack said, "We'll see about that. You have no actual objection to our following the rules of tradecraft?"

"No."

"That's good," Harley said, "because we jes' can't help it."

I told them the plan. Because of my physique I didn't think it wise to stop off in Rome and call on Zarah's ex-monk. Looking up from his deathbed at a six-foot-five American who speaks Italian like a Visigoth wouldn't put a man in the mood to share confidences. On the other hand, Jack had a soothing personality and he spoke fluent Italian. I told him what we knew about Paul's old friend and how we knew it, and handed him Zarah's slip of paper with the man's name on it.

"If he has anything to tell us," Jack said, "what do I do then?"

"Tell everybody everything you know over the satellite phone," I said. "Then follow up."

"By doing what?"

"Go wherever you think you should go, see whoever you need to see," I replied. "but feed every scrap of information to every single one of us by satellite phone as soon as it happens. Don't wait. Call the minute you know something."

They all knew the reason for this: if every one of us knew everything, only one of us had to survive to carry out the last stage of the op.

Ben Childress, our Arabist, knew Ibn Awad's German live-in doctor. This particular alumnus of the Schutzstaffel (SS) called himself Claus Bücher. If Bücher was still alive and still doctoring Ibn Awad, his whereabouts obviously would be unknown. We needed to know if he had dropped out of sight at the same time as his employer and, more important, if he had been sighted since. If he came into town every now and then, or flew somewhere for R & R, we might be able to get our hands on him, and if we did, miracles do happen. Who knows? If the incentive was right, he might take us to his patient.

Harley Waters had a wide circle of friends among the used-to-be's of the former Soviet bloc. He would find out whatever he could in Moscow, then go to Prague and Budapest and sniff around for recent traces of Paul and old folklore about Lori Christopher. Harley's prime target was the nobility of the old Austro-Hungarian empire. These people still existed, and in Lori's day they had been a nationality of their own, living in a world of their own, and so much intermarried over the centuries that they were nearly all cousins.

The old aristocracy had despised the Nazis, who came out of the gutters. By 1942, these people were an underground-in-waiting, and Lori was one of them. Had she gone to anyone for help in Prague, she would have gone to them. Unless they had come to her first and asked her help in liquidating Reinhard Heydrich.

Charley Hornblower, our scholar, would remain in Washington and work the files. He had an attic full of them and a Rolodex full of fellow pack rats.

I would go to Paris and sell the Hicks to finance the operation.

10

In my penury I continued to possess some of the accoutrements of the man of means: wardrobe, credentials, connections, manners, even a valid credit card. But I had almost no pocket money. I booked the cheapest available ticket to Paris and took a bus into town from the airport. At 8-bis, avenue Wagram, I presented one of my last calling cards to the burly servant who answered the door of Kalash al Khatar's apartment. He took it from my hand and shut the door in my face. A long time passed. Had I not been dealing with a descendant of the Prophet I might have feared that I had been refused entry. However, I had in the past been kept waiting by this haughty breed on many occasions in many parts of Islam, so I loitered patiently in the corridor. The windows looked down on a cobbled courtyard where a fountain played. I heard the muted gargle of midday traffic in the place de l'Étoile. This reminded me of how Paris had smelled at rush hour in my youth, when the proportion of leaded exhaust fumes to fresh air was only slightly lower than the level needed to commit suicide.

Forty-five minutes passed. An hour. More. When Kalash's man—a different one this time—opened the door, he was not smiling, he did not speak. He gestured me inside with a jerk of his bullet head.

He led me to an audience room. One very imperial overstuffed chair faced several smaller, unpadded ones. Also visible were a collection of knives with rhino-horn hafts on one wall, a bronze tray inlaid with silver and copper on the opposite wall, phrases from the Koran in beautiful calligraphy on the back wall. The room was imposing but not overwhelming. However, the surrounding apartment was vast. One felt this spaciousness without actually seeing the rest of the place. It must have cost a fortune. I wondered if Kalash's impoverished subjects made him an annual present of his weight in precious stones or metals, as did the followers of the Aga Khan.

After another hour Kalash appeared, wearing Arabian robes and carrying a carved and inlaid ebony staff. He was, indeed, remarkably tall—nearly a head taller than myself. He did not offer to shake hands, nor did he speak. Or sit down. I, of course, had risen to my feet when he entered.

"I apologize for arriving without notice," I said.

Kalash said, "What do you want?"

"I have a letter for you."

I handed over Paul's letter of introduction. He banged his staff on the marble floor twice. Yet another flunky appeared. Kalash handed him the letter. The flunky bowed himself out and a moment later bowed himself back in, with the opened letter on a silver tray.

Kalash read the letter. "Is that the painting?" he asked, staring at the rolled-up canvas on the chair beside me.

"Yes." I did not offer to unroll it. Kalash was a very annoying fellow.

He said, "How much do you want for it?"

"The price that you offered my cousin, plus ten percent. In cash."

"Let me see the thing," said Kalash.

I unrolled the painting and flattened it on the table. Kalash examined it inch by inch, like the expert he apparently was.

"This picture is not as it was when I saw it the last time," he said. "It has been damaged by all this rough handling. Take it away."

"As you wish." I began to roll up the painting.

"Stop that," said Kalash. "You'll make it worse."

"If the painting doesn't please you, what difference can that make? You'll never see it again."

"I don't wish to be an accomplice to this barbarous destruction," Kalash said. "So stop what you are doing."

"I can hardly carry it through the streets like a flag," I said.

Kalash's face was expressionless, as it had been throughout our encounter. I waited for him to speak again. At last he said, "Why did Paul send you on this errand, instead of coming himself or simply mailing the letter?"

There was no point in dissembling. I said, "We have a report that Paul died in China."

"Where in China?"

"Xinjiang province. It is very remote. . . ."

"I know where Xinjiang is," Kalash said. "What proof exists that this is true?"

"The Chinese have sent us his ashes."

"Are they genuine?"

"I don't know."

"But you mean to find out."

"If that's possible, yes."

We had been standing throughout this conversation. Now Kalash said, "Sit down." He himself sat down, not in the larger chair, but in one of the smaller ones. Evidently we were going to be equals for a few minutes.

He banged on the floor again with his staff, just once. In seconds the household slave appeared with two glasses of very hot, very sweet mint tea on a tray.

Kalash said, not unpleasantly, "So you are the man who killed my cousin Ibn Awad."

"So it was believed at the time."

"And now?"

"Paul left me a letter. I know what you told him."

"He wrote down everything?"

"The main points. An outline."

"So now you plan to kill my cousin again and you need money to do this and you think that I will give it to you? You *are* an extraordinary fellow."

I said, "I have no plans to kill Ibn Awad. Obviously I'm not very good at that. And I am no longer in the business of saving the world."

"Then what will you do with a million dollars?"

"A million one hundred. I'll carry on with Paul's search."

"For what?"

"For his mother, my aunt. For the Amphora Scroll."

"Do you plan to sell that, too?"

"Would you be interested in the right of first refusal?"

Kalash played deaf to this uppity remark. He said, "And if you happen to stumble on Ibn Awad?"

"We can talk about old times."

"You should have let him set off one of his bombs and *then* murdered him. In those days Tel Aviv would have been his preference, so America would have come to no harm. You would have been the toast of the West instead of being driven into the wilderness."

"Is that still your recommendation?"

"No. Times have changed. If I were the Crusader in charge of this manhunt, I would think it best to keep him from coming back from the dead."

"And how would you accomplish that?"

"Not by killing him again. That would inflame the pious, because they would never believe that he was not immortal. If he lived through one murder, why should he not live through another? Murder him again and you create a Hydra."

"What, then?"

"Capture him. I realize you're an American, but for once, renounce braggadocio. Say nothing to the world. Let him stay dead."

"And then?"

"Send him off to some Saint Helena in the Indian Ocean—
he couldn't be happy in a cold climate—and let him live out his
days in prayer and fasting. It would be a kindness to tell him that
all twelve of his bombs had gone off as planned in American cities.
Show him videos of the devastation. Lots of corpses clutching
crucifixes."

I said, "Very creative. But I thought we were doing all this to
prevent devastation."

"Obviously. But surely your organization can make very con-
vincing fake footage for a fraction of what it would cost to rebuild
New York, Chicago, Los Angeles, and so forth. It's said that you
faked the moon landings, so this should be child's play."

"You believe that?"

"About the moon landings? No. But I am not my cousin nor
one of his half-mad followers."

What, then, was he? His callousness was so matter-of-fact that
it was comical.

"Excellent advice," I said. "But do you really think such an
operation can be kept quiet forever?"

"You're in a better position to judge such things than I am. But
I say again, if this does not happen in impenetrable silence, if you
advertise Ibn Awad's return from the other world, if you describe
what he has in mind, if you plaster CNN with his picture and
pictures of his unexploded bombs, if you congratulate yourselves
on saving the world in the usual all-American fashion, you will
merely create another monster."

I said, "What's that supposed to mean?"

"If you show the world that Ibn Awad, just one pious man no
matter how rich, held in his hands the means to inflict a mortal
wound on the enemies of Islam, and that he accomplished this
miracle not once but twice, you will demonstrate that inflicting
the mortal wound is feasible. Therefore you will create the next
Ibn Awad. And if you kill *him*, yet another one. There will be no
end to it."

I said, "This is your cousin we're talking about."

"Exactly. I am trying to save his life."

"Naturally. But what else are you trying to save?"

Kalash said, "'What else?' I should think it was obvious. If the bombs go off in America, Islam will be incinerated by the United States Air Force. I'd like to prevent that."

Heaven help me, I found this fellow entertaining. How in the world had Paul done without his company for forty years? This did not mean I was prepared to become a co-conspirator in whatever tangled web he was weaving. For all I knew he had sent Paul Christopher to his death with an irresistible lie and was hoping to do the same for me.

I said, "Where is Ibn Awad now?"

"I have no idea."

"Who does know?"

"The people who are with him. But you will have to find them before you can question them, and if you find them you will have found him."

"And if I don't find them?"

"Then you must do what one does when lost in the desert," Kalash replied. "Go back to where you started and begin again. Do you have pen and paper?"

I handed over my Bic and a page from my notebook. Kalash scribbled a man's name and the name of a place, Manaus, on the paper.

"You should go talk to this man," he said. "He knows interesting things, and he has seen Paul Christopher quite recently."

Kalash stood up. The conversation was over. Apparently the negotiations were not.

He said, "Your demand for cash for the Hicks is ludicrous. Nevertheless I want it. I offered Paul one million dollars for the picture. I will have that sum deposited in Switzerland, if that's acceptable. Do you have an account there?"

It so happened that I did. I gave him the particulars.

He said, "Very well. Have you a phone number?"

"Yes."

I wrote it down for him. He recited his own number—rapidly, of course, saying *naught* for *zero* and repeating it only once.

"And one more thing," he said. "Ibn Awad has caused a fatwa to be issued against you. You understand what a fatwa is?"

"I think so." I attempted a smile. "Is there a reward?"

"Paradise is the reward. But money is also involved. You have to be a believer to collect, so you should avoid zealots with beards and wild eyes, but I'd be wary of all strangers if I were you. All you have to do to convert to Islam is say that there is but one God, Allah, and Muhammad is his prophet. There are good Christians in this world who would speak those words into a tape recorder, then pull the trigger and bring my cousin your head."

I said, "Is your man in Manaus one of them?"

"He loves money and hates Americans and thinks that Ibn Awad did good work in the world," Kalash said. "Whether he knows about the fatwa is another question. The fatwa is quite recent. Word of it has not seeped down very far."

I was passed along the avenue Wagram by loiterers with cell phones, just as I had earlier been handed along O Street, and when I boarded a Métro train at the Étoile, a thug with furry eyebrows got on behind me. He called whoever was next in line as I disembarked near the Gare Saint-Lazare. On the train to Geneva, I sat beside a very large Russian who smelled of unbrushed teeth (or maybe he was a Chechen, a Bosnian, an Albanian—the world was full of Muslims who looked like you and me). Across the aisle, a virtually fleshless woman with scarred wrists hiked her skirt and stared at me hungrily, stroked her meager leg, and talked Swiss-German to herself in a low incessant murmur. Or was she speaking to me, who couldn't understand a word, or maybe into a concealed hands-free telephone?

As far as I could tell, no one awaited me at the train station in Geneva, but I could not be sure because of the crowd and because all Genevese give the impression that they have us aliens under surveillance. I checked into a hotel behind the station and ate a gummy *truite au bleu* for dinner in its appalling restaurant. The waiter was an Arab. So was the cook; everywhere I looked I saw an Arab. They had always been numerous, of course. I just hadn't been so keenly aware of them as I was now. I decided not to go for a walk along the lake after dinner.

From my room I called Charley Hornblower. Had he ever heard of a man called Simon Hawk, Kalash's man in Manaus?

"Give me ten minutes," Charley said.

He called back in five. "True name Wolfram Ostermann, if I'm not mistaken," Charley said. "We came across him back in the fifties when we were trying to find Eichmann as a good-will gesture to the Mossad."

"Headquarters didn't tell the Mossad?"

"Apparently not, if he's alive and well and living in Brazil. Wolfram was a busy bee. He saw a lot of former SS men and we thought he might be up to something special. They'd talk to him, then head off to exotic destinations."

"Such as?"

"Pretty much everywhere. He seemed to be financing their travels by selling paintings, presumably stolen during the war. It was better to watch him than have him replaced with somebody we didn't know."

"And *was* he up to something special?"

"We never followed up. In those days the White House wanted to know about Russians, not runaway ex-SS men. We had a lot of those working for us in Germany."

"Anything else?"

"Just one faint marker," Charley said. "One of the people Wolfram dealt with in Brazil was a doctor who with called himself Claus Bücher. We never put a true name to him, but you know who he is—Ibn Awad's personal physician."

Small world.

11

Everything was in order at the bank. Kalash had actually deposited the money, all of it. After transferring $25,000 each to the Old Boys and withdrawing $25,000 in pocket money for myself, I collected from my safe deposit box an old Canadian passport bearing the name William O. Dyer and a picture of me as a somewhat younger man. At the airport I booked a ticket for Frankfurt with a connection to Manaus and paid for it in cash. Aboard the plane I fell asleep almost immediately. I had not seen a bed since leaving Washington thirty-six hours earlier. I could taste the awful meal I had eaten the night before. My bones ached. I dreamt of Paul and myself as a child on a sled. We crashed in a snowdrift. The sled overturned. I had a bloody nose. Offstage, a female screamed. Memory or symbolism? Who knew?

I had never been posted to South America, thanks be, so my first glimpse of Brazil revealed a sight that I could scarcely have imagined. From a height of thirty thousand feet, the rain forest stretched as far as the eye could see in all directions, the undulating spinach-green canopy carved into somewhat more comprehensible patches of territory by muddy rivers that glittered in the sun. As in song and story, a man really could disappear into this wilderness without a trace, enslaved by some dope-taking tribe of Indians, eaten by crocodiles or merely lost, following engorged rivers downstream in the direction of civilization as recommended by the Boy Scout manual but never finding anything but another muddy river. Most people, including me, would prefer to die another death someplace else. Yet here I was in this prehistoric world, under a false identity, on the recommendation of a man I scarcely knew who had no reason to wish me well, in pursuit of a cousin who might be dead and a mad Arab who might not be.

On payment of a handsome bribe to a passport officer at the Manaus airport, I was grudgingly granted a three-day tourist visa, which provided more than enough time to do what I had to do. The German I was looking for called himself Simon Hawk. I rang the number Kalash had given me from an airport phone and asked for Herr Hawk in German. When he came on the line I identified myself as a friend of Kalash.

"Your German is not as good as the last American Prince Kalash sent to me," Hawk said in English that could only have been learned in a British public school. This was the Schutzstaffel style: let this mongrel dummkopf know at the outset that you already knew all about him, that you could if necessary read his slow and simple and supremely uninteresting thoughts. That he had better come to the point.

"I apologize," I said in English, glad to have news of Paul. "I wonder if we might meet."

"Why should we do that?"

"Because I am a former officer of the American intelligence service who has excellent contacts in the Mossad, and if you do not talk to me, you will be talking to them."

This broke all the rules including the law of self-preservation, but it worked.

"How odd," said Hawk in an altered tone of voice. "I shouldn't have thought that a man with those connections would be a friend of Arabs."

"It's an odd world, Mr. Hawk. May I come to you or not?"

"Dinner tonight," he said. It was not a question; clearly I was all too available.

"That's very kind. How will I find you?"

"I'll send a car for you at the Novotel. Eight-thirty."

"I can easily take a taxi."

"The driver would never find me and you would be a fool to trust him," Hawk said. "I assure you that you will be quite safe."

Well, now, *that* put my mind at ease. If you couldn't trust an old Schutzstaffel man living in the jungle under an alias who happened to have a connection to Ibn Awad, whom could you trust? I decided to skip the Novotel and went instead to a hotel recommended by my taxi driver. The ride through Manaus was what one might expect in the tropics, a tour of a slum that appeared to have been built as a slum, punctuated by an occasional bank or office building made of the same scabby concrete and painted in the same garish colors as the rest of the city. In the central market sweaty butchers worked in the open air in hot sunlight, cutting up steers and hogs and selling the warm meat while blood spilled sluggishly over the edge of the table in a lacy crimson film.

Despite my driver's assurances that the manager was his brother-in-law, the hotel, a most humble one, was fully booked until I slid a twenty-dollar bill across the reception desk. The banknote vanished and an encouraging smile appeared on the face of the clerk, who almost immediately noticed a cancellation. I was soon under a lukewarm shower. After that I ate a dry room-service sandwich, wedged the door, and fell into yet another profound sleep. Evidently my brain wanted no part of the waking world into which the rest of my body had carried it.

After my nap, I put on fresh clothes and walked to the Novotel. I waited outside for my ride. The car that Simon Hawk sent for me at precisely eight o'clock was not the gleaming Mercedes that his telephone manner evoked, but a well-worn Subaru in need of a wash. The driver, a stringy Brazilian dressed in a clean but threadbare white suit, spotted me at once.

"You are the North American for Mister Doctor Hawk?"

Evidently Hawk had been willing to part with the name he was born with but not with the *Herr Doktor* that went with his origi-

nal identity. His house was some distance from the city. The road
ran through a sort of trench lined with brightly lit, open-fronted
shops and cafés. Music blared, people went about their business in
the trickled light of the shops. A fat drunk pissed into the road-
way and the driver steered around the arcing yellow stream as if
avoiding a pothole.

A mile or so further on, the driver turned the car into a narrow
driveway cut into a grove of enormous smooth trees. The house
itself was modest, overgrown with vines, in need of paint.
According to Kalash, Hawk had been in hiding from Nazi-hunters
since 1945, and by the look of things he was coming to the end of
his nest egg.

He greeted me on the doorstep with a Leica in hand and took
three rapid flash pictures before handing the camera for safekeeping to the driver, who disappeared.

"Hawk," he said, with a firm handshake.

"Dyer."

"No doubt."

I might have said the same, and did so with a lift of the eyebrows. Hawk showed me a small, just perceptible sneer.

"Do come in."

We stepped into a Sydney Greenstreet movie set: low ceilings,
concrete walls, small high windows, ceiling fans turning lazily.
Rattan furniture. Nothing on the walls except for a primitive tex-
tile or two. Several quite beautiful pieces of what I took to be
Amazonian Indian pottery. Outside, the low putt-putt of the
generator that drove the fans and supplied the dim light from a
couple of lamps.

Without having asked what I wanted, Hawk handed me a
drink.

"A Manaus Collins," he explained. "Rum, sugar, juice of local
fruits."

My host was dressed in a double-breasted blue blazer with a
crest on the breast pocket and white pants and sandals, no socks.
He was neither tall nor short, neither slim nor paunchy. He bore

himself as if still in the uniform he had last worn more than half a century before. He was swarthy for a German, especially so for a former SS man, but perhaps that had something to do with long exposure to the equatorial sun. He had a full head of springy steel-gray hair, worn long on top and combed straight back but cut short at the sides in the bygone military fashion of the Third Reich. Behind the small round lenses of his Himmlerian steel-frame spectacles, his eyes were brown, intelligent, and on full alert. The sandals were a mistake. The rest of him might be remarkably well-preserved, but he had an old man's feet, veined and splotched, with horny, broken toenails.

We sipped our sour drinks. He said, "Have you seen the opera house?"

"I'm afraid not. Jet lag."

The Manaus opera house, built a century ago by immensely rich rubber barons who imported Europe's most famous singers, was the city's great historical landmark.

"Don't miss it," Hawk said. "It's very nicely restored. There's a certain comic pathos to it. Imagine the greatest voices of the time traveling across the sea and then fifteen hundred kilometers by riverboat to sing for tone-deaf ruffians."

The driver appeared in a different coat and announced dinner. He served a tasty Amazonian fish with many unusual flat ribs, accompanied by pulpy vegetables I had never before encountered. Hawk ate his bony fish with two forks.

"Tambaqui," he said, naming it.

He rendered a full account of the natural history of this creature, which apparently grew to enormous size, had a gaping circular mouth, and was believed by the natives to have a taste for human infants, which it swallowed whole when they were carelessly dropped into the river.

"You do understand," said Hawk, "that Manaus is on the Rio Negro, not the Amazon. There are no fish in the Rio Negro—something about the black silt that gives the river its name—so this tambaqui and all fish eaten in Manaus come from the Amazon."

"How interesting."

"But not what you came to learn," Hawk said with a charming smile; yellow teeth. He rang a bell. "Coffee in the drawing room, please, Joaõ."

When we were settled in our chairs and had drained our tiny cups of coffee, Hawk came to the point. "So what is it, exactly, that brings you here, Mister Dyer?"

"You mentioned another American who visited recently. I said. "Do you photograph all your visitors?"

"Only the ones I've never met before. I have a bad memory for faces."

"Do you have the picture you took of him?"

"Yes. In my pocket, actually."

He handed over a snapshot of Paul Christopher, face bleached and pasted onto the black night by the flash. The date of his visit, less than a week after his disappearance, was written in neat Germanic script in the white space at the bottom of the picture.

Hawk said, "You know him?"

I handed back the picture. "Yes."

"You are in pursuit of him?"

"In a sense. He's my cousin. The family is concerned about him."

"So the first person whom you asked for assistance was Kalash al Khatar."

"Yes."

"Why?"

"He also sent my cousin here."

"And your name is actually Horace Hubbard, not Dyer?"

"Kalash has been in touch, I see."

"No, I watch CNN. I remember your hour in the sun. The spy who stole an election in his own country. Fascinating drama, so American."

"Indeed. You have the advantage of me, Doctor. I know you only as Simon Hawk. I have no interest in delving into any previous identities."

"Not even if your friends in the Mossad ask you nicely?"

"Not even then. My interest is in my cousin and the Amphora Scroll."

"Naturally. And beyond that?"

"Personal matters."

"That was what your cousin was interested in also."

"And were you able to help him?"

"Actually, yes," Hawk said coolly, and now he was enjoying himself. "As it happens, I knew his mother in Prague when she was the consort, shall we say, of a certain great man. *Baronesse*, he called her, which is the polite form of address in German for the unmarried daughter of a baron, as if her American husband and your cousin had never existed. She was the love of this great man's rather short life. Your cousin looks remarkably like her, a wonderful example of the archaic aristo type. He speaks German like a Bismarck. I showed him photographs."

"I hope that I may see them, too. As you know, the woman was my aunt."

Hawk smiled. "Perhaps a cognac?" he said.

I had brought along a bottle of duty-free VSOP Martell as a house gift, and it turned out after the second glass that my first impression was incorrect. Far from considering me a ridiculously clumsy American, Simon Hawk considered me a kindred soul. We had each of us in the past performed distasteful duties for our countries—in my case the murder of Ibn Awad and probably many similar abominations. In his case, actions unspecified but desperate for the Fatherland. Things had gone seriously awry for both of us, and here we were together, a couple of discards, war veterans who were free of former enmities, comrades of a sort.

"You are an interesting chap," Hawk told me. "Speaking German over the phone, using a ludicrously transparent alias, threatening me with the Mossad, and after all that, coming here to dinner all alone and putting yourself in my power. Why?"

"Just clumsy, I guess," I said, speaking truth.

Again he flashed his thin, knowing smile. "Do you know what

I think, my dear Horace?" Hawk said. "I think you *wanted* me to believe you were stupid and clumsy."

"Why ever would I want that?"

"To make me think I'm smarter than you are. To manipulate the well-known psychological need of my type to have the upper hand, the need to know more than his adversary, to outwit, then crush."

Sitting in feeble lamplight, one skinny white-trousered leg thrown over the other, tobacco-stain toenails in full view, Hawk looked even more sallow than before. Beside him on a table stood the Martell bottle, and next to that a large straw hat. Hawk reached for the bottle, then deftly slid his hand under the hat and produced a nine-millimeter Walther automatic. He pointed it at my chest.

"As you see, it would be quite easy," he said. "A short march down a hidden path, a tiny sound in a vast jungle already filled with inexplicable noises, then a grave in this amazing Amazonian soil that digests human flesh and turns it into something quite unrecognizable in a matter of days. Rather like a stomach at work on a big steak."

My, but this fellow could talk English. He cocked the pistol. I was seriously concerned. Hawk might have been bluffing, making a show. But for all I knew this urbane old nut had shot Paul and fed him to the worms and now intended to do the same to me. Certainly he had every reason to prevent people who had found him from telling others where he was, and as a chum of the Mossad I was living (for the moment) proof that rubbing out uninvited visitors was good policy.

We were seated about three feet apart. I am, as I have said, a tall man. My torso was just about long enough to bridge the gap. With trembling hand, I took a large mouthful of cognac, leaned forward, and spat it in Hawk's eyes. Then I took the pistol away from him, picked him up, and shook him hard. So hard that the cocked pistol in my hand went off, the bullet blasting a crater in the concrete wall. Hawk was quite light, all bones except for a few pounds of wasted muscle. His flaccid face quivered like Jell-O, his head snapped back and forth, his long gray hair flew. I was afraid that I might have gone on too long and broken something. So much for adrenaline and being out of practice.

Despite the gunshot and a loud glottal outcry from Hawk, Joaõ did not appear. This either meant that Hawk had given the only possible witness to whatever he'd had in mind for me the rest of the night off, or that Joaõ was not the sort of fellow to intrude on a private moment.

There is nothing like a good shaking to improve conversation. Generally no physical harm is done, but it does seem to awaken fundamental collective memories of encounters with cave bears. Only a moment ago Hawk had mentioned my being in his power. He now had a better understanding of who was in whose power, and was no doubt kicking himself for not just shooting me between the eyes without warning instead of making a fancy speech. Had I been a smaller man he might have done just that, but perhaps he doubted his ability to carry or drag a hulk like me to that churning stomach of a last resting place that he had mentioned. On the other hand, maybe he'd just been kidding. But in that case, why cock the pistol?

I poured him another glass of cognac. He lay sprawled in his chair where I had thrown him, twitching and gasping for breath. Apart from these involuntary movements he looked dead or close to it—eyes staring, skin a paler shade of yellow, nervous system apparently shut down. He was quite old. Perhaps he *was* dying.

"Sorry about that," I said. "But I don't know you well enough to have you pointing a gun at me."

His eyes regained some expression. Putting the glass to his lips I said, "Here, drink this. It'll do you good."

Hawk, eager to obey, took more brandy than he could swallow and went off into a coughing fit. I pounded him on the back. He recovered. I put the glass down on the table beside him and refilled it. He was living now in a world of surprise, and I believed that he was looking at me in an entirely different way. What I had done to him was, I admit, the act of a bully. I was a foot taller and probably forty pounds heavier than he was, not to mention at least twenty years younger. But playing the bully was the whole point, if you leave aside the element of self-defense. Hawk, after all, had belonged to a culture of bullies—people who punched old men into submission, set fire to rabbis' beards, shot children for sport, kicked women into filthy railroad cars. Bullying was something he understood. He was still in his chair, seemingly too subdued to move without permission.

This was hardly the moment to reassure him. I laid his Walther on the table beside me.

"Now I hope we can talk business," I said.

Hawk, avoiding my eyes, nodded his head. He was, as they used to say in the Schutzstaffel, at my orders.

12

When the interview began my intention was to help Simon Hawk calm down, so I chose what I thought would be a neutral subject.

"Why don't we begin with something that truly interests me?" I said. "May I ask where you picked up your amazing command of English?"

"I grew up in England," Hawk replied. "I was sent to the best schools."

"Which ones?"

He sensed a trap. This was vital information. If I knew his school and his approximate age I could ferret out his true name. And wouldn't the Mossad be delighted to have that information?

"Simon," I said. "Relax. I mean you no harm."

"Worksop College," he said at last, in tremolo, as if divulging the key to the innermost code of the Third Reich.

This was a new one on me. Where was it exactly?

"Nottinghamshire," he said.

"Ah, Sherwood Forest. You must have fond memories."

"Right," said Hawk with deep sarcasm. "Filthy weather, vile food, the jolly old birch drawing blood. Slaps, kicks, punches.

Pimply nancy boys fumbling at one's bedclothes. *Five years of that.*"

"But you did learn to be an English gentleman, or a reasonable facsimile thereof."

"Oh, quite. Monkey see monkey do, as my schoolmates used to put it. They knew I was a Jerry, you see. My father was posted to Manchester for many years as a representative of the German steel industry. Naturally the British regarded him as a spy."

You see what I mean about the benefits of a good shake. He would never have been this frank had he not made the mistake of pointing that pistol at me. You never know in an interrogation what will open the floodgates. Out of dumb luck I had pushed the right button by going around Robin Hood's barn to the gates of Worksop College instead of coming right to the point.

"Rings true," I said. "But it must give you deep satisfaction to know that passing through this ordeal made it possible for you to serve the Reich."

"What do you mean by that?"

"Obviously your command of English, your ability to pass as an Englishman if necessary—knowing how to dress, how to joke, knowing enough to eat your fish with two forks instead of a knife and fork like a navvy. Surely that attracted the notice of persons in high places?"

"It was people in high places who sent me to Worksop in the first place. I was regarded as an investment in the future."

He had stopped playing the eccentric Brit and was now quite openly his real self, a German Anglophobe with a bad past and a light conscience.

I will paraphrase what he told me by way of introduction. Hawk came back to Germany in the summer of 1934 as a nineteen-year-old. His father had given him a letter of introduction to a chum at ThyssenKrupp AG who was a secret member of the Nazi Party. Notwithstanding the disadvantage that Hawk's English education represented in German eyes, this man arranged for his admittance to Marburg University. In due course Hawk was awarded, with honors, a doctorate in what Americans would now call the history of art. By this time he was a dedicated member of the Nazi party. An assistant to the Gauleiter of Hessen took a liking to Hawk and gave him a letter of introduction to an art lover in Berlin. He was invited to dinner at a grand house near Unter den Linden and spent the greater part of the evening talking about art to the guest of honor, a tall blond long-faced man who, except for his rather large bottom, could have posed as the ideal Aryan for a Nazi poster.

"I need not tell you who this man was," said Hawk.

"Ah, Simon, but I'm afraid you must."

He hesitated for seconds before he spoke the name. "Reinhard Heydrich, head of the Reich security police and chief deputy to Himmler," Hawk said at last. "He wore evening clothes, not his uniform. He was perfectly charming, but a relentless questioner. He extracted fact after fact as if my mind were a safe to which he knew the secret combination. Mainly he wanted to know what were the most beautiful, what were the most valuable art objects in the world. And where, exactly, were they?"

Next morning, early, Heydrich sent two men to fetch Hawk to Gestapo headquarters in the Prinz-Albrechtstrasse. After an interminable wait he was marched into Heydrich's office, where the great man greeted him with a curt nod. He was all business today in a pinch-waist black uniform whose short tunic and tight riding breeches unfortunately emphasized his wide, almost feminine hips. Without preamble but with impressive solemnity, he offered Hawk the equivalent of an *Oberleutnant's* commission in the Schutzstaffel.

"Heydrich wanted me to join his personal staff as his artistic consultant," Hawk said. "My first job was to draw up a complete annotated list of great and near-great paintings and sculptures in private hands in Czechoslovakia and Poland. After that, Belgium, Holland and France."

"And by 'private hands' Heydrich meant Jews?"

"Not exclusively, but primarily, yes," Hawk replied. "It could hardly be otherwise since Jews owned a disproportionate number of the best European paintings and sculptures. Most of the rest were in America."

For which Hawk had not yet been asked to prepare an inventory.

Heydrich sent Hawk to his own tailor for uniforms, then to an SS officers' training camp for several weeks of military basic training and indoctrination plus instruction in secret police arts. He returned to Berlin inspired and ready to go to work. Hawk was allowed to hand-pick a small staff. The best art experts in Germany were Jewish, of course. He gave Heydrich a list of candidates for the project, all of them scholars of the first rank. Heydrich arrested the ones that were not already in custody and provided a large sunny workroom in Gestapo headquarters, complete with a first-rate library. According to Hawk, his helpers were quite happy in their work. It was infinitely less frightening than the fate they had imagined for themselves when the Gestapo knocked on their doors. Though young, Hawk was a genuine scholar, a rare bird among Nazis, and he took certain measures to keep up morale— for example, not wearing his SS uniform during working hours and letting his helpers wear ordinary civilian clothes rather than prison clothes. He also arranged for family visits and kosher meals.

Kosher meals in a Nazi prison?

"Heydrich had given me absolute authority, in writing, to manage the project as I thought best. His signature and stamp made anything possible." Hawk started to smile in fond memory, caught himself, but could not resist the pleasantry that had popped into his head. "We just ordered the arrest of a Jewish cook or two," he said. "Heydrich was a man who thought in spirals but acted in straight lines."

The lists of art objects for France and the Low Countries, complete with estimates of current market value, were completed in a couple of months. The combined value of works of art in private hands ran into hundreds of millions of reichsmarks. Heydrich ordered Hawk to form his own personal special unit of

SS troopers and began training them to locate the houses where the paintings on Heydrich's list were hanging, and to know these pictures when they saw them. Hawk's men spent their days memorizing works of art in the way that Luftwaffe trainees learned to recognize the silhouettes of Allied aircraft. When the war came, they would be among the first German troops into the target cities, and also among the first out as they sped back to Berlin with truckloads of treasure for Heydrich's art collection.

It was from one of his Jewish scholars, a specialist in ancient manuscripts who had done groundbreaking work in Jerusalem and in the Vatican library, that Hawk first heard about the possible existence of Roman manuscripts secreted in amphorae by confidential agents of the emperor for shipment back to Rome from the far corners of the empire.

"This man had a sort of informed obsession that such manuscripts must still be preserved in amphorae that had gone to the bottom of the Mediterranean Sea as a result of Roman shipwrecks," Hawk said.

Hawk kept this fellow upstairs for a few more days after the other scholars had been locked up. After exhaustive conversation and much consultation of Latin sources, Hawk made a trip to the Vatican library. There he found plausible evidence in ancient records that amphorae had in fact been used as moving dead drops aboard Roman ships, and that certain of those ships had sunk— many of them in relatively shallow waters off Crete while bound for Ostia or Brindisi from ports in Egypt, Phoenicia and Samaria.

"Any such manuscript would, of course, be a thing of great beauty as well as an object of inestimable value," said Hawk.

Hawk took his findings to Heydrich, who was tremendously pleased by his news.

"He saw the possibilities immediately," Hawk said. "Beyond that, he was quite moved by the romance of the thing. Imagine, from his point of view, the prospect of owning an authentic dispatch from a secret policeman who had worked for Caligula."

Imagine it, indeed. The harmonies must have been deafening.

In short order Hawk found himself on a small motor yacht off the sunny coast of Crete, commanding a dozen young troopers who could not believe their luck.

"My Jew had a pretty shrewd idea of where wrecks might be found," said Hawk, "and by a mixture of his scholarship and Heydrich's incredible luck, we found one in a matter of weeks. It had been a galley. Human bones had long since been dissolved by the salt, but the ship's keel and ribs were still intact. Coins bearing the head of Augustus and all sorts of corroded bronze objects were scattered about. And of course, masses of perfectly preserved amphorae."

The Roman amphora, smaller than the Greek one on which it was modeled, was an object whose combination of beauty and utility moved Hawk's soul. He had seen them in museums, of course, but it was quite another matter to descend three or four fathoms into the murk and behold by the bent light of the sun these marvels of ancient handicraft, so shapely, so perfectly symmetrical. They lay in profusion on the bed of the sea where they had rested since the time of Christ. The divers hauled the amphorae to the surface one by one. Except for a few empty or broken ones, they were still watertight and still held precisely 25.5 liters of whatever the Romans had put into them before setting sail. Under Hawk's personal supervision the beautiful jugs were carefully opened. Their contents included thick, sour wine that was sometimes still drinkable, water, grain and other foodstuffs, all duly numbered.

Number eighty-seven was filled with wheat ("so fragrant still that it made me sneeze," said Hawk).

And buried in the wheat was the Amphora Scroll.

"The scroll was sealed in thick red wax," said Hawk. "My heart has never before or since beaten so fast as when I loosened the seal with my razor."

Unrolled, the scroll was almost a meter in length. It was written in Greek, filled from edge to edge with the dense handwriting of a Roman official who signed himself Septimus Arcanus. Although

Hawk had learned the rudiments of ancient Greek at Worksop College and improved his knowledge of the language at Marburg, he was unable to puzzle out the text. Once he got used to the handwriting, he realized that the manuscript was written in cipher. Decoding it was beyond his abilities, so at this point he had no inkling that he held in his hands a world-shaking document that was beyond price. The fact that it was in cipher suggested that it was a secret communication, and that alone made it an even greater object of fascination than a decipherable manuscript would have been.

He was terrified that exposure to air and sunshine would fade the ink or cause the parchment to disintegrate. After all, it had been made from the skin of a kid that had been slaughtered almost exactly nineteen hundred years before.

Heydrich promoted Hawk to *Haupsturmführer,* the SS rank equivalent to captain, decorated him, and presented him with an engraved pistol. Heydrich was tremendously excited by the fact that the manuscript was in Greek and in code. He wanted to know without delay what it said.

The Jewish scholar whose brilliant theory had just been vindicated by his worst enemies was brought upstairs once again.

"It turned out that he had a good knowledge of ancient ciphers, and in no time at all he cracked the code," said Hawk. "It was a very simple one, based on a key that was easily deduced. Naturally he was also perfectly fluent in ancient Greek, so we soon had a complete translation. When I read it, I did not believe it."

Hawk had another scholar, even more eminent than the first man, arrested. His decipherment and translation matched the first man's almost exactly.

"It was all there, dated in the year we call A.D. 36—names, places, mysterious events," Hawk said. "Which of the disciples was the handler, the lot. What Roman purposes were."

Heydrich was overjoyed with the scroll. He was not, however, a man to live long without suspicions. He became convinced that the Amphora Scroll was a hoax, that the Jews who had translated it were playing a joke on him, making a fool of him with the Jesus story. It was just too good to be true. Hawk offered to find Aryan scholars who could decipher and translate the scroll, but Heydrich decided that Lori would do it. Hawk was detailed to arrest her husband and son and then to kidnap Lori as she rode in the park. His men delivered Hubbard and Paul to Gestapo headquarters for questioning and Lori to a Gestapo safe house in a wooded section of Berlin. There Heydrich asked her to do him the great favor of translating something from ancient Greek.

"According to Heydrich, she read and translated the language of Homer as fluently as English or French," Hawk said. "And so the Baronesse became, with Heydrich and me, the third person on earth still living to know that the Amphora Scroll existed, and the only one of the three who had seen with her own eyes exactly what it said."

Her translation of a Greek typescript of the scroll, completed at amazing speed, confirmed the accuracy of the scholars' version, which she had not seen.

"After this, more than ever, Heydrich was entranced by this woman," Hawk said. "And when he was named Protector of Bohemia and Moravia in September 1941, she went along with him. As did the Amphora Scroll, sealed now in a vacuum inside a glass tube. Heydrich kept it in a special cradle on his desk in his official residence in Prague. I think it amused him to hide the rarest treasure of the last two thousand years in plain sight."

I asked Hawk for a photograph of the entire Amphora Scroll. He professed not to have one. But he did let me see some of his many photographs of Lori in the company of her kidnapper. And he presented me with a copy of the picture of Lori's hand holding the manuscript, along with a shot of Heydrich and Lori in Berlin, heads close together, reading the Amphora Scroll with what appears to be a painting by Frans Hals hanging on the wall in the background.

The photograph was staged as if Hals had controlled the models, arranged for the costumes, imagined the props. But of course it was Heydrich, an artist in his own way, who had done all that.

TWO

1

During my brief absence spring had turned to summer in Washington. A fierce white sun burned over the city as my flight from Miami, where I had changed planes, came in for a landing at Reagan National Airport. Granted, I was in a classical frame of mind after all that talk about the Amphora Scroll, but from the air the shimmering Greco-Roman structures on the Mall looked more than ever like some misplaced imperial outpost from the time of the Caesars. Except for Charley Hornblower, our man in Washington, the Old Boys had scattered to their various operational destinations and I had hoped to slip in and out of town unnoticed. However, when I arrived home I found a long string of telephone messages from Stephanie. Each one was a bit higher on the treble scale than the one before, so I believed that she meant it when she said that she had something important to discuss with me. My bones ached. The tambaqui I had eaten the night before had had a bad effect on my stomach and so had Simon Hawk. I took a hot shower and had a large cup of espresso coffee before deciding not to call her back.

As I was drinking my second cup of coffee I heard the mail slot in the front door open and close. Had someone slipped a letter bomb through the slot? Had Stephanie entrapped me at last? Then

I heard heavy footsteps in the yard. Charley Hornblower's long foxy face—Ben Franklin eyeglasses, lantern jaw, claret nose—appeared in my kitchen window. When he saw me through the glass, he smiled. It was the same delighted grin he had had as the gung-ho young spook I had worked with thirty years before. Apart from the broken veins and a few wrinkles and white eyebrows and a glassy bald scalp instead of a bowl-cut thatch of rufous hair, senior citizen Charley looked pretty much the same as the junior officer Charley had looked.

I let him in and offered him coffee. He shook his head No. "Upsets my stomach."

Charley needed no caffeine; excitement was written all over his face. He did not refuse a glass of Laphroaig.

Before leaving for Paris I had given him the photograph of Lori's hand holding the fragment of the Amphora Scroll and asked him to decipher the portion that was visible.

"It presented no difficulties," Charley said, producing the photograph, now covered with notations in red ink. "It's written in a cipher using a simple transposition of letters. The Greek is a bit clumsy because of the cipher, and maybe because it was written in Latin first, then translated. However, it's easy enough to read once you break through. I think it's an intelligence report."

He went on a little longer about technicalities that had fascinated him. Charley, a doctor of philosophy twice over, liked to dwell on minutiae that did not necessarily excite the untrained mind. I waited. Something about the fragment had blown Charley away, and he wanted to delay the pleasure of sharing it with me.

At last he said, "It's only a fragment, of course, a couple of hundred words. This is the way it begins. 'Lucius Aelius Sejanus from Septimus Arcanus. In such-and-such year following the umpty-umpth Olympiad, I was commanded to proceed to Aelia Capitolina' . . . that's the Latin name for Jerusalem . . . 'for the purpose of weakening the power of the priests, whose arrogant disregard of

Roman taxes and other acts of disloyalty had caused the displeasure of the emperor.' You know about Sejanus?"

"Yes."

Charley gave me the pertinent facts anyway. "For a while he was Tiberius's right-hand man. For all intents and purposes, Sejanus was the dictator of Rome during the years that Tiberius was living on Capri."

"What else did the fragment have on it?"

"Enough to tantalize. The next sentence is cut in half by the edge of the photograph, but it mentions the name of one Joshua ben Joseph, who came from Galilee, and also refers to someone named Paulus, who may have been Joshua's case officer. And there it ends."

"No other ID for Paulus?"

"Only that he was a Roman citizen," Charley said. "You do understand that the Hebrew name Joshua translates as 'Jesus' in Greek."

"I understand." I am anything but a religious man. Nevertheless, the hair rose on the back of my neck as I listened to Charley's report. I said, "So what's your opinion?"

"That this scroll is a lot more dangerous than any twelve fission bombs ever manufactured."

"If it's authentic."

"Obviously," Charley said. "But if it really was found sealed inside an amphora in a first-century Roman shipwreck, how can it *not* be authentic? The cipher, the handwriting, the syntax, the context all match up with manuscripts for that period."

Charley had the gift of enthusiasm. His Rooseveltian diction, usually well under control, now burbled in my ear.

I said, "Slow down. When we have the original we can do the tests to see how old it is and whether the ink is right and all the rest of it. It's not authentic till then."

"*If* we get it first. I sincerely doubt that our pious friend in the desert is going to have it carbon tested before he pushes the button."

"Good point," I said. "And now, Charley, I really must go to bed."

As I went upstairs I heard Stephanie's voice on the answering machine.

"I know you're there, Horace," she said.

But I wasn't, not really.

2

The next afternoon, with a twinge of guilt (but nothing so serious as to cause me to ring Stephanie from the airport), I flew to Delhi. As arranged, David Wong and I met in an restaurant frequented, David said, by the movers and shakers of New Delhi, and indeed there were lots of men in business suits at tables glittering with silver and crystal. Midway through the soup, we were joined by a friend of his, an honest old uncle of a fellow whom David introduced as Yussuf. Although he was not Han—he wore Muslim clothes and his Turkic face with its beak of a nose was the color of strong tea—he was a visa clerk in the Chinese consulate, and he brought his stamps with him. He inked visas for Xinjiang into our passports while we dined.

It was a Hindu establishment. Yussuf declined the unclean food. He held up a hand in refusal when I offered to make a contribution to his children's education. Whatever old debt he owed to David, it wasn't hard to see that he was no happier than he should have been to be meeting a couple of Americans in a public place where an honest Muslim's food might be poisoned. I assumed that Yussuf would disappear as soon as he had taken care of us, but David and he were soon deep in conversation in a language that I could neither understand nor identify. I was glad enough to be left out. The long flight had done nothing to cure my aching bones. I had a burning thirst with nothing to drink but water that I did not trust. The gritty lukewarm Indian beer in its huge bottle tasted of dust. My tandoori chicken was dry; so was the rice. I ate a mouthful of each and put down my silverware. Sitar music came out of scratchy speakers and I was reminded, as if an iris had opened in my brain, of the everyday boredom of a life in espionage. One is always waiting for someone who does not show up, for something that does not happen. The obsequious waiter came and made an unhappy face at my uneaten plate.

In due course Yussuf departed, making half-hearted *namaste* to me. David had things to tell me. He flicked the ashes off the imaginary cigar of an imaginary Groucho and wiggled his eyebrows. He explained that the language he and Yussuf had been speaking together was Kazak, the Turkic tongue used in various dialects by Muslim tribesmen on both sides of the frontier between Kazakhstan and the Xinjiang Uygur Autonomous Region. The Kazak, like the other non-Chinese Muslim peoples along this border, did not acknowledge a line on a map drawn by their conquerors but drifted back and forth across it with their flocks and herds and trade goods. And sometimes, when fomenters of native uprisings like David got involved, they drifted back and forth with arms and ammunition and dangerous ideas.

Yussuf had news of Paul Christopher—third-hand news, hardly better than gossip, but news nevertheless. One of Yussuf's cousins had heard from another relative that an elderly white man who spoke rough peasant Mandarin—Paul had learned the language from his prison guards—had appeared on the Kazakhstan side of the border. He had somehow managed to get through the high mountains of the Borahora Shan on horseback and had reached the fringe of the quarantined territories. Apart from the polar regions, it may be the bleakest place on earth.

"I asked what questions Christopher was asking," David said. "The word was that the old man was inquiring about a very old European woman who he said was his mother," David said. "They thought he was crazy. The last they saw of him, he was riding east toward the forbidden area. They warned him that he would be locked up forever if the Han caught him, but he just thanked them and rode on."

I truly didn't know what to make of this.

David read my mind. "Christopher must have had some word from somebody to send him into the mountains," he said. "The people who saw him said he acted like a man who knew exactly where he was going."

"Based on what?"

"The way he acted. He seemed happy. That's why they thought he was nuts. There's not much to be happy about in that country for a foreigner who's all alone and sticks out like a sore thumb."

On the spot, David called the rest of the Old Boys and gave them this new information. Jack Philindros listened without comment, then asked to speak to me. He was in Rome. He had spoken to Zarah's monk.

"It wasn't a very productive conversation, though he did confirm Lori's presence in Prague," Jack said. "He was wary. He's a member of the Dominican order. He's dying and will soon be interviewed at the gates of Heaven, so he's reluctant to give up secrets that belong to God. Remember, it was the Church that sent him to Prague."

"Was he there at the right time?"

"Oh, yes, in January 1942. He was an art appraiser for the Church—an expert on private collections in the former Austro-Hungarian empire. Heydrich heard about him from one of his men and borrowed him from the Pope for a few days."

"That would make him the last person to see Lori."

"That's right," Jack said. "I showed him some pictures of 1930s women and he picked out Lori immediately. He remembers her vividly. She did live with Heydrich. She was under tight self-control but was so filled with hatred that he feared for her soul. He couldn't help her because she wasn't a Catholic, or even a Christian. That was all he was willing to say about her."

"Surely it's a short step from there to the scroll."

"You'd think so, but he hasn't taken the step yet."

"Then what was his mission?" I asked.

"He didn't specify," Jack said. "But the ice has been broken. I'm going to go see him again today."

I said, "Is he going to live long enough to talk?"

"Talking seems to revive him," Jack said. "He was much healthier looking when I left him than when I arrived. This time I hope to ask the larger questions."

An hour or two later, Jack called me back. When he reached the hospital, the Dominican's room was empty.

"According to the sisters he died in a state of grace," Jack said. "I'm going to knock on some different doors."

3

Vast and overpopulated though China is, the police know exactly who everybody is and exactly where they ought to be. They keep track of the teeming masses in the old-fashioned way, on 1.25 billion file cards. My own card, which had been gathering dust for fifteen years or so, popped up on the watch list when I presented my passport at the airport in Urümqui, the capital of Xinjiang. As I had expected, it caused a stir. I might now be an honest tourist with no evil designs on the People's Republic of China, but not so long ago I had been the chief American spy in Beijing, and the Chinese official had not been born who was willing to believe that I wasn't still what I used to be. The delay was long and the interviews gave my rusty Mandarin a workout. However, the visa that Yussuf had stamped in my passport turned out to be genuine, so they let me in, but without a welcoming smile. David Wong passed through the controls with far less trouble. The Chinese were just as suspicious of him, probably even more so because he looked Chinese and lived in China, but they had more recent reports of him and therefore had fewer questions to ask him. As we got into a taxi together, we saw that our minders were already on the job: two obvious sidewalk men, bored but competent, stayed close behind us on bicycles. The taxi driver kept an anxious eye on the rear-view mirror so as not to lose them in the snail's-pace traffic.

David and I had no reason not to behave like honest men. I had told my questioners at the airport a version of the truth—that I was here on behalf of my family to gather information about the death of my cousin. Playing shamelessly on Han reverence for graves, I said we were deeply unhappy that Paul's body had been cremated in Urümqui instead of being returned to us for burial among his ancestors. They could follow me around as much as they liked and never catch me asking questions about anything else.

As soon as we checked into the hotel, a brand-new Holiday Inn, we started making phone calls to the local officialdom. Out of a dog-eared pocket notebook, David provided the name of the policeman who was head of the section that dealt with foreigners. I called his office. According to the young policeman who answered, Captain Zhang Qiying was very busy. I should route my request through the American consulate.

I said, "Please write down two names."

My name in Mandarin is Han Huan Ren. Paul's prison name had been Yang Geng Qi. I described the ideographs in which the names were written, along with our dates of birth and other standard index-card content. This took a long time on the telephone, but that's one of the inconveniences of a language that has no alphabet. Clearly the man on the other end of the line thought that this was a waste of time, but he had been trained to copy down information. For political cops, from the FBI in the heart of our great American democracy to Captain Zhang in the backwater of the last big totalitarian state on earth, the possession of information is the object of the game. It doesn't really make any difference if the stuff in the files is useful, or even true. Getting hold of it and squirreling it away is the object of the exercise.

"Please ask Captain Zhang to consult his files to see if those names appear," I said. "I assure you he will be interested. I'll await his call."

While I waited I went for a walk, followed closely by one of our two minders. The other one, no doubt, was trying to keep up with David, who was hoping to collect some information at the crematorium. It's a tough job to follow a man one-on-one and I probably could have lost my minder even though my head with its big nose and ears and five o'clock shadow stuck up above the crowd. But I was glad of his company because I was trying to establish my innocent intentions, so I walked slowly and stopped often. Like most Chinese cities, Urümqui is a combination of medieval warrens and spanking-new office towers wrapped in a sulfurous pall of pollution. Cars crawled through a traffic jam comprised of pedestrians, bicyclists and the occasional horseman or camel rider, mixed in with coolies carrying astonishing loads. A man on a donkey talked on a cell phone at the top of his lungs. Half the crowd was doing the same when not coughing convulsively into each other's faces or spitting on the pavement. According to a tourist pamphlet I read on the plane, Urümqui means "beautiful meadow" in Mongol, but if there was a blade of grass in the whole city I did not see it.

David and I had arranged to meet on Red Square. This space turned out to be almost as vast as its namesake in Beijing, but David knew the ground and had named a meeting point. When I found it, he was already there. There is no such thing in China as a place to sit down in public unless you want to find a space on the curb where the saliva is fairly dry. Therefore we walked some more, followed now by David's tail as well as my own. The din of the crowd made conversation difficult. I was glad that it was David Wong and not Jack Philindros whose words I was trying to catch in this hubbub.

David had, of course, made friends at the crematorium; he showed me a picture of grinning workers in the viewer of his digital camera. They were not smiling, David explained, because they liked their jobs. They disliked the unnatural idea of burning corpses. It may have been state policy to cremate the dead, but it was an idea whose time had not come in China. David had brought with him from the States a gym bag filled with small gifts—pens and pencils, cheap watches, cigarettes, miniature bottles of liquor. A new watch, a pack of Camels and two ounces of firewater poured into a cup of tea at nine in the morning seldom renders anyone unfriendly.

"The fellows at the crematorium say they mostly burn Communists who are trying to make a good impression on their superiors, plus a few foreigners," David said. "Otherwise it's slow —so slow that it's hard to keep in practice."

"What about Paul?"

"They remember cremating two foreigners—one about a year ago and the other in September of this year. The first was a Russian who died of a heart attack. They have a good file on him—medical report, death certificate, photocopy of his passport. He was a fat man. They got a look at him because it's standard operating procedure to open the coffin to double-check the identity of the deceased before it goes into the flames. Also, I imagine, to harvest any valuables on the corpse."

And the other one, the one that was burned in September?

"It was delivered by the police," David said. "They didn't open that coffin because they were told that the body was badly decomposed."

"Decomposed?"

"Yep."

This was curious, because even in summer flesh does not quickly decompose in the parched air and weak sunshine of the Xinjiang high desert. Archeologists find mummies that are thousands of years old but still have the lustrous flowing hair and the fresh though tanned and shrunken faces of young men and women.

4

One of Captain Zhang's policeman, wearing plain clothes, awaited us when we returned to the hotel. At his polite invitation I plunged back into the mob and followed him to Zhang's office.

Despite his junior rank, Captain Zhang was no longer young—salt-and-pepper hair, office pallor, tired eyes, the slightly slumped posture of a man who has gone through the same motions too many times. However, his intelligence was as apparent as his fatigue. He worked from behind a clean desk, without notes, which told me that he had either mastered the details of Paul's case or, more likely, had no intention of telling me the truth. It was in his power to throw me out of China, so I was prepared to act out two different roles: elaborate politeness that would give him no reason to expel me, plus an informed curiosity that might give him a reason to let me run so he could keep an eye on me and maybe learn something. Unless Paul had changed all of a sudden, it was a safe bet that Zhang had little or no idea what he had really been up to when he was in these parts.

After the usual cup of tea and exchange of pleasantries, Captain Zhang was remarkably open and direct. Although we were speaking Mandarin he called Paul by his English name.

"We remember Mister Paul Christopher quite well," he said, gesturing with the stained fingers of a heavy smoker. "And you, too, of course, Mister Horace Hubbard."

I nodded pleasantly. How kind. Paul was the most notorious American spy ever captured by the Chinese, and in a more modest way I, too, had enjoyed an evil reputation in this country.

Zhang said, "And now we learn that the two of you are cousins. Is that correct?"

"Yes."

"This is new information."

"Is it? We certainly never made a secret of it."

"How strange. You spoke to us about him so many times in the past in your official capacity, when you were trying to secure his release from prison. Yet no notation was ever made that you are so closely related."

Zhang looked expectant, but I made no response to his remark. It wasn't my fault if the Chinese counterintelligence service didn't ask the right questions.

Finally I said, "On behalf of our family I wish to thank the Chinese authorities for returning the ashes to us, but I am sure you understand how bitterly we regret that our relative's body could not be buried in the family cemetery. Uncertainty has been created."

He made me wait just slightly longer for his reply than my own silence had lasted. Then he said, "Regrettable. But there are no embalmers in Ulugqat. I believe your friend Mister Wong has already ascertained that the body was not in good condition when it reached Urümqi."

Zhang knew that David had been poking around the crematorium. Zhang's eyes and ears were everywhere. He wanted me to know that. But amazingly for a secret policeman, he also wanted me to understand that he was willing to let himself be questioned. Or at least pretend to have a conversation instead of asking all the questions himself.

I said, "I wonder if you have any idea what my cousin was doing in Ulugqat."

Zhang did not exactly answer the question, but he did amaze me again by giving me information. "Mister Paul Christopher was brought down from the mountains by some Tajik herdsmen who found him lying at the bottom of a chasm. He was badly injured with many broken bones and unable to speak. They thought he had fallen off his horse, which was found grazing at the top of the defile."

"How far was this from Ulugqat?"

"A considerable distance, I believe. The Tajik don't use maps, so it's difficult to pinpoint."

"I see," I said. "But in any case these herdsmen left their herds and brought Christopher to Ulugqat for medical attention."

"Yes," Zhang said, with a look that told me not to mention how remarkable this was before he had explained the matter. "He was a foreigner and quite old. They thought he might be an important man. Or perhaps a spy. Unfortunately he died before they reached Ulugqat."

"They thought he looked old? Why?"

"He was, I believe, seventy-five years of age."

"I see. But they brought his corpse into town anyway?"

"Obviously. It was their duty to do so. He had been dead for some time when his body was delivered, and then it took several days to bring it into Urümqui."

"I don't understand," I said. "Why not just bury the man in Ulugqat?"

"Impossible," Zhang said. "There was no foreign cemetery. He could not be buried in a Muslim graveyard or in one of ours, for that matter. Secondly, the death of any foreigner on Chinese soil is a serious matter. Once we identified this particular foreigner, the matter became even more serious, because of Mister Paul Christopher's history. An autopsy was ordered. That procedure couldn't be done in Ulugqat."

"And the results of the autopsy were?"

"As I said, many bone fractures including a serious compression of the skull. A ruptured spleen, a torn liver, internal bleeding."

"They brought him down the mountain on horseback?"

"Yes. The Tajik had no motor vehicles."

"So he was alive when they found him?"

"That is my understanding."

"It's a wonder he could survive—how many days?—lying over a horse like a sack of grain."

"Indeed." Zhang nodded respectfully to Paul's admirable ghost. "He was a very strong and determined man, as we in China have reason to remember."

I said, "I suppose photographs of the corpse were made, fingerprints taken?"

"Of course, but these are official records that cannot be disclosed."

"Then you can show me no proof that the man the Tajik brought in was, in fact, my cousin?"

"Proof?" Zhang said in real astonishment. In China, proof was not something you asked a policeman for; it was something only a policeman had a right to demand. He said, "You have his ashes."

"We have ashes. We don't know if they are his."

Silence. Resentment. Zhang lit a rank cigarette, his fifth since we had started talking half an hour before.

I said, "I'm sure you wondered why Christopher had come back to Xinjiang."

Squinting through the cigarette smoke, Zhang said, "Not at all. He explained at the airport that he wished before he died to see the place where he had been imprisoned."

"And this was acceptable to you and your superiors?"

"Why should it not be? He already knew all about the place, and in any case it's no longer a secret location. It is now quite empty, abandoned. He went there on his motorcycle."

"On his *motorcycle*?"

You laugh? So did I.

"Yes, he bought one, a new Suzuki, soon after he arrived," Zhang said. "He brought camping gear with him—a tent, a sleeping bag, a small stove, dehydrated food, and so on. He rode around quite freely, chatting with people, asking questions."

"What sort of questions?"

"Strange ones. He seemed to be looking for his mother. This

was odd behavior for a man his age. I'm afraid we concluded that
he was not quite right in his mind."

"But you let him ride around asking questions?"

"They were harmless questions."

Zhang let me know by a small gesture and a change in tone of
voice that he had answered enough questions, harmless or not. I
asked another one anyway.

"When he was in prison, the political officer in charge of his
re-education, the man who questioned him every day for ten
years, was a party official known to Christopher as Ze Keli. Have
you any idea if Christopher contacted this man, or attempted to
contact him?"

"No," Zhang said. "And now, Mister Hubbard, I have these for
you."

Squinting through the smoke of his cigarette, he opened a
drawer and removed a package wrapped in cloth. He undid it and
placed before me, one by one, Paul Christopher's passport and
wallet, along with the Rolex watch he had been wearing since the
1950s. He had been wearing it when he was captured by the
Chinese. They had given it back to him when he was released. It
was a self-winding watch. I shook it and it immediately began to
run. I wondered if Paul had done the same after all those years in
prison where he had no means of measuring time.

5

The story Captain Zhang had told me was almost certainly hokum. At the same time, the delivery of Paul's personal effects was disturbing. On the face of it, they were evidence that my cousin was either dead or in Chinese custody. How else could Zhang be in possession of his watch, his passport, his wallet, his money—the entire contents of his pockets? But this was a hoary trick. By laying these familiar objects before me, Zhang wanted me to abandon hope and believe his story. Therefore I took it with a grain of salt.

"Christopher could have ditched his identity," David said.

This was possible. A switch of this kind was difficult for a white man to make while swimming in a sea of Han, but in his time Paul had done even more improbable things and gotten away with them.

Reading my thoughts—after all we had both breathed the same paranoid air of tradecraft for half a lifetime—David said, "He couldn't change names and nationalities while he was still in Xinjiang and under surveillance. But if he crossed a frontier . . ."

"What frontier?"

"Take your pick. But if his destination really was the forbidden zone, he could have crossed into Tajikistan, taken a train to Kazakhstan, and come back into Xinjiang over the Horgas Pass."

"Despite dire warnings that he was almost certain to be discovered and arrested."

"Correct," David said. "And looking on the dark side, if in fact Christopher was captured, that would explain how Zhang happened to have his personal belongings in his desk drawer."

Yes, it would. It could also mean that Paul was back in a Chinese prison. If that was the case, no one would ever see him again and it would be a far better thing for the Chinese if the family believed that he was dead.

This conversation took place on the bus to Ulugqat. Captain Zhang's men were waiting for us at the bus station. They made no effort to be discreet. They wanted us to know that they would be part of our lives as long as we were in China. This was fine by us; we were here for the honest purposes already stated, to find out whatever we could about my cousin and his death. After checking into a hotel, we began asking questions. We never asked about anything but Paul. Evidently Paul had made his usual good impression because people usually smiled when they heard his Mandarin name. A surprising number of people had seen Paul and remembered him, but none had anything interesting to tell us. He had come on a motorcycle, he liked their food. Ulugqat is not exactly a tourist destination, so for most of its citizens a visit by a foreigner was an interesting event.

David and I took long walks at night. It was our only chance to talk to each other with a reduced chance of being recorded. The streets were hardly less crowded after dark and you could find excellent food in the Tajik quarter—not the usual sticky Han delicacies but fat roast mutton with noodles and fried bread, and delicious yogurt made from sheep's milk. We found a particularly good restaurant and went back three nights in a row. On the third night, when we were still empty of new information and close to giving up, a Tajik with the butterscotch skin of a man who lives outdoors seated himself at a table facing us. Our minders were behind him, so they could not see his face. He engaged us in a jolly conversation about religion. He had the hearty, self-certain manner of an Episcopalian deacon. If Moses and Jesus Christ were among the Christian prophets, why did Christians call God by the wrong name? Why did they reject Allah's last messenger? As he got ready to leave, he came over to our table and leaned on it, and while David talked, slowly and distinctly whispered to me two short phrases in Mandarin.

One of these phrases was the name of a cemetery and the location of a grave. The other was a man's name, Yang Geng Qi. Paul Christopher.

On the way back to the hotel I told David what the man had said to me and what I thought it might mean.

David shrugged. "We can dig up the grave, Horace, but think for a minute. Maybe that's what they want us to do, so they can grab us in the act and get rid of us forever."

It was not impossible that he was right. Robbing graves is a serious offense anywhere in the world. In China, with its ancient reverence for last resting places, the penalty might very well be a bullet in the head. All the same, I wanted to know. David shrugged again and went along with me.

We set out for the cemetery in the wee hours of the morning. Even gumshoes have to sleep some time, and ours were exceptionally tired after the workout we had given them that day. They were dozing in the lobby. The receptionist was also asleep, but there was no question of tiptoeing past all three of them. We went out a back door, split up, and made our way through empty and silent streets, a strange and unsettling experience in China, where one never expects the crowd to be absent. It was a moonless night, but the stars were brilliant in the black desert sky. They gave off enough light for us to find our way among the markers.

It took time to find the grave of Yang Geng Qi. We had brought a metal tray from our hotel room and with this clumsy tool we dug through the gritty sand at the head of the grave. I had never before tried to be quiet in China, where noise is as omnipresent as the air itself. At this hour of the night the country was as quiet as sleep itself, and each bite of the tray into the earth sounded like the clash of cymbals.

At last we found what we were looking for. There was no coffin, just a body wrapped in cloth and trussed with rope. Feeling in the dark, I uncovered the face. Shielding ourselves under my raincoat, we shone flashlights into the grave. We found ourselves looking into the empty eye sockets of a young Han who had been shot through the back of the head. David slit the shroud to the man's waist. There was a gaping hole in the chest where the heart had been removed and another where his liver used to be. I felt beneath the body. The kidneys were missing, too. This was a criminal whose organs had been harvested immediately after he was executed.

David took several flash photographs of the mutilated corpse, which was well on its way to becoming a mummy.

Clearly Zhang *had* planned to show us a grave before presenting us with Paul's belongings. But then someone decided to send us ashes instead. A wise precaution.

6

I wanted to make contact with the Episcopalian again. David and I went back to the restaurant where the fellow had whispered his information. We didn't really expect to find him there—or if we did, that he would be fool enough to talk to us again—but there was no other place to start. Our minders went with us, of course. To all appearances they had not missed us the night before. Both had still been asleep in the lobby when we returned just before first light. Now they drank tea and watched stolidly as David and I once again ate the coarse barbarian food.

There was no sign of my informant, but David overheard talk among the customers about a buz kashi match. You may have seen this game in the movies or in *National Geographic*—polo as a blood sport with the carcass of a goat as the ball. The match between Tajik horsemen and some Kyrgyz from the north was planned two days hence somewhere in the mountains. The conversation was so free and easy that you might have thought we were in a free country and the two scowling Han policemen sitting against the wall were members of the family. We asked if it was possible for us to see the match. The owner, who had been leading the discussion, replied that we'd be as welcome as the day is long. As a matter of fact, he had an uncle who owned a Toyota

4Runner, and though he could not say for sure, it was possible that his uncle would be willing to drive us up the mountain. He was in the taxi business.

The uncle in his 4Runner arrived at our hotel at daybreak. He was a big sunburnt Tajik named Zikkar who somewhat resembled the Episcopalian, which could mean nothing or mean that they were related—or merely that both men possessed one of the half-dozen or so faces that the whole tribe shared after thousands of years of intermarriage. Zikkar asked for the equivalent of two hundred dollars to drive us up the mountain and back down. This was a large sum by local standards. Since we did not want him to carry passengers for whom he had no respect, David bargained him down to one hundred fifty.

Could he leave immediately? We were ready to go. We were already dressed in woolens and down parkas—it was cold in November even at Ulugqat's relatively modest altitude. Zikkar did not answer immediately. His eyes were on our two minders, who were sprinting toward us through the crowd like a couple of half-backs, spinning and dodging pedestrians. They were sleepy-eyed, frantic, panting. The senior minder let loose a torrent of Mandarin, too fast and slangy for me to understand, while the other gave David and me a burning stare designed to make us think of handcuffs and dungeons.

In Mandarin, David said, "We have hired this man to drive us to the buz kashi. We may never have another chance to see such a thing. You and your friend are welcome to come along."

As if a horn had sounded ending the game, the senior man stopped raving in mid-sentence. He considered the offer for a long moment, then stepped back into the crowd, turning his back in case one of us was a lip reader, and made a call on his cell phone. While he talked, the silent minder placed himself in front of the 4Runner. In moments the senior man reappeared. Without another word, he and his sidekick got into the car as if they had paid for it. The talker got into the front seat. Very politely, I asked him to move to the back with his friend and

David. There was no room for my legs back there. And besides, I had paid for the vehicle. Frozen-faced, he complied.

The buz kashi match would take place in a meadow at a high altitude. There was a road of sorts—actually a narrow track beaten down by hooves over centuries. The 4Runner, which had 200,000 kilometers on the odometer, made slow and bumpy but steady progress on a grade that got closer to the vertical with every turn of the wheels.

It took the better part of the morning to reach the point where, according to Captain Zhang, Paul Christopher had met his end. Zikkar halted by the fateful ravine as if this were a programmed stop on the tour. The gash in the earth was prodigious, with a cold torrent tumbling through mist at its bottom. The stony smell of the rushing water was apprehended as much on the tongue as in the nostrils. A brisk wind was blowing. The air was quite cold now, close to the freezing point and probably well below it on the wind-chill scale. Our minders wasted no time emptying their bladders and jumping back into the heated car. David took pictures. The vociferous minder rolled down a window and shouted at him to stop. This was sensitive country, a border region. We walked up the track a half mile or so, Zikkar trailing along behind us. In Tajik, David asked him if this was a dangerous place to ride a horse.

Zikkar grinned. "Only for a pregnant woman," he replied. "Or a Han."

"What about a white man?"

"They ride in cars."

"Has a white man every fallen off his horse and gone into the ravine?

"A white man?" Zikkar said. He gave us a long look before answering the question. "I don't think so. But you can ask at the buz kashi."

Zikkar faced the sun and looked at his shadow. It was about ten o'clock by this human sundial. With a follow-me jerk of his head, he strode down the mountainside toward the 4Runner. The Han policemen, dressed in cotton trousers and shirts and thin padded jackets, shivered miserably in the backseat.

An hour or so later we came to a notch in the terrain that framed a vista of whitened peaks marching into Afghanistan. According to the map, the altitude here was nine thousand feet. Below us lay an impossibly picturesque valley fenced by the sheer rock walls of snowcapped mountains. The Tajik village on the valley floor consisted of a couple of dozen stone huts straggling alongside a fast-running river. On the other side of the valley stood a half-dozen yurts—round, collapsible shelters made of thick felt.

Zikkar pointed to them: "Kyrgyz."

The visiting team. The blue smoke of dung fires drifted in the crystal-clear air. Yaks, sheep, and goats wandered about, with a few two-humped Bactrian camels intermingled. The horses, shaggy hammer-headed animals, stood apart in two groups. Zikkar maneuvered the 4Runner through the herd. The animals paid no attention to the stinking machine, which might well have emerged through a seam in time into this ancient world.

David and I were introduced to the village headman, a dignified fellow named Jafargul, who gave David and me cups of warm milk fresh from the ewe. He then invited us inside for more food and drink. Our Han minders were ignored, left to their own devices in the backseat of the car. I would have let them shiver, but Zikkar, a businessman thinking of the future, brought them tea and flatbread, along with a couple of sheepskins for warmth.

The buz kashi match, played mostly inside a cloud of dust, lacked the dramatic close-ups and sound effects of movie versions I had seen, but it was exciting enough. The smell of blood, sweat, dirt and fresh dung added a dimension that movies lack. Through my binoculars I caught glimpses of riders wrestling at a full gallop for the carcass of a young goat. Early in the game, two riders playing tug-of-war with the dead animal pulled off its head. Blood spurted. The man with the severed head pursued the other fellow, beating him on the back with it. As the match progressed, the goat's legs and tail were pulled off one by one, so it became more and more difficult to get a grip on the slippery dismembered carcass. Blood-smeared men were knocked off their horses, dragged, trampled, had their teeth knocked out—you could see them spitting incisors into the air. Injured horses writhed on the rocky ground. I have no idea which side won. Mayhem seemed to be the only rule. As far as I could tell, nobody crossed the goal—if there were goals—with what was left of the goat, so maybe the object was not victory but how murderously you played the game.

Injured men had been dragged off the field, but Zikkar assured us that no one had been killed today. "Many broken bones," he said with a delighted smile. "That's why they play now, so that they'll have the whole winter to heal."

7

The weather was changing. A great dark-blue bruise appeared above the craggy peaks to the west. The smell of snow was in the air. A few fat flakes were already drifting in on a soft west wind. There was no question of driving back down the mountain in darkness during a snowstorm. Zikkar led us back to the headman's house, where we would spend the night.

Jafargul awaited us outside his door. Beside him stood two men holding a wriggling sheep. They lifted it into the air, head down, and Jafargul slit its throat. He caught the blood in a bowl, then skinned the sheep with a few economical slashes of his knife, which evidently had been honed to a surgical edge. He then cut it up for the pot and with a dazzling smile of welcome, invited us inside. A dung fire burned cheerfully on the hearth, fumes rising through a smoke hole. The dirt floor, pounded to a sheen by many feet over many years, was covered with bright red-and-black tribal carpets. More carpets hung on the walls. There were no windows. The scene was lit by firelight and the flames of oil lamps. It occurred to me that I was seeing human faces and the mellow vegetable-dye colors in the rugs in a way that few Westerners had seen them since Edison brought the mischief of electric light into the world.

The Tajik believe that they are descendants of the armies of

Alexander the Great, and some of them do have Macedonian looks. Jafargul, for example, had green eyes and thick auburn hair and eyebrows. Women wearing pillbox hats with white veils attached were at work in the kitchen. The veils did not cover their faces. These particular Tajiks are Ismaili Shi'as, followers of the Aga Khan, and they have their own customs. In this house at least, abstinence was not one of them. Jafargul and his guests had a taste for whiskey, and we soon worked our way through the liter of Jack Daniels that David had brought along as emergency rations.

One of the guests, seated across the fire from me, was the Episcopalian. He sounded as if he were in the middle of another philosophical discussion. The Episcopalian paid absolutely no attention to us. Time passed. The feast and the whiskey took effect. Conversation dwindled to a murmur. Quite soon most of the men had stretched out on the rugs and fallen asleep. I, too, lay down and closed my eyes. What dreams would a man have in this place?

I was on the edge of sleep when a hand squeezed my arm. Zikkar. He beckoned, pointing to my parka. David was already on his feet, zipping up his own jacket. Zikkar put a finger to his lips, then led us outside. The wind had died. An inch or two of snow lay on the ground. More was falling through milky moonlight, forming a scrim between village and mountains. Boots creaking in the snow, we followed Zikkar to a small stone building at the far end of the village. It was surrounded by snow-covered animals. None of these ghostly beasts paid any attention to us except for a camel that swung its ponderous head toward our disagreeable scent and spat.

It was pitch-dark inside the hut. David entered first, and as I bent double to go through the empty door frame I heard him utter an explosive *oof!* A knife? A club? I dropped to my hands and knees and went inside like a defensive tackle—a slow one, but I still had bulk—and encountered two pairs of legs. One pair, wearing corduroys, belonged to David, the other pair, clad in rough wool, belonged to another man, who seemed to be holding my friend in a death grip. I was about to strangle the attacker when David, sounding as though the breath had been knocked out of him, gasped, "Horace, wait! It's okay."

A flashlight—Zikkar's—winked on and I beheld David in the embrace of a brawny tribesman. It was obvious that murder was the last thing this gentleman had in mind. He was delighted to see David. The man was dressed like the Kyrgyz I had seen at the buz kashi, and the language he spoke sounded different from Tajik.

"Good grief," David said in English. "It's Askar."

"Who?"

"Askar. He was Filibuster stroke one. We worked together on the frontier in the '80s."

Filibuster was the code name for David's infamous operation to encourage a Muslim uprising on the Sino-Soviet frontier. Askar's designation, Filibuster stroke one, meant that he had been the principal agent—commander of the Islamist network the Chinese supposedly had rolled up fifteen years ago. How could he still be alive and walking around, a free man?

Zikkar's flashlight went out. A lamp was lit. By its milder light Askar turned out to be a grayhead with bristling white eyebrows and a wiry pepper-and-salt Islamic beard. In the past David had given Askar hundreds of thousands of American dollars—I knew, because as chief of station I had signed off on every penny—but the affection the man was displaying toward his old handler could not possibly have been bought with money.

David introduced me to Askar in true name. There was no reason to do otherwise. Askar shook hands firmly, like a Westerner. "I know who you are," he said in slow Mandarin. "We were told to expect you."

I said, "Told by whom?"

"By the other American," Askar replied. "The one you're looking for. He said you would come and try to find him."

"When did he say that?"

"Not long ago."

"Where is he now?"

Zikkar shrugged. Exasperation washed over me. David put a hand on my arm.

"You'll get nowhere with direct questions," he said. "Step back. Let them talk. That's why they brought us here, to tell us something. Just listen."

Zikkar crooked a finger. David and I followed him to the back of the hut, where a large squared-up stack of thick felt—a folded yurt?—stood against the wall. He moved some of the material and I saw that the stack was hollow. Zikkar moved another bale or two and beckoned us closer. He shone his flashlight into the hollow space, revealing a bright-orange Suzuki dirt bike.

"This belonged to the other American," Zikkar said in Mandarin.

They had swapped Paul some food and two horses for the bike, Zikkar told us. He said no more than that. Zikkar hid the motorcycle again, then spread a carpet on the dirt floor. We sat down in a circle. David fished a pint of whiskey and three packs of American cigarettes out of the pockets of his parka.

As the tribesmen smoked and drank, Zikkar and the Episcopalian talked at length in their own languages. When they were through, David asked a question or two, then turned to me.

"Do you want to hear this now, or wait?" he asked.

"Now," I said. "The short version."

"Okay," David said. "One day Paul turned up on his motorcycle. Not here—higher up in the pastureland, because it was still summer and they were out grazing their herds. He spent a few days with them, long enough for them to get to like him. Apparently he had already picked up some of the language and was soon speaking it pretty well. Was he that quick?"

"Yes. A sponge."

"He said he was looking for his mother. He told them the story of her disappearance. This touched their hearts. As I said, there was something about him they liked, but they wanted to be sure he was for real. So he told them about his life, that he had spent all those years in a Han prison. Some of these people have served time, too, and he knew all the details of prison life under Mao. They'd heard about the ditch he dug."

"So?"

"So they almost trusted him, but at the same time he was a stranger in the wrong place. They were afraid that the Han would show up at any moment and they'd all be in trouble. They wanted to help him. They also wanted to get rid of him. Some of the old people knew a story about a European woman, not a Russian, who came to live with the Kyrgyz. She came when she was young. She lived among the Kyrgyz until she was very old. The last they heard, she was still living. They told him this."

"Was this story the truth?"

"They don't know. But it was enough for Paul. He asked directions and took off at once with the two horses he'd swapped the motorcycle for. He left one of the horses by the ravine with his belongings—the stuff Zhang showed you—in the saddlebag. Then he disappeared, riding west. The Han came up from Ulugqat and took the horse and saddlebag."

"What about the body they were supposed to have carried down to Ulugqat?"

"These people don't know anything about that."

David and Askar exchanged a few sentences in Kyrgyz.

Then David turned to me and said, "He says this European woman married his uncle. She had blue eyes and fair hair. She carried some sort of strange glass container with her wherever she went. He says she's still alive, living with her son."

"Paul found her?"

"Not that son," David said. "Askar's cousin, the child she had with his uncle. His name is Tarik."

"Does Tarik's mother have a name?"

"Yes," David said. "In Kyrgyz she's called Kerzira."

Askar told us the rest of the story, or as much of it as he knew. Fifty years before, Lori had appeared out of nowhere into another nowhere, arriving in a Kyrgyz encampment on a stallion, leading two mares. She gave the headman an admission fee in gold when she arrived. She lived with the headman's family. Despite her wealth—gold aside, the stallion and mares eventually grew into a large herd—she worked as hard as any other woman. The headman's wives liked her and taught her Kyrgyz household skills. Even in the beginning she spoke enough Kyrgyz to make herself understood. Before long she was fluent, and in tribal dress looked like a light-skinned, gray-eyed Kyrgyz. When Russian or Chinese police or soldiers came around, depending on which side of the border the herds happened to be, she veiled her face and withdrew along with the rest of the women. After a while she married the headman's youngest brother, putting up five colts and gold as a dowry. Soon afterward she had a child, and after that no one bothered to remember that she was not born a Kyrgyz unless reminded by one of her peculiarities, such as her refusal to be separated from her heavy glass tube and a habit of going for long, unwomanly gallops all by herself. No one knew where she had come from, though she had been wearing Persian dress and riding a Persian horse when she arrived. No one questioned her desire to live the wild bygone life of their mountain tribe. Who in the world would not wish to do so?

8

Snow continued to fall in big wet flakes. The jagged rocks that had made the landscape so beautiful yesterday were now softly rounded white globes. The snow was shin deep. Zikkar decided that it would be unwise to remain where we were.

"He says we won't be able to get up the hill and out of the valley even with chains if it snows much more," David translated. He was hoarse, poor fellow, from the long night of turning three difficult languages into English.

After tea and more naan and cold mutton, we were on our way. Our Han minders reappeared, wrapped in sheepskins. We hadn't seen them since arrival. They had been too thinly dressed to go looking for us in a snowstorm, and the one who did the talking launched into a tirade as soon as he saw us. David decided to pretend that he did not understand, and I really couldn't follow what the man was shouting. He was standing in eight inches of snow in cloth shoes. Midway through the outburst Zikkar took back the sheepskins, so it was a short tantrum. Both Han immediately leaped into the 4Runner, shuddering with cold. It was impossible not to take pity. Before getting into the car I stripped off the thick tight-knit Guernsey sweater I was wearing and handed it over. It was big enough for both of them, and by golly both of them got into it. Quite soon, thanks to the mingled heat of two scrawny bodies wrapped up in good English wool, they were warmer and quieter.

But no happier. The talker started trying out his cell phone as soon as we reached the crest of the hill above the valley. He had to operate it one-handedly because the other hand was trapped beneath my Guernsey sweater. There was no transmission tower for miles, so naturally the phone didn't work, but he kept on trying as Zikkar, barely in control of the creeping 4Runner, battled skids and spins and narrowly escaped going airborne over the brink of one precipice after another.

At last we arrived at the bottom, and as we rode through the outskirts of Ulugqat, our chief minder finally made contact with his headquarters. First the polytonal burst of his report, then silence while he waited for instructions, then the instructions, then the Mandarin equivalent of a very enthusiastic *ja wohl!*

He clicked off the phone and pulled out a pair of handcuffs. "You are under arrest," he said.

In any other country I would have smiled at the wondrous absurdity of being manacled by what appeared to be Siamese twins wearing the same baggy sweater. Not so in Xinjiang, whose prisons had swallowed so many people alive. We were loaded into a government car and driven straight to Captain Zhang's office in Ürümqui. This time, the captain was not alone. Two muscular cops stood behind us with drawn truncheons. Nor was Zhang the relaxed customer I had met the last time I was in this office. He wore his jacket and military cap and did not smoke a single cigarette. He asked us no questions and issued no recriminations. We were meant to take this as a signal that he knew all he needed to know about our nefarious purposes, and more than we could ever guess.

"Passports and air tickets," he said peremptorily.

We handed them over. Despite the manacles, we had not been relieved of our personal belongings or even searched.

Zhang examined the passports page by page as if seeing them for the first time, then wrote something in each of them and stamped them. He handed them back, but kept our air tickets.

"I have made a note in your passports that you are never again to be admitted to the Xinjiang Uygur Autonomous Region," Zhang said. "Do you understand?"

We nodded and kept quiet. This was a serious matter—especially for David because it meant losing some of his extra income, among other unforeseeable complications—but not so serious as awaiting trial in a prison camp in the forbidden zone for twenty or thirty years or however long it took a man to die.

Zhang said, "A plane leaves for Alma Ata in two hours." He handed two new air tickets to one of his thugs. "These men will accompany you to the airport and see you safely aboard your flight," he said. "I advise you to be cooperative."

We followed his advice religiously. But our banishment complicated matters tremendously. We had been tantalized in Xinjiang, but not enlightened, and now we could never come back to follow up our suspicions.

In theory.

9

David Wong waited until we were on the ground in Alma Ata, safe from Chinese ears, before he told me that his friend Askar had mentioned the Amphora Scroll.

"According to Askar," David said, "an all-points bulletin has gone out to every Islamist terrorist group in the world to find the scroll. A reward of five million euros has been posted for its delivery."

"Deliver the scroll where?" I said. "To whom?"

"Askar doesn't know. He says nobody knows, but the word is that the reward is being offered by a rich holy man living somewhere in Islam."

Who could this holy man be but Ibn Awad? If this was the fact, then this was our first confirmation that the old lunatic really was alive and on track to obliterate the cities of the crusaders. And Askar, a neutralized Islamist terrorist who wanted to get back in business, had the scroll within his grasp.

I said, "Does Askar know what's in Auntie's glass cylinder?"

"I don't think so," David said. "But he has a problem."

"What? Family feeling?"

"That may be part of it. But the real problem is that she and her glass cylinder have disappeared. She went for a ride one morning and never came back."

"Come on! On horseback? At age ninety-four?"

"I'm quoting Askar. She's a vigorous old girl. Still rides two or three mornings a week, though no longer at the gallop. "

"They didn't go looking for her?"

"Her son Tarik went after her. He didn't come back, either, so they figured he'd found her and she'd be okay."

"But they did go looking for them?"

"In due course, yes. She wasn't in the village. Neither was Tarik. The women think she's gone home to die, wherever home is."

I said, "David, how do you assess Askar's reliability?"

"In the past he never steered me wrong," David replied.

"Back then it would have cost him a lot of money if you caught him lying. And that's no longer the case."

"No," David said. "But he's not penniless. He gave me a satellite phone number to call in case I wanted to talk to him."

THREE

1

The last time I saw Moscow, twenty years before, her heart was barely beating. Now it seemed to be fibrillating. We were confronted everywhere by wonders. Restaurant food was edible, waiters smiled for tips. Bare skin and German cars were much in evidence, money was a more popular topic of conversation than the weather, the jokes were about sex instead of the Politburo. Darkness still fell at four o'clock in December. At four-thirty on our first day in town, Harley Waters pulled me out of my hotel room into a snowstorm.

"Everything in town is still wired," he said. "The only difference is, two organizations are listening in instead of one—the mafia and the Russian intelligence service."

Since the mafia was composed mostly of former members of the KGB, prurient curiosity remained all in the family. Harley had chosen a good night for the kind of walk he had in mind. Snow fell so thickly that it was pretty well impossible to see anyone who was more than a few feet away. Also, it was quitting time in Moscow and the trampling crowd left so many fresh footprints that tracking was impossible. The blizzard and Harley's knowledge of Moscow's nooks and crannies meant that we had little trouble ditching the three-man team that was following us.

He led me out of the storm and underground into a subway station. Our surveillance did not reappear, so we assumed we really had lost them. Even after miles of walking in circles this was chancy because of my height. I was less of a curiosity here than in Brazil or China, but I still attracted a lot of attention. I am used to this, but the fact remains that being six foot five is a handicap in a man whose profession requires him to be unobtrusive. That's why I worked inside instead of outside like Paul Christopher, the perfect singleton, who sat so still and said so little that waiters sometimes did not notice that he was at the table and neglected to take his order.

Very few people were left in our subway car when we arrived at our stop. We emerged into the blizzard in a benighted neighborhood on the outskirts of the city. Huge apartment buildings with snowdrifts on their flat roofs stood hunchbacked in the storm. Feeble light the color of urine showed in scores of tiny windows. One of these misshapen boxes was surrounded by a fence topped by barbed wire and broken glass. This meant that it had once been home to Soviet secret policemen and suchlike. The fence was designed to keep the masses out.

Harley's friend Mikhail Orlov, former colonel in the KGB, lived alone in a top-floor flat that smelled of cabbage, sausages, and garbage. Harley explained that Mikhail, who had lost a leg in Afghanistan, found it difficult to carry the trash down sixteen flights of stairs. Because of what he used to be, no one in the new Russia volunteered to help him. Not that Mikhail was interested in hiding his past: his well-pressed KGB uniform, boots, medals and all, hung on a hanger from a hook on the wall. Clearly he was ready to return to duty on a moment's notice.

Mikhail embraced Harley and kissed him on both cheeks. He locked eyes with me as if reading coded messages written on my irises and shook my hand firmly, letting me know how strong he was even when in a friendly mood. Obviously Harley and this KGB man were old friends. Mikhail was a stubby fellow with a shaved head, Slavic cheekbones and pale blue eyes with epicanthic fold. He wasn't wearing his wooden leg—it hung from another peg on the wall—but used no crutch or cane. Instead he hopped around on one foot, fetching smeared glasses for the vodka and a spoon—just one—for the caviar Harley had brought. Even after drinking half a liter of vodka, he never lost his balance. His good leg must have been incredibly strong.

Harley hadn't told me why we were here—only that Mikhail was an interesting fellow who had done some work for him in the past. When the level of the vodka bottle was right, Harley said, "After his wounds made it difficult for him to work undercover, Mikhail was the officer in charge of nuclear security at the Darvaza-76 scientific facility in Turkmenistan."

Mikhail locked eyes with me again. Up to this point we had been making small talk in Russian—haltingly in my case—but now he began to speak English.

Mikhail said, "You are the man who stole the American election, am I right?"

Ah, the old reliable icebreaker. "Something like that," I replied.

"You were on Russian television."

"Really?"

"Yes, very cheeky. Anywhere else besides America you would have been shot."

I smiled, the first time this had been tried by anyone so far this evening. "No doubt. But U.S. punishments are not so merciful as in the more enlightened countries."

"You think something is worse than death?"

His tone was contemptuous. What could an American possibly know about death? Admittedly, Mikhail himself was an expert. He had belonged to an organization that had hanged, starved, shot, and worked to death more Soviet civilians in time of peace than the whole number of combatants killed in action on both sides in World War II. Now the KGB had vanished into thin air, leaving him with a uniform and decorations that would get him stoned in the streets, a full colonel's pension worth less than $2,000 a year, and a wooden leg that did not fit. Harley, glancing with wry New Hampshire shrewdness from glowering Russkie to scowling Yank, decided that it was time to put the meeting back on track.

"Maybe we should talk business," he said.

Mikhail nodded—*about time!* He turned up his radio and hop-scotched over to the stove to fetch a pot of tea. After pouring the tea into the vodka glasses, he sat down and drew his chair closer so that we sat with our heads only inches apart. The music was so loud—the Red Army Chorus bellowing golden oldies—that we could not otherwise have heard a word.

Harley said, "Mikhail knows that we have an interest in missin' Soviet backpack nuclear devices, and he's got somethin' to tell us about that."

Evidently Harley had already made a down payment on the information, because Mikhail immediately came to the point. All traces of disdain and one-upmanship vanished as if by magic, and suddenly he was not a vodka-soaked, resentful used-to-be but an intelligence professional delivering a briefing.

"You are right to be concerned," he said. "Some of our devices are missing."

"How many?"

"Twelve, we think. The inventory was problematical. The missing devices are small, one or two kilotons each, but they are special weapons."

"Special in what way?"

"First, because they are compact," Mikhail said. "Second, because they are sheathed in cobalt, so the point is not explosive force but the effect and durability of the radiation."

I must have looked shocked because Mikhail paused and in an almost kindly tone said, "You did not know that?"

"We had been told that they were dirty," I said. "But not about the cobalt. You're absolutely sure of your facts?"

"Oh, yes. Just one of these devices, detonated in Red Square, would make Moscow uninhabitable for centuries."

"And you let twelve of them be stolen?"

"Somebody did, yes. It was a great mistake." Mikhail reached out and touched my chest with a blunt index finger. "It would be better, my friend, to hold your questions until the end."

He was right, and in any case I had no more questions to ask. There was nothing unbelievable about what he was telling me. The Soviets had manufactured and stored thirty tons of smallpox virus for use as the payloads for biological weapons, so why wouldn't they make cobalt bombs?

I said, "Sorry, go on," and picked up my glass of tea. It was scalding hot and even sweeter than Tajik tea.

"In the last days of the Soviet Union, just before the fall of Gorbachev . . ." Mikhail spat after mentioning the name, ". . . I was sent from the KGB hospital in Odessa straight to Darvaza-76."

"What's that?"

"A Naukograd, a secret science city. The 76 means that it is seventy-six kilometers from Darvaza, the nearest city in northern Turkmenistan. There are—were—-about fifty Naukograds in the USSR. New weapons were invented, developed, manufactured and stored in such places. I thought you knew this from your spy satellites."

"Maybe Harley knew it," I said. "But that wasn't my department."

"Lucky for us," Mikhail said. This man really didn't like me. Looking at Harley, he said, "May I continue?"

Harley gave him a priestly wave of the hand.

Mikhail drew breath and said, "Because of the lax discipline in the Red Army that followed the retreat from Afghanistan, not to mention the confusion in the Kremlin caused by Gorbachev's strangulation of the party, this problem of missing weapons had developed."

Mikhail had been selected to solve the problem because he had broken up a ring of Red Army officers in Afghanistan that had been selling Soviet arms to the mujahadin.

He said, "The great fear, you understand, was that these backpack bombs had fallen into the hands of religious madmen.

The mujahadin or, worse, the Chechens. We knew that arms paid for by the Saudis and others were flowing into Chechnya. Volunteers from all over Islam were sneaking into Chechnya. Large amounts of cash were crossing the frontier. The motherland was facing a second Afghan war, but this time on her own soil. And then there was the jihadist movement you people were financing on the China frontier as a second front in the Afghan war."

David Wong's project. Small world.

On arrival at Darvaza-76, Mikhail immediately arrested the officer in charge of security along with everyone else who had a key to the warehouse.

"I told them they would tell me everything they ever knew, everyone they suspected, every detail of their own movements and whereabouts for every moment of their lives," Mikhail said. "To encourage the others, I shot a couple of junior officers who were obviously innocent and therefore of no interest to my investigation."

The survivors understood what Mikhail was saying to them, but they had a problem. No one knew when the weapons had disappeared. Or even, at first, if the count was correct. They weren't exactly sure how many of the special cobalt weapons they had had in the inventory, or how many might be floating around inside the military apparatus. The army drew weapons for training purposes and sometimes forgot to send them back until forcefully reminded to do so by Moscow.

It took the remainder of the night for Mikhail to walk us through his investigation. His inquiries had been exhaustive. He had read every security record, every log, every sentry list. He had questioned everyone at the base, soldier or scientist, man, woman or child. But the long and short of it was that despite his meticulous detective work, Mikhail had never discovered who sold the bombs or who bought them. Or if they had simply been stolen, though this seemed unlikely because Darvaza-76 was a sealed city, surrounded by a concrete wall five meters high with electrified wire on the top, patrolled twenty-four hours a day by KGB troops.

Of course someone had to pay. The base commander and a dozen others, including three nonessential technicians and a handful of sergeants, were shot after a trial at which they saved their families by confessing to crimes the KGB knew they had not committed.

I asked Mikhail, "You weren't worried that one of these fellows hadn't told you all he knew before he was executed?"

"That was not a realistic possibility."

"But weren't you concerned about all those loose ends?"

"No," Mikhail said. "I assumed that sooner or later we would find the missing bombs. They were virtually unshielded to cut down on their weight, and they gave off so much radiation that they should have been readily detectable. However, I was wrong. We spent millions of rubles looking for them all over the Soviet Union with everything from satellites to soldiers with Geiger counters. We never found a trace."

Meaning what, in Mikhail's opinion?

"There were many theories," he replied. "They could be stored deep in a cave or a mine or an oil well. Or hidden someplace where there was already a lot of background radiation from old test explosions. We looked in all such places in the Soviet Union— Kazakhstan, Siberia, Kamchatka, the arctic testing sites, nuclear waste dumps, salt mines, coal mines. The old regime was not tidy about such things, so the country is full of possible hiding places. We found nothing."

"It did not occur to you that the bombs might have gone abroad?"

"Of course. But we had no responsibility to protect any other country."

"You still thought these bombs were going to be detonated inside the USSR?"

"Yes."

"There was one other probable target."

"The United States?" Mikhail said. "Not many in the Red Army or the KGB would have wept over a terrorist nuclear attack on New York or Chicago."

2

It was a long subway ride back to the hotel and when we got there, in time for breakfast, no hot water was left for a shower and shave. Harley and I were eating kippers and eggs in the dining room, waiting for the hot-water tank to fire up again, when a young man walked through the door and headed straight for our table. He was a muscular, keen-eyed type: Well-cut navy blue blazer, creased gray flannel pants, striped shirt, faux Eton tie, shoes too cheap for the ensemble. Everyone in the world who wears Western clothes looks like an American these days. Consequently I wasn't sure if this man was a Russian mafia hit man or one of ours or what.

He said, in a Midwestern twang, "Hi, Mr. Waters. Good morning, Mr. Hubbard. May I join you?"

Harley ignored him.

I said, "Pull up a chair. Coffee?"

"Had mine," the man said, lifting a finger to the waiter. He must have been a good tipper, well known in this place, because the fellow fairly ran across the room.

"Mineral water, please, Boris, and keep it coming," he said in good Russian.

Our visitor acted and looked like someone who not so very long ago had played quarterback in high school in a town where

127

that mattered a lot. He had one of those American heads on which a German skull combines with an Irish face, untraceable ears, and Mediterranean eyes. His smile was one hundred percent rich-kid American—$15,000 worth of flashing orthodontia.

I said, "You know our names. What's yours?"

"Kevin Clark," he said. No business card, no offer to shake hands.

Harley said, "Anything to add to that information?"

Kevin Clark gave him a charming smile. His mineral water came in the blink of an eye. He drank a full glass before speaking again. The waiter leaped to fill his glass, then hovered within earshot. Kevin paid him no mind.

"Well," he said loud and clear, as if barking signals, "I've been asked to be your friend while you're in Moscow."

"Really?" I said. "By whom? "

"By people who are worried about your safety."

"Can you be a little more specific?"

"Sorry, no," our new friend said. "It's a confidential relationship."

"I see. Why are these benevolent folks who want to protect us so worried about us?"

"It's the company you keep, Mr. Hubbard. Your recent activities in Xinjiang are worrisome, and the man you visited last night is a dangerous person."

"My goodness," I said, "but you seem to have scouts everywhere."

No smile for that one. Boris brought Kevin a second bottle of water.

"It would be best for everyone," Kevin said, "if you'd leave Russia before our hosts discover a reason to throw you out."

Harley, born before orthodontists were an American institution, replied with a glimpse of his own irregular, yellowing teeth. "We're not goin' anywhere, sonny. And you can go back to whoever sent you, like Tom Berger, and tell 'em that. Horace and I are just a couple of senior citizens on vacation, seein' the sights."

"I have no idea what you're talking about," Kevin said. "And I don't know anybody named Tom Berger. But believe me, I'm just trying to help you."

"You don't work for Tom in the American embassy?" Harley said. "Does that mean you're not a member of the Outfit?"

Kevin did not answer the question. He said, "Look, no matter what your friend Mikhail"—he dropped the name casually—"tells you, there are no lost bombs. This is an old KGB disinformation op designed to make people run around like chickens with our heads cut off."

"And this you know beyond the shadow of a doubt."

"That's correct. And it would be a great shame if the Russian police somehow found out that you're a convicted felon who had entered their country without making that known to them."

Harley said, "Frankly, son, I don't think they'd be too surprised or upset by that news. Maybe they'd rather follow Horace, here, around for awhile to see what he's up to instead of throwin' him out of the country."

"I doubt that. And besides, it's not the Russian police you should be worried about."

"Then who *should* I be worried about?" I asked. "I'm dying to know."

"I'm afraid you'll know soon enough," Kevin said. He drank another glass of mineral water—the whole thing, right down. He rose to his feet, leaving a big tip for the waiter, but leaving his check for us to pay. "See you around, gentlemen," he said.

Harley pulled a cell phone out of his pocket and dialed a number. He held the instrument away from his ear as if he expected whoever answered to talk too loudly. I could hear it ring, then hear the voice of Tom Berger, the local chief of station.

"Tom, it's me, long time since we last spoke," Harley said in a voice and diction no one could ever forget after hearing it once. "Quick question. Do you know the young fella my old friend and I had breakfast with this mornin'?"

The voice in the receiver said, "Nope. What's this all about?"

"Tryin' to find that out, Tom. No messenger sent to me from you?"

"No."

"Thanks, Tom," Harley said. He clicked off. "Sounds like Kevin don't belong to Tom—supposin' we can have faith in Tom."

Then who did Kevin belong to? It was all very mysterious.

3

Harley and I were too tired after our all-nighter to care. We went
straight upstairs after signing the bill for breakfast. Following a
five-hour nap, a shave and shower and a restorative pot of tea, we
went sightseeing. It was too cold to wander around outside, so we
took the subway to the Tretyakov Gallery. I had lost track of
time, but it must have been a day off because the place was
thronged with pink-faced girls in miniskirts, all searching for boys.
It seemed odd to be admiring female legs and breathing perfume
in Moscow. This happy crowd was a blessing, making it easy to
spot a gumshoe among the nymphs and fauns. As a counter-
measure to hidden microphones, their giggles were at least the
equal of Mikhail's tinny old radio.

Sauntering from one long-lost pre-Leninist Russian master-
piece to another, Harley and I talked business. Harley was speaking native New Hampshire now, whole paragraphs speeding by
without a final *g* or *r* being heard unless a word like *tomater*
cropped up.

"Could be all this business at breakfast was just new Outfit
clumsiness," he said. "But maybe it's got some basis in reality.
Somebody might actually know somethin'."

"Know something about what?"

"Well, that boy Kevin this mornin' mentioned the mob."

"You think the Russian underworld cares about us?"

"Might be prudent to acknowledge the possibility," Harley said. "Remember who those mafia bosses used to be. Might as well call it the KGB alumni association. Which brings us back to Mikhail. Notice anything funny about his story?"

This was like asking if I'd noticed that the girls in miniskirts had legs, but I replied, "Any number of things. What do you have in mind?"

"Told us all about the colonels, majors, captains, sergeants and first-class privates he'd put through the wringer, not to mention the scientists and so on who were interrogated. Cast of thousands. Talked about terrorists who may have burglarized the place. However, he never said a word about the likeliest suspects in a thing like this. Namely, the mob."

A couple of long-limbed girls moved between us and the painting and posed for a picture. The photographer was one of the boyfriends, and he was equipped with the latest thing in a digital camera. When he lifted the camera I saw that he was wearing a very expensive solid gold, blue-faced wristwatch. We moved on to avoid having our picture taken. The kids moved with us, innocent though their giggles may have been, until we lost them in the crowd, as we were conditioned to do.

In the next gallery, filled with Kandinskys, we were more or less alone. Then the same two beautiful girls and their boyfriends entered the room. Harley turned to them and said, in his flawless Russian, "Let me borrow your camera, young fella, and I'll get a *kulturny* shot of all four of you in front of this fine work of art."

The startled boyfriend handed over his camera. Harley took his time focusing and framing the shot—*Smile! One more!* At last Harley handed back the camera. We turned our backs and walked away.

"Two shots of us in the camera," he said. "Not very good likenesses. I let 'em be. Don't think they got close enough to do much listenin' or recordin'."

Was this street smarts or paranoia? "How would those kids know we were in that particular museum?"

"They got on the subway with us, all bundled up," Harley said. "Didn't start skylarkin' till we all got inside. You're slippin', Horace."

I wish I could say that Harley was wrong about this but the fact is, I had missed them because I hadn't been looking for golden boys and girls. I'd had an eye out for the old Peter Lorre type in black alpaca suit and oversize fedora. Obviously the times had moved on without me.

Not that I confessed my mistake to Harley. Instead I said, "You noticed the photographer's watch?"

"Yep. Unless the Russian intelligence service can afford twenty-five grand worth of costume jewelry, looks like those sparrows work for another employer."

"And how did they know to follow us?"

"Two possibilities," Harley said. "Mikhail or Kevin. Let's get out of here."

It took a moment to collect our coats and hats. Our four young friends were right behind us in line, and they spilled down the steps of the museum behind us, too. It was still snowing. One of the girls, her small round face piquant under its fur hat, ran to us and put her arms around Harley. She opened her burkha-like long coat before doing this, so that there was little between his old bones and her firm young flesh. Eyes dancing, she whispered in his ear. Harley was delighted, but I noticed that he put his hand in the pocket where he carried his money. He whispered an answer in Russian. She pouted and started to whisper a reply, but then her eyes changed, merriment to fear. I followed her glance and saw a man in a long overcoat reading *Izvestia* in the snowstorm. A little farther down the street were more men—not one but two complete surveillance teams, waiting for us. Harley saw them, too. The girl's companions were already fading into the falling snow, and she ran after them.

"Kind of flatterin', everybody takin' such an interest in us," Harley said.

"What did the little lady say to you?"

"She said Mikhail wants to see us. Urgently."

It was snowing harder now. Wearing his old sable hat and fur-lined coat, Harley blended with the crowd. I wore my brand-new Gore-Tex goose-down parka with the hood up. Slush leaked through my high-tech waterproof hiking shoes and I envied Harley his buckled early-twentieth-century black galoshes. The gumshoes followed us. Whoever they were, cops or robbers, they were glued to us. We ignored them as if we were innocent men; shaking them, even if that were possible, would only make them more suspicious. Besides, there was no reason to make a dash for it. I wasn't particularly worried about compromising Mikhail.

Darkness had fallen by the time we arrived at Mikhail's garret, Harley looking a little wan after the long steep climb up the stairs. Mikhail's flat was unlocked. And empty.

"Bad sign," Harley said.

We went inside anyway. I looked out the window. Three dark figures lurked in the slushy street—our watchers. A couple of hours passed before we heard footsteps on the stairs. They were unmistakably the tread of a man with a wooden leg. Mikhail opened the door, switched on the buzzing lightbulb that hung from the ceiling, and found Harley and me waiting for him.

"*Ooof!*" he said when he saw us. "Why are you here?"

Harley said, "You mean you weren't expectin' us?"

"Are you crazy?"

Harley looked Mikhail up and down. "Where've you been?"

"Waiting. This is still Russia."

Mikhail had regained control of himself. He looked less like a man who thought he was going to take a bullet, more like the disillusioned KGB colonel whom history, the thing he had trusted most, had stripped him of medals and uniform, dressed him in rags and locked him up in this rat-trap flat.

"Waiting for what?" Harley asked.

"This."

Mikhail pulled up his trousers leg and showed us the shiny metal shaft of a brand-new prosthesis. "Titanium, made in Germany," he said.

"Looks like a good one," Harley said. "How much did it set you back?"

"Every kopek you gave me."

"No wonder you need more money," Harley said. "Is it an improvement?"

"Anything would be an improvement," Mikhail replied. "Orphans in Afghanistan have better prostheses than that piece of junk I was given."

Mikhail switched off the light and peered out the window. The watchers were still there, small black figures in a field of phosphorescent white.

"You were followed," he said.

"We know," Harley replied.

Because I irritated Mikhail so, I was letting Harley do the talking until the Russian calmed down.

"There are three of them," Mikhail said. "And now that they've seen my light go on, they know I'm home."

"But not that we're here. We didn't touch the light."

"Ha! That's exactly what they would have noticed."

"Does that mean you're the only suspect in this building that's got a thousand windows?" Harley said. "Calm down, Mikhail, and turn on the light. We have to talk."

"We can talk in the dark."

Harley got up, closed the curtain, and pulled the chain on the light fixture.

"Better to see faces," he said. "Horace, here, has got a few more questions for you."

"What questions?" Mikhail said, registering deep affront. Then greed conquered resentment. "For how much?"

"You'll be taken care of in the usual way, honorarium in the dead drop," Harley said. "You wouldn't want those roughnecks outside to find you with a pocketful of dollars."

He fixed Mikhail with a headmaster's all-seeing eye. *Better think twice, my boy.*

"All right," Mikhail said. "But it would be quicker to tell me what you want to know and let me summarize."

I was not going down that path again. The night before, Mikhail had summarized us to sleep, spouting irrelevant detail like one of those old Steinberg cartoons in which a little man in the corner of the drawing spews nonsense into a balloon that fills up the rest of the frame.

"The questions won't take long," I said, "Just loose ends, really."

I handed Mikhail a photocopy of the list of stolen nukes with their serial numbers that Paul Christopher had left for me in his table-leg safe. Charley Hornblower had puzzled out the, to me, illegible signature.

I said, "Is this an authentic document?"

Mikhail glanced at it, lips twisting in disdain. *How could it be genuine if a cretin like you has it in his possession?* But then his expression changed.

"Where did you get this?"

"The question was, is it authentic?"

"That, or a very clever forgery," Mikhail said. "How much did you pay for this document?"

"It was a gift. Do you recognize the signature?"

"Y. A. Kirov," Mikhail said.

I went to the gas ring he used for cooking, lit it, and burned the list of nukes. I didn't want it found on me if I was arrested after I went downstairs.

Mikhail, hands trembling slightly, throat dry, looked like he needed a drink. We had brought no vodka this time. He had had little sleep the night before, and if his account of his day was correct, he must be worn out.

I said, "It was not just Kirov who was omitted from our discussions last night. . . ."

Mikhail bristled. "Omitted? What are you implying?"

"Nothing. But we took longer than we should have to come to the point, so I will come to it now. Did it not occur to you that criminals—what's now called the Russian mafia—may have been the thieves?"

"Of course it did," Mikhail said. "But this was not an American movie where criminals are smarter than the police. Darvaza-76 was a walled city, alarmed and guarded by the KGB with the strictest security measures. How would they get in?"

"By having a friend inside," I said. "Just like in the movies."

"Impossible. Even if they did get into the city, how could they penetrate the nuclear storage facility, which was the most closely guarded section of the installation?"

"How many people had access to the nuclear storage facility?"

"Only two could authorize access," Mikhail said. "The base commander and the head of security."

"One of whom is dead. The other is Yevgeny Alexeivich Kirov, whereabouts unknown."

"Kirov was an officer of the KGB," he said.

"And therefore above suspicion?" I asked.

"Of course not."

"Just a man thinking of the future. Playing the game. Putting away a few million toward retirement."

Mikhail smiled a long tight-lipped smile. "I see you're a show-off all the time, not just on television," he said. "You should be a little more modest about your brilliance."

I had gotten under his skin. I made no reply, hoping that he would go on telling me off. I was not disappointed.

"Moscow used to be the safest city in the world," Mikhail said. "However, now that these gangsters are in charge and money is everything, that is no longer the case. They use real bullets. People die. You should bear that in mind, my friend Horace. All foolish people should bear that in mind."

He turned off the light and looked outside.

"They are gone," he said. "Now you should go."

4

By the light of a flashlight, we started down the sixteen flights of stairs. About halfway down, Harley called a halt.

"Got to sit down for a minute."

His voice quavered. He sank onto the stairs, fumbled in an inside pocket, and handed me a bottle of pills. He held up one finger of his left hand. With his right hand he was clutching his heart. I shook a pill out of the bottle and placed it on the palm of his trembling hand. He put it under his tongue. After a moment he seemed to be all right, but his face was pale and his voice weak.

"Nitroglycerin," he said. "Helps my angina. Had a little flutter there, nothin' to worry about, happens all the time. Give me a hand."

"Are you sure?"

He grabbed my arm and pulled himself upright. "Not stayin' here."

He was still unsteady. The stairs were steep. There were no handrails. As we started down again, I took his arm. He shook me off. Not much strength in the gesture, though. Harley was seventy-eight years old, but until this moment you wouldn't have guessed it.

My satellite phone, set to vibrate instead of ring, vibrated. I got it out and answered, expecting to hear Charley Hornblower or another Old Boy on the line.

Instead, a youthful but faintly familiar voice said, "Hi, Kevin here."

Kevin?

He said, "Don't hang up. I thought you'd be interested to know that the light in your friend's window went off, then came back on again just now. Now it's off again."

"Maybe he's gone to bed."

" One of the men who followed you here blinked back with a flashlight."

Turning lights on and off was typical KGB tradecraft. I put my hand over the mouthpiece and told Harley what was going on.

He pointing to his chest. "Nice timin'."

"Now two of your watchers are going inside," Kevin said. "Are you on the stairs?"

Where else would we be? "Yes."

"What floor?"

I saw no reason to tell him that. I said, "How many does that leave outside?"

"Just one. His weapon is drawn."

I hung up. Harley had already turned off his penlight. I said, "Sit down, Harley. Stay out of this."

"Not spoilin' for a fight just now," he said. "But I can do the talkin'."

"We'll see," I said, wondering how much talking was going to be done. "If Mikhail comes down from the rear, trip him."

I moved down the stairs, turning a corner onto the landing just below us. There was no sign of a light further down, but I could hear rapid footsteps and hard breathing. The two men were running up the stairs. I had no weapon, of course. When they reached the landing, breathing hard, I stepped back around the corner, pressed my body against the wall, and switched on my flashlight, holding it as far away from my body as possible. One of the men fired an entire magazine. Sparks flew from the barrel of the pistol.

Red-blue-yellow muzzle-flash lit up the shooter's moon face, unshaven under a tall fur hat. High-velocity bullets ricocheted from wall to wall and ceiling to floor, drawing fiery lines on the concrete and filling the air with the smell of burnt gunpowder.

I dropped the flashlight and groaned loudly. An empty magazine clattered on the concrete floor as the shooter reloaded. The second man, the one who had held his fire, now rushed up the stairs, pistol held rigidly in the approved two-handed grip. I could see him clearly in the light of the fallen flashlight, and I guess maybe he saw me, too, before I kicked the gun out his hand, then smashed him in the nose. His gun went off when it hit the floor. The other man fired another full magazine, creating more pyrotechnics. The noise was deafening. My ears rang.

Without pausing to reload, this wild shooter threw himself up the stairs. He saw his friend lying on the floor and me on my feet and stopped in his tracks. I was taller than he was to begin with and stood above him on the stairs. I lunged and grabbed him by the skull and put my thumbs in his eyes. He tried to get away with a sudden violent spin of his whole body. His fur hat flew off. He was a big, compact, powerful man. I planted my feet and held on. Halfway through his bearish pirouette, the man broke his own neck. I felt it go and with it, the life from his body.

I dropped him and picked up his gun and held it on the partner, who lay facedown on the stairs. I spoke to the man in Russian. He did not answer. I gave him a hard kick in the ribs. No sound from him. His body hardly moved. He was dead, too, maybe struck by a ricochet.

Harley picked up my flashlight and shone it on the corpses. The dead men were leaking blood. One of them had his head on backward. He looked a lot like the man who had sat next to me on the train from Paris to Geneva. I fell to my knees and sniffed his open mouth. He smelled the same, too, a stranger to toothpaste.

"Quite a mess," Harley said. "Better go get Mikhail unless you want him behind you."

Harley pilfered a full magazine from one of the dead men and handed it to me. That left him with the empty pistol. I hesitated.

"Go," he said, and rolled over a corpse to look for more ammunition in its clothes.

My satellite phone vibrated.

"Kevin here. Heard shots. You guys okay?"

"Yes."

"We'll be right up. And don't worry. The third man is out of it."

By now Harley had harvested another magazine. He slapped it into the pistol.

As I mounted the stairway three or four treads at a time, adrenaline flowing, ears still ringing, I was even more terrified than I had been three minutes before when bullets were flying around my head. The stairway was as black as the Pit and just as silent—not a single light showing, not a curious head in sight.

Mikhail knew too much and had told me too little to be left behind, but he worried me. He was cornered—no place to go but up onto the roof—and that is never a good thing. The fact that he had only one leg didn't mean that he was defenseless. I had to assume that he was armed, if only with a kitchen knife or his spare leg. There was only one way into his flat, through the flimsy door. I was a big target. If he had a gun I was dead. Even a whack on the head could do me in—not instantaneous death, perhaps, but unconsciousness at the very least and, consequently, capture by Mikhail or whoever came up the stairs next.

Far below, a single gunshot rang out, creating a string of echoes in the staircase. As in playing football and making love, it is best not to think too much when engaged in mortal combat. When I reached the top landing I did not stop to ponder the situation, but without even knowing why I was doing it until I had done it, took a running step or two, and launched myself horizontally, feet first, against his door. It splintered under my weight. I landed inside the room on my back.

Mikhail was armed, all right. The blinking muzzle-blast of his pistol outlined his figure. Rounds flew over my prostate body. I kicked out at what I hoped was Mikhail's artificial leg. He fell with a crash, still shooting into the ceiling until the hammer clicked on an empty chamber.

I kicked Mikhail in the groin—no easy trick because the harness of his prosthesis gave him protection. He howled. I picked up his pistol, shone my flashlight on him, and patted him down. No hideout weapons, but a large wad of cash and a spare magazine in the pocket of his baggy pants. He gasped out curses in Russian.

I said, "Roll over and take off your leg, Mikhail."

His eyes widened in fear and hatred.

"Now," I said, pointing both guns at him Tombstone style, "before I shoot it off."

To my own surprise, I was shouting. I was also shaking with anger and would probably have drilled him full of holes if he had demurred. Luckily for both of us—who would want to go through life knowing he had shot a one-legged man when he was down?—Mikhail did as he was told. In a matter of minutes he was hopping trouserless down the stairs. It was a remarkable display of balance and athleticism, especially for a man who had just been kicked in the testicles. I brought up the rear, a pistol in one hand and Mikhail's made-in-Germany titanium leg, heavy Russian boot attached, in the other.

The dead bodies lay where they had fallen. I turned on the flashlight to make sure that Mikhail got a good look at them. He hopped on by without sign of recognition, careful not to slip in the blood, as if the dead men were bags of garbage that had split open and spilled their contents.

5

When we got to the bottom, we found a dead muzhik sprawled wide-eyed in a corner of the stairwell. He had been shot between the eyes.

Mikhail, breathing heavily, looked at the body and said, "You are going to die in Russia, my friend Horace."

"Why do you say that, Mikhail? Is there something special about these fellows?"

"Special? Yeah. They're Chechens. You should say your prayers, wise guy."

Wise guy? Had Mikhail been watching gangster movies? An image of a roomful of KGB men learning English in the dark from Jimmy Cagney popped into my head. I laughed loudly.

"That's right," Mikhail said. "Laugh."

Just outside, Harley was chatting with Kevin Clark while another all-American boy stood lookout. Beside them, an Audi sedan with driver at the wheel waited, motor running.

"We should get started," Kevin said.

"Where to?"

"Anywhere but here, Mister Hubbard."

I looked to Harley for a sign. He shrugged and smiled. We didn't have much choice.

"Okay," I said. "What about our friend here?"

"He can ride in back," Kevin said.

One of Kevin's silent men patted Mikhail down, bound his wrists with plastic shackles, and heaved him bodily into the trunk. He then produced a syringe and plunged the needle into Mikhail's buttocks before tossing his titanium leg in after him, covering him with a blanket, and closing the lid.

"Better get in front, sir, more legroom," Kevin said to me. "If either of you has to pee, we'll stop somewhere. Don't do it here. DNA and all that."

"What about Mikhail?"

"He'll sleep for a while."

Kevin said nothing about the gun in my hand. I kept it there.

The Audi's Quattro drive took us steadily through snow and ice. This car was a big improvement over Zikkar's 4Runner. So was the driver, who kept us moving without headlights under a sky unpunctured by moon or stars. He drove at a steady 80 kph through unlit empty city streets, and after we left the city and entered open country, much faster over narrow highways in which snow had drifted into windrows. The compass in the rearview mirror indicated that we were headed east-northeast. Sometimes the direction changed briefly as we took yet another back road. I noted the numbers on the odometer. We passed a few big trucks, but not a single car besides our own was on the road at this hour.

Harley said, "Where're we headed—Leningrad?"

"Not quite that far today, Mister Waters," Kevin said. "We'll stop soon. You fellows must be tired."

"Any idea who those dead fellows were?"

"Chechens," Kevin replied. "Very angry people."

Hello, fatwa.

As dawn broke we turned into a narrower road that cut through a forest of birches. I wasn't at the moment attuned to the beauties of nature, but I had to agree when Kevin remarked on loveliness of the chalky tree trunks in the watery morning light. He had said little during the trip, the other two men nothing. Through the trees a sugar-cake dasha, frosted with snow and decorated with icicles, a flat aluminum sun behind it, came into focus. Wood smoke curled from the chimney.

"Home sweet home," Kevin said. He smiled and pointed fondly at Harley, who was sound asleep, ashen hair disheveled, steel-frame eyeglasses askew. Harley uttered a loud snore. His eyes snapped open.

"What is this place?" he said.

"A dacha," Kevin said.

"Who does it belong to?"

"We have the use of it for the day," Kevin said.

He got out of the car and stretched. This was nothing so simple as reaching for the sky and bending over backward to make the joints crack. He did the entire set of regulation stretching exercises.

While Kevin exercised his helpers got a groggy, barely awake Mikhail out of the trunk. They had taken the precaution of taping his eyes. Each man took one of his arms. He hopped between them into the dacha, leaving a trail of single footprints in the dusting of fresh snow that had fallen during the night.

Inside the dacha a cheery log fire burned in a stone fireplace. A furnace was running full blast as well. The smell of coffee and frying bacon mingled in the stale scorched air trapped inside the dacha.

"My suggestion," Kevin said, "is that we have some breakfast, get some sleep, and then talk."

"Talk about what?" I said.

The orthodontia flashed. "Oh, I think we both have a thousand questions," he said. "The bathroom is down that hall, first door on the left."

Still the very model of hospitable courtesy, he said nothing about the pistol that I still held in my hand.

Kevin's men served an excellent American breakfast—orange juice from concentrate, scrambled fresh eggs and thick-cut bacon, toasted English muffins and super-sweet strawberry jam. Coffee that took the enamel off the teeth.

Kevin showed Harley and me to our room. Our bags were already unpacked, spare suits hanging in the closet, shoes lined up beneath.

Harley said, "You checked us out of the hotel?"

"Yes, sir," Kevin said. "It seemed best."

"You did this before the episode on the stairway?"

"Yes, but after you went upstairs to see Mikhail."

"So you were going to abduct us when we came downstairs no matter what?"

"Abduct you?" Kevin said. "Look at what happened to the guys who actually tried that. Our plan was to extract you in case you needed help."

"'Extract us?'" I said. "That has a ring to it."

Kevin smiled with his eyes. What a likeable old curmudgeon I was turning out to be. "We're all tired, sir," he said. "Get some sleep. No one will disturb you, I promise."

"That's good to hear."

Another smile. "One request," Kevin said. "Please don't use your satellite phones."

The room was cozy, with its own bathroom. While Harley showered I wedged the door and the window and checked our arsenal. Two Glocks from the man with the broken neck and his friend, one Makarov belonging to Mikhail, one full magazine for each with a few rounds left over. Expensive ordnance. I took the rubber bands off Mikhail's plump bankroll and counted the money: Five thousand U.S. dollars in crisp new hundreds stuck together by static electricity.

Harley came out of the bathroom in a cloud of steam. "How much did you pay Mikhail?" I asked.

"Twenty-seven-five U.S."

"Thousand?"

Harley snorted. "Hundred."

I showed him Mikhail's money.

"I wondered why he didn't hold out for more," Harley said.

In the shower I scrubbed the smell of dead Russians—

fresh blood, old perspiration—off my skin, but not out of my nostrils. Harley was already asleep when I came out of the bathroom, and I followed him to dreamland as if falling off the roof.

6

"If I may say so, gentlemen," Kevin said, "that was impressive work on the stairway last night."

It was late in the afternoon and from the look of Kevin, he had just woken up, too. We were drinking coffee by the fireside and eating tuna sandwiches, heavy on the mayonnaise. A quiet moment went by—sparks popping from birch logs, snow falling outside, the scent of the food.

Harley finished his coffee, put the cup down gently, and turned to Kevin. "Excuse me if I ask a question," he said. "Who in the wide world are you, son? And what're you tryin' to do? I know you can't tell us, but tell us anyway. We won't breathe a word."

Kevin gave each of us a long look.

"Gray Force?" Harley said.

Kevin was astonished. So was I—not because Harley knew something I didn't, but because it wasn't like him to just come right out and reveal something he knew but wasn't supposed to know.

Harley explained. "Gray Force is one of those outfits that doesn't exist," he explained. "Doesn't belong to the Outfit, doesn't belong to Defense. Doesn't belong to anybody. It's private enterprise, kind of like a civilianized Delta Force. Their people are ex-Green Berets or Navy Seals or whatever. Guns for hire. They do things like look for connections between organized crime and terrorism, like drug lords in Colombia and what used to be M-19 before Maoist freedom fighters went out of style, then bust up the connections."

It sounded like useful work. I said, "Unless you want to correct Harley's information, Kevin, we can work from that. You're working under some sort of contract. Is that it?"

Kevin was smiling. It must have been sincere this time because he was doing so in spite of himself, teeth hidden behind puckered lips.

"It's funny," he said. "Our motto is *Never Underestimate*." The smile broke loose.

"Meaning what?"

"If you want to make that assumption, it's okay with me."

"Who's the contractor?"

"You'll understand if I didn't quite hear that question," Kevin said. "The way you guys operate you stand a pretty good chance of falling into the hands of the enemy and we wouldn't want to be compromised."

"The only operation we're interested in is the one you've already involved us in," Harley said.

I said, "I've got an easy question for you. Do you really think there are no stolen missiles, and that it's all an old KGB disinformation op designed, as you put it, to make the Outfit run around like chickens with their heads cut off?"

"From what I've observed, the Outfit already knows how to do that," Kevin said. "The answer is, I don't know."

"Don't know or don't know yet?"

"You ask tricky questions, sir."

"You know what Mikhail says about the bombs. Have you checked that out? Was he in Turkmenistan, doing what he said he was, at the right time?"

"I believe he was, based on other data. The problem is, the folks back home don't believe Mikhail's story because they can't bring themselves to believe him. He's a retired torturer and assassin, so how can he be trusted?"

Harley said, "Well, Horace, here, and I don't have to worry about Mikhail's past. And I'm part of it. I'd like a chance to say good-bye to him."

Kevin gave Harley another puckered smile. "Okay," he said. "But I'd appreciate it if you didn't give Mikhail's money back."

Harley said, "Why's that?"

"To take away his alternatives," Kevin said. "In order to restore his bankroll he'll have to go back to the mob, show them his bruises, and tell them how he was kidnapped and beaten up and robbed by you two crazy old Outfit types who had a grudge from the Cold War."

Harley said, "You make him do that, tell them that, and he's a dead man."

"Fifty-fifty chance," Kevin said with a shrug.

"One hundred percent, son. And before he dies, he'll lead 'em back to this dacha."

"Let him. The owner doesn't know we're here. Doesn't know us, for that matter. We'll clean it up before we leave—put the transmitters back where we found them, wipe prints, all like that."

"You mean you just burgled this place and turned it into a hideout for a day?" Harley said.

Kevin gave us his full high-noon smile, but no further explanation.

7

Our last conversation with Mikhail was not especially friendly. I asked him a few more questions, he snarled at me.

"Why should I tell you anything?" he asked.

"Why not?" Harley said.

"I work for pay."

My, but Mikhail was a single-minded Russian.

"How much do you want?"

"Five thousand American dollars in hundreds."

"We can cover that," I said. "But first the information. What was the code name for the cobalt backpack bombs?"

"They were too secret to have an official name," Mikhail said. "The troops called them Uncle Joes. To save weight, the bombs were unshielded."

"So why Uncle Joe?"

"Because to have Uncle Joe Stalin on your back meant you were going to die young."

We had been standing while Mikhail reclined on a bed. His titanium leg was nowhere to be seen. Harley sat down on the mattress beside him.

"One last thing," he said. "This has been troublin' me right along, so I'd appreciate it if you can ease my mind."

Mikhail nodded mutely. In spite of everything he *liked* Harley.

Whatever else the two of them were, they had been professionals together for years.

"It just seems peculiar that they'd take a wounded officer out of a hospital in the Crimea, like they did with you, and send him all the way to Turkmenistan to handle a case as big as this one," Harley said.

Mikhail said nothing.

Harley said, "They must've had a lot of faith in you."

Again, silence, but Mikhail's frozen face was thawing.

Harley said, "So the question is, Mikhail, why did you shoot the wrong people?"

Mikhail laughed an explosive liar's laugh. "That was not a crime in the Soviet Union."

"No, but there was usually a reason for it. What was the reason this time?"

"Do I get my money?"

"If the answer's truthful."

"They knew about you and me, Harley," Mikhail said. "They had photographs of our meetings, recordings of our conversations, everything. So my ethical choices were limited."

Harley was holding Mikhail's bankroll. He handed it to him.

"Best use this to get across the border," he said.

"For these people there are no borders," Mikhail said.

Harley gave him a paternal pat on the arm and left the room.

Now that he was alone with me, Mikhail's eyes, so shiny in his last moments with Harley, turned back into dry ice. He said, "I still think you will die in Russia, my friend Horace."

By now it was pitch dark and snowing hard. When I emerged from Mikhail's room I found my bag packed and waiting in the sitting room, my parka draped over it. An electric sweeper howled. Kevin's men, mute as ever, wiped surfaces clean of fingerprints and put listening devices back where they had found them. All the windows were open. I wondered if that would be enough to get rid of the smell of fried bacon.

I said, "No surveillance cameras?"

"The techs installed a loop," Kevin said. "Shows the rooms empty like they should be, over and over. Transmitters are voice-activated, so if they hear nothing, that's normal. The snow will take care of footprints and tire tracks."

"Best sweep 'em anyway, son," Harley said. "Can't depend on the weather."

He had opened his own suitcase and was rummaging through it. "Found it," he said, unpacking an out-at-the-elbows heirloom wool cardigan and putting it on. "Chilly in here."

Kevin nodded amiably. "Sorry I can't ask you to stay to supper, but as you can see we're moving out."

He beckoned us to a table where a Michelin map was spread out. It showed highways in red, back roads in yellow, dirt tracks as dotted lines.

"We are here, about three hundred klicks from Moscow, as I'm sure you noticed," Kevin said, pointing to a spot between two lakes. "The Latvian border is about one hundred fifty klicks to the west. When you come to the end of the drive, turn left. At the second intersection, eighteen klicks south, you're going to turn right. That will take you to the main road to the border. The usual no-hassle exit fee for the Russians at the checkpoint is one Ben Franklin per head. The Latvians will let you in for free when they see your passports."

He handed me a set of keys with an Avis tag attached. "You should get started if you want to stay ahead of the snow. The car is outside, full tank. Please leave it, locked, in the parking lot at the Riga airport, keys, papers, and parking stub in the glove compartment."

Kevin handed me an open paper bag. Sandwiches and two Cokes, our supper. He looked me straight in the eye and shook hands very firmly.

Harley shambled over and offered his hand. "You're quite a lad, Kevin," he said. "Best of luck to you."

"You, too, Mister Waters," said Kevin.

"Don't be too hard on old Mikhail," Harley said. "We made him what he is today."

"That's charitable, sir."

"Simple truth, son."

In the car, headlights reflecting from hypnotic whirling snow, Harley said, "What I was lookin' for in my valise back there was the water glass I swiped from the dinin' room in Moscow."

"The one with Kevin's prints on it?"

"That's the one. It was still there, but it'd been wiped."

Harley threw the brown-bag lunch Kevin had packed for us out the window.

"Best not eat the sandwiches," he said.

FOUR

1

During my five days in Russia I had not had a single thought about Paul Christopher. This changed on my first morning in Latvia when Jack Philindros called me from Jerusalem.

"I've been talking to a friend of your cousin's mother," he murmured. "It seems she passed through Palestine right after the war."

He meant World War II. I said, "On her way to where?"

"The impression here is that even she didn't know. Just wanted to disappear. However, she left a bona fide with her friend. Her wedding ring."

"Why?"

"In case her son ever showed up. Which he did, about six months ago, taking the ring with him when he left."

While Harley Waters flew to Prague in search of people who might remember Lori, I took a plane to Tel Aviv. No one met me at the airport. Jack's strict obedience to the rules of tradecraft ruled that out, but I knew that he would materialize before the end of the day. I took a taxi to Jerusalem, checked into the King David hotel, and waited. My room overlooked the deserted gardens and in the middle distance, the old city. I went to sleep and was awakened from a dream by a burst of faraway Uzi fire. Or maybe the weapon was fired in the dream. I wasn't sure.

At five o'clock precisely the bedside telephone rang. "Welcome to Jerusalem, Mister Hubbard," Jack said. "I wanted to confirm our appointment."

This meant he was waiting for me downstairs.

I had just come out of the shower. "Can you give me ten minutes?"

"Certainly."

Jack met me at the elevators without a sign of recognition, turned on his heel, and led me out of the hotel. He was a little more olive-skinned than usual after three weeks in the Mediterranean sun. In a city where few wore coats or ties, he was dressed in his usual style—black senior bureaucrat's suit, crisp white shirt, dark-blue silk tie, burnished wingtips.

He led me along King David Street to a courtyard where his rental car was parked. It was the sabbath, so traffic was tolerable.

Jack said, "We'll be there in about ten minutes. It's pretty secure."

Our destination turned out to be a Greek Orthodox monastery in the old city. Jack was staying there. As monasteries go it was pleasant enough—dusty shafts of honeyed sunlight and the muted clatter of pedestrian traffic coming in through open windows, gilded icons on whitewashed walls, old monks with youthful voices singing vespers in a chapel at the other end of the building.

"I've asked Lori's friend to join us," Jack said. "He's not so likely to be compromised by coming here as to the King David hotel. The monks know him."

"He's a Greek?"

"No, Israeli. A scholar. The monastery has a very good library, going back to Biblical times."

The man awaited us in an anteroom. Jack had told me nothing about him apart from what he had reported over the phone. He was younger than I had imagined—about Paul's age. Despite his short stature, balding head and small paunch, he was still an almost theatrically handsome man. As a youth he must have looked a lot like the movie actor John Garfield. He wore snow-white sneakers, brand-new jeans, a blue chambray work shirt, a leather jacket. He had very small hands.

He closed the book he had been reading, stood up, and offered his hand.

"Norman Schwarz," he said. He had a ringing actor's voice, brimming with hearty good will.

"Horace Hubbard."

"Paul's cousin. He described you to a T."

"How was he when you saw him?"

"He seemed well. Happy, even. Not much changed, except larger and older, from the last time I saw him when we were boys."

"You knew him back then? Where?"

"In Berlin. Our parents were friends. We went to school together, went hiking together, played football. My memories of him and his father and mother are vivid. Because of the Christopher family I am alive today. I have had more than sixty years of life that otherwise would have been taken from me."

I knew what was coming next but waited for Schwarz to make his own explanation.

"In 1939, when I was fourteen," Schwarz said, "at the last possible moment, the Christophers smuggled my parents and my sister and me out of Germany. On a sailboat to Denmark. There were many others who also escaped Hitler on that sailboat. Paul says we were the last."

"The yawl *Mahican*."

"Exactly. So you know about the things they did?"

"Just the bare facts. Paul and his father rarely spoke of it. And of course his mother was lost to the Nazis."

"So we heard at the time," Schwarz said. "So we believed for a long while. But it wasn't true, at least not in the sense that they killed her."

"You know this for a fact?"

"I saw her here, in Jerusalem, in 1945. It was a memorable thing. I was old enough by then to realize how extraordinary she was."

He pulled some snapshots from the pocket of his jacket.

"Look," he said. "Here she is with my mother and father and me."

One of the bleached figures in the overexposed photographs was a pale slender woman who could well have been Lori. She was a bit taller than the Schwarzes. Young Norman wore British army hot-climate uniform—short-sleeved khaki shirt with a row of campaign ribbons, voluminous starched khaki shorts and brown knee socks. In the pictures, Lori was the only one who wasn't smiling.

"How on earth did she end up in Jerusalem?" I asked.

"On a ship to Haifa full of Jewish refugees."

"And how did that happen?"

"I think the Mossad helped her. Their original mission was to rescue Jews in peril, as you no doubt know."

"But she wasn't Jewish."

"No, but many Jews who would have gone to the camps were alive because of her."

"The fact that she had lived with Reinhard Heydrich was known?"

"Oh, yes."

"That didn't enter into it?"

"I imagine it had a bearing," Schwarz said, "A positive bearing. My father said that Heydrich was dead because of her."

"He knew this?"

"He seldom guessed at things," Schwarz said. "He was with the Mossad before it was the Mossad. Even when we lived in Germany he did that kind of work. He sent a lot of people to the Christophers. They saved them all. That's why we were so late in leaving Germany. There was always one more to rescue. Finally, when it was very late, he was ordered to go, to save himself."

"The Christophers knew all this?"

"Oh, yes. That's why they helped us." He gripped my forearm with his childlike hand. "Imagine the courage that took."

I said, "Why do you say that Heydrich was dead because of Lori?"

Schwarz's cell phone rang in his pocket. He ignored it.

He said, "Why do you ask?"

"As I understand it, Heydrich's assassination was supposed to be a British operation, carried out with British weapons."

"It's true that Heydrich was killed with Sten guns. But the British weren't the only people in the world who had Sten guns. Or friends in Prague. Or even the strongest motive to eliminate Heydrich."

"Are you telling me Heydrich's assassination was a Jewish operation?"

"If I were, I'd only be guessing," Schwarz said. "Let me tell you what I know about Lori Christopher."

Her ship had sailed from Bari, on the heel of Italy. To get from Czechoslovakia, across Austria, and down nearly the whole length of Italy through the chaos of Europe in 1945 was no easy matter. The roads were clogged with displaced persons fleeing the Russians or simply trying to get back home after having been kidnapped by the Nazis. Lori had no papers, but neither did anybody else. The trains weren't operating. Almost no one had a motor vehicle and there was no gasoline for civilians in any case. There was no way to get anywhere except by walking.

"She lost herself in the mob until she was out of Czechoslovakia," Schwarz said. "Then she walked across Austria, alone, traveling at night, her belongings wrapped up in a shawl."

"What belongings?"

Schwarz said, "I think you already know the answer to that question. The Amphora Scroll."

His phone rang again. This time he answered, speaking in Hebrew.

"Please excuse me," he said. "But I really have to go now."

And with a charming smile he was gone.

2

Jack Philindros and I dined with the monks, who did pretty well for themselves at table. Greek salad, roast lamb, fruit, sour red wine mixed with water, gritty sweet coffee. Except for the coffee, Septimus Arcanus might have eaten a similar supper two thousand years ago in this same neighborhood.

Afterward, in Jack's whitewashed cell, we talked about Norman Schwarz. The walls and door were thick. One tiny shuttered window was set high in the wall above an ornate Byzantine crucifix. The silence was almost perfect, so Jack was almost audible.

I said, "Likeable fellow, your man Schwarz."

"Everybody notices," Jack replied.

"Do you believe what he was telling us?"

"With the usual reluctance, yes," Jack said.

"You've dealt with him before?"

"Yes."

"Then why the reluctance?"

"Truthful men sometimes lie and liars sometimes tell the truth," Jack said. "All things being equal, Norman is a truthful man."

"I was a little surprised at his suggestion that Lori was an agent of Zionists."

"It's not impossible. Norman's mother, who was Lori's contact in the *Mahican* operation, was Yeho Stern's sister."

"Oh."

The late Yeho Stern had been head of the Israeli intelligence service during the earliest years of Israel's existence. Yeho was legendary in the original sense of the word. During his long tenure as Memuneh, meaning the Big Boss of the Mossad, no one outside his service, and not everybody inside it, could be absolutely sure that he really existed.

I said, "What about the Brits?"

"Maybe Yeho piggybacked their operation," Jack replied. "Taking free rides on better-financed services was one of his many specialties."

"So you see no holes in what Norman has told us so far?"

"I didn't say that."

"What, then?"

"A possible funny coincidence," Jack said. "Norman was in the Jewish Brigade, a unit of the British army that saw action in northern Italy in the spring of 1945, just before V-E Day. In the summer of 1945 members of the Jewish Brigade were active all along the Italian frontier with Yugoslavia and Austria, helping escaping Jews to get aboard the underground railroad for Palestine."

"So?"

"Norman may have met Lori in Italy on Uncle Yeho's orders and put her on the right boat for Haifa."

This made sense. No introductions would have been necessary, no explanations required. Lori already knew Norman from Berlin days, and anything he did for her could be explained as payment of a personal debt.

Having planted this seed, Jack fell into a silence. Monastic surroundings notwithstanding, I was in no mood for silent communing and besides, he had aroused my curiosity about Norman.

"You said that Norman is a scholar," I said. "What's his field?"

"Byzantine art," Jack said. "That's why he's a regular here.

He uses the library. Some of the monks are Byzantine scholars, too."

"Don't tell me he's another doctor of philosophy."

"No, he took it up in retirement. For most of his life he was a professional poker player."

According to Jack, Norman had learned the game from seamen on the Australian tramp steamer that had taken his family from Copenhagen to Haifa after their escape from the Nazis. Norman showed an immediate flair for poker. He had phenomenal eyesight, which meant that he could read every card that fell, a retentive memory, and a gift for arithmetic. As a result of a boyhood spent in the company of people who mostly wanted to see him dead, he was also good at reading faces and body language.

Soon after Norman came home from the war he sat down to a game of five-card stud with his Uncle Yeho and some of his Mossad friends. He cleaned them out.

Yeho immediately saw his nephew's possibilities. The kid was young and handsome and smart and already a cool experienced killer—as a soldier he had been an unusually competent sniper in Italy. This résumé would have made Norman interesting to Yeho even if he had had no other qualifications. His skill at poker made him special. Needing no other cover, he could go anywhere in the world and play cards with anyone, and because gamblers lived at night while the rest of the world slept, he could get away with just about any kind of operation.

That very night, Yeho popped the question.

"Norman made a condition," Jack said. "He insisted on keeping whatever money he won at cards. Yeho said okay. How could he play without an incentive?"

"And did he come out ahead?"

"After a few years in the field he used his winnings to buy a small hotel in Miami Beach," Jack said. "It didn't really matter to Yeho where Norman lived, of course."

"Did he go on playing poker after he became a hotelier?"

"Until he began to lose to younger players, but that didn't happen until years later," Jack said. "He played in high-stakes games all over the world. Norman met a lot of interesting people, rich Arabs and so on. Rich Germans, too."

Jack had something to tell me, but he expected me to ask for it.

I said, "Tell me more about the rich Arabs and Germans."

"You can ask Norman when you see him again." He looked at his watch. "Midnight. You know, Horace, I think you'd be better off staying here tonight. The monks will be glad to have you, and Norman does come by almost every day."

"What about tomorrow?"

"We'll see what we see," Jack said. "Meanwhile, you're welcome to stay here for a few days. The King David is a goldfish bowl."

"You want me to go into hiding?"

"No, but you have nothing to gain by being conspicuous. I know you don't care about security anymore, but Israel is full of Russians and not all of them are innocent returnees."

"Meaning?"

"From what I've heard about what you and Harley were up to in Moscow, you may have created resentments in Russia."

I said, "Is this a warning on general principles or do you know something specific?"

"There's some local anxiety about your safety," Jack said.

"You're telling me both the Russian mob and the Mossad are after me?"

"Not the Mossad, as far as I know. Why should they be when you might have better luck than they've had so far in finding the missing bombs? They'd rather just watch you work."

"And Norman is the watcher?"

"One of them, maybe," Jack said. "But I think he represents an offer of friendship. A broker between two parties who have similar objectives."

The other party was Yeho's old organization. I had never heard

165

of anyone going into partnership with the Mossad and coming out ahead.

I said, "A broker who belongs to the competition and just happens to be one of the best poker players in the world?"

"Yes, but he's also Norman."

"Meaning what?"

"Meaning I really don't think Norman is going to lie to a cousin of Paul Christopher's or betray him," Jack said. "He may have an agenda of his own, but he has his memories, too."

In his elliptical way Jack was saying that Norman was an Old Boy who lived by old principles. The Christophers, who had saved his family at the risk of their own lives, were his friends. So were their friends, and especially their families.

We finished our breakfast. Jack said, "Why don't you take the day off? Stay in your room and wait for Norman to show up. I have some things to do."

The monks did not speak to me, but they didn't seem to mind my presence. After wandering around the monastery for half the morning looking at icons and books, I settled down in my cell with a novel I had brought with me. Around one o'clock I heard the monks shuffling by my door and then, drifting down the corridor, convivial sounds as they tucked into lunch. Jack had vanished and I felt diffident about going down to the refectory by myself. I ate an apple and went back to my book.

An hour or so later came a tap on the door. My caller was Norman Schwarz, carrying a tray covered with a napkin.

"The monks were afraid you might be faint with hunger," Norman said. "And I have this for you."

From a string shopping bag he produced a package containing clean socks and underwear, a razor and toothbrush, and a secondhand sweater old enough and large enough to have been made for Goliath. Apparently Jack had asked him to do some shopping. Again I noticed his small hands. His Uncle Yeho, whom he did not otherwise resemble, had been a tiny man. Imagine a hairy ten-year-old.

Under the napkin I found a bowl of soup based on last evening's roast lamb, a chunk of bread, a slab of cheese, a jug of water.

"Eat," Norman said.

While I chewed, he talked. Norman had vivid memories of Lori Christopher as she had been after she came ashore by night in Palestine.

"She had been emptied out," Norman said. "Everything she had been before Heydrich had run down some psychological drainpipe. She was alive, yes, and apart from being thinner and very, very quiet, she was the same as she had been in Berlin. Back then she had crackled with intelligence, exuded vitality. She was still beautiful, but you felt that she was someplace else emotionally. And so she was—she was between her last self and her next self."

"I'm not sure I follow you," I said.

"Before the war, even with the Nazis in power, she had been a reckless person. She said whatever came into her head, she did what she wanted. She had everything—an ancient name, enough money, beauty, a husband she loved, Paul. She lost all that, even ownership of her own body. So she was not the woman she had been, and never could be that woman again."

"This is speculation?"

"No," Norman said. "She told me this."

"Whatever for? Were you her psychiatrist?"

"No," Norman said. "Her lover."

I could not have been more astonished if he had pulled out a pistol and shot me with it.

It was Lori who started the affair. She had been staying with the Schwarzes in Jerusalem. Norman was on terminal leave from the army. One night she simply got into his bed. In Norman's experience it was usually the woman who made the first move, but this surprised him. There was not that much difference in their ages. He was in his early twenties; she was still in her thirties. But the last time he had seen her he had been a boy and she had been Paul's mother.

"I was startled," Norman said, "but I was young and she woke me out of a sound sleep in which I was probably dreaming of a girl, so I didn't think twice. She had the body of a girl, she smelled like a girl, but she had the sexual intelligence, the bed language, of a woman to whom nothing is new and nothing is forbidden."

This was my aunt he was talking about. I was quite uncomfortable.

I said, "You told Paul this?"

"Of course not."

"Then why are you telling me?"

"You have a reason to know and no reason not to be told," Norman said. "And I assume you can keep a secret."

Norman fell in love with Lori. "I was under no illusions," he said. "She didn't love me. She couldn't have been better to me in bed and in every other way if she had loved me. But she didn't."

"Your parents didn't notice what was going on?"

"I saw little smiles on their lips. Mothers like their sons to get laid. My parents were old-fashioned radical socialists, believers in free love. To them, sex was like eating an ice-cream cone on a hot day. Who doesn't like ice cream?"

"If she didn't love you and she was still in shock from what had happened with Heydrich, what was she getting out of it?"

"She was burning a bridge."

"Using you?"

"Asking me to collaborate." Norman stopped talking, bit his lip, looked at the crucifix on the wall of my cell. "I had no idea that I was still so sad about all this," he said. "Give me a moment."

In a lifetime of listening to secrets, I had seldom before encountered one that shook me up as this one was doing. Human beings, women in particular, step out of character all the time and do unpredictable things. If Norman had been telling me about anyone else, short of my own mother, I would not have been shocked. But Lori Christopher—Paul's mother, my uncle's wife— had been the heroine in a romance that had transfixed me and the rest of the Hubbards and Christophers for half a century. It was a surprise to discover that this maid of the mists had been flesh and blood after all, and that she had been trying to run away from the husband and son who had spent their lives believing that she was waiting for them to find her.

"Anyway," Norman said. "I would have done anything for her. There was no other woman like her. I don't mean her looks or her mind or the sex, even though all of it was wonderful. It was what it came wrapped up in—profound sorrow, never mentioned, not even in the form of a sad face or a tear. But always there. Accepted. Her fate."

"You didn't find this in any way theatrical?"

"Are you serious? She didn't have a theatrical atom in her being. She was a person to whom the unbearable had happened, a person who had been in the power of maniacs. What had actually happened to her was already a nightmare. What was there to embroider?"

Lori told him the story of the Amphora Scroll, showed it to him sealed in its glass cylinder, described its contents.

"She must have trusted you."

"She had good reason," Norman said. "I have never told anyone that it existed from that day to this."

"Not even your Uncle Yeho?"

Norman was not at all surprised by the question. "Not even him," he said. "What Lori told him, I don't know."

I said, "Lori knew Yeho Stern?"

"He came to our house for dinner every sabbath so he could light matches and make phone calls without giving offense to the orthodox. He was a chain-smoker in those days and there was always somebody he had to talk to."

"He met Lori in your parents' home?"

"They met through my parents, but earlier, I think."

"In Berlin?"

"Maybe."

"You don't know for certain?"

"With Yeho nobody knew anything for certain," Norman said.

"Did you ever ask Lori?"

"I never asked anybody any questions about anything having to do with Yeho," Norman said.

3

In the winter of 1945–46, a bitter one all over the Old World, Norman awoke one morning in Jerusalem to find Lori gone. In true Christopherian fashion, there were no good-byes. She left a letter, addressed jointly to him and his parents.

"What the letter said, essentially, was thanks for the hospitality and good-bye forever," Norman said. "No hint of where she was going or why. Of course I knew why. My mother and father didn't. They were shocked by her bad manners. For a minute or two what she had done turned Lori back into a German for them. Then they remembered who she was and what she had done."

Travel in those days, especially in the Middle East, was no simple matter. The British still controlled Palestine and its frontiers. They were already nervous about the work of Yeho Stern and other Zionist activists—the smuggling of European Jews into Palestine, terrorist incidents designed to frighten the British out of the country. As far as Norman knew, Lori still had no papers. In 1945 the chances of a German national, no matter how heroically anti-Nazi, moving freely across borders were close to zero. Unless she had help. Fortunately Norman was in a good position to ask the right person about this. As first light broke, he woke up his Uncle Yeho, pounding on the door of his room in the Old City. This was risky business.

"Yeho was not happy to see me," Norman said. "He came to the door with a big revolver in his hand. At the time, of course, he was considered the most dangerous terrorist in Palestine. But when I explained, he was sympathetic. He had the facts at his fingertips, of course."

According to Yeho, Lori had acquired a Red Cross passport identifying her as a displaced Czech. She had left for Haifa to board a Lebanese freighter, the *Amin Gulgee,* that was bound for the Persian Gulf. Norman arrived that same morning, an hour before the ship sailed, and bought deck passage to the last port of call.

"Lori and I met on the deck as soon as the ship was beyond the twenty-kilometer limit," Norman said. "She was not happy to see me, but short of throwing me overboard there wasn't much she could do about my presence. She must have known that Yeho had a hand in the situation, just as I suspected that she owed her Red Cross papers and who knew what else to him."

The *Amin Gulgee* was not built for speed or comfort, but the weather was cool by the standards of the region, and the long wallowing sun-scorched passage through the Red Sea and around the Arabian peninsula was pleasant enough. There was no possibility of lovemaking and very little opportunity for conversation. Lori shared a cabin with ten other women. The deck where Norman slept teemed with seamen and passengers day and night.

They disembarked at Bandar-e 'Abbas, the first port of call in Iran. The journey had taken more than a month.

"The British were thin on the ground in that part of Persia and anyway I had a British passport," Norman said. "So after paying bribes we went ashore without difficulty. However, this was Balochistan. A woman could not travel alone. Lori agreed that we would pose as man and wife. She had acquired a chador aboard ship and she put this on. I look enough like a generic Semite to pass for an Arab or even a Baloch."

"You spoke the local languages?" I asked.

"Enough Palestinian Arabic to be understood by other people who didn't speak it very well," he said. "Lori just kept mute inside the chador, as any Muslim woman would. Everyone assumed we were what we said we were."

Then as now there were no railroads and virtually no roads in those parts. Air travel was far in the future. Norman and Lori took an ancient bus to Kerman, a journey of about two hundred miles as the crow flies.

"We traveled as the worm wiggles, assuming a worm could live in that dehydrated wilderness," Norman said. "Half the time there was no road. Everyone would get out and push. The bus stopped at dark and we slept inside it until sunrise, when the starter would grind and wake us up. This was always a moment of suspense while the ancient diesel engine made up its mind to fire up. It took five days to get to Kerman, but when we got there we were welcomed, naturally, by a friend of Yeho's."

It was Lori who had the man's name and address and the spoken phrase in Hebrew that told him that she was under Yeho's protection.

"This fellow, Ibrahim by name, was in the caravansary business," Norman said. "His inn was a hollow square made of tin sheets that buckled and boomed in the wind. Inside the square was a courtyard with a well. Dozens of camels were hobbled in this space. Swarms of huge black flies fed on their manure. It was stark, I tell you—not a pane of glass or a screen in the place. Sun beating down on a metal roof, the flies and the stench and dust drifting into the room on a delightful desert breeze that was the temperature of blood. Lori swathed in that chador."

Until they saw the camels and the ruffians who owned them, Norman and Lori intended to join a caravan headed eastward toward Afghanistan. This was Lori's plan, or as much of it as she cared to reveal.

"Ibrahim was horrified," Norman said. "'They already know you are not Muslims,' he said in Hebrew, so that Lori would not understand. 'These people are primitive. They will kill you on the second night and take the woman. They will pass her around, make a slave of her and beat her, and when she wears out they will leave her naked in the desert to die.'"

Norman was convinced. He knew savages when he saw them, and so did Lori. But she still wanted to travel by caravan.

"She simply had no fear," Norman said. "It wasn't that she wanted to die, but danger just didn't matter to her. This would have been strange in a man. In a woman it was uncanny. It was enough to make you wonder if a fortuneteller had described some other fate to her and, out of character as it seemed, she believed what the cards had told her."

Norman feared that he would wake up one morning and find her gone again. Ibrahim forestalled this by providing alternative transportation before night fell on the day he delivered his warning.

"Who knows where he found it, but Ibrahim found us an old British truck," Norman said. "Prewar vintage, but it ran."

Ibrahim dealt in firearms as in many other things, and from him Norman and Lori bought two old but serviceable English sporting rifles, one equipped with a scope, and five hundred rounds of ammunition. Also water and spare gasoline in goatskins, a small tent with carpets in which, they soon discovered, a metropolis of fleas dwelt, and three sheep, a ewe to be milked and two wethers to be killed and eaten. All this did not come cheap—Ibrahim was a businessman, after all—but Lori paid for it with an open hand.

"Money seemed to be as irrelevant to her as caution, as though it was something that she wasn't going to need much longer," Norman said.

In the bazaar in Kerman, Norman bought men's clothes for both of them. Lori wore her chador until they were well out of town, but then ordered Norman to stop the vehicle and went behind some rocks. She came back as a slender youth in pantaloons and baggy caftan, her bobbed hair concealed beneath a turban that she somehow knew how to wind. She no longer moved like a woman or even like a European, but like the fellaheen she had evidently been studying aboard the *Amin Gulgee* and ashore in Balochistan. On the ship and the journey from the sea to Kermin she acquired a deep tan, and though she was more golden-skinned than most Balochi, in addition to being gray-eyed, she might—with a cloth across her face—pass for a boy whose mother had spent a night with an Englishman or a blue-eyed Afghan.

The only road north out of Kerman ran through a hilly salt desert. There were two or three oasis villages between Kerman and the point on the map, three hundred miles distant, where the road turned eastward across the Afghan border. And beyond that to the city of Herat.

Norman said, "I fully expected that I would die for love long before we got to Herat. Lori did not say that this was our final destination, but I couldn't imagine a more hidden place on the face of the earth."

On the second morning out of Kerman they were attacked by men on camels who rode out of a blinding white sunrise and riddled their tent with bullets.

"Because of the fleas in the rugs Ibrahim had sold us, Lori and I had taken to sleeping on the ground in the open," Norman said. "On this particular morning we were on a little hill above the camp. We had our rifles with us. There were seven men in the attack. They were armed with jezails, old black powder muzzle-loaders, and they riddled our empty tent with bullets. Without saying a word, Lori began firing. I had no idea how well she could shoot. But she knocked one man off his camel at a range of at least two hundred yards before I got in my first shot. My weapon was the one with the scope on it, which rendered it useless because we were shooting into the sun."

By the time Norman got the scope detached, a matter of a few seconds, Lori had downed another man and wounded a camel, which threw its rider and was now running in agonized circles. The rest of the bandits were fleeing back into the blinding disk of the sun. Norman, who as you will remember was a trained sniper, downed one of them and wounded another, who held onto his mount and kept going. The survivors were now out of range over open sights.

"Before I could stop her, Lori was running down the hill toward the camp," Norman said. "She wasn't wearing her turban and her hair was flying like a blond flag. I grabbed the scope and a box of ammunition and followed. No choice. I caught up with her just as she was leaping into the truck. She started it up with a roar and took off after the fleeing men."

They were off the road, driving through open country. In such circumstances the old rattletrap could not go much faster than a running camel, but even a camel gets tired, and after a few minutes the men stopped on a hilltop, made the animals lie down, and began firing on the truck from behind a screen of rocks.

"Lori made a wide circle around the hill, then put the truck in low gear and drove it to the top of another little hill about a hundred yards away from the first," Norman said. "The enemy's jezails were pretty well at the limit of their range."

This time the sun was behind Norman and Lori. She parked the truck behind a big rock, climbed to the top of it, fell on her stomach, and began methodically shooting the camels.

"Head shots every time," Norman said. "The camels just jumped in their skins and died. I lay down beside her. She said, 'The men are yours.'"

Norman had not been made a sniper by the British army because he was faint of heart, but this seemed extreme. The men were defeated, and where could they go without camels?

Lori said, "Kill them, Norman."

"I understood what she was telling me," he said. "If we didn't kill them all they'd have a motive for revenge and we'd never be free of them."

He put the scope back on his rifle and one by one he shot the men, the last one being a mere boy, judging by his agility, who tried to escape by running down the hill, dodging from rock to rock.

"In minutes they were all dead, men and animals," Norman said. "Lori was as composed when the smoke cleared as a woman coming out of a theater."

They left the dead brigands and their camels where they lay, as an advertisement to others.

4

Even in Herat Yeho had a friend. Although this is not much mentioned in radical Islamist circles nowadays (and I never knew it until Norman told me), the local people still believed in 1946 that they were the descendants of an Israelite tribe that had been captured and marched to Babylon by Nebuchadrezzar after the destruction of Jerusalem in 586 B.C. Eventually these people made their way into western Afghanistan, founded Herat, became the tribe called the Pathan, and started conquering their neighbors. Like their purported ancestors under Joshua and modern Israelis under men like Yeho, they were ferocious and merciless warriors and conquerors. They called themselves the Ben i-Israel, sons of Israel. They lived under a semblance of ancient Hebraic law, spoke a different language from the rest of the Afghans, and believed that their lineage made them the most noble people in Afghanistan and its destined rulers.

In the thirteenth century they ran up against the Ghuzz, a Muslim Turkoman people whose missionary army attacked Herat. The forty inhabitants of Herat who survived the siege converted to Islam—just how wholeheartedly one can only guess—but their legendary history and law were recorded in sacred books. The hereditary keeper of these texts was Yeho's friend Habibullah.

Once again it was Lori who knew where to find Habibullah and what to say to him.

"With Yeho you never knew, but I don't see how Habibullah could have been expecting us," Norman said. "He took us in anyway when we mentioned Yeho's name."

From the outside, Norman said, Habibullah's house looked like a hovel, but inside it was spacious, with divans and tables and Persian carpets laid edge-to-edge. It swarmed with servants. The windows were closed against the stench and the heat and the flies. Little boys stirred the fetid air by pulling the ropes on fans suspended from the ceiling. Habibullah took it for granted that Lori and Norman were a married couple.

"Or maybe he didn't, since we were infidels and it didn't matter anyway," Norman said. "For whatever reason, he put us up together in an apartment of our own. As soon as we were inside the door, Lori ripped off the chador. She was fully clothed underneath, of course, but Habibullah rolled his eyes to heaven to avoid looking at her face. She immediately pulled a scarf across it and covered her hair. Habibullah relaxed. But he let us know that Lori should not wander around the house veiled or unveiled, and that he would conduct business with us in our own apartment. I would eat meals with him. Lori would be fed in her room by women."

All the business was done by Lori, reciting briskly from mental lists. She wanted three good horses, a stallion and two mares, clothes suitable for a journey through the mountains, and at least two hundred rounds of ammunition for her pistol and each of the two rifles. Also one good saddle for a rider and two packsaddles, food for thirty days and such medicine as was available, and large-scale maps and verbal directions across northern Afghanistan and India as far as China. She would pay in gold through Habibullah.

The horses must be the very best available and she must inspect and ride them before any deal was made. She communicated in English with Habibullah, who spoke the language well, like most educated Afghans and so many others who lived on the pink parts of the map as the sun was setting on the British empire. Lori found the horses she wanted—not the beautiful Arab steeds Norman had imagined, but wiry surefooted animals that were not much larger than ponies.

"Naturally she rode like a Cossack and knew all about horse-flesh," Norman said. "Her repertoire of skills amazed me. She had acquired most of them as a child. Before Hitler the Germans were great believers in overeducation, and I guess these accomplishments were just things that were expected of the daughter of a Prussian baron. Except maybe the marksmanship. Her father taught her to shoot when she was ten, she said, in case the Russians ever came."

In less than a week Habibullah acquired everything Lori needed, including the sporting ammunition she had specified. This was something of a miracle, considering where Herat lay on the map and the fact that Europe had been at war for six years and in all that time no one had been making ammunition for civilian use. Knowing what she wanted and never taking no for an answer had been important parts of Lori's Prussian education.

"She said nothing about her plans or the future, but then she never had," Norman said. "One morning I woke up and she was gone. Again. I knew this was going to happen eventually, of course, and the way she made love the night before—as if orgasm was a period at the end of a sentence—should have told me that I was getting the only good-bye I was ever going to get. Still, it was a shock. I knew what had happened from the moment I opened my eyes, but I gave no more thought to following her than if she had cut off my feet and taken them with her. There was no place for me where she was going, and I didn't want to spend the rest of my life among the people she was going to find when she got to wherever that might be."

This time, Lori left him a letter.

"It was quite impersonal, written in German, which was the language she and I spoke to each other," Norman said. "She enclosed her wedding ring, with her initials and her husband's, the date, and a word or two about love engraved around the inside. It was not for me, or even for her husband, but for Paul in case he ever showed up. I was to give it to him and say nothing."

"Say nothing?"

"I guess she wanted him to think of the ring as evidence that she was dead. Why else would she ever part with it? But she wouldn't ask me to lie about it."

"And did you do as she asked when Paul finally found you?"

"No."

"Why? Did you think she had changed her mind?"

"Hardly," Norman said. "The fact is, I wanted someone to find her. I've spent my life wishing that I had had the balls to do it myself, but I wanted to be with her in Paris, not in the middle of nowhere."

He fell into a silence. His large brown eyes, as keen as a youngster's, were unfocused, looking into the past. He left without saying good-bye.

FIVE

1

Our Arabist, Ben Childress, and I had agreed that we would never meet in a place where there was even the smallest probability that we might be seen together by Arabs. He chose Ireland, a country hotel on Lough Swilly in Donegal, about as far north and as much out of the way as one can go in Ireland. Ceaseless rain and icy wind chilled your bones. Ben arrived on the second day in time for tea. He was a Massachusetts man, raised on a stony mountaintop farm. As a boy, he had milked cows and chopped wood and walked to a one-room school. His people talked with a twang that made Harley Waters sound like a radio announcer. Ben himself sounded like a fellow who had gone to Princeton, which in fact he had done on the GI Bill of Rights after going ashore on D-Day with the First Infantry Division and somehow living through the remainder of the war.

Ben said, "Sorry, Horace, but what I've got for you may make you feel like the white hunter in the storybook."

"Which white hunter?"

"The one tracking the tiger who comes across his own footprints on a jungle path and realizes that he's walked in a circle and the tiger is stalking him."

I said, "Do go on, Ben."

"Ibn Awad knows you're after him again."

"You know he knows?"

"Yep."

"Then you know he's alive?"

"I have reason to think so."

"You've seen him with your own eyes?"

"Not yet. But I saw the fatwah he's issued against you. All believers are instructed to kill you on sight. Very good description of you appended."

"Ibn Awad signed this fatwah?"

"That's a trick question," Ben said. "You know he can't read or write. Just like the Prophet. And since he's officially dead and wants to stay that way, he had the fatwah issued by somebody else. But it came from him."

"You know where he is?"

"Not yet. He keeps on the move. From what I'm beginning to suspect, not just from one part of the Arabian desert to another. From desert to desert all over Africa and Asia, wherever there are Muslims."

That *not yet* was pure Childress. If Ben said he knew something, he knew it. He had the lofty certitude of Sherlock Holmes —achieved in his case, as far as I know, without the help of cocaine. He even looked like Holmes or, rather, like Basil Rathbone in the role of Holmes—dark hair, large aquiline nose, tight smile, white crooked teeth, a bachelor through and through, though not nearly so indifferent to the ladies as Holmes had been. Nor as rotten to the Watsons of this world, whose ranks, in Ben's estimation, included me and nearly everyone else he'd ever known.

Except Arabs. After Princeton, Ben had taken a degree in oriental languages at Oxford. From his tutors or the language he was studying or maybe from a desire to escape the musty gloom of England, he had contracted Arabitis. After getting his degree Ben had spent a year living in the Ar Rub al Khali desert with a band of bedouins who claimed to be the last descendants of the Quraysh tribe, who were thought by scholars to speak the purest Arabic. Many people who have lived among the bedu end up wanting with all their hearts to be as unlike them as possible. Ben, however, thought they were wonderful. He converted—sincerely—to Islam and became one of them, and for the rest of his life could become one of them again whenever the occasion demanded. This was a tremendous asset to the Outfit, which had recruited him in college and paid his way through Oxford. He was an Arab at heart, but an American do-gooder by instinct. He wanted to rescue the Arabs from their own ignorance and from sword of Christendom. Above all he did not want to become an American T. E. Lawrence, one of a long line of idealists who had been entranced by the Arabs and ended up betraying them. However, he was an idealist. He wanted above all to save the Arabs from one another, which was why he had helped me out in the original Ibn Awad operation. He had understood before anyone else that the old man was insane, and that he had it in his power to bring down the unholy wrath of the West on his innocent people.

Ben was protective of his sources. Nevertheless I asked the necessary question—but cautiously.

"Can I have some context for all this?" I asked.

"You mean names?" Ben said.

"Not necessarily, Ben. But it's my skin we're talking about here."

"Same type of sources as usual," Ben said. "I have an old friend whose grandson is a member of a terrorist cell. My friend used to be a terrorist himself, so like any grandfather who had a wild youth, he worries about the kid, wishes he had listened to him and practiced medicine."

"But he skipped med school?"

"No, he's an M.D., a surgeon trained in the States. It's just that his practice is confined to terrorists. He travels constantly, patching up the wounded—kind of like an Outfit medic."

"How does he know where to go?"

"He gets an e-mail from whoever controls him and gets on a plane."

"So how does he know anything about Ibn Awad?"

"Because the last patient he treated, in a desert camp, in Tunisia, was Ibn Awad's German doctor. He has cancer."

Tunisia? Did this mean that Ibn Awad had relocated to the Sahara? Ben Childress didn't think so.

"For one thing, our young doctor—call him Mubarak—wasn't sure he was in Tunisia," Ben said. "He deduced this from the fact that he was flown in a private plane to an airstrip among sand dunes like the ones in the Tunisian desert. When he got home, he described the German doctor to his grandfather and the old man knew it was Claus Bücher."

"How could he be sure?"

"He couldn't be sure. But he knew Bücher by sight and behavior. Lots of people did in the old days, before Ibn Awad was allegedly assassinated. At that point, Bücher disappeared. But before that, he was a man about town. There was nothing secret about Bücher's position in Ibn Awad's household."

Tea arrived on a tray carried by a fair-haired young waitress. Ben engaged her in conversation and in a matter of minutes was in possession of her entire curriculum vitae. She may have begun by thinking that she was talking to a nice old gentleman, but after the first five sentences Ben's age ceased to matter. He was simply a lean and hungry male with an interested look in his eye. Ben had learned much from the bedu, but asceticism was not one of the lessons. He was famous for the spell he cast on women. At cocktail parties I had watched other men's wives take off their shoes, remove their earrings, shake their hair, dance to inaudible music while merely chatting with Ben in a corner of the room.

When the waitress left us, reluctantly, I asked Ben why he thought Ibn Awad was moving his hiding place. He finished eating a buttered scone before replying.

"Because Mubarak was called back to treat Bücher," Ben said.

"This time he flew to Tehran by commercial jet and was given another ride in the private plane. Then a long helicopter ride. He wound up in an entirely different place from the last time."

"Also in the desert?"

"Yep. Different landscape altogether, different feel. But the same tents, which included a fully equipped portable hospital. Operating room, all the latest instruments and gadgets. He says it was a U.S. Army field hospital."

"How would he know that?"

"Maybe he watched *M*A*S*H*. Anyway, that was his opinion."

"Why did he go back?"

"To report biopsy findings," Ben said. "The tests confirmed that Bücher had cancer of the pancreas. This is invariably fatal. The patient didn't accept the diagnosis. They argued in Arabic. This time Bücher told Mubarak who he was. He mentioned his degree from the University of Vienna, the most famous medical school in the world when he was there. He emphasized the fact that he had been personal physician to Ibn Awad for many, many years."

"Bücher just blurted that out?"

"He wanted professional respect. He wasn't quite ready to stand before the Judgment seat. He wanted Mubarak to *do* something."

"Save him."

"Operate. But Mubarak wasn't qualified to perform this kind of surgery. Besides, even when it's successful, which is rarely, it only increases life expectancy by a few months."

"How long can Bücher live without surgery?"

"With the latest drugs, which are being administered, somewhere between three and six months. He was diagnosed about three weeks ago."

"What happens now?"

"He already has jaundice and itchy skin that can't be treated," Ben said. "Next come pain, sleeplessness, weight loss, deep fatigue, anemia."

"Amnesia?"

Ben gave me one of his frigid Sherlock Holmes glances, up and down, as if he were the much taller man. What made me think that he would omit such an important detail?

"Not inevitably," he said. "But of course the pain and fatigue soon reach a point where the victim doesn't care about remembering anything, or is so drugged that he can't remember."

Ben rose to his feet. "Time for a walk," he said.

We strolled in a freezing mist along the gray beach beside the gray sluggish water of Lough Swilly. We had to shout to be heard over the rain drumming on our hats, the bottled-up sea sloshing in the lough, the moaning wind. We walked on in silence for a mile or so before turning back. Dark was falling and the whitecaps became less visible, then phosphorescent. We reached the path to the hotel. By now it was full dark and Ben and I could not see each other. I could smell him, though—wet tweed, tea and cakes on his breath, shaving soap.

He said, "I suppose you'd like to talk to Bücher before he dies."

"That would be useful."

"You can hardly do it yourself," Ben said. "So the question is, who can, without getting himself killed?"

"Mubarak."

"The prime candidate, but unapproachable."

"He doesn't seem to have all that many scruples about spilling secrets to his grandfather."

"True, but Mubarak doesn't know what we need to know, i.e., exactly where Ibn Awad is, exactly where the bombs are."

"Exactly what we want to ask him."

"Bücher may not know, either," Ben said. "There's no reason why he should. For that matter, especially now that Bücher is dying and is of no medical use, there's little or no reason why he and Ibn Awad should be in the same place at the same time."

Ben had always irritated me. "I'm not interested in what Bücher *doesn't* know," I said. "I'm interested in what he does know."

"Then all we have to do is snatch him from his deathbed or send him someone he trusts," Ben said. "Someone he wants to confess to."

Elementary, my dear Watson.

2

It does focus the mind wonderfully to be the subject of a fatwa. Add to that the vengeful mood of the Russian mob, the homicidal impulses of a couple of Schutzstaffel golden-agers, the cheery ambiguity of Kevin and his Gray Force (if that's what it was) and the arithmetic of being a frequent flyer in the age of terrorism, and you've got yourself an actuarial crossword puzzle. Paranoia was nothing new in my life. You can't let it get in the way of work or spoil your leisure hours. The trick, as I was told as a trainee by what I then regarded as wise old instructors, is to avoid getting into situations from which there is no escape. Always case the joint before you go in, always sit with your back to the wall, always make sure there's a back door. A majority of my classmates took this advice to heart and were not much good to themselves or anyone else thereafter. In practice, you have to walk right in and sit right down. Sometimes getting out the back door involves breaking somebody's neck on a dark stairway.

Actually, if I may lecture for a moment, the trick is to find a way to turn the threat back on the threatener. He has committed himself to an action, so it's jujitsu time; you use your attacker's energy to destroy him. This means getting close to the adversary, and that means overcoming the instinct to get as far away from the person who is trying to destroy you as you can, as quickly as you can. However, in operations the question is not, How do I get myself out of this? It is, What can I do to the other fellow next? One must always be the aggressor, never the defender. Always the joker, never the butt. Always the carefree American boy (think of Kevin) who is never suspected of guile until it's too late. The odds are never what they seem. Your opponent, taking his three-point stance across the line of scrimmage, might have more hair on his knuckle than you have on your entire body, but you have the inestimable advantage of his belief that you're going to be no trouble to him merely because you *are* less hairy than he is.

However, theory is one thing, reality another. After saying good night to Ben I lay abed in Donegal, doing what I had done as a cross-country schoolboy runner, as an infantryman, as an operative, as a prisoner of my own government—counting a hundred reluctant footsteps, then another hundred and then another as a way to keep on advancing into an undesirable future. We had collected a lot of information, far more than I had expected, in a relatively short time. Time is supposed to fly for people with gray hair, but it seemed a long, long while since David and Harley and Jack and Ben and I had left Washington. My mind was in the future. Images of Simon Hawk in Manaus, Captain Zhang in Xinjiang, even the fresh recollections of Mikhail in Moscow were already fading in my memory. In fact the Old Boys had been in the field for scarcely a month. Nevertheless we were moving too slowly; we *were* behind schedule. We knew more now than we had known to begin with, but not enough to take action. We were still in a passive state, watching, listening, sniffing the wind. We did not yet know exactly where to go or exactly what to do when we got there. There was nothing unusual about this. Operations develop like the seduction of a woman who knows that she's worth any amount of trouble—false hopes, faux pas, misunderstandings, rebuffs, zones of silence, long gazes into seemingly candid eyes that will not answer the simplest question. And then, when you have despaired of ever seizing the moment, it arrives.

Although Ben Childress and Jack Philindros might differ with me on this point, it is not necessary to know everything, to tie up every conceivable loose end, before making the leap. At least we were beginning to sort things out. Choices had emerged. Philindros and Childress had provided excellent leads. Jack had reminded me that the quarry was Ibn Awad and the prize was his bombs. Ben had pointed out that finding Claus Bücher was not the same thing as finding Ibn Awad. But then, neither one of them understood that finding Paul Christopher might be the key to everything. And neither had mentioned something that was obvious to me—that wherever Ibn Awad was, he and the bombs were not necessarily in the same place. If he was moving from one place to another, he could hardly take twelve unshielded nuclear devices with him in his luggage. Finding the bombs without finding Ibn Awad, or vice versa, would be a good outcome, but the only acceptable outcome would be to find both. The bombs without Ibn Awad meant that whoever was guarding them for him would be free to use them as he saw fit. Better the madman you know, etc.

What we wanted was the bombs and Ibn Awad's head. No apocalypse, no more resurrections. And the way to achieve this— the only way, I truly thought—was to possess something that Ibn Awad wanted with all his twisted heart.

The Amphora Scroll. But how to let him know I had it, even though I did not have it?

After breakfast, the traditional Irish eggs-and-everything-including-black-pudding affair, Ben and I went for another walk in the misting rain. On the beach we saw the fresh hoofprints of two galloping horses and before long the horses themselves coming back, riders up, kicking up sand and sending pulses of sound through the porous ground beneath our feet. There was no other sign of life under the pewter sky, not even a gull.

I said, "Tell me, Ben. Do you really think that finding a use for Mubarak is beyond our capabilities?"

"As a witting asset, forget it," Ben said. "But even if he didn't know what was happening to him, the motivation to cooperate would have to be very strong."

"Like what?"

"Time was when money was always in good taste in that part of the world, but money means nothing to a man like Mubarak. Even if we had enough of it to rent him for awhile, and I assume we don't."

"Not enough to compete with Ibn Awad," I said. "He'd have to be unwitting. The invitation would have to come from someone he trusts."

"If you mean his grandfather, forget that, too," Ben said.

"I mean Ibn Awad."

"You've lost me."

"Ibn Awad is going to need a new doctor. It's possible he's put out a want ad on the terrorist Internet and Mubarak is the first candidate to be interviewed."

"That's creative thinking, all right," Ben said. "But what good would that do us?"

"Mubarak could put Ibn Awad in our hands."

"How would we get close enough to induce him to do that?"

"Suppose we had the item that Ibn Awad most wants in the world?"

"A hydrogen bomb?"

"Think smaller."

"The Amphora Scroll."

"Bingo."

He trudged on into the sodden wind, head down, unspeaking. Of course he knew perfectly well what I had in mind. I waited in vain for him to say so. In Lough Swilly a sail appeared, white against sky and water that were the same shade of gray. On the errands of mercy that had cost them their future, the Christophers had sailed the *Mahican* in waters like these and in the same kind of weather.

"What's needed is a messenger Ibn Awad can believe, like his doctor," I said. "If Mubarak tells him who has the Amphora Scroll, that should do it."

Ben stopped in his tracks. "That's what I was afraid you were going to suggest," he said. "Horace, you're crazy."

"You don't think Ibn Awad wants the scroll?"

"He wants your severed head."

"Not before I tell him what he's dying to know."

Ben said, "But you don't know where the Amphora Scroll is."

"Then I wouldn't break down under questioning, would I?"

Ben quickened his pace, leaving me behind. I didn't try to keep up, though my legs were longer than his and it would have been easy enough to do. This went on for considerably more than a hundred paces. He was thinking, deducing. Ben didn't like ideas that were not his own. This was a weakness that had preserved him from the inconvenience of senior leadership in the Outfit. The old Outfit's lifeblood had been a combination of bright young men with freedom of speech and older men who listened to them because they had once been bright young men themselves. Ben had once been a bright young man. The problem was, he had remained a bright young man well into old age. Headstrong. Not a good listener. But a man who loved daring ideas as long as he thought they were his own.

I watched the sailboat tacking in a twenty-knot wind—very good sailor at the helm and sheets. At last Ben stopped, turned around, and waited for me. When I reached him he said, "I see your point, but I also see big problems."

"I knew you would, Ben. That's why I need your thoughts. After all, it was you who gave me the idea."

"Not me, pal."

"Really? You do remember saying I couldn't do it myself—that is, get close enough to Ibn Awad to lay hands on him? That was what began the train of thought."

"I remember the words. But I don't remember advising you to put your head in the lion's mouth. You're acting like Christopher."

"There are worse role models."

"Right. And look at all the happiness being Mr. Intrepid brought Paul," Ben said. "Horace, this plan is pointless unless you can tell us exactly where you are and stay alive long enough for the cavalry to arrive."

"And if I could manage that?"

"We still wouldn't have any cavalry. Are Harley and Jack and David and me—combined ages roughly three centuries—supposed to drop from the sky, slay the evil-doers, and rescue you and the maiden?"

"No," I said, "but I'm not planning to be taken prisoner. I just want Ibn Awad to come closer or else give us a signal so that we can move closer to him."

We stayed where we were, shivering, the wind snatching our words as they were spoken, while I told him what I had in mind.

At the end of the speech, he merely nodded.

I said, "Does that mean you're on board?"

"I signed on for the whole voyage," Ben said. "But you do realize that you're shaking a coffee can full of old watch parts and hoping you'll find a Rolex inside when you open the lid, don't you?"

"Maybe. Do you have a better idea?"

"Any idea would be a better idea," Ben said. "But I'll pass the word that you have the Amphora Scroll, God help you."

3

Technology is a friend to man. A case in point is caller ID. My satellite phone was equipped with it, and stored in its memory was the number of the telephone Kevin had used to call me on the stairway outside Mikhail's Moscow flat. A dead giveaway of that kind is not so rare in clandestine circles as you might think. Long ago I had an asset in the bowels of the Chinese government who always wrote his true name and return address on the envelopes containing the reports he sent to me through the mail. A dyed-in-the-wool bureaucrat himself, he felt that the absence of a return address would be more likely to attract more attention from routine-addicted postal snoops than its unabashed presence in the upper left-hand corner of his treasonous communications. He must have been right, because he was never caught.

When I called Kevin's number I got voice mail—no surprise—that asked me in a chipper female voice, in Russian, to leave a name and number. I said, "This is Horace Hubbard calling Kevin Clark with a fabulous one-time offer. Please call me back at the number you already know. Bye!"

I ate the dry sandwich and drank the bottled water that I had bought that morning at a gas station convenience store on the road to Belfast. I stood on a hilltop beside my tiny rental car on a tiny unpaved road in a place so lonely that it hardly seemed possible that it could be hidden away on an island as crowded as Ireland. Nothing so wild and unpeopled existed in Xinjiang or among Russian birches. Apart from the road, there was no sign that the human hand had ever disturbed anything in eyeshot. Hundreds of untended black-faced sheep, wool beaded with rainwater, grazed like wild game. Birds fed on their droppings. Both sheep and birds were mute; cottony silence reigned. Moist green turf, hue intensifying as the sun found a rift in the perpetual clouds, covered the earth from horizon to horizon.

Satellite phone traffic among the Old Boys had dwindled as the novelty of the thing wore off. These were people whose life's work had taught them not to trust telephones. Old spies like to work alone, in silence, watching the faces of their sources for telltale signs, such as greed and fright—sometimes even selfless idealism—that tell the practiced eye whether the all-believing ear is hearing truth or trash.

My satellite telephone rang. I thought, *That was fast, Kevin.* The phone was in the car, inside my canvas briefcase. It kept ringing till I unzipped the briefcase and answered.

Harley Waters said, "You're still in Jerusalem?"

"No, I'm tending my flocks elsewhere."

"Are you now?" said Harley. "Watch out you don't get too lonesome. I think I've got somethin' for you. Can you get to Budapest from where you are?"

His tone of voice told me that he was dying to tell me something that he could not tell me over the phone.

4

Madame Károlyi, the little goldfinch of an old woman whom Harley took me to meet in Budapest, talked about dark days as we sipped coffee and ate pastries in her parlor. It was a small dusty room above a narrow street: fringed lampshades, fringed shawls draped over the furniture, dark oblongs on the faded wallpaper where paintings formerly hung. She wore what looked like a Chanel suit from the sixties; it was pink with large glassy buttons. The skirt was short. Her stockings bagged at the knees.

"It was quite curious how trusting people were in sexual matters under Communism," she said. "One believed that the only escape into privacy from the secret police was to get into bed with somebody. A love affair is something everyone knows how to keep secret—maybe that was why God spit into the handful of dust—so we believed that we were safe if we were naked with a lover. The Soviet occupation may have been the most erotic period in Hungarian history, which is saying a lot."

She offered me another éclair. I regretted the interruption. It had been years, if ever, since I had encountered a woman who played the role of herself so beautifully. Every shift of tone, every gesture, her museum clothes, the coy angle of her ancient feet in their fetishist's pink shoes, was a flashgun exposure of the beauty she used to be. You saw the invisible jewelry she once wore, the haughty faces in the missing paintings. No wonder Harley, who had run her as an agent for twenty years, looked at her like a man hopelessly in love. He must have collected his reports from her in a four-poster.

"And the *dénouement!*" she said. "A Molnár play! It turned out, when the secret police files were opened up after the Communists were overthrown, that everyone—*everyone*—had been reporting to the secret police every word of pillow talk, every shiver of ecstasy, every political joke whispered by their lovers. And it wasn't just the *cinq-à-sept* adulterers. Wives were tattling on husbands, husbands on wives. That, of course, was only to be expected. But tender lovers? *Quel chagrin!* Mass forgiveness and forgetfulness were necessary when it all came out or no one in Hungary would have had sex ever again."

Madame Károlyi, Christian name Marie, bore one of the most ancient surnames in Hungary, though she married into the family after the arrival of the Red Army, too late to make much of a fuss about being a member of the highest aristocracy. In her own right, she was a remote descendant of Sigismund Bathory, who defeated the Turks at Walachia in 1595, and of the famous Blood Countess Elizabeth Bathory: "Of course you know about her; she bathed in the blood of virgin peasant girls as an aphrodisiac." Madame Károlyi delivered this information in the same twitter of high amusement in which she had described the ménages à trois in which the AVH, the Hungarian secret police, was the one in the middle. As a young case officer in Budapest, Harley had been the third party in some of her affairs with prominent communists. Among these was a Soviet ambassador who went on to become head of the KGB. Also a puppet prime minister of Hungary who had been one of her lovers when she was a teenager and came back from Russia after the war in an altered state: the KGB had castrated him, a time-honored oriental technique designed to ensure his undying obedience. Madame Károlyi's detailed eyewitness report to Harley on this man's condition, delivered during the failed Hungarian revolt of 1956, had been regarded as one of the more titillating intelligence coups of the time. There were others, some illustrated with photographs. By the time she was no longer a sex object, Harley's deposits into her Swiss bank account had made her a rich woman by the standards of ruined aristocracy. She lived as she lived now, shabbily, because she knew better than to draw attention to herself. Those newly in power in Hungary thought that she had been a collaborator with the Soviets. She could hardly defend herself by revealing that she had done it all for Western civilization and the Outfit's money. For Madame Károlyi this was the final irony in a life that she seemed to regard as one long joke.

Harley, who must have heard her stories many times, listened with a sparkle in his eye and a reminiscent smile that were reflections of Madame Károlyi's own vivacious expression. Maestro that he was, he knew that his agent's chatter was just her way of coming to the point.

The point was, she was Lori Christopher's third cousin once removed. She provided the full genealogy—a Prussian great-grandfather had married a Hungarian great-grandmother, I think. In 1942 Madame Károlyi had been a twelve-year-old countess named Marie Bathory who lived with her parents, siblings and various aunts, uncles and cousins on the family estate near the Czech frontier.

"The estate is no longer even in Hungary, but in Slovakia, but it was never really of this world," said Madame Károlyi. "Three thousand hectares of land so poorly managed that not even the peasants could grow enough food to feed themselves. Of course they fed us first because we owned the land, and they worked without pay as servants in the house for the same reason. Their families were as old as ours and had always been in bondage to the Bathory family, so what else could they have done? If they had not done their duty, my family would have evicted them from the land. Social injustice? Unbelievable. But at that time no one, neither master nor peasant, had ever heard of the concept."

In 1942 Hungary was not yet occupied by the German army,

although the country had a fascist government and was an ally of the Third Reich. The Hungarian army was fighting alongside the Wehrmacht on the Russian front and taking ruinous casualties. Marie's family were trying to isolate themselves from the right-wing Horthy government, whose suspicion of aristocrats was almost as lethal as that of the German Nazis and the communists who came after them. The estate was about seventy miles from Budapest, well beyond the last railroad station, and for the second half of that distance could only be approached over footpaths or wagon tracks.

"No electricity, no telephone, no running water," said Madame Károlyi. "Once a month all of us children took a bath together in a big wooden tub filled with tepid water heated over open fires by the peasants. On my twelfth birthday I was banned from the tub and after that washed merely my face and hands, crotch and armpits like the rest of the grownups. Time was a blank. Nothing happened, nothing. No card games, no hunting, no charades, no conversation, no walks in the woods except for purposes of incest. I ask you to imagine! The boredom was so intense that one of my cousins became a famous theorist of boredom. As a professor of philosophy in America, he wrote treatises explaining that boredom was the root of all evil, especially politics. In my opinion this was the most brilliant intellectual breakthrough of the present age, but of course no one paid the slightest attention."

Another éclair? No, thank you. Are you quite sure? They're delicious. Really, no. But how fascinating all this is.

"Fascinating?" said Madame Károlyi. "You would not have thought so if you never changed your clothes, never tasted a sweet, lived among people who had been perfectly charming in Budapest but were now a collection of sleepwalkers who never laughed and hardly ever even talked. They had lost their money, for them the same thing as losing their souls. It was beyond Chekhov, my dear man. It was pure Kafka! And then, out of nowhere, came this vision. Lori."

Lori Christopher arrived, on foot, a pack on her back, in the early winter of 1942. No one knew how she had found her way. She had spent a summer on the estate as a child. How could she have remembered the paths through the woods, how had she escaped rape, robbery, murder, being eaten by wolves? Yet here she was.

"'I have come to you,' she said, 'because I have no other place to go,'" said Madame Károlyi. "It was like a novel. She was running from the Nazis, at that time the most dangerous people in the history of the world. Yet she looked beautiful. When they saw the look in their husbands' eyes the women said, shaking their heads in unison, 'She is putting us in danger.' But my mother, who was the highest ranking female on the estate, said, 'She stays!'"

During Lori's childhood visit to the estate, she and Madame Károlyi's mother had become fast friends, and all their lives afterward, until war broke out and the mail stopped, they had corresponded regularly. Long before the war the mother, whose name was Nandine Bathory, and her new husband visited Lori and Hubbard in Berlin. Nandine had known Paul as a toddler. His existence had inspired her to become pregnant with Marie.

"Maman dreamed that Paul and I, who were only a couple of years apart in age, might marry someday, even though he was half American," Madame Károlyi said. "It was the usual friendship between girls, one beautiful and brilliant, the other, my mother, less so. One the ardent friend, the other politely accepting the situation."

Lori did not explain to the Bathorys why she was in Upper Hungary in the middle of a war Germany was winning or where she had come from. Actually no one wanted to know; such knowledge was dangerous. From Lori's letters Nandine knew her political sympathies, but she thought it wise not to make a point of this to her husband or other members of the family.

"Not many of them actually remembered Lori," Madame Károlyi said. "But everyone knew where she belonged on the family tree, and that, along with Maman's positive identification and insistence on giving sanctuary, sufficed. Lori told my mother her story—not all of it, not enough to put her in danger in case she fell into the hands of the Gestapo, but enough for Maman to believe that Lori had a right to be very, very sad. However, as I remember it, she was not sad, at least not outwardly."

Lori had money. "German marks and also gold coins," Madame Károlyi said. "Naturally this made her very welcome indeed. She purchased little luxuries like soap and sugar. It wasn't that there was very much one could buy in those times, but it made people feel better to know that in some way things were as they should be again because money was hidden somewhere in the house. She hired gypsy musicians—at this time the Germans had not yet started to liquidate the Roma—and we danced. She was very good at dancing the *csárdás,* which is a fast Hungarian dance, and the *lassú,* which is a languorous one. All the men wanted to be her partner."

Madame Károlyi actually paused for a moment and excused herself. As she disappeared into the bathroom, Harley grinned after her tottering figure, pleased as punch with himself. He had reason to be. In no other operation had I ever been so fortunate in my sources of information as in this one. All of them were old and garrulous. You merely had to put them on the sled and give them a push down the mountain. After that it was Marie, Marie, hold on tight! This did not mean that they were without malice or duplicity or that their memories were always accurate or that they did not strive to please the audience. But at least you had a lot of material to choose from, as long as you kept in mind that they were still the slippery characters they always had been. As aren't we all?

To Harley I said, "How much of this is the truth, do you think?"

"The parts I already know about are accurate—or at least they jibe with the stories she told me in the first place," he replied. "The bits about Lori are new to me but they probably have a basis in reality, too."

"I hope so. What comes next?"

"I've got no idea. She knows every ghost in Central Europe."

Madame Károlyi returned, bearing a tray on which bottles and glasses were balanced. It was four in the afternoon.

"The witching hour," she said. "Harley, darling, will you do the honors? We have scotch, sherry, and something Hungarian."

She had freshened her vivid makeup, fluffed her canary-yellow hair. Harley gave her a stiff scotch, neat.

"I'm afraid I've been boring you," Madame Károlyi said to me.

"Far from it, Madame Károlyi. Please go on. I'm fascinated."

"Not everyone is kind enough to say that. I have lived to be an old bore. *Santé!*"

She drank the scotch straight down and held out her glass to Harley for a refill. I must have raised an eyebrow, because Madame Károlyi tapped me on the knee and said, "This business of sipping cocktails is something the new people invented. They are *very* genteel. In my day it was bottoms up." She drank the second glass.

"So," I said. "What happened next?"

"Next? After what?"

"After Cousin Lori organized the dance."

"A terrible winter. There were wolves in the garden. No one had ever actually spent a winter on the estate. It was hell—coughing, sneezing, frostbite, water frozen in the washbowl every morning. A whole generation of our young relations were killed that winter, fighting in Russia. The Bathory were a military family. They had all been reserve officers. Those who survived the war were shot afterward by the Russians. My cousin András, for example, a major in the guards, handsome as a dream, sang like an angel . . ."

I interrupted. "Actually I'm fascinated by your cousin Lori."

She frowned, then drank down a third scotch, about three ounces of it. Not a tear in her eye, not a catch in her throat.

"Ah, Lori. Why are you interested in her? She was *de passage.*"

"Still, a romantic figure," I said. "What happened to her?"

"You think she was a romantic figure? Of course she was, madly so, but she avoided that impression. She said almost nothing about herself, and of course this heightened the romance, but she meant her silence to be taken for modesty, not mystery. From her I learned that the truly mysterious never behave mysteriously. A valuable lesson to me in later life. Ask Harley."

She held out her glass. "Another drop, Harley, if you please," she said. "Let me see. Lori. She bought a horse from a peasant, quite a nice one, a bay gelding, and went for long rides through the snow. On her outings she carried a pistol, and with it she shot a wolf. This wolf and some of its friends were following her through the forest. Scent of blood. She was menstruating. My father fell in love with her. Her shooting the wolf must have excited him."

"That must have been distressing to your mother," I said.

"Why should it have been? Men are men. Lori was beautiful, she was exotic, she shot wolves. There was no privacy in the house. Father lusted from afar—not, of course, by choice, but Lori kept him at a distance. Lori and my mother laughed about it."

I grew impatient with all this twittering sophistication. It showed, and Harley gave me a look that said, *Don't push it, let her talk.*

"Eventually the Gestapo came, of course," Madame Károlyi said as she pointed to her glass while giving Harley another dazzling smile. "They were looking for Jews or Roma or whoever they were shooting that week. By then Lori looked like one of us. Anyway they were not especially interested in women. She had papers. Before Horthy sacked him, my father had been in the foreign ministry. All the Bathory men were civil servants if they were not soldiers. They had no idea of business or politics. To them land was money, even when it was a sinking ship. In any case, Father still had discreet friends in the ministry and he got Lori an identity card under a Hungarian name, so she was all right. The Nazis were only interested in people they wanted to slaughter. Even in rags, smelling like a peasant, no one ever looked less like a Jew or a gypsy than Lori."

"When was this, do you remember?"

"Nineteen forty-four, probably. The Germans came in forty-three, left in forty-five. Don't ask me the month. We had no idea of time. It must have been summer or fall because they could not have gotten through the snow in winter or the mud in spring."

By now she had drunk roughly fifteen ounces of Dewars whisky and was asking for yet another glass, but showed no more effect than if it had been mineral water. Her emaciated body could not possibly absorb all that alcohol. She was skin and bones. She must have had an amazing liver.

"The Germans made it even more inconvenient to live in the countryside because they marched most of the peasants away," Madame Károlyi said. "But at last the war ended. We were liberated by the Red army. I don't know why, but no one had any idea the Russians were going to stay forever. By then I was fifteen, longing to live. Lori was my confidant. She advised me to find love in the world because it made sex much more enjoyable. I asked how long that would take. She said three to five years. After that I should live as if I were going to be alone because in one way or another all women ended up alone. 'Love will come, if it comes, in a form that will surprise you,' she said. 'Accept it for as long as it lasts.' My hope was that it would come several times, beginning very soon. She saw nothing wrong with that even though she seemed to be a fanatical monogamist."

"She spoke of her husband?"

"Never. One morning in the spring of 1945—the Germans had left and the Russians had not yet found us—I woke up and found twenty Maria Theresa gold pieces, a fortune, wrapped up in a handkerchief pinned to my nightgown. Lori had departed."

"She left a note?"

"No. And not even my mother had any inkling that she was going to decamp."

"What about her horse?"

"It was a bay. Its name was Maxel."

"She took it with her?"

"No. She left it for my mother."

"Did you ever hear from her again?"

"How would we have heard? Hungary was sealed by the

Russians and stayed sealed for almost fifty years. Maman believed that Lori had made it to Shangri-la. But the Red Army was a great fishnet stretched across Europe. She must have swum into it like everyone else. I assume the Russians caught her and killed her, after doing what Red soldiers did to stray women."

I said, "One question, if I may. Did she have anything with her, any possessions besides the pistol?"

"Her money, of course," Madame Károlyi said. "Some sort of glass tube, large and heavy. It was precious to her. After the Germans occupied Hungary she wrapped it up in canvas and hid it inside a hollow tree I showed her. God knows if she ever found the hollow tree again. I never could."

"Tell me," I said, "did you ever meet Lori's son?"

"No, of course not," Madame Károlyi said. "Did he find love in the world?"

"He certainly looked for it," I said.

5

Madame Károlyi had connected a dot or two. But she had also erased a couple of things. We now knew that Lori had somehow found her way to Hungary after the assassination of Heydrich. There was a certain logic in this. In 1942 Hungary was the only country within walking distance of Prague that was not occupied by the German army. We knew that she had left her Hungarian cousins without notice or explanation just as she had left Norman's parents and Norman himself and before that, her husband and child. You may ask, What difference does it make? Perhaps none; perhaps all the difference in the world. Knowing her habits as a young woman—the behavior that rose from her fundamental nature—gave us an idea of how she might behave as a nonagenarian. What we now knew about Lori after all our trouble was that finding her was not enough. She might be glad to see us, she might stay the night, she might dance the *csárdás,* commit kindnesses, or casually shoot a wolf or nine camels. But sooner or later she would be gone in the morning. We heard in Xinjiang that Paul was very near to finding her. Being Paul, he might even have done so. But his mother had left him before and if she ran true to form she would do so again. All of her life since Heydrich she had left everyone, everything, giving no notice. And Paul was just like her.

She had abandoned everything, that is, except the Amphora Scroll. And it was the scroll, not Lori, that we had to have. If we found her, would she hand it over, even if we didn't tell her we intended to use it as bait for a lunatic who regarded it as a license to blow up Washington and Manhattan and Chicago?

On the day after our exhilarating chat with Madame Károlyi, I waited for Harley in a rundown coffee house that had a fine view of one of the Danube bridges, which through the smeared window glass seemed to be pasted against the Wehrmacht-gray gloom of the wintry afternoon. Harley had taken Madame Károlyi to lunch, a sentimental occasion because it would almost certainly be their last meeting. I kept out of the way. The coffee was instant Nestlé's with whipped cream in it. In a place where a gypsy should be playing the zither, Nat King Cole sang "Sweet Lorraine" and "Embraceable You" over scratchy loudspeakers. Halfway through "You're Nobody Till Somebody Loves You," tall, bony Harley arrived and folded himself like a stick figure into the bentwood chair opposite.

"This is for you, a present from Marie," he said, drawing a packet from an inside pocket and placing it on the table between us.

"Know what that is?" he said, tapping the packet, which was wrapped in some sort of slippery yellowish material.

"No."

"Oilskin. Nobody's made oilskin since Hannah was a pup."

"What's inside?"

"Open 'er up," Harley said.

Inside the oilskin was an envelope, an old one with grease spots on it that smelled faintly of lanolin. The envelope was unsealed, unaddressed. It contained five pages of velvety prewar writing paper, covered front and back with decisive vertical script written in black ink with a fine-nib fountain pen. Lost art, lost tool. The lines ran straight across the page as if ruled. No words were crossed out or corrected. In direct light the aging black ink showed greenish highlights.

"You can read German, can't you?" Harley said.

"Barely," I said. "What is this?"

"Marie doesn't know. I believe it's Lori's translation of the Amphora Scroll. She left it with Nandine. Marie found it when the old woman died."

I was nonplussed, deeply skeptical. It's not that I don't believe in windfalls. Like more respectable pursuits such as scientific research and brokerage and practicing law, espionage is an organized search for windfalls. But this? In Budapest, where no one has ever given anyone anything, not even love, for free?

I said, "Why is she handing this over to us?"

"Again accordin' to Marie, everybody she's related to is dead or lost or in exile," Harley said. "She thought it ought to stay in Lori's family, of which you're a member."

"What a noble impulse."

"That's what I thought. So I bought her a fur coat."

Despite the value of the merchandise I held in my hand, I was startled and showed it. A fur coat? Did he think money grew on trees?

"Don't worry," Harley said, reading me perfectly as usual. "'Twasn't sable. Or even new."

Harley went to the men's room. For the past ten minutes he had commanded my entire attention, but before that I had noticed a young man across the room. He arrived shortly after I did, took a table in the window, and ordered coffee. He wore tiny headphones. Maybe he was listening to music, though it did not seem so because he was not swaying to the beat or singing along as his generation is wont to do. He wore a forest-green parka over a sweatshirt with "UCLA Football XXL" on the chest. Baseball cap, corduroys and multicolor sneakers with thick corrugated soles completed the ensemble. This costume made him noticeable in a room filled with shabby old men and women dressed like Ronald Colman and Bette Davis. He looked vaguely Middle Eastern—not quite an Arab, perhaps a Turk or an Armenian.

Was he following me? The fact that he chose to sit in the window—there were less exposed tables all over the room—earned him the benefit of my vague doubts. No trained man would do such a thing—unless, of course, he was maintaining visual or electronic contact with someone in the street. The afternoon light, such as it was, was behind him and this made it difficult to see his face. Was this technique or happenstance? The face, close-shaven, open and friendly, could even have been an American face.

Harley returned. I called for the check. While I was paying it the youth stood up and left. The asthmatic old waiter, even more paranoid than I, scuttled to the abandoned table, wheezing in anxiety. He seemed reassured, even pleased, by the banknote he found under the youth's coffee cup.

Outside in the street there was no sign of the youth. I described him to Harley. He took a look around and said, "No sign of him now. Want to go for a walk?"

"I could use a German-English dictionary," I said.

"Follow me."

He stepped off at his usual 120 paces per minute. After walking in a circle through a warren of medieval streets, we arrived at an international bookstore. The youth was already inside, headphones in place, browsing through a French-language Michelin green guide to Hungary.

"Wonder how he got here first," Harley said. "Could have somethin' to do with the earphones."

I found a pocket German dictionary, paid for it, and left. Harley lingered till the youth followed me. Then he followed him. Would the youth detect the sandwich? Apparently not, but at this point what did appearances mean? He window-shopped along behind me in his many-colored sneakers.

After ten minutes of this, I stopped at the mouth of a narrow alley that ran between the blind sides of two large buildings and waited for the youth to catch up.

When he did, I stepped aside and said in English, "After you, son."

Without fuss or change of expression he walked into the alley. Harley waited at the entrance. After a moment another young fellow, also dressed by Land's End, crossed the street against the light, tapped Harley on the shoulder and said, "After *you*, sir." Now Harley and I were the ham and the cheese in the sandwich.

To the original youth I said, "What can I do for you?"

The youth was in tip-top physical condition. Broad shoulders, flat stomach, square jaw, keen brown eyes without a single speck of red in the whites; a nondrinker. He had large bony hands that could turn in an instant into large bony fists. Nothing on his breath but coffee and strongly perfumed toothpaste. His backup pretty much fit the same description.

The youth said, "When a man your age invites a man my age into an alley, the question usually is what can the young man do for the old man, and at what price."

He spoke English with an accent, faint and to my ear undefinable. I heard Harley say, "Watch out!" He choked on the words. I took my eyes off the youth for an instant and saw that the other youth had his left forearm across Harley's throat. In his other hand he held a knife, blunt edge of the blade across the bridge of Harley's nose. I felt metal against my own skin, looked down, and saw that the youth was pressing the muzzle of a cocked pistol against my Adam's apple.

He was much shorter than I. He said, pleasantly enough, "Please do not do anything foolish."

At least for the moment, he had nothing to worry about. However, I was worried about Harley's heart. He looked pale and limp and seemed to be breathing with difficulty.

"My friend is in trouble," I said.

"So are you," said the youth. He unlimbered a cell phone, punched in a number with his thumb, and spoke into it. In broken Arabic. In Russian he said to me, "In a moment a car will come for us at the end of the alley. You will come with us quietly. Your friend will stay here. We have no interest in him."

"What is your interest in me?" I asked.

His phone rang. He answered it. Harley was now breathing convulsively, as if these were the last lungfuls he would ever inhale.

Suddenly he went limp, his joints collapsing as if his spinal cord had been severed. The youth who had charge of him—suspecting a ruse, I suppose—tightened his grip on Harley's throat and lifted his knife as if to stab him. My own captor was still busy on the telephone, speaking Arabic too fast for me to understand. He had his back to Harley and the youth with the knife. I made the mistake of thinking twice about doing something violent while he was distracted, but I was afraid Harley might get stabbed if I made a move. It looked as though Harley was already dead, but somehow it seemed worse that his corpse should be knifed than his living body. The eyes of the knife man moved slightly, as if he saw somebody behind me. I heard the discreet pop of a silenced pistol. His right eye, which had been dark and liquid, turned into a gob of blood. He dropped the knife and went over backward. I pushed backward against my own captor as hard as I could, and we fell down together, him firing his pistol into the air as he went. The shots were virtually noiseless. He fell over the entangled bodies of Harley and the other man. A man wearing a black watch cap and a black leather jacket leaped by me, kicked the gun out of the gunman's hand, then knocked him senseless and voiceless, if he did not kill him, with a karate chop to the Adam's apple. He stood the unconscious man up, threw him over his shoulder, ran down the alley to an open window and dumped him through it. Another man, also wearing a black watch cap and leather jacket, did the same with the corpse of the youth who had had the knife. It was all very businesslike.

A third man, dressed just like the other two, said, in flat Ohio English, "Sorry about this."

It was Kevin. I said, "Nothing to apologize for."

His men were cleaning up the ground where the dead man had lain. It didn't take them long, partly because they knew exactly what they were doing and partly because he had fallen on his back and bled into his own skull.

Mere seconds had been consumed by all this action. Harley stirred and clutched his chest. I shoved Kevin aside and took hold of him. His whole body was trembling violently. In his breast pocket I found his tube of nitroglycerin pills and put two of them under his tongue. He breathed more easily.

In a faint voice Harley said, "I feel like puking. Bad sign."

He lost consciousness again.

Kevin and his troops immediately went into action. One of them punched a number into a cell phone and spoke into the mouthpiece in Magyar. Kevin and the other man stretched Harley out on the pavement and began giving him CPR. Kevin administered mouth-to-mouth resuscitation while the other fellow ripped the buttons off Harley's shirt and pounded his chest. Under the pasty skin on his torso Harley had a rib cage like a robin's. I was afraid this bodybuilder would splinter the ribs.

Kevin said, "He's breathing." The other man felt Harley's wrist, then his forearm. He said, "I can't get a pulse."

Kevin took over the chest massage. After a moment he said, "The heart is beating. But it's slow and very faint. His skin is cold. Let's cover him up."

Cover him up? I began looking for a head to twist. But what they meant was "keep him warm." They laid him on his own fur-lined coat and wrapped him in their parkas. I added my old raincoat. Harley's face, shiny with cold sweat, was the color of suet. The gun that the youth had pressed to my throat lay in plain sight on the pavement next to Harley's head. A fellow could end up with quite a firearms collection hanging out with these cowboys. I pointed to the weapon. Before the medics arrived, Kevin picked it up and put it in a pocket of his parka.

They carried Harley to the mouth of the alley. A car arrived, instantaneously, it seemed. Kevin took the wheel. The others loaded Harley in the backseat. I got in with him and held his head on my lap during the trip to the hospital. When we arrived at the emergency exit, two men and a tall gawky woman with mop of flying dark ringlets dashed across the driveway, pushing a rattling gurney. They took Harley.

Kevin parked the car, then joined me inside. The gesture sur-

prised me, but not so much as his obvious concern for Harley.
You might have thought that he was the sick man's grandson. As
we waited for the doctor to emerge with a report, Kevin kept going
up to the wicket and asking for bulletins in what sounded to me
like fluent Magyar, a language practically no non-Hungarian
speaks. He had to wait in line. The husky woman on duty looked
like Leonid Brezhnev after a sex-change operation. She told him
nothing.

There were no chairs left in the crowded waiting room. Kevin
touched me on the shoulder and led me outside. The din of traffic, the warped minor-tone *DOOT-doot* of approaching ambu-
lances, the confusion of the loading dock, made conversation relatively secure.

I said, "What was that all about?"

"Beats me," Kevin said. "Those fellows were Chechens, hired
men."

"Whose hired men?"

"There's a fatwah on you. Did you know that?"

"I'd heard something about it."

"It could be connected to that," Kevin said. "There's a big
reward for you. Or it could be something else. You did make enemies in Moscow."

"And you just happened to be in Budapest and decided to
come to the rescue in the nick of time?"

"Actually, no. We were watching over you."

"Thanks a lot. But why?"

Before he could answer, I saw the doctor through the glass
door. Kevin saw her too. He said, "Meet me at midnight on the
bridge by the coffeehouse where you met Harley today."

Then he turned on his heel and walked briskly away toward the
parking lot. I went inside. The doctor wore a long, white medical
coat with her name, Józsa Fodor, embroidered above the pocket.
She had the wary unwavering eyes of a woman who knew how
attractive she was but wanted no sign from me that I might have
noticed this, too.

In staccato American English she said, "Your friend has had an episode of ventrical atrial fibrillation. He will recover."

She waited for a question, and when I asked none, kept talking. "His pulse was below thirty, his blood pressure very low. He had no injuries except for a small cut on his nose. Can you explain that?"

"No."

"We have given him drugs to restore the rhythm of the heart and thin the blood. He could have a stroke. He should have a pacemaker-defibrillator implanted. But in America, where it will be covered by Medicare. European pacemakers cannot be monitored properly in America."

"You trained in the States?"

Instead of answering the question she said, with strong eye contact for emphasis, "He should be more careful in the future."

I quite agreed. "Clearly he should take better care of himself," I said. "When may I see him, Doctor?"

"Now, if you wish. He will stay in the hospital tonight. Tomorrow he'll be released, barring complications, which I do not anticipate."

"Where is he?"

"Come with me."

She showed me to his door and left us alone. Harley was propped up in bed. His color was a little better than it had been in the alley, but he looked old and exhausted. He was hooked up to an intravenous tube and a heart monitor. His thin hair was disheveled, his sharp collarbones stretched his parchment skin. He looked up at me with milky eyes.

I said, "Sorry about all this, Harley. My fault."

"Seemed like a good idea at the time," Harley said. "What happened to those fellows? D'you wring their necks?"

"Didn't have to. The cavalry arrived."

"Ours or theirs?"

"Kevin and a couple of his commandos came to the rescue. He said the whole thing was just a coincidence."

"He did? You'd better have a talk with that boy, Horace. He needs counselin'."

Harley's voice trailed off even before he dropped the final *g*. His eyes closed. His mouth fell open. He uttered a wordless gargle. Frightened, I spoke his name. When he didn't answer I stuck my head out the door and shouted for the doctor. She came at the run, ringlets bouncing, but Harley had merely fallen asleep.

6

I met Kevin on the bridge at the appointed hour. The murky city seemed to be sound asleep. Street lamps traced the outline of a hill with a bulbous church steeple at its summit. During the Soviet occupation, Harley had told me, this bridge had been such an ideal rendezvous point for spies and counterrevolutionaries and subversive lovers that the secret police had planted microphones in the railings. Under Communism there had not been enough traffic noise to interfere with the mikes. Evidently Kevin had never heard this story or believed that the new democratic Hungary had torn out the wiring, because when I asked him again why he had Harley under surveillance, why he had gone into the business of rescuing us, and what I was supposed to think of him, he began to talk as if there were no tomorrow.

"Look," he said. "You're being tracked. Every phone call you make, every flight you book, every car you rent, every person you meet shows up on the screen. Example: Yesterday you met with Marie Károlyi, a former party girl of Yuri Andropov's, among other enemies of humanity, and every word of your conversation, which lasted two hours and forty-two minutes, was picked up by a transmitter. You're on somebody else's turf, trampling on the footprints, sir. They want you off it."

I said, "Who wants me off it?"

"It's not just you. It's the whole gang of you. The Over the Hill Gang—that's what they call you guys. They're very annoyed."

"I've got the picture. Now let me ask you again, Who is *They*?"

He said, "The system."

"Ah, the Keystone spooks. For whom you're the designated messenger?"

Kevin winced. "The world has changed," he said. "No matter what you and your chums used to be, you're amateurs now. You're out of date, out of the loop, senile, a danger to yourselves and everybody else. After all, we're talking about nuclear weapons."

"You concede that Ibn Awad has nuclear weapons?"

"I'm talking about the hypothesis. That's one of the objections to you. You've got this hypothesis you're trying to prove instead of relying on cold facts."

Cold facts, in my experience, mean about as much in relation to one another as a spoonful of iron filings stuck to a magnet. It is what people actually do that counts, not what you think you know about their intentions. I said, "Is that your personal objection?"

Kevin smiled. He said, "You mentioned a fabulous one-time offer in the message you left for me."

"That seems to have been bad timing," I said. "Maybe I'll get back to you."

Kevin nodded and handed me an engraved calling card: *Mr. Osborn Denison*. A number with an unfamiliar country code was written on the back.

"If you do, use this number," Kevin said. "Call on a land line, from outside the United States."

My turn to smile. Was it was possible that I had made a friend?

7

My German was never more than adequate. During my appren-
tice tour in Frankfurt, English-speaking German assets—supercil-
ious veterans of the Abwehr who acted, not without reason, as if
their American handlers were working for them instead of vice-
versa—did all the sidewalk work. I scarcely ever set foot outside
the I. G. Farben building. After staying awake most of the night
with Lori's translation of the Amphora Scroll and my German-
English dictionary, I realized that deciphering the manuscript was
beyond me. I would need help from someone I could trust and
trust absolutely. A member of the family. I made two reservations
on an afternoon flight to Washington.

At the hospital I found Harley wide awake and bright-eyed,
reading *Hetek,* a Budapest newspaper. He seemed to read Magyar
as easily as Russian.

I asked him how he was feeling.

"A-number-one applesauce," Harley said. "Waitin' for the doctor to set me free."

"Good, because we're on the two o'clock flight to Frankfurt."

"What's in Frankfurt?"

"Nothing except a connection to Dulles. We both need a little
R and R."

To my surprise, Harley didn't argue. He hardly had time to do so because in the next moment the long-legged Dr. Józsa Fodor arrived on the fly. Without a word of greeting to either of us she applied her stethoscope to the patient's breast. Commanding him to take deep breaths, she tapped and sounded his chest and back for a moment or two, took his blood pressure, pressed his bare ankles with a fingertip to check for fluid.

"You are no longer in fibrillation," she told Harley. "Your heart rate and blood pressure are low, but back in the normal range. All this is thanks to electrical shock and drugs and it will not last. You should see a heart specialist as soon as possible. In America."

"Does that mean I can travel?" Harley said.

"Today, if you wish, and I advise you to go immediately to America. But avoid situations that excite."

Dr. Fodor touched Harley's rumpled newspaper with a forefinger and asked a question in Magyar. He replied in the same language, and being Harley, went on for a few more sentences. She smiled in surprise, a glowing transformation, and replied, also at length. I noticed for the first time that the doctor had freckles—strange in a dark-haired girl. I imagined her in love, arriving headlong at a tender rendezvous. She gave me a female sidelong glance as if intercepting my thoughts. I was as surprised by these stirrings within my disused body and imagination as she seemed to be by Harley's idiomatic Magyar. I had not thought about a woman as a woman since I went to prison.

Then, with a brisk handshake for Harley and a curt nod to me—was there womanly amusement in her eyes?—Dr. Józsa Fodor dashed away.

I said, "What was all that Magyar about?"

"You, mostly," Harley said. "She wanted to know if you were the same big, tall fella she saw on American TV a couple of years ago."

Ah, fame again. I said, "Did you get her phone number?"

"Yep," Harley said with a lascivious grin. "How much is it worth to you?"

Alas, nothing.

SIX

1

There was nothing to be seen between Budapest and Frankfurt from the window of the Airbus. At thirty thousand feet the sunlight was brilliant, but an uninhabited continent may just as well have lain beneath the unbroken ceiling of clouds that sealed Central Europe from the winter sun. Down there, I knew, the world was the color of concrete, joyless and dank, and would remain so until June. No wonder the summer solstice had been such a fun day in northern Europe before Christian missionaries arrived from the sunny south. If priests had not driven sex underground, what would the north have been like? Would art have flourished in the absence of sexual repression? What about artillery and fortification? The Reformation? The Thirty Years' War? The French Revolution? The final perfection of murder as blood sport at Verdun and Dresden and in the Gulag?

In short, where would we be without Jesus? I had understood enough of the letter of Septimus Arcanus to make me wonder. What the Amphora Scroll told us, assuming that what I had read was a faithful translation of a document that had, in turn, been a faithful description of events, was this: Joshua ben Joseph had in fact existed, and had done the things the Gospels said he had done. Whether his acts were miracles or the result of clever manipulation by a Roman case officer was a matter of belief, so we were right back where we started from. It was entirely possible that the case officer who handled this particular operation made the common mistake of overestimating the importance of his own role. He could not possibly have overestimated the unintended consequences of a minor dangle project that he probably regarded as a lark. For the second time that day I was feeling something human move within me. First Józsa Fodor had made me remember passion. Now across centuries Septimus Arcanus was making me remember religious feeling. What a miraculous joke it would be on everyone if this letter from Jerusalem which seemed to cross out the Jesus story ended up by confirming it.

Harley Waters, back from the door of death, slumbered restlessly at my side, talking Magyar in his sleep and dreaming, perhaps, of Marie Károlyi when she was young. Or, the old lecher, of Józsa Fodor as she was now.

2

The last person I wanted to encounter in Washington was Dr. Stephanie Webster-Christopher, so naturally hers was the first familiar face I saw after landing at Dulles. She was getting out of a taxi, great swollen purse like a sheep's stomach slung over one shoulder, laptop over the other, hanger bag on wheels bumping along in her wake, bulging attaché case in her free hand.

I tried to slip away, but Stephanie hallooed. I was looking straight at her, so I could hardly pretend I didn't see or hear her.

"Stephanie!" I said. "Coming or going?"

"Going," she said, bowed and unsmiling under the weight of her luggage. "That's why I got *out* of the taxi."

Score one for the girls. Stephanie was a small woman and she always seemed to be in tip-top condition. She ran five miles a day, worked out at the gym, and for all I know, boxed. All in all she tended to expect more of herself physically than her body could deliver.

I said, "Let me take those bags."

"Not necessary."

This was a two-word political autobiography of the give-no-quarter feminist that she was. Stephanie's maladroit patterns of speech had been rather endearing when she was younger and prettier and softened by her love for her husband. They were less so now.

"So," she said, packing all the exasperation she seemed to feel into the little word. "Have you proved the negative?"

"What negative is that, Stephanie?"

"That Paul is not dead."

"Proved it? No."

She stared at me, expressionless. "What, then?"

"I've heard some interesting stories, but I haven't gotten close enough to take Paul's picture."

"Where Paul is concerned there are always interesting stories and no one ever gets close," Stephanie said. "Has it occurred to you that you're creating false hope, and that that's a very cruel thing to do?"

She spoke forcefully. This drew knowing glances from other travelers as they hurried by. Clearly she had been thinking unkind thoughts about me in my absence. It was pointless to reply. Information was not what she was after, and no answer I could make would mollify her.

"You might think in term of the peace of mind of Paul's children," she said. "Lori has nightmares about her father being back in a prison camp in China. Who knows what goes through Zarah's mind since her father has already been presumed dead and come back to life once before in her lifetime."

Stephanie had a good loud voice and as she spoke a steady stream of total strangers, conditioned by a lifetime of watching television to be entertained while their attention was elsewhere, caught bits and pieces of her monologue as they hurried by. We must have sounded mighty like a husband and wife whose marriage was on the rocks.

There was little I could say in my defense, since there was at least a chance that Paul was, in fact, back in a Chinese prison camp. This was a thought I had not permitted myself to have for several weeks. What a good psychotherapist Stephanie must be, to summon hidden thoughts to the surface in the way that she did.

I said, "Sorry about all that, Stephanie. Where are you off to?"

"A conference in Cancun. How long will you be in town?"

"I'm not sure. When will you return?"

"What, so you can be sure to clear out before I come back?"

Talk about mind-reading. I was beginning to think that it was I, not my unfortunate cousin, who had once been married to this woman. On the other hand, it was impossible to imagine anyone talking to Paul as she talked to me. Silence and an understanding smile were the best defenses.

Stephanie said, "I'll be gone for ten days. Are you going to be staying at your house?"

"As far as I know, yes."

"I'll call you when I get back."

What a happy prospect.

She said, "I've got to run."

Then, unaccountably, she smiled—a complete girlish smile, impish eyes and all. She was pink in the face from emotion and also, I guess, from the strain of refusing to put down all that luggage while she read me the riot act.

"I really am fond of you, Horace," she said. "But you've gone around the bend again. You do know that, don't you?"

Fond of me? I said, "Already? I've been standing here thinking that I might go around the bend at any moment."

But she was gone before I could finish the sentence, dragging her hanger bag, weaving her way through the crowd.

3

My house, hardly larger than a garage, was tucked away between two far more imposing structures. It looked the same, but I assumed as a principle of tradecraft that it must have been entered by stealth in my absence. Perhaps listening devices had been planted, the phone bugged, the coffee poisoned, a trip wire connected to a bomb installed. I entered by the back door—the front door was blocked from the inside by a knee-high drift of junk mail—and checked the various traps I had set to tell me whether someone had been here in my absence. The hairs I had stretched across the cracks between the doors and doorframes had been broken, but then removed in a professional manner and replaced with substitute hairs of a slightly different color. Also, Uncle Horace's patented waylay to catch meddlers had caught one. A toilet that I had left unflushed had been flushed in my absence. Very few intruders, no matter how highly trained they might be to leave everything exactly as they found it, can forget their mothers' scolding voices when confronted by an unflushed water closet. They pull the chain before they think.

My stomach cramped. I sat down. Soon I was lost in thought. How would I avoid Stephanie? How would I see Zarah without exposing her to risk?

My body finished what it had been doing. Automatically, I

reached behind me for the lever on the water closet, I saw in my memory an image of the flushed bowl. A message snaked up my arm and into my brain. I took my hand off the lever, pulled up my pants, and went into the kitchen to find a paring knife and a flashlight. With these tools I examined the lid of the tank, and finding no wires, gingerly lifted it and peered beneath. And sure enough, folks, just like the tired old pulp fiction cliché that it was, there in the beam of the flashlight was about a pound of *plastique* taped to the underside of the lid. It was rigged with a simple trip wire to go off when the toilet was flushed. The bomber had flushed the foul toilet to make sure no one else did before I came home and pulled the chain myself.

I disarmed the bomb, which was about the size of an orange, then wrapped the *plastique* in aluminum foil and put it into the pocket of my raincoat for safekeeping. That done, I ate a bowl of instant oatmeal, then went upstairs and took a shower. I entertained more long thoughts while the hot water poured over me. What next? Who *were* these guys? Not that I didn't know who they were in the abstract: in the particular, of course, they were nobodies and I wouldn't have known who they were if someone whispered their names in my ear or showed me their pictures. But why all this thrillerish nonsense with bombs? Why not just shoot me or stab me? Who would care? I myself was too tired, too nauseated to care. Before retiring for the night I set a few traps just in case, but it didn't seem likely that the people who rigged the bomb would wish to reenter my house until it had gone off. Wearily I climbed the stairs and lay down for the first time in weeks in a bed that fit my body and slept the sleep of the just.

4

When I awoke it was dark, but still only six o'clock in the evening. There was nothing in the house to eat or drink, so I walked down the hill to M Street and dialed Zarah Christopher's home number from a sidewalk pay phone.

"It's Horace. Can I take you to dinner?"

"Come to my house," Zarah said. "You can cook."

Since it behooved me to suspect everyone, I could hardly take a cab in a town where a clear majority of taxi drivers wore luxuriant whiskers and behaved like lookouts for the jihad, so I walked the whole way, a couple of miles as the crow flies but farther than that by the circuitous route I took. I kept a sharp eye behind me, of course, but Washington is not a walker's town and I was the only pedestrian in the posh neighborhoods through which I passed, and was probably in less danger of assassination than of being mistaken for a prowler and reported to the police.

Zarah lived in an old underheated Tudor-style house that overhung, rather than overlooked, a brambly section of Rock Creek Park. Its former owner had equipped it with all sorts of gadgetry including a restaurant-style kitchen with a six-burner Viking stove, a full set of copper pots and pans dangling from an overhead rack, and a large selection of razor-sharp German knives. I loved this kitchen. Cooking, for me, is what golf seems to be for more clubbable men, something that gets your mind off your everyday work because it requires a certain amount of skill and concentration, yet at the same time is a means to sociable ends.

While I made a *poule au pot* with the groceries I had picked up on my way to Zarah's place, she sat on the countertop, ankles crossed, sipping a glass of Grgich chardonnay. An uncorked bottle of Beaune stood on the kitchen table, breathing. A wedge of Reblochon cheese softened on a board beside a bowl of black grapes. Zarah had provided the wines, fruit and cheese. Also the conversation. She said nothing about people we knew in common. She mentioned movies she had seen, books she had read, something out of her own childhood experience about hunting with falcons.

Zarah, it turned out, knew all about birds of prey—how they are trained, how they are handled and rewarded, how they kill. In the Atlas Mountains of Morocco, where she had grown up while her vengeful mother was concealing her existence from her father, the Berbers had hunted gazelles and jackals with golden eagles. It took a very strong man to carry one of these birds on his arm. To desert people, as I already knew, falconry was a mystical art, worth any amount of trouble or money. My superficial knowledge of such matters was nothing compared to Zarah's. In ancient times, only kings had been permitted to hunt with eagles. Lesser nobility had been assigned peregrine falcons, the swiftest and most powerful of the many kinds of falcons and hawks—she named them all—used in the sport. Rich Arabs will pay almost any price for a particularly fine specimen. If they have unlimited money, like Saudi princes, they might own scores of the birds, gathered from all over Asia. The peregrine falcon can spot its prey at tremendous distances and when dropping out of the sky for the kill can fly at amazing speeds— diving as fast as a small airplane can fly. Zarah described explosions of feathers in blue desert skies, noted the absence of memory from the falcon's yellow eye after a kill.

"Do falcons remember the last victim or does the brain send

them some imprinted instruction each time they spot their prey?" she asked. "Nobody seems to know."

"Ibn Awad was a falconer," I said. "His birds sat on perches behind him when he dined in company—twenty or more of them all in a row, wearing hoods."

"Twenty?" Zarah said. "That's about half a million dollars worth of birds."

I'd had no idea. "He could afford it," I said. "And he had no other vices."

Except a thirst for murdering infidels, of course.

We drank what remained of the chardonnay, then moved on to the chicken and the burgundy. Conversation—at least Zarah's half of it—sparkled until we arrived at the cheese and grapes. Then, all of a sudden, her smile faded.

She said, "Horace, do you think they're alive?"

"Let's go for a walk."

Zarah lived in a quiet, not to say hushed neighborhood, and at that hour of the night we encountered no other pedestrians except dog walkers. It was cold and damp, but nothing compared to northern Europe. We walked for as long as it took me to tell her everything I had learned on my travels. Hours. She never once interrupted until I had finished.

Then she said, "Then you think they're both alive?"

"I work on the assumption that the answer is Yes. Otherwise what would be the point of going on with this? Whether Paul and Lori are together is another question."

"Even though he was on the point of finding her?"

"Lori may not have wanted to be found."

"By her own son?"

"You're asking me to read her mind. As nearly as I can make out, nobody has ever been able to do that. Not even Paul, and in a way he's devoted his life to the effort."

Zarah stopped. We were on the other side of the park, standing under a large tree in a softly lit, sleeping neighborhood of mansions. I had no idea where exactly we were.

"I've done the same, you know," Zarah said. "When I was a child, long before we met, my father was my imaginary friend. He told me wonderful stories."

"Even though he was not present?"

"Exactly. He was in China, though I didn't know that at the time. My favorite story was about dinosaurs. In his story they were feathered creatures and they sang as birds do except the sound was much grander, pipe organs instead of piccolos. He described a grassy plain crowded with them, a rainbow of color in the sunlight, each kind of dinosaur with its own plumage and its own voice, but all of them in some wonderful kind of harmony."

"How old were you when you thought this up?"

"I was about ten. And I didn't think it up. It came to me."

I said, "You were an imaginative child."

"Was I? I wonder."

A figure approached out of the shadows—a middle-aged woman in a Gucci babushka and a Burberry coat, reeking of whiskey, staggering slightly on high heels and glaring at Zarah and me as her yapping miniature schnauzer tugged her down the street.

Zarah and I walked back to her house. Fortunately, she knew the way out of the strange neighborhood into which we had wandered. I had in my pocket the only copy of her grandmother's translation of the Amphora Scroll. While still in Budapest I had realized, out of the blue, that Zarah was the person—the only possible person—to translate her grandmother's German version of the Amphora Scroll. Now I handed her Lori's manuscript, still in its oilskin packet. She opened the packet and saw the handwriting.

"Whose handwriting is this?"

I told her.

I said, "Can you translate this into English?"

She read another page, then nodded. We walked back to her house in silence. I left the manuscript in her care. I will tell you a curious thing: I had not bothered to make a copy of this unique and irreplaceable document. This contravened the habits of a lifetime, but there you are. I seemed to be turning into a Christopher, suddenly trusting impulse in the same blind way I had always before put my faith in calculation.

5

Though I had seen most of them one by one and talked to them all by telephone, usually to my great benefit, the Old Boys had not met with everyone present since our last get-together at my house less than a month before. Time had flown for me because I had been having such a good time in Xinjiang and Moscow and Jerusalem, but I sensed that it had dragged a bit for some of the others. It was time for a meeting. Despite my deeply held belief, based on hours and hours of boredom, that meetings of more than two people are thieves of time in which nothing important is ever accomplished, I asked Charley Hornblower to set one up. In the circumstances we could hardly get together at my house, so we put on neckties and gathered at the club in time for tea.

The clubhouse was more or less deserted between lunch and dinner except for a few shabby derelicts like ourselves. Because Ben Childress and David Wong were in the field, there were only four of us at the meeting—Jack, Harley, Charley and myself. I was still a member in good standing. While in jail, in fact, I had been charged the reduced dues of an out-of-town member. Naturally it was Paul, to whose address all my mail was forwarded, who paid these for me. The club rules said nothing about banishing convicts as long as they did not commit the mortal sin of discussing club business in their testimony or anywhere else where the newspapers might get hold of it.

We met in the billiards room, which had no windows and was better heated than some other parts of the old mansion. As the ranking used-to-be among us, Jack presided. Jack loved meetings. He was bursting with questions. As so often in the past, the object of his curiosity—I might even say his exasperation—was me.

Before he could launch into what I knew would his lengthy list of whispered questions, I unwrapped my pound of *plastique* and slammed it onto the billiards table. All present recognized it immediately for what it was. No one asked a question but all eyes were upon me—resentful eyes, because I had violated the prime rule of all meetings: never surprise anybody.

I told them the tale of the bomb and filled them in on the rest of my adventures. Still there was no commentary—no "Gosh, Horace! That was a close call!" No "What kind of person would do such a thing?" We all knew exactly what kind of person would do such a thing. But there are no answers to empty questions and we had all been taught never to ask them.

Harley said, "Are you movin'?"

"No. Under the circumstances it would be unethical to rent the place or sell it. Anyway, I'm hardly ever there and anyway, they probably won't try the same thing twice."

"But apparently you would," Jack said. "Horace, what's this we hear from Ben about running a dangle operation on Ibn Awad?"

A dangle, I should explain, is an operation in which one dangles somebody or something before an adversary in the hope that he'll take the bait. If he does, the benefits can be considerable. If, for example, the infamous Aldrich Ames had been a dangle instead of a genuine rotten apple, he could have falsely identified the Russians' best operatives as American agents and smiled while the Russians fed them into the fiery furnace. Instead, of course, he fingered actual American assets, and they were the ones who were cremated alive.

I said, "What has Ben told you?"

"That you're going to dangle the Amphora Scroll."

"That's correct."

"What if it doesn't exist?"

"It exists, all right."

Jack's blank brown eyes examined me as if reading the big E on an eye chart. He knew me. And I knew him.

"You realize that they're going to come after you?"

"It's beginning to look like they already have."

"Maybe," Jack said. "I'd just like to have your assurance that you have no plans to expose yourself any further than you already have."

"No such plan exists."

"I'm glad to hear it," Jack said. "As I'm sure every man here is, too."

The expression on his face—more accurately, the absence of expression on his face—told me that he did not really believe me. The other faces in the room were just as bland as his. If Ibn Awad decided to kill me, he'd have to kill us all, and septuagenarians are no more philosophical about a bullet to the brain than anyone else. Less so, if anything. The closer one is to the inevitable, the more desirable postponement becomes. The six of us were probably paying more, collectively, for pills than we had ever spent as a group on alcohol, and that's saying a lot.

Time to change the subject, Charley thought. "We should stop using the satellite phones," he said. "Those fellows in Moscow, whoever they are, got hold of Horace's number and called him up. They followed him to Budapest. Didn't they also tell you they were intercepting all our calls, Horace?"

"They said that someone was," I replied. "But I doubt if that's the fact. There's just too much conversation bouncing off satellites and relay towers, millions of different instruments tuning up twenty-four hours a day, for anyone to hear half a dozen harmonicas at the back of the orchestra."

"Vivid metaphor," Jack said. He *was* annoyed. "Then how did they get your number?"

"Maybe they checked out the stores in the Washington area, found the one where I bought the phones, and leaned on the manager until he remembered he was a good American and gave them the number."

"You didn't pay cash for the phones?"

"Sure I did, but that's a suspicious act in an age when every honest man pays with plastic. However, if you described me to a clerk and hinted that I was a terrorist, don't you think he'd remember me?"

Jack said, "You've always been noticeable, Horace."

What was the *matter* with him? I wasn't the only one who wondered. Harley Waters, pale and shrunken, had been silent through all this. Now he said, "I've got a suggestion. Jack, Horace—stop bickerin'. It's bad for the digestion."

After throwing off this spark, Harley retreated into silence. He slumped in his chair, eyes averted, mind elsewhere.

I said, "There's an unreported development. Thanks to Harley, we have in our hands what we think is an original copy of Lori Christopher's translation of the Amphora Scroll."

Charley said, "Translation into what language?"

"German."

"I can handle that."

"I know you can, Charley. I've asked Zarah Christopher to do the first translation into English. We'll want you to do an independent reading."

Jack said, "Did you say Zarah Christopher?"

"Yes. She's fluent in German."

"She is? How did that happen?"

"She studied it as a child. She wanted to surprise her father when they met. And then she polished it by talking to Paul after they were reunited."

"But she's not part of this group."

"True, Jack. But she's a Christopher. The translation belongs to the Christopher family if it belongs to anyone."

"Lovely sentiment, Horace."

It isn't often that I am charged with sentimentality. I said, "My thought was that Zarah might see things, understand things that a non-Christopher might miss."

"Understand or romanticize?"

Harley stood up. "I'm leavin'," he said.

I didn't blame him. Charley said, "Come on, Harley, we need you."

"Nothin' personal," Harley said. His voice squeaked. He coughed to clear his throat. "I've got a doctor's appointment in half an hour."

Jack offered him a lift.

"No thanks, I'll take shank's mare," Harley said. Although he seemed unsteady on his feet, he was out the door before I could speak to him.

"Look, I'm going, too," I said. "He shouldn't be alone."

Jack stood up at the same moment I did. "I'll join you," he said.

We had no trouble catching up to Harley, who was walking across the broad avenue so slowly that the light changed before he made it to the opposite sidewalk. Taxi drivers from all over the Muslim world blew their horns. Most of them had never seen a clock in their native villages. Now America had worked its magic and time was money. They were shaking their fists at this marooned old codger who was robbing them of precious seconds.

Jack and I dodged through traffic to reach Harley. Jack, always the one with presence of mind, grabbed a taxi. We got Harley inside. He put his head back on the seat and closed his eyes. He looked bad—little blue veins on the lids, a visible pulse in his temple. Shortness of breath. Sweat on his forehead. Pallor.

"G. W. emergency room, fast," Jack said to the driver in a baritone so resonant that it startled me. Anything louder than a whisper would have done the same, coming from Jack.

It even roused Harley. "Didn't know you had all those decibels in you, Jack," he said, in a voice so labored that I could barely make out the words.

5

We were surrounded in the waiting room by the wretched of the city. Because most of them talked nonstop on cell phones or to each other, we knew that gunshot wounds and knife wounds and overdoses and the sudden onset of labor pains were on their minds. Even Jack understood that these people had no interest in eavesdropping even if their hearing was keen enough to pick his words out of the hubbub.

Half an hour later, as we waited for a doctor to bring us news of Harley, I said, "Jack, what was all that about, back in the club?"

"We're all concerned," Jack said. "You're fixated on the Christophers."

"And that signifies what?"

"It makes you unpredictable. Zarah is the last of the Christophers. You regard that as reason enough to break security and entrust her with the most important piece of evidence we've yet discovered. And you do this without consulting anybody."

Jack's summation amounted to an impeccably accurate reading of the situation.

I said, "I'm not sure I understand why this should be so disturbing to you. She's not going to mail a copy to Ibn Awad."

"That's not the point."

"Then please tell me what the point is, Jack."

Jack stared at me as if confounded by my thick-headedness. His face worked—actually changed expression. In anyone else this would have been a sign of emotion. But Jack?

He inhaled. "I did the damage control when Zarah came back from that shambles that David Patchen led her into," he said. "That, too, was a dangle op. As director of the Outfit—*director of the Outfit*—Patchen himself was the primary bait. She went along with him—she was part of the dangle—I suppose because she wanted to be like her dad."

"And?"

"She had a bad time. Patchen set it up so that he'd be kidnapped. The timing went wrong and she was kidnapped with him. He had some demented notion that if he was taken and tortured the Outfit would be so compromised that they'd have to reorganize it. Take it away from the presidency. Make it independent. Start over. He'd save it from its enemies."

I said, "That's exactly what happened."

"Yes. And hasn't it all turned out wonderfully?"

"Not so great for you and me, granted."

"It didn't turn out so great for Zarah, either," Jack said. "Do you have any idea what happened to her?"

I did. In fact I knew exactly what had happened to her. But I had heard the facts as a family secret, confided by Paul. I had no business sharing it, even with Jack Philindros. Besides, I didn't want to hear it again.

I said, "No need to confide."

Jack ignored my words. He said, "They shot her full of dope and ganged her while she was unconscious. She had no memory of this."

His formerly impassive face was unmolding as if something under the skin was about to burst forth. I might have said any number of things at this point to make things easier for him. But there was good reason to say nothing.

"It was my job to tell her what happened," he said.

Again I offered no encouragement. It would have done no

good to tell him to shut up. Jack was spilling a secret. This was a rare, maybe even a unique event in his life.

He said, "I *had* to tell her. Two of the rapists were HIV positive. Paul and his rescue party shot them all dead, but it showed up in the autopsies."

He looked ravaged.

I said, "Did you give her a blood test first?"

Jack said, "We would have to have had her permission to do that."

"Needed her *permission?*"

"It's the law."

"But she had the test?"

"Yes, it came back negative." Jack said. "But she didn't believe the results."

I was speechless. I had always wondered what genius had given Zarah the news. Jack Philindros, tomb of discretion, was the last person I would have suspected. At this point, in the nick of time, Charley appeared.

Harley was going to be all right. They had given him a pacemaker.

Exactly what the Hungarian doctor ordered. Charley was even happier than usual because he was the bearer of good tidings. And so he should have been.

"When are they going to do this?" I asked.

"They're doing it right now," Charley said. "If all goes well he can go home tomorrow. Harley will be right as rain. He can come to my place."

After Charley left, Jack said, "Look, I'm sorry about the outburst," he said. "I guess I didn't know how much that business about Zarah had affected me until I started to talk about it."

"Then it's just as well you got it out of your system," I said.

"Maybe. But she shouldn't have to go through anything like that again."

"I agree," I said. "But it's up to her, isn't it?"

"That's probably what Patchen told himself," Jack said.

"He was a headquarters man."

So was Jack, of course. Even when he was posted overseas he stayed behind a desk in an embassy while third parties made the messes and cleaned them up. He just read about it, wrote about it, and signed the vouchers. For that matter, I wasn't so very different.

Jack said, "'He was a headquarters man?' What's that supposed to mean?"

"Blood and ink don't smell anything alike."

Jack looked me over, shrewd eyes the color of brown eggshells and just as expressive.

7

By now it was rush hour. The automobiles on Massachusetts Avenue alone, bumper to bumper from Union Station to the Maryland line, were probably worth more, collectively, than the gross national product of most of the countries that owned embassies on Embassy Row. I have never in my life commuted. Like Harley, shank's mare has been my transport and I've been lucky enough, thanks to taxpayers like these idle folks in their idling Fords and Toyotas, to live most of my life in cities where walking is a pleasure.

Washington is one of those towns, if only in the cool weeks between mid-October and mid-March when open-air exercise is possible without drowning in your own sweat. Right now I was walking past the vice president's fortified residence, on my way to the Wisconsin Avenue Whole Foods store to buy some groceries and be snubbed by the politically fastidious regular clientele, who could tell at a glance if one's shopping cart contained vegetables contaminated by chemicals and pesticides or chickens that had not ranged free before their heads were chopped off.

I felt oxygen-deprived after breathing exhaust fumes during nearly an hour of uphill walking. No wonder the drivers looked so dazed, so overcome. Someone had fallen into step beside me. I looked over my shoulder and saw two more pedestrians, one about ten meters to the rear, the other across the street. Our old friends A, B, and C again. This time they weren't Russians or Chinese or clean-cut Ohio boys with Glocks in their jeans, but fellows in matching dark raincoats and polyester tweed hats.

As I turned into the cross street that led to Wisconsin Avenue, the one beside me, a stocky broad-shouldered man with Nixonian five o'clock shadow, looked up at me and smiled.

"Hi," he said.

Let's call him "A."

I said, "Good evening."

A said, "My friends and I would like it if you can join us in for a drink. Our place is just around the corner."

"Very kind of you," I said. "But I have some shopping to do."

"This won't take long. For old times' sake."

"Maybe some other time."

"Right now would be better for us."

A was showing me something. It was one of those flip-open leather cases you see on television when federal agents flash their ID and everyone either becomes cooperative or starts shooting. Plainly A regarded it as a talisman. I took it out of his hand—no tug of war; he let me have it. A picture, unmistakably A, a fictitious name, Robert F. Gordon, and the official name of the Outfit embossed above its official seal. What, no badge?

I handed it back to him and said, "I thought that secret agents never carried credentials."

"Times have changed, Horace," A said. "This way, please."

Squat and muscular and sure of his strength, he reminded me of the man on the stairway in Moscow.

We were standing next to the iron fence that marks the boundary of the vice president's grounds, not the best place for a clandestine conversation. This perimeter bristled with hidden cameras and listening devices and motion detectors, and the times being what they were, maybe even atomizers filled with some kind of secret gas that freezes trespassers in their tracks. His feet planted on the sidewalk, A had taken what police training manuals call the stance of authority, not exactly blocking my way but giving me a broad muscle magazine hint that it would be unwise to try to step around him.

I said, "Tell you what, my friend. I'll meet whoever's waiting for me around the corner at the café in Whole Foods in half an hour. Alone. He or she should pick up two tomatoes on the way in and place them on the table when sitting down with me."

"That's not what we had in mind," A said.

"Life is full of adjustments."

"You're making unnecessary difficulties."

"Well, you and your friends can overpower me if you think that's a good idea," I said. "But for all you know I have a friend watching over me, ready to dial 911 and take pictures of the mugging with a fancy cell phone while waiting for the cops to arrive. Or maybe the vice president's security cameras will pick up the action. 'Goon Squad Jumps Notorious Ex-Spy.' The ten o'clock news should love it."

"One minute," A said. He stepped away, turned his back, and made a call on his phone. Then he said, "Okay, the Whole Foods café at seventeen fifty-five hours."

"I'll be there," I replied. "And no offense, but I'd rather not see you or your friends in the elevator or shopping for cabbages."

A controlled himself quite nicely.

At precisely five minutes of six, just as I had begun to drink a scalding hot caffe latte that had too much milk and too little coffee in it, a thirtyish couple wearing barn coats over office attire joined me in the café. The man glumly placed two bright-red vine-ripened tomatoes on the table. He had palmed them like a shoplifter, as if they might be of overwhelming interest to whoever was shadowing us. The woman was slender with buzz-cut hair and discreet gold earrings and slightly unfocused eyes, large and blue, behind contact lenses. She did not return my smile. Neither did her colleague. Both wore wedding rings. The rings were of different designs. Apparently they were not married to each other except professionally. They looked like GS 12s or 13s, go-ahead young officers who had just started to rise through the career bottleneck that would probably be corked, for them as for most, at GS-14.

They looked around in dismay. All the tables in the café were occupied by homeward-bound lawyers and such, so we were cheek by jowl with a roomful of fruit-juice and latte drinkers, none of whom had a right to overhear our conversation.

"These are not ideal circumstances for this meeting," the man said.

How right he was from his point of view. Clearly and distinctly I said, "My name is Horace Hubbard. What shall I call you?"

"I'm Don," he muttered. "This is . . . Mary."

"Just act like you've never heard the word *security*, Don and Mary, and everything should be all right. Want something to drink? My treat. Mary? No?"

They shook their heads in unison. Their eyes were fixed on me, matching what they observed to whatever description had been provided to them. I guessed that I had been painted as a difficult, unpredictable, a dinosaur in disgrace. I had the impression that I was going to conform to their worst expectations no matter how hard I tried to be good company.

I said, "If you're not thirsty why don't we just get this over with? What can I do for you?"

"We have some unpleasant news for you," Don said. "You're wanted for murder in Moscow."

Of course I was. I asked no questions and, I hope, showed no sign of worry.

"I'm innocent."

"They have an eyewitness," Don said.

Of course they did. I said, "Do they also have an extradition treaty with the United States?"

Don's turn not to answer.

Mary said, "That's not all, Horace. A rare and valuable painting by Edward Hicks, known to have belonged to the late Paul

Christopher, has surfaced in the Paris art market." To go with her big blue eyes she had a sweet little-girl voice. "According to our information, the painting was sold privately," she said. "If it was sold by an American citizen, that person has broken federal law."

I sipped my latte and held my tongue. This had the usual effect. My questioners filled the silence.

Mary said, "You've spent a lot of money lately, Horace. Airplane tickets, hotels, fine restaurants."

I didn't remember the fine restaurants, but denied nothing.

"This spending pattern is interesting," Mary said. "It makes people wonder."

"Makes what people wonder about what?" I asked.

"Well, two things, actually," Don said with an edge of sarcasm in his voice. "Why you're spending all this money and where you got it."

"The answer to the first question is common knowledge," I said. "I'm trying to find my cousin, Paul Christopher."

"But he's dead."

"That's the official report. I happen not to accept its accuracy."

Don said, pouncing, "Where did you get the money?"

I said, "What a rude question, Don. That's none of your business, is it?"

"The IRS might consider it their business."

"You mean you're not with the IRS?"

Mary blinked rapidly, as if the insult—IRS indeed!—was a speck of grit that had gotten into her eye. Don flushed and injected more menace into his tone.

"You may think this situation is funny," he said. "But I assure you it is not."

"Then maybe you should tell me what this is all about."

"We've been trying to do that."

"Then please try harder. You're too subtle for me."

After a long moment of hard eye contact, Don said, "Mary, you try."

Mary, the good cop, said, "Actually, Horace, it's pretty simple. We're just trying to give you a friendly heads-up."

"Thank you very much. About what? And why?"

"For old times' sake," Mary said. "You're in danger. You should take precautions before it's too late."

First you try to kidnap a fellow in broad daylight, then you advise him to take precautions? Who wrote this comic strip?

"Funny," I said. "Just days ago I had this same talk with some fine young folks in Budapest and before that in Moscow. Except that they were armed to the teeth. Friends of yours?"

Don said, "We don't know anything about that."

I believed him. He and Mary weren't high enough on the totem pole to be told about such interesting people as Kevin.

"Look, it's very simple," Mary said. "We're fond of people like you. You're well and gratefully remembered. But you and your old-timer friends are causing a lot of unnecessary trouble. You're getting between our people and an important target. What is desired—and this comes from the very highest level—is for you and your shuffleboard team to get out of the way. And stay out of the way."

Maybe Mary wasn't the good cop after all.

"I don't quite follow," I said. "All I'm doing is looking for my missing cousin who, if I may say so, should really be remembered fondly and gratefully."

Mary's glassy eyes came into focus behind the contact lenses. Through her teeth she said, "Look, Horace. The message is simple. I'll deliver it one more time. Get out of the way. If you'd rather make fun of us than do the sensible thing, be my guest. You can be debonair or you can be something else that starts with *d*."

What a shocking thing for Mary to say. I stared at her.

"You've embarrassed us in the past," she said. "All we're asking is that you don't get you and your pathetic friends killed and embarrass us even worse." With a squeal of chair legs, Mary got to her feet. "I hope that's not too much to ask," she said. "Because this is the last time we'll ask you nicely."

The Outfit certainly was using a tougher vocabulary since it started recruiting female case officers.

Mary strode away. Clattering heels, shapely legs, shortish skirt. Don followed along behind. He forgot his tomatoes.

8

When I emerged onto Wisconsin Avenue with a shopping bag full of groceries I found A, B, and C waiting for me. They stood in a cluster at the crosswalk like so many high school boys meeting on the corner. All three stared boldly at me, letting me know that they had testosterone to burn and no friendly intent. I joined them at the curb and waited for the DON'T WALK sign to change. With his eyes fixed on the traffic signal, A said, "Take a good look at the crowd."

"What am I looking for?"

"Try ethnic characteristics."

Across the street I saw three Middle Eastern types, one of them talking into a cell phone. A bit farther down the avenue, another one was talking into *his* cell phone. I assumed they were talking to each other and perhaps to others elsewhere in the crowd. Then I saw them everywhere I looked. It was like quitting time at the mosque. It was hard to believe, but it looked like I was being swarmed. This was an unexpected compliment. An exercise of this kind, called waterfall surveillance in the jargon, is very, very expensive and can also be seen as an admission of defeat on the part of the people who are watching you. Waterfall surveillance involves walking right at the target face to face and making eye contact instead of sneaking along behind in the usual way. It requires a small army of agents, all targeted on a single person who would, of course, have to be blind and stupid not to understand what was happening.

The whole idea is that the victim *does* understand what is happening, that he cannot fail to understand. The objective is to make a show of intimidation, to spoil the day if not the life of someone you know to be a bad guy but who for one reason or another you cannot neutralize by the usual dirty tricks. Unless you want to keep this up for the rest of the subject's life and bust your budget, the idea is to scare him so badly on day one that he'll go into another line of work or flee the country. Or if you're really upset, you can kill or maim him when you're through playing big cat, little mouse with him. Was this some sort of zany Outfit operation? It seemed unlikely, but we were living in a new age with a new ethic and it was entirely possible that the people of the new Outfit had become what Hollywood and the media and academia had relentlessly taught the young the old Outfit always was—a ruthless outlaw agency staffed by homicidal maniacs.

Waterfall surveillance works most efficiently in deserted neighborhoods where the target can clearly see his adversaries and wonder when the fear in his heart is going to be extinguished by a bullet. However, this was a Friday evening in upper Georgetown, the day and hour when young people with money in their pockets, educated voices and radiant smiles hit the bars and restaurants. Apart from the ones with beards and angry eyes, these kids looked and sounded like a convention of Kevins. This was not the sort of crowd into which I could disappear. Of course, neither could the other guys. However, this was America, not Xinjiang or Russia, and all was not lost—at least not yet. Rescue was possible, at least in theory. I could call the police and tell them exactly what was happening. In that case the cops would have taken me to St. Elizabeth's, the local loony bin, for a night of observation, and I would have been inaccessible—not such a bad outcome. What I needed was sanctuary, a place where my enemies could not enter. It was next to impossible to elude them, but I might be able to confuse them, if only for the fraction of a minute I needed to slip out of the net.

The light had not changed. It was rush hour and cars had the right-of-way, so the signal was set for a long, long pause. A and his friends still stood beside me. Still gazing fixedly at the DON'T WALK sign, lips barely moving, A muttered, "Like we told you, you've got problems. And there's not a thing we can do to help you."

"I was thinking of calling the cops."

"Nothing they could do. These guys haven't done anything except stand on the sidewalk and talk on the phone. It's a free country."

Ah, was *that* the problem?

Still, I had certain advantages. Tactically, this was a bad place to execute a waterfall surveillance because we were in the middle of a steep hill and there were no cross streets for a couple of blocks in either direction. The way an operation like this works is that the operatives walk past the subject, turn into the first cross street, jump into a waiting car or van, and are ferried two or three blocks in the direction in which the subject is walking. Then they hit the sidewalk again and walk right at the poor fellow, making awful faces. This is great fun if you have the temperament for it.

My advantages were these: (1) I knew where I was going and my tormentors did not; (2) my pursuers stood out in this crowd at least as much as I did; (3) it was getting dark fast; and (4) I do have the temperament for it.

Needless to say I wasn't thinking as sequentially as this suggests. The moment I've just taken such pains to describe was just that— a moment. What I did next I did without conscious thought. The only nanosecond in which it's possible to escape the waterfall is the first one, before you are swept over the edge. So far all the thugs I had spotted were downhill from me. My house was only a few blocks in that direction. Evidently these people were thick-headed enough to assume that I was human enough to head for home.

Looking uphill, the only way out, I saw a Metro bus approaching and people waiting for it half a block away on the opposite side of Wisconsin Avenue. The signal clicked at last and changed to WALK. I charged into traffic even before it stopped. It took about thirty seconds—though of course I remember all this in slo-mo—to dash across the street and leapt through the door of the bus just before it closed behind me with a whoosh and the vehicle lurched into motion. Along with a couple of other people who also had not had time to find seats, I fought for balance. I had never before in my life been on a Metro bus, and I had no idea where it was headed or what the fare was or how to pay it. A motherly Haitian woman wearing a maid's uniform under her coat helped me count out the change as the bus rolled down the avenue, gathering speed with every turn of the wheels.

I rode the bus to M Street. No gorillas got aboard at either of the two stops in between, maybe because they were all pointed in the other direction and had to be reprogrammed. Leaving my groceries on an empty seat and hoping the Haitian lady would take them home with her, I exited by the rear door, jumped into a taxi that already had two witnesses in the backseat—sharing taxis is a quaint old Washington custom—and asked the Punjabi driver to take me to the club.

He turned out to be a natural-born getaway driver. While he weaved in and out of traffic and jumped red lights, we chatted about his cousins, half a dozen of whom were also cabdrivers in the District of Columbia. Finally he made a hard left turn across traffic, tires squealing, and sped into the club's circular drive and dropped me at the door. I didn't even have to cross the sidewalk. I gave him a handsome tip, walked into the foyer, and was as safe from my enemies as one of Dumas's noble fugitives in the Cathedral of Notre-Dame. None could enter here except members and their guests, and nobody I had met so far this evening had much chance of being nominated for membership—or, for that matter, even being invited to lunch.

Happily—this seemed to be my lucky day—the front desk had just received a cancellation from someone who had booked one of the larger upstairs bedrooms for the weekend, so I was able to move right in. This had many advantages besides a comfortable bed, unlimited clean towels, and a shelf of unreadable books written by members. Chief among these was an unbugged telephone, safe to use at least for the time being.

I immediately called Zarah and described my circumstances. I invited her to lunch at the club the next day. Zarah accepted calmly. There was no need to explain to her that it wasn't wise just now for me to go to her house. This would likely remain the case until the present excitement faded away. The way things were going, this might not happen in my lifetime.

9

"I'm finding it mind-boggling," Zarah said.

"The fatwa?"

"No," she said. "The job you asked me to do."

We were seated at a small table in an alcove of the club dining room. I was conscious that Zarah wore no perfume and realized for the first time that she never had. She smelled of skin and hair, scrubbed teeth, the wool of her dress, the leather of her shoes, the tang of metal polish on the handsome Arabian silver belt that she wore.

"You're finding the translation difficult?" I asked.

"No, Lori's translation is in words that cannot possibly be misunderstood," Zarah said. "But it's disorienting to read a fifth Gospel that sounds like it was written by an investigative journalist. This man Septimus Arcanus has his own slant on the miracles. He sees them as a series of pranks cooked up by Roman case officers. He's *laughing* at these dupes."

"Does he describe Roman purposes in running this operation?"

"In the clearest possible terms. The Israelite priesthood was a thorn in the side of the Roman governor, fomenting unrest. The Romans wanted to put the priests in their debt so they could control them. So they manufactured a threat to their authority, namely one Joshua ben Joseph, financed the mischief he made, and then made the problem go away by crucifying him."

"And that bothers you?"

"Something keeps telling me not to believe it."

"A voice from above?"

"From within," Zarah said. "I feel as I read Septimus Arcanus's dispatch that I'm doing something forbidden just to read it. I don't feel alone in the house."

She was serious. No deprecating smile.

"My goodness," I said, "I didn't realize you were a Christian. Had I known, I wouldn't have put you in such an uncomfortable position."

"I'm not a Christian. I wasn't raised as a Christian. The Jawabi, the Berber tribe we lived with in Morocco, believed that they were Jews who had fled Israel in the time of King David. They regarded the God of the Old Testament as an unpredictable psychopath who would send plagues or floods or war or exile unless he was constantly appeased. They thought he was a local god they'd left behind, but they were still praying to him and sacrificing animals four thousand years later just in case he ever showed up again. Mother hired an English clergyman to teach me the Bible. He was very learned and devout, but after reading the whole text line by line, I came away with the impression that the Jawabi were right about Yahweh and that the story in the New Testament was just plain unbelievable. I've never been able to understand its power over so many minds."

"Until now."

"That's right," Zarah said. "In daylight I tell myself it's just the effect of two thousand years of superstition. When the sun goes down I'm not so sure."

"Maybe it's the history of the Christophers rather than the story in the scroll that's bothering you."

"Maybe," Zarah said. "It's in my grandmother's handwriting, after all, as if she were writing to me."

The food arrived. Zarah, usually the soul of kindness to waiters, behaved as if the grilled grouper—we had ordered the same thing—and the woman who brought it were invisible.

She said, "You must think I've taken leave of my senses."

No Christopher I had ever known ever came this close to asking for reassurance. I was taken aback.

I said, "Not at all. I've put in a lot more time as a heathen than you, and I've had similar thoughts about the Amphora Scroll. But frankly, I don't know why, it makes me nervous."

Zarah had brought Lori's translation with her. "I really don't want custody of the original," she said.

"But it's yours by right of inheritance," I said.

"If it hadn't been for you I would never have known it existed," Zarah said.

"Does this mean you don't want to do the translation?" I asked.

"I've done it."

She handed it to me, printed out in Times New Roman on sheets of white paper.

"You have this stored in your computer?"

"No. It's on a diskette."

"And that's in a safe place?"

"It's in the safe that doesn't exist."

It took me a moment to realize that she meant Paul's table-leg safe—the one in which Stephanie refused to believe.

"Did you make a photocopy of the original?"

"Yes, three. One is stored with the diskette, the other is in a safe-deposit box, and the third is the one you hold in your hands. I also made a diskette for you. Everything is in this envelope."

She slid that across the table, too. A couple of nonagenarian members, watching all this from the next table, frowned in disapproval. It was against the rules to have papers in sight in the precincts of the club. Besides, the whole idea of a men's club was that it was a refuge from women. So what were women doing here?

A telephone rang. The old duffers glared at Zarah—just like a woman!—but it was my satellite phone. Ordinarily I would not have broken the club rules and answered it, but in the present circumstances a higher duty required me to do so. It was Ben Childress, calling from Yemen. He was outdoors, apparently in the middle of a sandstorm. I could hear the night wind howling. Ben was brief and to the point, as usual. He had excellent news about Claus Bücher. Of course he didn't call him that over the phone, but he made me understand whom he was talking about. As he spoke, an idea—no, an inspiration—formed in my mind.

I hung up and said, "Zarah, how would you like to go to Vienna?"

10

We traveled on separate flights, me via Frankfurt on Lufthansa, Zarah a day behind me by way of Paris on Air France. I saw no surveillance on leaving the club and none at Dulles, but this did not mean that it wasn't there or that it wouldn't be waiting for me when I landed. The motive of the Outfit in shaking me down time after time was a mystery to me. I said so. Charley Hornblower, playing solitaire on a laptop in the seat beside me, expressed an opinion.

"The world as we knew it is no more," said Charley. "No rules, no out of bounds, no penalties. This war-on-terrorism apparatus is Tyrannosaurus Rex, very small brain, only one idea: 'If it moves, eat it.' You moved."

"Charley, that's truly poetic."

"Allegorical, actually. When do I get to see the beautiful lady's translation from the German?"

I handed him Zarah's diskette. Charley inserted it in his laptop and brought the text up on the screen. While he scrolled I gazed out the window. Far below, low clouds scudded eastward across the North Atlantic toward the wintry gray city for which we were bound. How romantic such destinations had seemed when Charley and I were young and the Outfit was handing out scraps of the trembling Old World to kids like us and instructing us to preserve them from evil. How dreary they seemed, now that we had slain the dragon and discovered that the damsel, far from crying "My hero!" pined for the loathsome creature.

Charley finished reading with a grunt. "Quite an artifact," he said.

"Your thoughts?"

"Burn it before somebody burns us. At the stake."

11

This was Ben Childress's good news: Dr. Claus Bücher had gotten his wish to be saved by Viennese doctors. Of course, there was no saving a man with his type of cancer, and his name was not really Claus Bücher, and he was an Austrian rather than a German, but the important thing was, we knew at last where to find him.

"It was a case of '*Wien, Wien, nur du allein,*'" said Ben Childress when we met in a deserted museum. "Only Vienna would do. Mubarak yielded to Bücher's hysterical insistence that a cure for pancreatic cancer had been perfected by Viennese medicine."

"Has it?"

"Of course not. Bücher's real purpose seems to have been to come home to die. For the first time since 1945 he can do that without going to prison for the rest of his life. In Bücher's case that would mean a one- or two-week sentence, according to Mubarak."

"You've talked to Mubarak in person about this?"

"Hardly. But his grandfather filled me in. And there's this."

Ben handed over a photograph of a pretty blond woman holding a pretty blond toddler by the hand. From the woman's clothes and hairstyle, it looked as though the picture dated from the 1970s. She was smiling, her child was chortling. They were outdoors, perhaps in a park, watching something outside the frame that amused them. The child, a girl, pointed a chubby finger. The images were slightly distorted. From a lifetime of looking at surveillance photos I had an idea why. The photograph had been taken through a telephoto lens, then cropped and enlarged.

Ben tapped the photograph. "That's the reason why Bücher is in Vienna. The child is his only granddaughter. She's in her thirties now. He wants to see her before he dies, see her children if she has any, have a good cry. It's a sad story."

"Tell it."

Ben said, "Bücher had a wife and children. When he bugged out in '45, he left them in their quarters at Treblinka with no money and no place to live. When the precise nature of Bücher's service to the Reich came out, his family were shunned by decent folk, naturally. His wife, who made her way to Vienna, was disowned by her own family. For a couple of years after the war she had to work as a prostitute to feed and clothe the kids. There were three of them. One boy died of peritonitis while his mother was spending the night elsewhere, a second simply vanished. That left the youngest, a daughter, given name Renata. She hated her father, wouldn't communicate with him after her mother died, but Bücher kept tabs on her through old comrades. He even got hold of some pictures of her. That's her in the picture. The child is her daughter."

"He's in touch with this grandchild?"

"No. Never has been. But he knows she exists and he knows her Christian name, Gretchen. He doesn't know her married name, if she has one. He thinks she'll come to him if she knows he's in Vienna."

"Do we have the married name?"

"No," Ben said. "But neither does Bücher. He's put ads in all the papers. 'Former monster of Treblinka, true name on request, now dying of incurable cancer in Vienna hospital, seeks granddaughter Gretchen, child of Renata, for deathbed reunion. Please call this number.'"

He handed me a tiny scrap of newsprint clipped from yesterday's *Wiener Zeitung.* If you read between the lines, the actual message was not so very different from Ben's burlesque version.

I said, "He thinks she'll see this and respond?"

"I doubt it. I think he's looking for publicity. Bücher hopes a city editor will see it and send a reporter to interview him. If he gets a story with pictures, including that one"—he pointed to the photo in my hand—"she'll see that. And magically appear."

"So she can have *her* picture in the paper and ruin her life and the lives of her children if she has any?"

"We're not dealing with a man who has a great track record as a realist," Ben said. "But it gives us an opportunity."

I had already had the thought I knew Ben was about to express. Nevertheless I gave him an encouraging look. Opportunities to be of a single mind with Ben Childress were few and far between.

"If we can find her and persuade her to visit her grandfather," Ben said, "we can maybe listen in on the conversation."

"You mean, wire her?"

"Something like that. Give her some questions to ask, at least."

"You think she'd let herself be used by a couple of evil Americans?"

"Do you have a better idea?"

Actually, I did—Zarah would impersonate Gretchen. I told Ben what I had in mind. It would be an exaggeration to say that admiration dawned in his eyes, but I believe I can say without false pride that I surprised him. Pleasantly? That's another matter.

Ben said, "This is Paul Christopher's daughter we're talking about?"

"That's right."

"The one David Patchen and her father almost got killed?"

"I don't think her father had much to do with that."

"She's in Vienna, she speaks German well enough to carry it off, she's willing to do this?"

"She arrives tomorrow. The answer to your other questions is Yes."

"I can't wait to meet her," Ben said.

"It might be just as well to avoid that for the time being," I said. "Meanwhile, we'll get Charley to search the local archives for the granddaughter. Her identity shouldn't be too hard to pin down, inasmuch as we have Bücher's true name and her maiden name and the Austrians are great record keepers."

"So they are, bless them," said Ben.

12

In cheap eyeglasses and a wig streaked with gray and a shapeless dress from the Viennese equivalent of Good Will Industries, Zarah looked a bit like Donna Reed as the timid old-maid librarian in the out-of-body sequence in *It's a Wonderful Life*. Even so, she was all that Claus Bücher had ever dreamed of in a granddaughter and then some. When she identified herself as such, Bucher said, "You have a Berliner accent, Gretchen."

This was a reassuring moment. Charley Hornblower's Austrian friend had vetted Zarah's German from a tape recording and pronounced it out-of-date and too Prussian for his ear, but arguably native. Zarah merely smiled at Bücher's remark as if taking it for a compliment. It really wasn't necessary for her to say anything to Bücher. Despite the fact that he was well advanced into congestive heart failure and had barely enough breath left in his lungs to gasp out more than one or two words at a time, he did all the talking. This was the last role he would ever play after his long life of playacting. He was not interested in the details of his granddaughter's life. He was here to tell her his own life story so that she and her children would remember him as the dashing Black Pimpernel that he had been.

Bücher told Zarah how heartbreaking it had been to part from her grandmother and the children in the chaos of the German surrender. However, he was required by his conscience to continue to do his duty to the Reich. His Schutzstaffel oath was an oath for life, so he had no choice. One wondered, Zarah said later, how a real Austrian granddaughter would have reacted to that particular sentiment. Bücher could not tell her all that he had done—it was better that she did not know—but the work to which he had devoted his life had been done for her sake and for the sake of her children. By the way, how many children did she have?

"None," said Zarah sadly. She and her husband Horst Zechmann, a wonderful man, simply had been unable to have any.

And what did Horst do?

"He's a chef."

A *chef*? His granddaughter—the flesh and blood of a German officer and medical doctor educated in Vienna—was married to a cook and was actually trying to produce a child by this *Untermensch*?

Zarah, reading the outrage in his eyes, said, "Last year Horst won the competition for best Black Forest cake for the entire Austrian association of small hotels."

Bücher responded to this prideful statement with what sounded on tape like the collapse of a lung.

Zarah's little joke about the Black Forest cake nearly cost us the farm. Bücher clearly wondered—you could hear it in the condescension in his voice—if this déclassé drab was worthy of knowing the great things he had accomplished during a life of solitary sacrifice. At last he decided that she was—or at any rate realized that he had no one else to tell if he did not tell her. So Bücher went on. This was a painful process because of his breathing problem, which seemed to worsen by the moment. From time to time he coughed spasmodically. Heaven knows what it cost Zarah psychologically merely to listen to him, given her own family history vis-à-vis the Nazis. But she played the nurse, giving Bücher sips of water, wiping phlegm from his lips with Kleenex.

He said, "When I returned from the front"—apparently that's where he thought he had been when he was performing his experiments in Treblinka—"and saw the wanton damage the British and the Americans had inflicted on German cities and the poor German people, I knew I could never rest until those who had committed these crimes against our people and our culture themselves felt the pain and the loss and the sorrow that we had felt."

He had wandered the world, Bücher said, living in secret, doing his duty, but always looking forward to the day when things were once again what they used to be. Never for a moment had he ever doubted that this would happen. His granddaughter should not doubt it, either. And because they would never meet again, and because in his mind his children and their children had always been messengers to this wonderful future that he had tried all his life to achieve for them, he was going to tell her some marvelous news.

His wheezing, stoked by emotion, grew worse with every word.

"I have taught you by the example of my life the power of an oath," Bücher told her. "Now you must swear to me that you will never tell the secret I am about to tell you."

Zarah nodded. This was not enough.

"Put your hand on my heart and swear," Bücher said.

Zarah did this. Again I cannot imagine how she overcame her own blood memories and actually touched this man, but somehow she did.

"Good," Bücher said. "Now listen. There is a man, an Arab, a sort of king, who is the enemy of our enemies. Fate works in marvelous ways. I could never have imagined that this hook-nosed old man, bearded and circumcised and looking so amazingly like . . ."

Here Zarah's stomach warned her not to let him go on. She said, "Save your strength. Who is this man?"

"I cannot tell even you his name, but you will soon know it. Our worst enemy, America, destroyer of the old Germany, thinks that its assassins killed him years ago. But they are wrong. This man lives. Only last week he embraced me and thanked me and said good-bye to me. We both knew we would never meet again. Nor will you and I, my dear. For years I have lived with this man. I saved his life after he was wounded by an American assassin. I have taken care of him ever since, because he has a great plan and the means of carrying it out."

Zarah waited in silence for the rest.

"Soon he will come back to life—that's what the Americans will think—and do to vulgar ugly American cities what American bombers did to our beautiful ancient German cities. New York will burn like Hamburg. San Francisco will be pulverized like Dresden. Washington will be turned to ashes."

Zarah said, "This Arab has nuclear weapons?"

"Many, many, many," said Bücher. "Hidden in the desert. No one will ever find him."

"Which desert?"

Bücher actually answered her with what sounded like a name. But the name, if that's what it was, was wrapped up in such a paroxysm of coughing that the rest of us could not understand it, no matter how often we listened to the tape, no matter how Charley's wizards tried to enhance it.

It really was his last word. We could not trick him into repeating it because he sank into a coma immediately after speaking it. It took him almost a week to die, but during that time he never regained consciousness. The nurses said he did not know he was suffering, that mentally he was elsewhere, in some place where the dying often went.

One wondered where that might be, in Claus Bücher's case.

SEVEN

1

After her interview with Bücher, Zarah passed the tape recording she had made to Charley Hornblower, who bumped into her by prearrangement in a hospital corridor. She then went straight to the railroad station and took a train to Istanbul. When Charley and Ben and I got to Istanbul a few days later—we waited in Vienna until Bücher died and then traveled separately—we could not find Zarah. She was not registered at the Hilton as expected. According to the front-desk clerk, she had no reservation. This was alarming. We had not actually seen her board the train, nor had she telephoned or communicated in any other way.

Had she been snatched by the same pack of nitwits who were bloodhounding me—or, worse, fallen into the clutches of some Schutzstaffel equivalent of the Old Boys? Claus Bücher must have had money squirreled away somewhere. According to Charley Hornblower's information and my own impressions of the threadbare Simon Hawk, Bücher's old apparatus was starved for funds. Zarah had gone to the station in her Gretchen Zechmann disguise. Had Bücher's old comrades assumed that she was the real heiress? Were they at this moment shining a blinding light into her eyes and asking her where her grandfather's money was?

Ben Childress thought that my imagination was running amok.

"Get a grip on yourself," he said. "She may have gotten off the train somewhere. Did you say exactly when we'd be in Istanbul?"

"No."

"Then why would she hurry?"

"Why would she get off the train?"

Ben gazed down from Olympus and said, "The train to Istanbul goes through Prague and Budapest, doesn't it?"

Of course it did, and Zarah may well have gotten off to do some genealogical research on her own. Everything Ben said made sense. Making sense was his specialty. Nevertheless I had never in my life felt more anxiety than I felt now, gazing out the window over the endless jumble of roofs under which Istanbul was hiding itself.

Courtesy of another classmate of Charley's, this one the heir to a Turkish chewing gum fortune, we were staying in a waterfront villa on an island in the Bosporus. We were being circumspect, of course—everyone arriving from a different point of the compass, no more than one of us outside the house at any one time and then only after dark, no telephoning, no faces in the windows, no loud music. Because our makeshift safe house was a summer place and it was now midwinter, the house was empty of servants. However, it came with a full larder and an unlocked wine cellar stocked with quite drinkable Turkish reds and whites and sparkling rosés. There was nothing to do but wait and sort through what we knew and talk about what might be next. We really had no idea. Pieces of the puzzle were missing. We had had our little successes but we didn't know which way to go. We spent a lot of time listening to the tape of Bücher's last conversation with Zarah. There were words we did not understand, references that baffled us.

"Does it mean *anything*?" Ben asked.

"This thing is not coming together the way it should," Jack said.

What we really needed was a stroke of luck. All operations get to a point where nothing makes sense. Then one small isolated fact falls in your lap and the whole thing comes together. As Harley might say, this always happens, except when it doesn't.

We were increasingly anxious about Zarah, Jack especially. He spoke Turkish and he had bought a cell phone in Istanbul. He used this, walking a long distance from the villa before switching on, to call the Hilton and check up on Zarah. At the end of the third day—that is to say, the eighth day since she left Vienna—there was no word. Even Ben began to look preoccupied.

On the fourth night, late, I was watching a Turkish-language version of *Bonanza* when I heard the doorbell ring. Ben, who was supposed to be asleep, beat me to the door. Zarah walked in. She wore jeans and sneakers and a black leather trench coat. Her hair was tucked under a knit cap that looked like the Roaring Twenties cloche my mother wore in family snapshots. All in all, this was a far more fetching costume than the one she had worn as Gretchen. I suppose I should have felt like kissing her, but no such thought crossed my mind. I settled for what I hoped was a warm smile but may have been more like a grimace of pain, judging by the puzzled look in Zarah's eye.

I said, "Hi, there. Good trip?"

"Interesting," Zarah said. "I stopped in Prague and Budapest You haven't been worried, I hope?"

"A little impatient, maybe."

Ben said, "Before I go back to bed, may I ask a question? How did you find this place?"

"Horace mentioned the name of this island in case we missed contact," Zarah said. "I went down to the waterfront and asked a boatman if three Americans your age had hired a water taxi lately. He said, 'Is one of them very tall?' I said yes, and he brought me over to the island. After we landed, he asked a question or two of other boatmen and gave me directions to this house."

"Wonderful," Ben said. "Good night, my dear."

2

The next morning, Zarah appeared at breakfast at six-thirty, looking as though she had slept for eight hours instead of the three or four she had actually spent in bed. I cooked a mushroom omelet with yogurt beaten into the eggs. Charley had found an electric coffeemaker and a pound of Maxwell House. Ben, who preferred Arab coffee, sipped this mild brew as if his tripes were being dissolved in battery acid. Before the dishes were cleared, Ben produced a Walkman into which was loaded the tape of Zarah's conversation with Claus Bücher.

"This is you and Bücher," he said to Zarah. "He speaks a word at the very end that none of us can quite make out. Maybe you can, since you were there."

Zarah put on the headphones and listened. The expression on her face was perfectly neutral. She rewound the end of the tape once or twice, listening to the mystery word.

Finally she said, "He's speaking Arabic, or thinks he is. At the time, I thought the word was *houbara*. Now I'm sure of it. He's swallowing the final syllable, but maybe that's the way the Arabs he knows pronounce it."

"Houbara is an Arabic word?" Charley said.

"It's a bird," Zarah said. "The houbara bustard. I had just

asked him where Ibn Awad or the bombs could be found and he was answering my question."

"With the name of a bird?" Ben said. "What is it, a code name?"

"I don't think so," Zarah said. "The houbara bustard is the bird of birds if you're a falconer."

Ben already knew this, obviously.

"There are still falconers in the world?" Charley asked.

"Lots of them," Zarah said. "Rich Arabs will travel hundreds of miles to hunt the houbara bustard with falcons. They do it partly for the thrill of the thing, but also because they believe this bird is an aphrodisiac. They eat them by the hundreds in season."

"Flying Viagra," Charley said. "Wow. Any truth in that belief?"

"You'd have to ask the man who ate one," Zarah said.

Ben was annoyed by this badinage. This was no light moment. He was processing new information. I too was deeply interested.

Charley said, "Where is this bird hunted?"

"Any number of places, but always in the desert," Zarah said. "It breeds in Central Asia and western China in summer, then migrates to Africa. During the later winter it flies north again. There's a big hunt in Balochistan every January."

"So where are the bustards now?" I asked.

"After Balochistan they continue on to Central Asia and beyond," Zarah said. "Turkmenistan, northern Iran, western Afghanistan. After that, Kazakhstan, Tajikistan, Xinjiang, Mongolia. They don't all start from the same place or at exactly the same time, so they don't all arrive at the same time."

"What's the time spread?" Ben asked.

"I don't know exactly."

Ben was visibly disappointed by this gap in Zarah's knowledge. So were the rest of us. We all understood what this information might mean, if it turned out to mean anything.

Ben said, "Zarah, how do you happen to have all this lore at your fingertips?"

"I knew people who hunted the houbara bustard with falcons in Morocco," she said. "They were fixated on the houbara. That's why I thought I understood the Arabic word Bücher was using."

I said, "So where do we go from here?"

Zarah said, "The key is the exact migratory pattern of the houbara."

"Why is that the key?"

"Because Ibn Awad is a very rich Arab and you told me, Horace, that he was a keen falconer when you knew him."

Charley said, "I thought he was an ascetic."

"Once a falconer, always a falconer," Zarah said. "If that's true in Ibn Awad's case, he will hunt the houbara bustard, maybe in several different desert places along their migratory route. Pinpoint those places and the time of arrival of the houbara and plot them on a map and you'll know where to look for Ibn Awad."

Ben said, "Brilliant work, Zarah."

And so it was—a breakthrough. I said, "Charley?"

"I'll get right on it," Charley said.

"How long will it take to draw a map?"

"Not long if all goes well. I know a bird man at the Smithsonian. We can use Landsat images."

Ben nodded. This meant Charley would have to go back to Washington, a happy turn of events from Ben's point of view. His thoughts were like slides projected clickety-click on a screen: Let Charley do the donkey work. I'll do the thinking.

Ben said, "Zarah, will you be working with us?"

"From a distance," she said. "I'm planning a little trip."

A little trip?

Where to? Not, I was sure, to the faubourg Saint-Honoré for a shopping spree. In my bones I knew the destination would not be a safe and civilized one even if such a place existed in the chainsaw-massacre movie that was the world in the twenty-first century.

Any plan I may have had to discuss Zarah's itinerary with her in private went aglimmering because Ben decided that the lazy minutes after breakfast provided a good opportunity to test her Arabic. They sat at the table, conversing in that tongue, while Charley and I did the dishes. For me, who had not lived with the language for years, this was something like watching a film in Arabic without subtitles. At first I understood almost nothing. After ten minutes I was catching about half. Another ten minutes and I half understood nearly everything but the slang and the jokes. Both Ben and Zarah were too much at home in Arabic for me ever to understand everything they said. Had they wished to do so, they could have shifted into another gear and left me behind completely.

Ben was impressed. He treated Zarah as if she were a promising young man he was sizing up for recruitment. Given his reputation with women—I admit I had been reluctant to introduce him to my lovely young cousin—this was something to behold. Suddenly he was gender-neutral. It was not Zarah's looks but her brain that enthralled him.

Ben's conversation with Zarah was an interrogation, of course. "Where exactly in the Maghreb did you grow up?" he was asking Zarah when I finally plugged in.

"In the Idáren Dráren," Zarah said.

"That's the Berber name for the Atlas Mountains?"

It was Zarah's turn to be impressed. Not many people knew that.

"That's right," she said.

"You speak Berber?" Ben asked.

"We lived with Berbers."

"Which tribe?"

"The Jawabi."

"Ah, Joab's people. The hidden Jews. Are they still pretending to be Muslims?"

"If that's what they're doing it's kept them alive for twelve hundred years."

"You spent your childhood with the Jawabi and you don't *know* whether they're faking it?"

"Religious questions have never interested me," Zarah said.

It was clear even to Ben that this was the only answer he was going to get. In a sense, this pleased him. Zarah certainly knew the answer to the question, but she could keep a secret. She had a sense of duty to others who knew the same secret. Good signs. You could see Ben putting a mental checkmark beside "loyalty."

Ben said, "Do I have the basics correct? The Jawabi believe that they left Israel under the command of King David's great general, Joab, and after wandering all the way across Egypt and the Sahara, ended up in the mountains of the Maghreb?"

"In the highest place in the world, yes."

"There were a number of tribes of Jewish Berbers," Ben said. "All converted when the Arabs conquered the Maghreb except the Jawabi, yes?"

"Berbers have their own way of being Muslims," Zarah said.

"Like eating wild boar and drinking alcohol and not fasting for Ramadan and not being too fussy about ablutions?"

"All of the above," Zarah said. "However, the Jawabi go to the mosque and pray five times a day like everybody else."

"Yes, and the Maranos in Spain went to mass like everybody else after they were converted to Catholicism by the sword, but continued for generations to worship in secret as Jews."

No reply. Not even a change of expression.

Ben soon understood what was going on and to my amazement, apologized. "I'm sorry," he said. "But the world you lived in is the one I've always wanted to experience."

Zarah said, "You speak Arabic like a man who grew up with Arabs."

"I've lived with Arabs, but I grew up in Williamstown, Massachusetts. Where were you born, may I ask?"

Ben was back in all-wheel drive. By the look in her eyes I could see that Zarah understood this and knew that the only way to escape Ben's questions was to answer the ones it was convenient to answer and feign deafness to all the others.

Patiently, Zarah said, "I was born in a cave in the Idáren Dráren when my mother was on her way to live with the Jawabi."

"She'd been invited?"

"She was traveling with a friend of my grandparents who was a Jawab. They met in Europe when Mother was pregnant and alone. The friend, whose name was Lla Kahina, more or less adopted her."

"Why?"

"Because she saw how unhappy and how out of love with life my mother was. And because Mother was carrying her friends' grandchild and Lla Kahina was afraid that the child would be lost to the Christophers. She thought they had already lost enough."

"This Jawabi woman told you all this?"

"After I was grown up and my mother died, yes."

"Died how?"

"She was killed by terrorists. She camped by mistake near one of their training camps. Mother was a horsewoman. She liked to race ostriches on horseback. An ostrich is much faster than any horse and can go on at top speed for hours instead of minutes for the horse. The race was hopeless. That's what Mother liked about it."

"Is that why you dislike terrorists?"

This took my breath away. Didn't he *know*? An elastic moment of silence ensued.

"It depends on the terrorist," Zarah said at last, letting go of her end of the invisible rubber band. "And now, if you'll excuse me, I have to pack."

Ben practically exploded with disappointment. He was in a state of excitement. Zarah knew things that he had always hoped to know. And now would never know even if they met again, because she had made it clear that their conversation was over forever. Zarah was perfectly still, as if under Ben's onslaught she had turned herself into an oil portrait of herself—beautifully lighted by the golden sun of Asia Minor, perfectly attentive and frank of gaze. But silent, inert.

3

I tapped on the door of Zarah's room.

Without opening the door—I suppose she had heard my tread in the hallway—she said, "Come in, Horace."

She was standing in front of the mirror, combing her hair. She had changed into a soft wool sweater and a gray pleated skirt. A blue blazer lay on the bed beside her traveling bag, which was hardly larger than a briefcase.

"Did you have that outfit packed in that little bag?" I asked.

"Along with a couple of others," Zarah said. "I pack like a sailor, everything rolled up so it won't wrinkle."

"Who taught you that?"

"The Jawabi." She smiled at me in the mirror. "The Sahara is a sea of sand, no?"

I said, "Look, I apologize for Sherlock Holmes."

"No need," Zarah replied. "Ben would have made a terrific psychoanalyst, founder of the listen-here-young-lady school of therapy, asking questions instead of avoiding them. Quite refreshing in his way."

Her voice was light, but she kept her back to me. "Before you go, I want to thank you for all you've done," I said.

A Gioconda smile in the looking glass. She was winding

her hair into a coil and pinning it with a barrette. Another painting.

"Sorry to apologize twice in the same breath," I said, "but I had no idea that Claus Bücher was going to be as bad as he turned out to be."

"Don't worry. It wasn't much of a surprise to me. I'd heard a lot about Heydrich from Lla Kahina. Same species."

"I really appreciate your work in Vienna," I said. "And now you seem to have solved the problem of finding Ibn Awad."

"You think so?"

"It's the first time we've had a pattern to work from."

"It's just a hunch," Zarah said. "Even if it's correct, we'll be dealing with an awful lot of territory. Half of Asia, half of Africa, most of the biggest deserts in the world."

I said, "Your point being . . . ?"

"The hypothesis could be wrong, a wild guess."

I didn't think so. For most of my conscious life I had watched her father have what might be called memories of the future. Feathered dinosaurs were the least of it. Why should Zarah, who was so much like her father, be different?

Zarah, coat on, bag in hand, hair covered by a scarf, ready to go now, watched me as though my thoughts were visible to her.

I said, "May I know where you're going?"

"Kyrgyzstan."

"Why?" I said, flustered.

Zarah did not have an automatic American-girl smile. She looked gravely into my eyes and said, "There are things I want to know, questions I have to ask."

"What things, what questions?"

"I'm not sure."

"Ah. Well, keep in touch."

"You can count on it."

Her room had French doors that opened onto a winter-brown garden. Beyond the garden lay Istanbul with its domes and minarets washed by watery morning light. She walked through the doors and down the steps, a straight-backed young woman in a blue blazer, and as far as I knew, all alone in the world. And on her way to Kyrgyzstan.

4

Zarah had given us a new direction. Ben Childress left on the morning plane for Cairo, Charley Hornblower on the afternoon flight for New York. They had work to do. I had run out of things to do next and had nowhere to go unless I wanted to hang my birding binoculars around my neck and start walking toward Xinjiang, looking for the houbara bustard. As happens in life, especially in a life devoted to trying to catch slippery trout with your bare hands, I had come to an impasse. Thanks to weeks of methodical labor by the Old Boys and brilliant thinking by Zarah, I now knew far more than I had any right to know about the targets I had set out to acquire. But I did not yet know enough and I could not proceed further until I knew more. It seemed a good moment to read Zarah's retranslation of the Amphora Scroll.

Bright sunshine notwithstanding, it was too cold to read in the garden, even if there hadn't been sound reasons not to show myself outdoors in daylight. I put on a sweater, switched on the electric fire in the sitting room, made myself a cup of tea, and sat down with Zarah's typescript. She had printed it out on heavier paper than is usual. Several minutes passed—long enough for the tea to cool—while I stared at the thing as if it were still written in the Greek alphabet. When at last I steeled myself to begin, I found things to enjoy. It was uncanny how closely the voice of Septimus Arcanus, confiding and worldly, resembled the voices in the top secret cables and dispatches I had been reading for most of my adult life. Arcanus was a type I knew by heart—intelligent, truthful to a nicety, diligent, and infinitely condescending to the outlandish persons on whom he was reporting. It was no comfort whatsoever to remember that Simon Hawk had told me that he and Reinhard Heydrich had felt pretty much the same sense of kinship to this dead Roman. No doubt the similarity would have been even stronger had I been able to read the original in the author's Greek but, as Homer and the New Testament have taught the world, translations from the Greek are quite powerful enough. In any case, the manuscript soon made the world I lived in go away.

Septimus Arcanus began by describing a lazy slave being beaten in the street by his red-faced master.

"Puffs of dust sprang from the slave's filthy tunic with every blow of his owner's staff," he wrote. "These caused the master to sneeze but he went on with the beating anyway: Whack! *Ah-choo!* Whack! *Ah-choo!* It was hot in Jerusalem. As you know, dear Sejanus, Judea is a waterless country where the masses are caked with a lifetime accumulation of dirt and for the most part never feel water on their skins. Recently I watched a baptist at work dunking converts in a river. I am told that the baptized feel that their sins have been washed away, and no wonder. According to my information it was the specialty of a religious eccentric called Yohanan, a Hebrew name meaning 'Yahweh has been gracious'— Yahweh being the local god who, unlike Jove, feels no need for subsidiary gods and runs the world unassisted. I say *was* because Yohanan, who had attracted a considerable following among the unwashed by predicting that a messenger from Yahweh would soon arrive and supplant earthly rulers, got his head chopped off by Herod for his troubles."

It was the decapitation of Yohanan that awakened Septimus Arcanus to the operational potential of religious dissidents.

"I reasoned," he wrote, "that if a half-mad derelict like Yohanan could get under the skin of Herod to the point of being arrested and then beheaded merely for making prophecies about the imminent arrival from heaven of a messiah who was going to rule over the Jews, then zealotry was an asset worth looking into. These are primitive people, driven by superstition, who had lived so long in fear of their angry absentee god that they trembled at the smallest sign that he might be coming back to visit another of his catastrophic punishments upon them. "

All of the above and everything that follows, I wish to emphasize, represent Septimus Arcanus's interpretation of what Christians know as the stories of John the Baptist and Jesus of Nazareth. At the time, of course, there was no such thing as a Christian. Jesus was attempting to perfect Judaism, not found a new religion, and until the eminently practical apostle Paul pointed out that the movement would attract few converts if gentiles were required to observe the bewildering requirements of Hebraic religious law, all followers of Jesus were intensely observant Jews. Since reading Septimus Arcanus's report I have refreshed my memory of the Gospels, and I have inserted references to chapter and verse that seem to resemble his version. Often the similarities are striking. For example, according to Acts of the Apostles 1:15, a total of 120 believers in the Resurrection existed in Judea soon after the crucifixion. This accords more or less with the information available to Septimus Arcanus, who lists by name 123 believers in the immortality of the late Joshua ben Joseph. The names included eleven of the original disciples or "bodyguards," as Arcanus persisted in calling them.

In the beginning, as described in Arcanus's report and in the gospels, the priests were suspected by the Romans of encouraging the evasion of Roman taxes. Because the whole point of having an empire is to milk it for taxes, this was deeply upsetting to Rome. What if this madness spread to Egypt or even beyond?

"I called upon the services of an agent, already in place, who specializes in keeping an eye on religious agitators," Septimus Arcanus wrote. "This man, a Pharisee who lived in Tarsus, was a Roman citizen, quite picturesquely called Gaius Julius Paulus. I instructed Paulus to find the most outrageously radical preacher then at large and surround him with bodyguards so that he could travel about the country attacking the priesthood as heretics. The objective was to disrupt the priests' anti-tax campaign by challenging their theology. This must be done rudely, openly, even blasphemously. Doing violence to a few priests was an option to consider. If Paulus's man could put in a good word about Roman taxation now and then, so much the better.

"The most important point was this: This preacher, whoever he turned out to be, must never know that he was working for the Romans. Nor should his bodyguards be aware of this. It was essential that he and they believe absolutely in their own authenticity. This meant that one Roman agent—but not more than one—must be infiltrated into the group as a handler. This man would provide the preacher and his retinue with money for food and lodging and alms for the poor. I authorized the expenditure of two hundred pieces of silver for these purposes. Our man would also, of course, report on the doings of the group to Gaius Julius Paulus, and Paulus in turn would report to me. Strict secrecy was essential. No one else in Judea or anywhere else, not even the governor, was to be told anything about the operation. With the fate of Yohanan in mind, I supposed that this endeavor would end with the death of the preacher. Best not to kill any of the others, I thought, because this would rob the central figure of drama. What was needed was a martyr, not a gang of ruffians who got their just deserts for thumbing their noses at Yahweh's priests."

As all chiefs of station should be, Arcanus was well-versed in the local languages, politics and ethnology. He spoke Aramaic and read Hebrew. He knew all the Israelite tribes, and provided

Sejanus with a brief tutorial: "Gaius Julius Paulus, for example, is a member of the tribe of Benjamin, to which King Saul belonged, and which was renowned for its fierce warriors. Its slingers had the remarkable ability to twirl two slings at the same time, one with each hand, thus doubling the number of stones catapulted on the enemy."

In the overt portion of his life Paulus was a teacher of religious law who had studied philosophy at the renowned university at Tarsus. He came from a well-to-do family and was trustworthy in the first place because he was not only a Roman citizen himself but also the son of a Roman citizen. Paradoxically, Paulus was trustworthy above all because he was a patriot. This did not surprise me. I have never known a political dissident who did not have a deep-seated need to describe their own treasonous thoughts and actions as patriotism. My own experience had taught me that this is true in all countries, including my own. Paulus's love of his people and religion constituted a solid-gold guarantee that he would serve Roman interests. By accepting Roman money and protection to overthrow a corrupt regime, he served the true interests of his people. His Roman citizenship was the door that Septimus Arcanus knocked upon, and Paulus opened it as duty required. But he had his own purposes and he was under no obligation to show the visitor through the whole house.

"After receiving his instructions, Paulus returned to Tarsus," Septimus Arcanus wrote. "Soon after that he requested a meeting. We met in Damascus, where the chance of either of us being recognized was smaller than in Tarsus or Jerusalem, in a Roman house. Paulus dressed in the toga of a Roman citizen and he has the manners of a Roman when he chooses to have them. Paulus observes Roman social amenities with an impatience that would amuse you, dear Sejanus. At heart, he is an ascetic who has little taste for wine and none for Roman food, which is against his religion. We had hardly wet our lips when he burst out with his news. There was no need to invent the preacher we were looking for. The man already existed. He was an Amharetz, one of the common people of Galilee, and so were the eleven followers who traveled with him. This preacher, Joshua ben Joseph by name, was an uneducated nobody. Unlike Yohanan, he had no great speaking voice. So far this had not been a handicap because he had drawn very small crowds, almost all of them Galileans. However, he was by far the most reckless preacher Paulus or anyone else had ever heard. He attacked the Pharisees, who are the learned priestly authorities on Hebraic law and tradition including such fascinating questions as Judgment Day, the resurrection of the body, and the coming of the messiah. Joshua used blunt, not to say blasphemous language. His fundamental message was profoundly subversive: the priests misunderstood Yahweh's law and his intentions. So far, this message had not struck sparks into the tinder of the rabble. But in Paulus's judgment, Joshua was going to develop, with or without Roman help, into a thorn in the side of the priesthood."

Paulus was authorized to infiltrate Joshua's entourage. This was both easy and difficult—easy because Joshua and his followers were very poor, a band of beggars scrounging for pennies and food, difficult because they were all Galileans, many of them brothers or cousins or old friends. Theirs was the sort of cell that remained relatively secure even if penetrated because the brothers and cousins did not confide in members of the cell to whom they were not related. It was difficult to pin down their identities because Joshua had arbitrarily changed some of their names and others had changed their own, ostensibly as a sign that their lives had been changed by their master's message. (Arcanus, naturally, regarded these name changes as tradecraft). Status among the disciples derived from closeness to Joshua. Some were closer than others. Three brothers named James, Peter and John were the closest. Others, even most of the others, fell outside the circle of trust and friendship and hardly counted at all. They were sycophants and Joshua treated them as such, lecturing and scolding them. He told them over and over that they did not understand him or his message and probably never could. And then in the next breath he told them that they must carry on his work after he was gone. He was obsessed by the idea that he was going to be killed for speaking truth.

"In Julius Gaius Paulus's opinion," Septimus Arcanus wrote, "what Joshua needed were the usual items—money and information. These could only be provided by someone outside the circle who had reliable information about what the priests were planning, what the Romans were thinking and so on. None of Joshua's current disciples answered this description. Paulus recommended a man named Judas. He came from Kerioth, a wretched town lying east of the Dead Sea in Moab. His full name, Judas Iscariot, meant Judas of Kerioth. In addition to being likeable and presentable, Judas was described to me as highly intelligent, experienced, diligent to a fault, devoted to his work, and trustworthy as long as your ideas and objectives were exactly the same as his. This was Paulus's assessment. I understood from this description that Judas was another version of Paulus.

"Paulus understood that none of the Galileans would like or trust Judas. They would hate him and scheme against him and warn Joshua that he was not to be trusted. However, their enmity would be Judas's great advantage because it would give Joshua an independent adviser who owed everything to Joshua and nothing to the group—no brotherly affections or old loyalties applied. Also, Judas would finance the operation and this, too, would remain a secret between Joshua and Judas. If it stirred up more animosity, as sudden money usually did, so much the better. To Joshua this could only mean that Judas was useful to him and to nobody else."

Septimus Arcanus was impressed by Paulus's operational plan. Two thousand years later, so was I. A mind like Paulus's occurs perhaps once in a millennium, the Prophet Muhammad being the next case and Karl Marx the one after that. When one of these bent geniuses appears in the world and decides to reinvent salvation, woe to the status quo. We never understand them for what they really are before it's too late. Their cover, like Paulus's and the other two just named, is never blown—and even if it were, few would believe that they were not what they had claimed to be. What came next caused me to put the pages down for a moment and gaze out the windows at the sloshing dark waters of the Bosporus.

"Paulus suggested to me that it might be a good thing for Joshua to do a few signs," Septimus Arcanus wrote. "Wonders would swell the crowds and, besides, this sort of thing was expected of prophets. I asked what he meant by signs. Paulus said conjurers' tricks, such as turning a staff into a snake, or transforming one liquid into another, or curing a cripple or a leper or a blind man."

Septimus Arcanus approved Paulus's idea and duly recorded the miracles that followed. His sense of place and sequence of events was vague, probably because he was hearing about them by word of mouth whispered down a chain of cut-outs, but the events themselves are usually recognizable. In his version, the changing of water into wine at the wedding in Cana (John 2:1) was a simple matter of filling all but one of the water jugs with wine (better wine, Paulus grumped, than it was strictly necessary for Judas to buy with operational funds) while no one was looking. Judas bribed the servants, hired for the day, to tell the guests about the magical transformation and give Joshua the credit. Joshua got his startling information about the five ex-husbands of the Samaritan woman at the well of Jacob (John 4:15) from Judas, who had heard it from a village gossip. A blind beggar was cured when Joshua rubbed spittle in his eye and sent him to bathe in a pool whose name no one present recognized. He came back an hour or two later, but apparently as a different man who resembled, but did not seem actually to be, the original blind man. He was denounced as an impostor by some in the crowd and thrown out. But as usual in such matters, others believed in the cure (John 9:1). Lazarus (John 11:1) had awakened from a coma and Joshua just happened to be there when it happened. That Lazarus did not stink after three days in the tomb, as his own sister Mary warned Joshua he would, was proof enough to the literal-minded Paulus that Lazarus had never been dead in the first place.

"Now the amusing thing, dear Sejanus, is that this Joshua seemed to believe that he had actually performed the signs that Judas had set up by bribery and trickery," Septimus Arcanus wrote. "So did the other eleven disciples—or at least they pretended to believe. However, they were colder to Judas, and although they were eating better than before, accused him of stealing money from the group. Still, he stayed in character. He outraged them all after Lazarus's sister Mary rubbed a highly perfumed ointment on Joshua's feet and wiped it off with her hair [John 12:3] by asking why the ointment had not been sold and the money given to the poor. Joshua brushed the criticism aside by saying to him that the poor would always be with Judas and the others, but he would not because it was his fate to be slain by his enemies."

Arcanus was delighted with Paulus's report on Joshua's raid on the Temple. Kicking over the tables of money changers and sellers of birds and animals intended for sacrifice and driving them out of the Temple with a whip improvised from a piece of rope was exactly the sort of rowdyism he and Paulus had in mind. And Arcanus was beside himself with amusement on hearing about Joshua's answer to a man who asked if it was permissible for the pious to pay Roman taxes. The phrase about rendering to Caesar the things that are Caesar's is so familiar that I won't reshuffle the words by providing Arcanus's more vivid and quite possibly pepped-up rendition.

"Now strangely enough, Judas apparently had nothing to do with staging either of these events," Septimus Arcanus wrote. "This was hardly surprising, since even Judas never knew what Joshua might say or do next. For example, he had begun to say that those who believed in him would eat his flesh and drink his blood. This caused converts to leave him in disgust. His following, tiny to begin with, shrank. On at least one occasion a crowd threatened to stone him, but he hid and then escaped without harm. However, obscure and unpopular as Joshua remained, our plan was bearing fruit. The Pharisees were beginning to worry about him. I made sure that they worried by sending emissaries to inquire about Joshua and suggest that he was developing into a dangerous man. If the Pharisees let him go on, he might attract new believers and the Romans might have to get involved. Soldiers might even seize the Temple. The high priest of the year, a man named Caiaphas, called for his death. After this, Joshua and the disciples were convinced that the preacher truly was in danger of his life, just as he had foreseen. Judas was so worried that he persuaded Joshua to hide out for a while in the mountains at Ephraim, a city far removed from any other. Of course I instructed Paulus to countermanded this mistake as soon as I learned of it. Of what use was a preacher who did not preach?"

Along with a purse containing an additional fifty pieces of silver in case more money was needed, he sent word to Paulus to step up the pace—and if such a thing were imaginable, to encourage Joshua to be even more confrontational with the priests. On the downside, two worrisome things seemed to be happening. Judas was becoming fond of Joshua to the point where he often, even usually, chose Joshua's interests above those of the mission. This is by no means unusual. Handlers in intimate situations like Judas's often come to love the agent more than the operation. Emotional isolation has something to do with this. So does propinquity and the guilt of lying about everything to someone whose life is in your hands. Moral confusion is a problem when the handler is more intelligent than he strictly needs to be to handle the job. The Judas of the Amphora Scroll certainly seems to have had a high IQ.

"Through all of this," Septimus Arcanus wrote, "Joshua appeared to be distancing himself from Judas. In the midst of one of his lectures to the disciples he said, 'One among you is a devil.'

Such outbursts were frequent, but Joshua's words encouraged
Judas's enemies within the group. He became more and more isolated, he had less and less access to Joshua. This was because he
kept urging caution and recommending such measures as the period of hiding at Ephraim. Obviously we wanted no interference
with the fatal outcome. I ordered Paulus to remind Judas who he
was working for and what his real job was. Because Joshua's
crowds tended to be larger in Galilee, and because his disciples
believed that he was not safe in Judea, he spent most of his time
on home ground. Word of his signs had spread through the
province—he had recently predicted the dramatic recovery of a
dying child and then, on the sabbath, cured a sick man at
Bethesda. The sabbath cure and his growing tendency to suggest
that Yahweh was his actual father was shocking to his listeners.
The Galileans knew him as the son of Joseph the carpenter, one of
several brothers and a couple of sisters. How then could he be, as
he put it, the bread that had come down from heaven?"

Although the gospels speak of multitudes coming out to hear
Jesus speak, Septimus Arcanus insists that the crowds were small.
However, they grew in size in the wake of the miracles.

"You will be amused, dear Sejanus, to be told that Judas had
no explanation for some of these incidents. Joshua seemed truly
to be able to cure the sick, cast out demons and produce other
signs without Judas's help or anyone else's. Of course this was
nonsense. Either the people whom Joshua cured were malinger-
ers who feigned their illnesses or he had found some other way
of fooling the credulous. Neither Judas nor Paulus put any stock
in episodes in which the dead were brought to life. It wasn't
always possible to tell if a person who appeared to be dead really was dead. The Judeans have little or no medicine. Mistakes are
made. A good many people are buried alive. The local custom of
burying the dead before the next sunset added to the risk of having unconsciousness mistaken for death. That's why at their
funerals shrouded corpses were pelted with handfuls of dirt
before the grave was filled—to test whether they could be awak-

ened. The lucky ones sat up or cried out before the shoveling began."

Septimus Arcanus explains the miracle of the loaves and fishes as the work of a conjurer who had learned this elaborate trick from Egyptians. He suggests that he himself sent the conjurer out, since a trick of this magnitude required professional skills and hidden confederates and expensive props that Judas could not possibly organize without ripping gaping holes in his cover. Although the Scroll estimates the crowd at around 500, rather than the 5,000 mentioned in John 1:10, the enterprise was a huge success. Joshua, however, walked away from the feast while it was still in progress, leaving the disciples behind, and disappeared into the hills alone (John 6:15). Judas reported this as Joshua's disgusted reaction to the trickery. Even Joshua could not possibly believe, Judas told Paulus, that he was capable of turning five fishes and five loaves of barley bread into a hundred times that many. Judas warned that no more such surprises must ever be sprung on him.

"Joshua had not returned from the hills by nightfall," Septimus Arcanus wrote. "And now something happened that shook my confidence in Judas. Although a strong wind blew and night had fallen, the disciples decided, inexplicably, to get into a boat and row in pitch darkness across the Sea of Galilee in search of Joshua. Three or four miles from shore, the water turned very rough. They thought the boat was going to capsize. Then, up ahead in the stormy darkness, they saw Joshua walking toward them *on the water.* In Judas's account, he appeared and disappeared depending on whether he was standing on the phosphorescent crest of a wave or walking in a trough. The next thing the mesmerized disciples knew, their boat bumped ashore on the other side of the lake.

"Now this would be utterly unbelievable to a Roman or any civilized man, but all in that boat agreed that they had seen the same thing and that what they had seen was a miracle. Judas was no exception. He assured Paulus that what he had seen was real. I asked myself, Was there any such thing as a sensible native, no matter how much Roman education had been pounded into his thick skull? Could we believe anything Judas reported from now on? Could he even be trusted to carry out the simple tasks assigned to him, or was he so besotted by superstition that he was useless and needed to be replaced? Paulus advised patience: Judas was an intelligent boy who knew where his true interests lay. It was no easy thing to live a deception for weeks or months, to be continually under suspicion, to exist as an unwelcome stranger inside a group of men who despised him for the favors he did for them. Judas would wake up to his own foolishness sooner or later. Give him time and the benefit of the doubt. The charade would soon be over."

Septimus Arcanus agreed to do as Paulus advised. He had no choice, since Judas was irreplaceable, but he ordered Paulus to give Judas a stern talking to. Judas's reporting had become more and more emotional and spotty. He was deeply worried about Joshua. Passover was approaching. Joshua was planning to show himself in Jerusalem on this highest of holidays.

"He could not resist doing so," Septimus Arcanus wrote. "The priests had arranged for the preacher to be arrested on sight. Anyone who saw the wanted man must report this to the Temple at once. After Joshua's provocative entry into Jerusalem—a band of followers waving palm fronds greeted him at the city gate and he rode a donkey, the traditional mock-humble mount of a king coming to assume the throne of Judea—Judas was more concerned than ever that his friend was inviting arrest and death."

Judas appealed to Paulus for help in saving Joshua from himself. This was, of course, the last wish Septimus Arcanus was likely to grant. While Paul and Judas talked in a safe house in Jerusalem, Arcanus listened from the next room. Judas was emotional to the point of tears.

"It was obvious that this young man had changed so much that he could not be depended upon to help deliver Joshua for arrest unless he was tricked into doing so," Septimus Arcanus wrote. "Therefore, Judas was told that the only way to rescue Joshua was to deliver him up for arrest by the Romans. Once in Roman hands, he would be safe, because only the Romans could carry out an execution and Arcanus would make sure that there would be no execution. Interrogation by the high priest? Yes. A Roman trial? Yes. Imprisonment? Possibly, but it would be brief. But death? No. I myself gave Judas these necessary assurances, making sure that I was magnificently dressed and wearing the badges of my office. His gratitude, dear Sejanus, was profound. He kissed my hand and wetted it with his tears, an extraordinary gesture for a man of his religion. They are haughty, these penniless worshippers of Yahweh. As you can imagine, I was deeply moved as I looked downward on this sobbing fellow's unwashed hair in which I saw legions of tiny creatures on the march, and smelled the dusty rags he wore and the sweat he had carried in his armpits all the way from Galilee."

Septimus Arcanus omits a description of the Last Supper. A dinner party of nobodies talking nonsense in Aramaic would not have interested him. According to Arcanus, Judas confided the Roman plan to Joshua, who gave him no immediate answer. Later, however, in the presence of the other disciples, he gave Judas (or did not give him—Joshua was cryptic as usual) what the latter understood as instructions to go ahead and fetch the Romans to arrest him. "If you're going to do it, do it quickly," Joshua told him.

"Judas departed trustfully into the night," Septimus Arcanus wrote. "Quite soon he returned with the squad of Roman soldiers, together with some of the high priest's men, whom I had arranged to wait upon him. Although it was a cold night, Joshua awaited them in the garden. He showed no sign of surprise on seeing the soldiers and calmly identified himself to the officer in charge. He instructed his bodyguards not to interfere. Nevertheless, one hothead called Peter drew a sword and with a shout of rage tried to split the skull of one of the high priest's men, a fellow named Malchus. Fortunately he missed, cutting off Malchus's ear instead [John 18:10]. He then fled, along with most of the others. Joshua was arrested and led away."

For most of the remainder of the report, Septimus Arcanus

describes Pontius Pilate's outrage over having been put in the position of cleaning up after Arcanus and his agents.

"You know how small and bald and nearsighted our friend Pilate is, dear Sejanus," he wrote. "His questions were delivered in a shower of spittle. I answered as many as I could out of kindness but confided as few details as possible. Nevertheless, he understood that he had been left out of a secret plan. This took his breath away. He was suffocated by the insult. He commanded that the prisoner be brought into his presence, an extraordinary thing to do, and turned on him as if the poor fellow were Septimus Arcanus instead of the miserable ragged beggar that he was. Had he ridden a donkey into the city because he thought he was the king of Judea? 'If you say so,' the man replied with the utmost insolence. Joshua answered Pilate's questions with riddles and treated him with the contempt with which Pilate should have been treating him. Pilate's temper rose and rose. Finally he had the wretch whipped in hopes of teaching him manners and loosening his tongue. This had no effect. At one point the prisoner, still babbling what he obviously considered to be the most profound philosophy, said something about Truth. Pilate, glaring at me with red eyes, cried out, 'Truth? Truth? What is that?'

"After all this I had thought that nothing Pilate might do could surprise me, but right after this outburst he turned to me and said, 'This man is guilty of nothing.' As you may well imagine, dear Sejanus, I was taken aback. Of course he was guilty of nothing. *That was the whole point.* Was Pilate going to release the prisoner out of spite and ruin everything? I reminded Pilate of what was at stake and where my orders came from. He was too angry, too insulted, too humiliated to listen to reason. It was impossible to speak frankly to him in the presence of the prisoner even though the lash had left the wretched fellow half-dead.

"A crowd—next to nothing by Roman standards, but large enough to make noise—had gathered outside, awaiting Pilate's verdict. He said, 'Very well, we'll leave it up to them.' He meant the crowd! I could scarcely believe we were speaking in our own language. Before I could protest, Pilate seized Joshua by the arm (adding to this comedy, the soldiers who whipped Joshua had dressed him up as a king of clowns in a purple robe and jammed a crown of thorns on his head) and dragged him out onto the balcony. The crowd hooted at this comical sight, then hushed in anticipation of Pilate's words. These were not at all what they were expecting.

"'I find no case against this man,' Pilate bellowed. 'Shall I let him go?'

"What an enormous voice Pilate has for such a little fat fellow! His words silenced the crowd. They certainly silenced me as I stood behind him in the shadows, wondering whether it was better to push Joshua over the balcony or put him to the sword. The prisoner seemed to take no notice. He seemed to be quite indifferent to his fate. In fact he seemed to welcome it, but this is often the case with condemned men. He was, perhaps, in too much pain to understand or even hear what was happening. The crowd's silence lasted no more than a moment. Then a scream of protest rose from a thousand savage throats. Pilate stood his ground, repeating that the prisoner was innocent. He even offered to set him free as a holiday gift to the crowd. A gift! The only gift they wanted was this man's death, and the more painful it was, the better. Finally, with a mighty shrug worthy of an actor on the stage at Rome, Pilate gave them what they wanted. And then, dear Sejanus, he *called for a bowl of water and washed his hands of the whole matter in front of the crowd!* You can imagine my amazement. He might as well have washed his hands on the steps of the palace at Rome after touching the emperor. It was, I respectfully suggest to you, the grime of his wounded pride and his disgust with duty that he was attempting to wash away.

"And so that, dear Sejanus, is how the fates worked in this particular case. We Romans were commanded by the rabble to kill one of their own—a man the Roman procurator himself would have permitted to live out of hatred for me and for those in Rome who sent me to this place. However, we were saved from Pilate's folly by the very people we had deceived. The priests and their followers had demanded that we take them into our power. It was a pretty ending. Even Pilate will someday relish its irony. But not soon, dear Sejanus, not soon."

In a postscript, just a line or two, Arcanus records that Judas has disappeared and that he suspects that Paulus has arranged for him to go abroad, perhaps to Greece under a new identity, out of the reach of the vengeful bodyguards. Perhaps the two will meet again, Arcanus remarks. Paulus was not a man to let a good agent go to waste.

"As for the very loyal and useful Roman citizen Gaius Julius Paulus," Arcanus wrote, "he pursues and destroys Joshua's believers with the greatest zeal. I have told him that he must leave the eleven bodyguards in peace. This has given him a new idea. He wishes to see what he can do to turn Joshua's followers into a sect that might be useful to Rome. Obviously they are at loose ends and need an organizer. He wants to plant the idea that they must go into exile and make converts. Apparently Joshua suggested something of the sort during one of his tirades. I see little prospect of profit in this, for who could believe that a half-mad vagabond who let himself be killed by mere men was an immortal god in disguise? However, I see no danger in it either. Certainly it would be a good thing to maroon these louts on a Greek island. Perhaps they can write their memoirs. It would be useful, and amusing, to have a report of these events by people who actually believed their own eyes and ears. Therefore I intend to indulge the good Paulus. When next we meet in Damascus I shall give him a little money and my permission to go ahead with his plan."

As all who have read the ninth chapter of the Acts of the Apostles will remember, it was on the road to Damascus that Saul of Tarsus, the Roman citizen afterwards known as Paul the Apostle, was blinded by the radiance of a vision in the sky. A thunderous divine voice spoke to him. Soon afterward, his blindness cured by a miracle that caused the scales to fall from his eyes, he began preaching that Jesus Christ was the son of God. Surely Septimus Arcanus, who had so many reliable sources, knew about this. One wonders what he made of it. Not much, probably. By that stage in his career he must have been beyond surprise.

EIGHT

1

Suddenly, in the here and now, everything depended on the houbara bustard. How could this have been predicted? But then, how can anything be predicted? If Septimus Arcanus had recruited any other principal assets besides the unstoppable Gaius Julius Paulus and the schizophrenic Judas, would the Holy Roman Catholic Church be named after the empire instead of the triptych divinity it worships? Reading the Amphora Scroll had created a mood from which I was not sure I would ever escape. As if I were twenty again, existence seemed mysterious, events inexplicable, outcomes uncertain, meaning unknowable. Irony may be to life what gravity is to the universe, the invisible force that holds everything together and keeps everything apart.

On the spur of the moment (I really wanted to leave behind me, before dark if possible, the dank villa into which I had introduced the ghosts of Septimus Arcanus and his assets and targets), I decided to make myself useful by going to see Kalash el Khatar. I cannot account for this impulse, but I followed it. If hunting the houbara bustard was the favorite sport of the Prophet's descendants, Kalash must know something about it. Or about Ibn Awad's favorite hunting grounds. In any case it could do no harm to ask. I took a boat to the city and a taxi to the airport. Security was very tight—so tight that one of the black-jawed unsmiling Turks guarding the outer doors of the terminal took my satellite phone apart and handed it back to me in pieces. Among other inconveniences, this made it impossible to call any of the Old Boys and tell them what I was up to. I supposed that any attempt to put the phone together again while in the airport or aboard a plane would lead to my arrest on suspicion of building an infernal machine, so I stowed it in my pocket. I bought a phone card and used a pay phone to call the number Kalash had given me after our meeting in Paris. To my amazement, he answered his own satellite phone. The word *allô* rang like a coin tossed onto the pavement in front of a beggar who was expected to scramble for it.

In English I said, "This is Paul's cousin."

Silence.

I said, "I have something to discuss with you."

In French, Kalash said, "What could that be?"

"Are you in Paris?"

Kalash switched to English. "My phone says you're calling from Istanbul. Take a flight to Cairo. Call again after you're through customs."

He disconnected.

Cairo? I had had my heart set on Paris, on a *plateau de fruits de mer* and a bottle of Meursault, on French girls, on the light of the Impressionists, on thugs I knew, Kalash's men, rather than Egyptians I did not know. The last place I wanted to be was in a city full of crazed louts, every one of whom was licensed to kill Horace Hubbard.

At Cairo airport, the passport control officer, who wore a full Islamic beard, examined my blue U.S. passport as if it were the head of a pig that I had passed through the wicket with my left hand. However, he waved me through after spitting on his stamp and slamming it down on a fresh page. Customs paid no attention to me. Neither did anyone else as I stood against a wall outside the arrival hall and put my phone back together.

This time, I got Kalash's voice mail. I left a message. Two minutes later, my phone rang. In the earpiece, Kalash's voice said in English, "You are in Cairo?"

"Yes."

"Where?"

"At the airport."

"Go to the general aviation terminal. Ask for my pilot. His name is Captain Khaldun. Like the dead historian."

"How will I know him?"

"He'll know you. He will bring you to me. Do you have warm clothes in your kit?"

"Yes."

"Good. It's cold here at night and the women won't sleep with a heathen."

Click.

Captain Khaldun turned out to be a handsome fellow in his thirties, mute as a stone. We took off at dusk in a venerable Learjet and landed about three hours later at an airstrip in a desert. Kalash was right about the temperature. It was cold. A sickle moon hung in a velvety field of stars, so bright against the blackness that I began remembering the names of constellations I had learned in the planetarium at the Museum of Natural History. Captain Khaldun disappeared. I was all alone in the desert (but which desert?) with nothing to be seen except the stars and nothing to be heard except the piano-tuner ping of the jet's engines cooling in the frigid air.

A Greek sniper who hunted Turks when he was young told me that he always took a position downwind from the enemy when working at night. When a Turk urinated, as one almost always did sooner or later, he fired a whole clip of ammunition at the smell. He often got his man. It was a particular satisfaction, he said, to kill an enemy you hated while he held his most precious possession between his fingers and his thumb. I emptied my bladder. Urine drilling into the sand made quite a loud noise. Apart from the discordant music of the cooling engines, the silence was total, so any rifleman assigned to take me out would be able to put at least two of the five senses to work as aids to marksmanship. It seemed unlikely that Kalash, even if he had had a reason to kill me, would have gone to all the trouble of flying me to a mysterious destination in order to shoot me. It would have been far easier and more economical to rub me out at the airport. One more dead Yank. Killer unknown, motive obvious.

An edgy wind blew. I dug my parka out of my bag and put it on. It was more than I needed against the desert chill, but it was all I had. Outside the bright spot created by the Lear's parking lights, a vast noiseless pool of darkness stretched in all directions. I decided to take a little walk. I kept the Big Dipper over my left shoulder—not that I needed the stars as long as I did not lose sight of the airplane and the glowing bulbs on its tail and wingtips. There were shrubs and rocks in this desert. Walking in a straight line was difficult. After about ten minutes I turned around to orient myself with the Lear and saw nothing but darkness. Somebody had turned off the lights.

I sat down on a rock and searched the sky. There, by golly, was the Big Dipper, with the North Star off by itself just where a former second-class Scout would look for it. Since I had no idea where I was, this knowledge wasn't particularly useful. In the absence of a map I had no way of knowing where I'd end up if I steered by Polaris. I said aloud, "Nice going, Horace." I have been alone for most of my life—in half-empty houses smelling of absence after my parents divorced, in underheated snowbound schools where everybody else wanted to be a lawyer or a stockbroker, in a profession where no one was called by his true name, in Pennsylvania. I am in the habit of talking to myself. Even when not engaged in one-man conversations with him, I think of Horace as "he," a man apart whom I am watching, listening to, not quite understanding.

A voice said, "You will end up as hyena dung if you keep this up. Do you know what hyena dung looks like?"

It was the inimitable Kalash. I said, "Hyena dung? Not actually, no."

"It looks like pulverized crockery because hyenas chew up the bones and digest them."

It was not so dark as I had thought. There was enough light from moon and stars to make out my host, a very tall figure wearing Arab robes. The darkness in which I had imagined myself lost had been darkness only because there had been nothing to see.

Kalash said, "Why are you wandering about like this?"

"Enjoying the stars. They're very bright tonight."

"They're very bright every night in the desert unless there is a sandstorm. Follow me."

He turned around and strode off into the night as if walking up the Champs-Élysées with the Arc de Triomphe as his landmark. Now that my eyes had adjusted to starlight I found it possible to keep him in sight. I heard a noise behind me, looked over my shoulder, and saw two squat figures who looked like wrestlers dressed in windblown kaffiyehs and caftans. They carried AK-47s, unmistakable even in silhouette.

A couple of hundred meters away we came upon two Range Rovers, parked with their lights out. I must have walked right by them, or near enough. Another wrestler, Kalashnikov slung over his shoulder, held open the door of one of the vehicles for Kalash. I made a move as if to follow him. The two bodyguards behind me steered me to the other car. Except for the driver I was alone in the vehicle. Melancholy Arab music played—a contralto singing in heartbeat rhythm about how the airplanes of the Great Satan had killed her one true love in Afghanistan.

For the moment the use of hereditary titles was inconvenient in Sudan, but by all that is holy and eternal, Kalash was an emir. In the desert as in Paris, he lived like one. The tent into which I was shown after the drive from the airstrip was used for dining. Handsome carpets, heavy and thick, covered the sand floor. There were the usual big pillows and a long low dining table. Tapestries embroidered in gold thread with verses of the Koran hung from the eaves, stirring gently in the moving air. Hidden musicians tuned their instruments. Servants scurried about. One of them brought me a gin and tonic in a tea glass. Not my favorite drink, but I was glad to have it. Another offered me figs. I ate two, my first food since Istanbul. Behind the table, all in a row, a half dozen hooded peregrine falcons perched motionless on shoulder-high T-shaped perches inlaid with what looked like ivory and lapis lazuli.

After a half hour or so, Kalash entered. He had changed into camel's hair robes. A servant followed, carrying a large, hooded falcon—Kalash's favorite, I guessed—on his arm. Other servants marched in with five more falcons and placed them gently on the perches. When Kalash sank to a sitting position—a considerable sight to see in a white-bearded man dressed in flowing robes who could not have been less than six foot ten inches tall—the first handler took up station at Kalash's elbow, falcon on his forearm, every muscle frozen. I wondered how much the bird weighed.

I wondered, too, when Sir Cecil Hardwicke would enter, costumed as a British general in scarlet tunic and decorations, and convey the best wishes of the Queen Empress to the emir, who would smile like the original serpent at this eunuch who was in the service of a woman.

Kamal gazed with affection at the birds. "Do you know what these are?"

Yes, I knew. But even on short acquaintance I also knew how much Kamal liked to instruct, so I lifted the end of the word with a question mark when I said, "Falcons?"

"Peregrine falcons. They are used for hunting."

"What is the quarry?"

"Other birds," Kalash said. "Sometimes small animals. A peregrine falcon kills its prey by grasping it in its talons while flying at more than two hundred miles per hour."

"That must make the feathers fly."

"Yes. And the blood. A man from *National Geographic,* an excitable fellow named Wilbur something, took some photographs of kills."

"Do you still have them?"

"No. Pictures lie. The colors were wrong, like a cartoon, and a kill really doesn't look like that at all, frozen into a single instant, silent."

"What *does* it look like?"

"Like what it is, an epiphany. Many things happen in a split second but it can seem much longer if you know how to look at what is happening. The impact, the talons, the prey fighting back, trying to escape, not dying at once. Tomorrow you will see."

"I can't wait."

Kalash said, "My father hunted with eagles. An eagle can kill jackals, even antelope."

"Not hyenas?"

"The hyenas would eat the eagle, then probably the other hyena because it was bleeding from the eagle's talons. Once my father's eagle attacked an ostrich. The ostrich ran away with the eagle. The eagle held on like a jockey for miles, trying to kill this enormous thing, then finally let go and flew back to the wrist."

A servant arrived, holding aloft a huge platter on which an entire roast lamb was arranged. Other men followed with other platters of rice, vegetables, figs and dates, hot unleavened bread.

"As honored guest you're supposed to eat the eyes, brain, tongue and so on," Kalash said. "It's a great honor."

"No, thank you. Roasted sheep's eyes and half-cooked brains disgust me."

"Commendable honesty. Most kaffirs gobble them down to be polite. They are anxious not to insult the ancient customs of desert hospitality. They look like they're going to vomit at any moment. 'More, take more!' we say. And usually they do. It's a great joke among the servants."

While we ate the delicious greasy meal with our right hands only—more difficult for a kaffir than you might suppose—Kalash continued his lecture on falconry. All the falcons in the room responded to his voice only, Kalash said. Most falconers of his rank employed underlings actually to launch the birds, but Kalash's father had taught him that a man who did that was a mere spectator.

"He even launched eagles by himself?"

"Certainly. Of course he was larger than I and very strong. With a sharp sword he could cut a man in half with a single stroke. The bird is always held on the right arm. This strengthens it for the sword."

He was less imperious than he had been in Paris. I was content to listen. It's rare in my experience that a descendant of the Prophet says anything interesting in the interminable interval that it takes him to come to the point. During our lengthy friendship, Ibn Awad was rarely coherent and even more rarely came to the point. Of course his only subject was God's will, in which my interest is limited. Kalash, on the other hand, was teaching me a lot about a practical matter.

For training purposes, Kalash was explaining, only a fresh-caught wild falcon will do. It must be female because in all species of hawk the female is larger, stronger and fiercer but easier to dominate.

"She falls in love with her master," Kalash said. "That is the object of the training. You keep her in a dark room, always hooded, with a bell tied to her leg by a leather thong. The thong is tied to the perch. Of course the bird falls asleep. You go in and speak to her in the dark. She wakes up. She must hear no other voice but yours and you must always make the same sound."

"What sound?"

"I can't make it or all these falcons would fly. Each time you visit the falcon and wake it up you must speak to her and give her something to eat. Raw meat at first. Then a live mouse or a pigeon. You don't put it in the beak, you touch the bird's legs and feathers with it and let her lunge for it. You wear a thick glove for this. You must whistle, two short notes, while she swallows. In time she will connect the sound to feeding and will grip with her talons when she hears it. After this phase you can carry her about among people to accustom her to the sound of them, then do the same with the hood off so she will see what men look like from ground level. Wild birds do not know this. Falcons always see us from a great altitude, so they don't realize how big we are, even though their eyesight is eight times more powerful than ours."

He went on: Gradually the bird is accustomed to light and movement and is fed outside the dark room. She feeds in broad daylight while perched on the hunter's arm. More training follows. Eventually she flies, kills, abandons what she kills without eating it, which is against her nature. Then she comes back to the falconer's arm.

"The falcon does not tear and eat her victim because you have fed her before the hunt, so she is not hungry," Kalash said. "Now she is a pure killer, killing for pleasure only and always ready to kill again. Training a virgin is quite similar. In the case of the virgin, one uses chocolate and new clothes and perfume and sometimes jewels instead of raw meat and dead pigeons. But both things happen in the dark and the voice of the master is very important. Obedience creates desire and desire creates obedience."

Coffee was brought. Kalash drank it down, a thimbleful, then rose to his feet.

"Tomorrow we hunt," he said.

He strode from the tent. His exit was anything but unceremonious. His bodyguards, who had been standing behind the perched falcons, followed him out, Kalashnikovs at port arms. The music stopped in mid-chord as he stepped across the threshold into the dark.

2

I was not alone for long. A servant entered from outside and said something rude to me in Arabic. It never occurred to him that I understood. I did not enlighten him. Smiling now, he beckoned me to follow him. He led me to a small tent. It was decorated in the same way as the dining tent, but this time with a bed in the center. The covers were turned down, as in a hotel. I was more tired than I had thought. The flights, the heavy supper, the sheer effort of listening to Kalash's certitudes for the simple-minded, had worn me out. I undressed, washed my face in the bowl of water the servant had left, and got into bed. It was an extra-long bed. Kalash was the first host I'd ever had who was taller than me.

When I put my head on the pillow, something crackled. I looked underneath and found an aircraft map of Central Asia. I spread it out on the bed. It was a very large, detailed map. The area covered stretched from the Arabian peninsula to northern Iran and northern Afghanistan and beyond that to Turkmenistan, Kazakhstan, Uzbekistan, Tajikistan, Kyrgyzstan, Mongolia, and Xinjiang. This vast territory was essentially a patchwork of deserts. At various points on the map, airstrips had been drawn in by hand, with latitude and longitude and the length of the strip entered in a neat draftsman's hand.

I knew what the map meant. I thought I knew why it had been given to me. However, I wondered about the lengthy inventory of other possible motives. But not for long. I fell asleep as if drugged. Judging by my dreams, in which Mikhail assured me that absolutely no one was my friend and Kevin showed me Christopher in a box, perhaps I had been.

The stars were still out when I was awakened by the sulky servant who had put me to bed the night before. He brought tea and yogurt, flat bread and figs. I took the tea outside. Venus was large and bright among the fading constellations. Septimus Arcanus's sky must have been something like this, but (I had read this someplace) with a Venus the size of a lemon.

Suddenly Kalash's voice, close behind me, said, "Do you know the zodiac?"

"By heart."

"So did Christopher. A strange expertise for a man who didn't believe in fate. Do you believe in fate?"

"In luck, maybe."

"Luck is the fate of the unbeliever."

As we drove away with the windows open I heard a voice in the camp calling the faithful to prayers. Kalash paid no attention. The driver was in radio contact with someone who was telling him which way to go, where to turn. At our destination, a patch of desert that looked very much like the ground we had been driving over, we were greeted by a dozen of Kalash's men. Half of them were wrapped in blankets against the lingering night chill. The rest carried falcons on their right arms.

"This is a good place to find the houbara bustard," Kalash said. "Have you ever seen one?"

"Not even a picture of one."

"Even cameras cannot see them when they do not wish to be seen."

It was no longer dark but it was not yet light, either. The sun came up over the rim of the desert. Long rippling shadows formed. The falcons, all hooded, did not move. The human beings had already turned their backs to the sun to protect their eyes. From the first instant you could feel its heat through your clothes. Kalash walked away very fast, heedless of the rough footing. I was able to match him stride for stride. The others trotted to keep up. A few yards farther on, two lookouts in sand-colored clothes were sprawled on their stomachs in the sand. The men behind us stopped in their tracks in unison, as if in response to a silent command. Kalash sank to his knees. He crooked a finger to me and to one of the falconers, then crept toward the lookouts up ahead. We followed and reached the lookouts in moments. They made hand signals. It was quite strange to be in the company of four Arabs and not hear a word spoken.

Kalash's men were gazing intently at a bush about twenty yards to the front. At first I saw nothing. Then I remembered my birder's lore and looked for shadows in the horizontal light. I spotted a likely one and followed it back to a brown speckled bird about the size of a partridge but with a longer neck and longer legs and pointier beak. It was frozen in position, head thrust forward, one leg raised. Its camouflage was amazing. It looked like nothing living—like a divot gouged from the desert floor. Without the shadow as guide I might never have seen it, though I have spent many happy moments sorting birds out of foliage. I snorted in admiration.

Kalash did not see the houbara yet, but he knew by the noise I had just made that I did. He rose to his feet and took the falcon from its bearer, who removed its hood in the same motion as the one with which he passed the bird to Kalash. The lookouts also stood up and ran toward the houbara. It fled—not into the air but across the ground, moving at almost unbelievable speed for a two-legged animal. Outside of Road Runner cartoons, I had never seen a bird move so fast afoot. One of the lookouts fired a gun at it. He missed, then missed again. I realized that he was trying to make it fly rather than hit it. A third round kicked up dirt about two feet to the bird's left. At last the houbara took flight.

It flew like a woodcock, fast and close to the ground, zig-zagging around obstacles as if equipped with sonar. Another shot. The houbara climbed. The sun had been up for less than ten minutes but already the sky was an inverted bowl of indigo, utterly cloudless, fingernail moon still visible on the western horizon, pinprick Venus to the east. Even when climbing the houbara flew very fast. When it was between the horns of the moon from our perspective, Kalash gave a two-note whistle and released the falcon. It rose into the sky quicker than the houbara and in seconds was above it.

The falcon then dived, overcoming the resistance of the wind with its big wings. Kalash had been quite right. What was happening was beyond photography's power to capture or even suggest. The falcon fell, the houbara took desperate evasive action. The falcon drove its prey back toward Kalash, who had taken off his sunglasses and was gazing upward, his ebony face shining in rapture. The falcon, talons extended, hit the houbara bustard at speed that I would call blinding except that the opposite was true. At the moment of impact the many elements of the image fragmented. Talons gripped, the houbara twisted in agony, feathers exploded, blood spurted then separated into a spume of vermilion droplets. The falcon's beak struck, the houbara went limp. The falcon, gripping its prey in its talons, braked its fall with outspread wings.

The falcon dropped its prey several hundred meters to our front. All four of the servants ran toward the spot, human retrievers gone to collect the kill. Kalash waited calmly, arm outstretched, face lifted toward the circling falcon. He whistled. After what seemed a long time but was probably less than a minute, the falcon settled onto Kalash's arm. Its curved beak was bloody; so were the feathers on its breast. Kalash gave the bird a piece of meat and spoke to it in a kind of wordless baby talk. The bird's eye was exactly as Zarah had described it, without memory or mercy. If it remembered anything, I thought, it remembered its dinosaur ancestor doing to the houbara's ancestor what the two of them had just reenacted in a new world where everything was smaller but outcomes were the same.

Kalash said, "Did you see everything?"

"I doubt it. But enough."

"Enough?" He paused. "I'm glad to hear that because it's time for you to go. Captain Khaldun will fly you to Cairo."

"All right, thank you for letting me see this."

"Remember it and you will understand other things. You understand the map?"

"I think so. It shows the flight path of the houbara bustard's winter migration."

"You understood. Ibn Awad is an enthusiastic falconer—or did you perhaps already know that? He follows the houbara. It is his only pleasure."

Kalash looked at me for a long moment. "I can't help you more than this and still meet my cousin in paradise," he said.

If he was being sardonic I saw no sign of it. I held my tongue. Questions would have been useless even if I had any. As for expressions of gratitude, I supposed that thanking one descendant of the Prophet for betraying another is bad form. Bad Kismet, too, probably.

Kalash said, "Don't procrastinate. Ibn Awad is enjoying himself now, but when the houbara are home again, a short time from now, he will act."

The lookouts and the bodyguards approached, one of them holding the dead houbara at arm's length by the feet, the others grinning in celebration.

Kalash said, "Remember, he's an old man to whom you owe something for the inconvenience you have already caused him. No assassins this time. Fate will not permit an assassin to succeed. No bullets, no sword, no humiliation. A new Saint Helena's, but warmer, and with more intelligent guards."

He put on his sunglasses and handed off the falcon to its bearer. The lookouts were already far ahead of us, scouting for more houbara bustards.

3

"Assuming you were averaging three hundred fifty to four hundred miles an hour, that means that Kalash's camp was somewhere in the empty quadrant," Ben Childress said.

We were in Rome. The time had come for a meeting of all the Old Boys. Ben and I had arrived first and let ourselves into the apartment in the Campo dei Fiori that Charley Hornblower had rented through the Internet. The apartment was on the top floor. We had it for a week. Ben and I were drinking bottled Campari and soda on the tiny terrace. A troupe of acrobatic cats made its way across the face of our building, leaping from balcony to balcony. By craning the neck one could see the wonderful stretched dome of Michelangelo's St. Pancrazio. Traffic moaned all around us, making discreet conversation difficult.

Ben was extrapolating the location of Kalash's camp on the basis of the rough information I had compiled on the flight back to Cairo, when I placed my trusty compass in front of me on the tabletop. This told me that the Learjet was flying northeast. The flight took three hours and thirty-seven minutes from takeoff to touchdown. This was enough data to permit Ben to put his finger on his mental map of the Arab world.

I had no notion what or where the empty quadrant was, and

when Ben surprised me by not explaining his reference in detail, I said, "The empty what?"

"Quadrant," Ben replied. "The region where Sudan, Chad and Libya meet. You say there was vegetation?"

"Low bushes. And rocks."

"Hilly?"

"Somewhat."

"Northern Chad, most likely," Ben said. "Somewhere near the Aouzou Strip. Jef Jef el Kébir, maybe. That neighborhood, anyway. Nothing there, not even an oasis, for hundreds of miles. You were lucky that the natives were friendly. Mostly they're not."

He named a tribe of brigands, told anecdotes of robbery, rape and murder of wayfarers. Ben was pulling this esoterica out of his head as if flipping the pages of a guide book. There was no reason to think he didn't know what he was talking about. Ben had probably used Jef Jef el Kébir as a dead drop at some point in his career or recruited an agent who called it home. And of course he had always been a fellow who knew where every well in the Sahara was.

I said, "There was a well where we were camped, I believe."

"Really?"

It was plain to see that Ben doubted that, but he wasn't going to argue with a man who did not know what he was talking about. The truth was, Ben was miffed that Kalash had dropped Ibn Awad's itinerary into my lap. Ben himself had arrived with great news. With our money, though the young doctor did not know this, Mubarak had bought himself a GPS monitor. When I asked, Ben explained that GPS means Global Positioning System. On his most recent visit to Ibn Awad's encampment, the one during which he sent Claus Bücher on his way to Vienna, Mubarak's device had triangulated on U.S. space satellites and calculated his position on the surface of earth to within a few meters.

"And guess what?" Ben said. "He wasn't so very far from where you met Kalash."

"How far?"

"I'd have to have an exact fix on Kalash's camp, but Mubarak thinks he was in southern Libya. The distance between him and Kalash couldn't have been very much."

Kalash's map was spread out between us. I put my finger on the airstrip I thought was the one used by his Learjet. There was no other airstrip within hundreds of miles.

"Same airstrip, maybe," Ben said. "Mubarak was choppered north for half an hour or so after landing. You were near the airstrip?"

"Within fifteen minutes by Jeep."

"Maybe you were both guests of Ibn Awad," Ben said. "Wouldn't *that* be rich, if his falcon was catching a houbara bustard just over the next ridge at the very moment that Kalash's was doing its thing?"

"Priceless," I replied.

However, there was a catch. If Ibn Awad really had been nearby while I was visiting Kalash—and I had to admit the possibility that he was—why was I still alive?

Ben answered my question even though I had not spoken it aloud. "Maybe what Kalash's hospitality and the miraculous map really mean is that Kalash is a cat's-paw of Ibn Awad's and has been from the start. If so, chances are he's sending you in one direction while his illustrious cousin goes in another."

"Anything is possible," I said.

But I didn't believe it. It was almost impossible to imagine Kalash, the very model of egomania, playing cat's-paw to anyone. It's a great thing to have a devil's advocate on your team. That's why Ben was on ours. His stock in trade was the dark side of human nature. He was more interested in shadow than sunlight, he never trusted virtue, he had observed that people were never so happy as when they were betraying a trust. He had suborned too many men to betray other men in return for money and the illusion of friendship that he offered. Too many wives had taken off their clothes for him, then washed off his smell and fixed their hair and faces and stepped back into the boring matrimonial movie from which they had escaped for an afternoon while their costar, John Q. Cuckold, was playing his big scene at the office. On the other hand, Ben had his limits. A man who is good at taking advantage of situations—and this was Ben's forte—usually lacks the imagination to create situations that can be exploited. He must wait for opportunity to come to him.

I said, "Ben, I hear what you're saying to me. But we can't start over. We have to go in the direction in which we're headed. Everything we know, or think we know, pushes us that way. If I'm wrong I'm wrong."

Charley Hornblower was the first to join Childress and me in Rome. This raised the prospect of being locked up with two compulsive pedagogues, but I was glad to see Charley just the same. He brought good news about Harley, who was back on his feet and, according to Charley, entirely himself again. Perhaps even more so if such a thing were possible. He had more energy, less shortness of breath, better concentration since the implantation of his pacemaker. Needless to say Charley had lots to tell us besides this, but before he could begin his briefing, the bells of St. Pancrazio began to toll. The noise was so huge, coming in waves, that you felt that you might be able to reach out and take a handful of it. A yellow cat, frozen now with back arched, tail stiffened and teeth bared, shook its head and yowled back at the bells. It was several moments before any of us could hear again.

The houbara bustard's migration, Charley told us, had been tracked from space. Lightweight transmitters—miniaturized versions of Mubarak's GPS device—had been attached to individual birds. These broadcast to the three GPS satellites in stationary orbit six hundred miles above the Earth's surface. One bird, released in Abu Dhabi in February, flew 6,600 miles. It stopped in Iran, Turkmenistan, Kazakhstan and Uzbekistan before arriving in Xinjiang in April after fifty-four days en route. It traveled at an average speed of 18.64 miles an hour and covered an average of 787.92 miles between stops. Other birds had also been fitted with transmitters and released. This research established that there were two migratory flocks, one of which bred in western Kazakhstan, the other farther to the east.

We spread Kalash's map on the floor, got down on our hands and knees, and measured the distance between airstrips. The desert runways lay about eight hundred miles apart, corresponding roughly to the distance between stops by the migrating houbara bustards. "And look!" said Charley, drawing a path with his index finger. The landing strips staggered toward the east, along the flyway of the houbaras who were headed for Xinjiang and Mongolia.

"Bingo," he cried, rubbing his hands. "A perfect match."

Too perfect, Ben suggested in body language, though for once he held his tongue.

That afternoon, Jack Philindros and Harley Waters arrived. David Wong turned up an hour or so later, haggard after the long flight from Hong Kong. Without speaking a word, a wonder never before observed in the voluble David, he took a shower and fell into bed. While waiting for him to wake up I played gin rummy with Philindros. This was a dispiriting experience. Jack took cards as seriously as he took everything else. He showed no mercy, picking up good cards and sticking me with bad ones and whispering "Gin" like an automaton with a one-word vocabulary. This had nothing to do with luck. He simply skunked me. I ended up owing him more than two hundred dollars. The experience reminded me why I had never liked games.

By the time David woke up, it was after nine o'clock in the evening. This is no very late dinner hour on the Mediterranean. Rome was experiencing a false spring and this had its effect on all of us. In the overheated dusk, young people kissed and fondled by the fountains. Grown-up Romans were even nicer and more talkative than usual. The restaurants had put tables on the sidewalk. We set out for an evening on the town—walking separately, to be sure, but all headed for the same restaurant, a kind of ritzy catacomb. The walls were made of fragments of old columns.

Noseless marble faces peeked sideways or upside down out of the rubble. All were fakes, made of plaster. Had they been genuine, Charley said, he would have dated them to the first century B.C.

David loved Italian food. He ordered antipasto and a full plate of pasta, followed by a large steak and topped off by stewed pears and ricotta. This would have been a lot of food even for a man my size, but David had no trouble putting it all away. The restaurant had the high noise level that good restaurants often have, dishes clattering and everyone talking at once. David responded happily to this. Conviviality was important to him. Not a word about business was spoken during dinner.

Afterward we left separately. Finding the way back to the apartment was a challenge for me. In old neighborhoods, Roman streets are narrow and dark with imperceptible changes in direction that can lead you far out of your way. Everyone who understood the hidden logic behind their twists and turns is long since dead. Before very long I was lost. I didn't really mind. I liked the smell, the colors, the sound of this city. No matter how many times you had walked down a particular street, there was always some new detail to see—a window, a statue, a fountain. To get lost in Rome was to be civilized by its past. At last I emerged into a small piazza, cobbled and colonnaded and lit by floodlights that illuminated its prettiest features—a small church, a niche in which water flowed from the mouth of a stone fish into a scallop-shell basin. Outside a small restaurant a few late diners sat at sidewalk tables. A very old tenor, accompanied by a very young female guitarist, sang a quavering "Come le rose." I knew the tune and the name of the song because I had heard it many years before while dining outdoors in Rome with Paul and his first wife, Zarah's mother. Same tenor, maybe.

Behind me David's voice said, "*Americano, Lei?*"

I wish I could say that I knew all along that David was following me. But I didn't. True, I had been absorbed in the night and the city, but the fact is, I probably wouldn't have detected him even if I had been fully alert. Even when not in a crowd of other Chinese he had the knack of rendering himself invisible. He had been practicing all his life, but still, he was an alley cat.

David said, "I smell coffee. Let's find it."

We followed his nose. To my surprise the Pantheon was just around the corner—obviously I had been wandering about longer than I thought—and just down the street was a coffee bar. At this time of night, it was empty. David paid the sleepy cashier and amazed her by ordering a double espresso for me and a cappuccino for himself in pretty fair Romano. Evidently not many Ashkenazi-Chinese came in here speaking the local dialect.

David drank his cappuccino in one long swallow and then belched, as he had every reason to do, considering what he had had for supper. He leaned back in his chair as if to relax and let the clock tick. However, I knew that he was merely casing the joint and watching the street. David had something to tell me. It was written all over his face. I did not read what I saw there as a sign of good news to come.

"There's been a development," David said at last. "I wanted to tell you about it before reporting to the rest of the group."

He looked solemn. This was very far out of the ordinary. I said, "David, you're making me nervous."

He made no effort to reassure me. "I don't know if you remember mentioning a certain Ze Keli to Captain Zhang when we were in Urümqui."

Ze Keli was the name used by the party functionary who had been Christopher's interrogator when he was in prison in Xinjiang, the man who had questioned Paul every day for ten years. I had made a mighty effort to recruit or bribe him, using David Wong as the enticer. The effort has failed. Ze was incorruptible, a sort of Maoist Jesuit who thought that Paul was a soul worth saving for the revolution if only he could be persuaded to confess his sins.

I said, "I remember, but you weren't present when I asked about Ze."

"I heard about it later," David said, "when the boys from Guoanbu came to see me in Beijing."

Guoanbu is jargon for Guojia Anquan Bu, the Chinese Ministry of State Security.

David said, "They were very curious. This bothered me a little, considering my history with Ze."

I said, "What did they want to know?"

"Why you had brought up this name after so many years. They asked how you even knew the name. Good question. I pleaded ignorance."

"And?"

"They went away. Needless to say my curiosity was aroused. Why were they so fixated on this one small detail? Especially if Christopher was dead, like they said. So I put out some lines."

"After all these years?"

"Ze's family lived in Shanghai when I was trying to cultivate him. I had other business there. I paid the family a call. They were still there."

"And you got a bite?"

"Christopher's name was the bait, so yes, I did. A day or so later Ze Keli came to see me. Walked right into my hotel in broad daylight."

It was midnight in Rome. The coffee bar was silent. In English the cashier called out, "Signori, it's closing time."

We left immediately. The coffee shop's metal shutter squealed down behind us. The cashier locked it and strode off into the night, high heels clicking. David turned right; I would have gone the other way. We walked by the Pantheon. Not a soul in sight. Shadows, weak bulbs, cobbles underfoot, the lingering smell of coffee.

I said, "And?"

"There weren't a lot of preliminaries," David said. "Ze was very up front about Christopher. He told me the whole history of ten years of questioning, how the man had never yielded, how he would rather die than lie to save himself, as Ze put it. This behavior won Ze's undying admiration. Apparently Christopher was his first sinless sinner. This prisoner was like an ancestor, he said, so removed from weakness and vanity. He actually said this."

Paul did stick in people's memories. I said, "How old is Ze now?"

"I don't know exactly. Soon to be an ancestor, however. Maybe that's why he didn't seem to care what he said to me or who was listening. He must have know that hotel rooms for foreigners are bugged by the Guoanbu, but it didn't seem to matter to him."

"Maybe he was running an errand for Guoanbu."

"Or maybe not. Emotionally he's out of the Party, I think." Very quietly, after letting a puddle of silence form, David said, "Ze had word of Christopher."

"What word?"

"Some people from Guoanbu had come to him to ask about Christopher. They pumped him out, actually. They wanted every detail, everything he could remember, every character trait, every gesture, every weakness. Ze told them Christopher had no weaknesses except that he had lost his mother when he was a child. He said Christopher always talked about her when they came to an impasse in the interrogation. Which was every day, more or less."

"Is Ze making this up?"

David said, "I don't think so. Ze says that the young bucks who were questioning him suddenly perked up when he mentioned Christopher's mother. They had arrested a man they thought was Christopher and a very old woman in the forbidden zone. They had no papers. The old woman dressed as a Kyrgyz and spoke Kyrgyz to them. The man spoke illiterate Mandarin. They didn't know what to make of either one of them."

These words took my breath away. My skin crawled, I was shaken to the bone, I was speechless, I trembled like a leaf. Clichés are clichés for a reason, my friends.

We were standing in the middle of the street. David put a hand on my arm. He said, "It may not be as bad as you think. They asked Ze to go with them to Xinjiang to talk to his old friend

Christopher. He was on his way to Xinjiang on the day I talked to him. I gave him my satellite phone."

"What satellite phone?"

"The one you gave me. I have another. The point is, he took it. I gave him your number."

All around us the underwater hush of the sleeping city simulated deafness—sound remembered instead of sound itself.

"I don't think you understand," David said. "This is good news, Horace. Cheer up. Christopher is alive."

I understood, all right. Paul's luck had not changed. Nor had his gift for confusing the issue as a means of clarifying it.

4

Two hours later David delivered his report to the full group. Eyes went cold, faces froze. In the opinion of the group, Ze Keli's information about Paul and Lori was hearsay. Worse than that, it was speculation upon hearsay. It was a diversion, a thing apart from the real purpose of the mission. The reality was that we were very close to success or disaster. Willy-nilly, which is always the way things work in our business, we had come into possession of a body of facts. We knew that Ibn Awad was alive. We knew where he was likely to be during the next month or so. Success was possible at last. It was time to act.

Jack Philindros said, "What do we do about Christopher?"

"Same mission," I said. "Always was. Paul wasn't wandering around the forbidden zone in Xinjiang for the fun of it. He knows something."

"Like what?"

"We'll know that when we find him."

"Find him?" Jack said. "What does finding Christopher have to do with it?"

"You've been asking that question from the beginning, Jack. The answer hasn't changed. I owe it to him. We all do. And even if that weren't the case, I say again: He knows something we need to know."

Jack said, "Even if we don't know what that might be. I give up. What's the plan?"

I told them. They listened carefully, with expressionless faces. After I had laid out the details nobody broke the silence for a while. Ben smiled. He was the quickest mind in the room, as always.

"To state the obvious," I said, "this could get us all killed. It could all come to nothing."

"What's different about that?" Harley asked.

Nobody answered. But nobody said he wanted to forget the whole thing and go home.

Something like enjoyment—or maybe the memory or anticipation of it—seemed to be present in the twitch of the lips that was Jack's idea of a smile. "We're going to rely on the kindness of strangers," he said. "Is that the idea?"

I said, "What choice do we have? Nobody who knows us is going to help us out."

I took a vote. The shrugs had it.

NINE

1

Points of interest to tourists in Sofia, formerly the darkest capital in Eastern Europe, are connected by a yellow brick road—or at least by a trail of yellow bricks embedded in the sidewalks. Maybe that's why Mr. Osborn Denison, formerly known to me as Kevin Clark, chose Sofia as an appropriate place for the two of us to meet even though it was crawling with Russian mobsters. According to Kevin, the local wise guys were provincials, not really connected to the central nervous system of Russian crime. On the other hand, they were used by the Russians as assassins and kidnappers and no-nonsense interrogators, just as they were in Soviet times when what was now the Moscow mob were still members of the KGB and the Bulgarians were an off-brand copy of that famous service.

Neither one of us had ever been to Sofia before. Kevin seemed to think this provided a margin of safety, and in a way he was right. It takes a day or two to organize surveillance on strangers who arrive by surprise, and by that time we would be out of town. All the same, regarding Sofia as a safe haven required a leap of the imagination. We met as arranged in an underground passage near the National Palace of Culture. When Kevin saw me coming he bought an ice-cream cone, the signal that we were not under surveillance. He was dressed in a suit, tie, trench coat and crushable hat and, for once, grownup shoes. Perversely, this outfit gave him a boyish look. I followed him upstairs to the street and then along the yellow brick trail. It was evening, cold and damp. The crowds were eerily silent. The police-state hush, the costuming and the whey faces created the illusion that we were walking through an underlit scene in a silent movie made by a devoted Marxist in the 1920s. Kevin led me through a labyrinth of streets to an improbable restaurant called the Mexicano. It featured Tex-Mex food along with other Latin-American specialties. Entertainment was provided by a duo called the Singing Twins, who dressed as cinema Mexicans and sang south-of-the-border favorites complete with coyote yips and *ai-ai-ai-ai*s. The place was mobbed. The din was terrific. I guessed that Kevin had chosen the Mexicano because he thought it would be a good place to talk, but we couldn't hear ourselves think. This left the dubious pleasures of the menu. We both ordered beer and the combination plate. After the first taste I shouted, "How did you ever *find* this place?"

Kevin replied that it was recommended by a friend. The Tex-Mex was not bad, though not up to Texas standards, Kevin said. I wouldn't have known. Texas was another place I'd never been. After finishing our beans and rice and several unidentifiable gummy things, we wandered back into the street. As a steeple clock struck nine, we found ourselves sitting on a bench in a small park beside the Russian church. Apparently Sofia went to bed early. The streets were deserted. We were alone. Because Kevin and I had been unable to outshout the Latin beat at the Mexicano, the ice had not yet been properly broken. How to begin?

I said, "You'll be glad to know that Harley is all right. He had a rough week or two, spent more time in the hospital, but he's doing fine now."

"Thanks for sharing," Kevin said.

This New Age phrase set my teeth on edge, but the look on Kevin's face was nothing if not sincere. In spite of all that had happened between us—more likely because of it—I was rather fond of him. In my palmy days I had kept an eye out for young fellows like Kevin. He had, in spades, what it took to do the work he did—the ability to mistake the absurd for the significant. That's why I was about to try to recruit him. In a way this was a maidenhead experience for me. He represented my first try at turning an American against his own government, but I didn't see why that should be any more difficult than suborning a Chinese or an Arab. The principle was the same—make him believe that I was asking him to do something for his country. In this case, that happened to be true. The other magic ingredient, gratification, was also present. I knew what he wanted to do and I had it in my power to make it possible for him to do it.

I said, "Kevin, I need your help."

Of course he had been expecting something like this. Why else would I have asked to meet him? Not a flicker of surprise. No response, either. He simply waited to hear what I was going to say next.

"You've been trying to get me and my friends to get out of the way," I said. "We're prepared to do that."

This got Kevin's attention. "You mean you're giving it up?"

"Up to a point. The target is beyond us."

He put a hand on my arm. It was a filial gesture, I thought. "It's beyond everyone," he said.

I said, "What do you mean by that?"

"I mean we don't have a clue, either. Really."

"Do you expect me to swallow that?"

He hesitated, but only for an instant. Then he said, "No. I think you and Harley and whoever else is involved have got it right. So do a lot of people, deep down. That's the problem."

Ah ha. The seed of doubt. I said, very softly, "Then why are you going along with this exercise in denial?"

Kevin was mute. Hands in pockets, legs stretched out in front of him, hat tilted over his eyes, he gazed intently at the unremarkable church. This was no weather for a long conversation in the open air. Damp cold seeped through three layers of wool. A clammy lump of undigested Bulgarian Tex-Mex lay heavy in my stomach.

At last Kevin said, "An exercise in denial? That's one way to put it."

"How would you put it?"

"Word choice is not my job."

"It's not your job to protect and defend the United States?"

This was a low blow. I was trying to trick him into revealing that he worked for U.S. intelligence—or, depending on how devious one's mind might be, giving him an opportunity to deceive me into thinking he worked for America when in fact he worked for someone or something else. Kevin retaliated by letting me think he had been tricked. Or maybe was pretending actually to be tricked. Or both. I wouldn't have given a nickel for him if he had done otherwise.

"What am I supposed to do?" he asked. "Do as you did and run an operation against the Constitution?"

"I wouldn't recommend that," I said. "But let me ask you this. How much leave time have you accumulated?"

"Why do you ask?"

Kevin was fully alert now. He recognized Beelzebub when he saw him.

I said, "Because I think we'd all be better off if you took a vacation from hound-dogging us. It's distracting to all parties."

"Meaning what?"

I said, "If you have a month or so to spare, off-duty and on your own, I wanted to invite you to go hunting with me and some of my friends."

"Hunting what? The sheik of Araby?"

"No. The houbara bustard."

This time Kevin was truly puzzled. He even forgot to smile. The *what?* I told him everything—or nearly everything—I knew about the bird and Ibn Awad's enthusiasm for hunting it with falcons. I described Kalash's map, outlined my plan to let the houbara bustard lead us to Ibn Awad. There was little risk involved in spilling all these beans. Even if Kevin shared what I told him with his employers, whoever they were, there was little chance that my theory would be believed. In their wisdom, his masters would almost certainly mistake the truth for a ruse.

At the end of my spiel, Kevin wasn't so very sure that he himself believed me, but I had aroused his interest.

He said, "So why are you telling me this?"

"Let's just say I've learned to like you," I said.

"Horace, I do believe you're trying to recruit me."

"On a temporary basis, yes."

Frankness pays. Kevin smiled. It was nice to see the Ohio quarterback again. He said, "You're crazy."

"I am? Why?"

"Why on earth would any sane person think I'd be open to such an offer?"

It was my turn to smile. If Kevin hadn't been open to the offer he wouldn't have asked that question. He would have jumped to his feet, denounced me for an enemy of all that was good and decent, and walked away in a dudgeon.

"Let's just say I have a feeling about you," I said. "I think you've got a sneaking sympathy for us. I also think you're not entirely happy with the people you work for."

"That doesn't mean I'm ready to betray them."

"What does betrayal have to do with it?"

Kevin said, "Don't tell me, let me guess. I've got you all wrong. You're giving me an opportunity to do something really special for humanity."

Such cynicism! Who would have guessed that such bitter wit lurked behind that wonderful all-American smile?

I said, "No, I'm giving you a chance to make the Outfit look like a bunch of jackasses."

"Why?"

"For the satisfaction of the thing. You say yourself that you think us old fogies are right about Ibn Awad and the Outfit is wrong. Think about the consequences if you take the easy way out and go along with these dopes and this man of God blows up a dozen American cities."

A silence. Under the rules of recruitment I couldn't be the first to break it. Kevin had to speak first. And if he did, I was across the goal line.

Finally he said, "Okay, let's take this a step further. What do you want from me?"

Hallelujah. I said, "Two things. Your commando skills and cover."

"What do you mean by commando skills?"

"I want to take Ibn Awad alive. He has bodyguards, lots of them. I hope that you and your men can kidnap the old fellow in the night and be gone before his people wake up."

"You think we can do that?"

"I've seen what you can do. The question is, will you do it?"

Kevin answered as though his mind was already made up on that point and he had moved on to practicalities.

He said, "Take him alive? I can't promise that."

"I know that. But do you think it's possible?"

"It depends on the circumstances. And what you have in mind for him afterward."

"Not torture or death," I said.

"Why the change of heart?"

"We live and learn. This time I mean the old lunatic no harm. All I want to do is stop him and find his bombs and disarm them. Really."

Kevin thought this over and decided to answer the question. He said, "Yes, it's theoretically possible to take him alive, assuming that we can find him and assuming that his men aren't under orders to kill him to save him from capture."

"Understood."

"I have another question," he said. "You want me to provide cover for you. Exactly what does that mean?"

I thought he'd never ask. I said, "Somebody has to take the credit. We don't want it."

"What if I don't want it, either?"

"Then you'll just have to depend on Washington to take all the credit for themselves."

Kevin was smiling again, but this time to himself.

He said, "And I will have the deep satisfaction of having saved the world. Is that the deal?"

"What more could you want?"

Kevin laughed out loud. "Okay," he said. "What's the timetable?"

We settled the details then and there.

2

That left the budgetary questions. I discussed these with the Old Boys. We had plenty of money in the bank—almost $900,000, plus a few thousand left over from the $25,000 advanced to each of us at the beginning of the operation. These weren't government funds, meant to be scattered to the winds before the end of the fiscal year. It was real money, Paul's money, and everybody understood this. It doesn't cost much to fly tourist class. Staying at cheap hotels and monasteries and eating mutton in backstreet restaurants in remotest China consumes very little cash.

Charley said, "How many people is your friend Kevin bringing with him?"

"Half a dozen," I replied. "Not his own men. Independent contractors. Former special-ops types. He's recruiting them as we speak."

"We'll have to pay them?"

"They want Ibn Awad. I said they could have him."

"Handsome gesture, Horace."

I handed Charley the list of arms and equipment Kevin wanted. It was detailed and specific. He looked it over.

"Saints preserve us," he said. "Belgian assault rifles with grenade launchers and grenades, sniper rifle with scope, Swedish 74U submachine guns, nine-millimeter Beretta pistols, hand grenades, Semtex explosive, detonators, ammunition, knives. A month's ration of Meals-Ready-to-Eat. Medical kit. Two-way low frequency radios. Satellite phones. GPS whatchamacallits." Charley peered over his reading glasses. "I thought the idea was to take Ibn Awad alive."

"It is. The firepower is for those who might try to prevent us from doing that."

Charley didn't like guns. Neither did the rest of the Old Boys. In our day gunfire was regarded as the sound of inexcusable failure. The mission back then was to tiptoe in and tiptoe out, leaving no one the wiser. The adversary (never rudely called *the enemy*) wasn't supposed to find out what you'd done to him until it was too late, if ever.

"I have no idea where to find this stuff or what it costs," Charley said. For once he wasn't the smiling volunteer.

"Kevin will take care of all that," I said. "It will be cheaper than you think. Figure fifty grand up front, not including vehicles."

"If it's all the same to you," Charley said. "I'd rather not know."

"But you do know," Jack Philindros said. "Don't be such a liberal, Charley."

Jack was now fully on board. So was Ben. Washington etiquette applied. After the decision is made, the time for criticism is past. You support the plan or resign and keep your mouth shut. This didn't mean that the worrywarts weren't nervous about the ad hoc nature of my plan. Improvisation didn't come easily to either of them. But in the absence of a cast of thousands, improvisation was our only option. Neither spoke the thought that was uppermost in both their minds: By involving Kevin we were opening the gates of Troy to a wooden horse. Who knew what and who might be inside it? This *was* a risk, no question about it. But how refreshing of Jack and Ben not to point that out to the rest of us, who already knew it. The others, needless to say, were all in favor of the rousing game of dirty tricks that lay ahead. They hadn't had this much fun in years.

We were back in Italy—this time in Florence, in a different apartment near the Ponte Vecchio. This place was far more elegant than the walk-up in Rome and much farther removed, thank goodness, from church bells. After the Restaurante Mexicano, I needed a good dinner, so I did as Disraeli used to do when he wanted to read a good novel. I cooked one. Prosciutto and asparagus, spaghetti with clams, a whole roasted sea bass, and more Tuscan wine than was good for the old pipes inside the assembled company. Harley proposed a toast.

"To the life in the Old Boys yet," he said.

Everyone drank to that. But it was late. Quite soon the conversation stalled, the laughter dwindled. Charley and I did the dishes. The rest were all in bed by ten. Sometime during the night I woke up from a dream. Every single one of the Old Boys was snoring—tenors, baritones, an "Old Man River" bass. On a still night in the desert, with the constellations wheeling overhead, these old fellows could have been heard for miles.

In the morning we scattered, each to his own task. David Wong and I headed east, toward Xinjiang.

3

We met Zarah in Karakol, close to the Chinese frontier with Kyrgyzstan. The three of us breakfasted on tea and yogurt in the tiny dining room of the guest house where we were staying. Men in peculiar felt hats, shouting at each other in Kyrgyz, filled the other tables. The smell of dung fires permeated their clothes and this pungent odor mixed with the aroma of the warm sheep's milk they were drinking and the smell of horses and wet fleece and their own bodies. The guest house was badly out of plumb. Slivers of daylight shone through its window frames and door jambs. You could imagine its being built long ago by people with fingers numbed by cold who lacked all but the most primitive tools. Through its isinglass windows we had a smeared view of the Ala Tau Mountains, snow-clad peaks pink in the early light. American eyes had not beheld such a sight and lived to tell the tale in my lifetime—until recently. Now all you had to do to visit places that had been forbidden to outsiders for three generations was click a few computer keys and take a plane. In summer these mountains crawled with American and European backpackers. Capitalism! How right the apparatchiks had been to fear it.

I told Zarah about Kalash, about Mubarak's GPS readings, about Charley's research.

"Then Ibn Awad *is* a falconer."

"So it would seem, unless we're being set up. To the suspicious mind it all fits together a little too neatly."

Zarah gave me a wry look. She said, "A man I know is a dealer in contraband falcons. He says that the falcon of choice for hunting the houbara bustard is not the peregrine but the Saker falcon."

"And why is that?"

"The Saker is larger than the peregrine, with a much broader wingspan," Zarah said. "It lacks the peregrine's big talons but it has an uncanny ability to fly very low to the ground. This means that it finds the houbara bustard on its own, chases it when it runs and flushes it into the air, where it finishes it off. Because of its smaller talons it does much less damage to the carcass when it kills than the peregrine. This is important if you're going to eat the houbara."

"And?"

"It's an endangered species," Zarah said. "Because of its rarity, the Saker falcon is coveted by Arab falconers. Sakers come in all colors from dark brown to blond, from ash to white. White is the rarest color."

"It must be difficult to find one."

"Very. Also illegal. But not impossible. A pure white, wild female Saker falcon could be worth up to a hundred thousand dollars."

I said, "Let me guess. Your friend knows where you can buy one."

"Yes. A pure white female. It's in a village not far from here."

"I'd love to see it. But what are we going to do with a pure white wild female Saker falcon?"

"I thought it would make a nice present for Ibn Awad," Zarah replied. "Something that would catch his eye, bring him to us."

After breakfast David Wong went off to find a Kyrgyz friend who would drive us to the village where the Saker falcon and its owner awaited. The Kyrgyz friend turned out to be Askar, the revolutionary we had met in the Tajik village after the buz kashi, the man who had told us that Lori had been living among the Kyrgyz.

He was the same jovial customer as before, full of patriotic fervor, glowing with heroic reputation. He knew exactly who Zarah was, and after telling her how much she looked like her grandmother, he recited his entire genealogy.

"My grandfather and your great-grandfather were first cousins," he told Zarah. To me he said, "Zarah is your first cousin's child. So you and I are cousins, too."

In my case the blood-tie was honorary, but this was a moment that called for a gesture. I offered my hand. Askar took it and very nearly crushed its bones.

Askar and David had arrived in a Subaru pickup truck. Zarah and David rode in the cab with Askar. For the sake of the legroom I chose to ride in the truck bed. This was an unwise decision. The combination of Askar's driving—he could have gotten work as a stunt man in Hollywood—and the road, built to the most dismal collectivist standards, made me regret it before we had traveled a mile. It was very cold. Snowflakes swirled in the vortex of the truck's passage.

The village, when at last we reached it, turned out to be a collection of stone huts huddled against a mountainside. Just above the jumble of houses, a hot spring bubbled from the rocks, giving off wisps out of steam. Askar told us that there were caves nearby where, in the good old days, he and his men had hidden after raids into China. During the struggle to unite the Kyrgyz people the village had been a nest of lookouts, warning Askar and his partisans of approaching Russians. And what had Askar and his men done when Soviets troops came looking for them?

"We crossed the mountains into Xinjiang and hid in different caves on the other side," he said. "The Han and the Muscovites never told each other anything."

Askar knew everyone in the village, of course. He was given a celebrity's welcome. We were included in it—or at least David and I were. Zarah, her pedigree having been explained by Askar, was swept away by the women like a long-lost sister. In the headman's house, we men were offered fermented mare's milk. I was happy to have it. It made my body feel less sore, and while I can't say I preferred it to scotch whiskey, it did have a nice malty taste. The headman assured us that although a lot of vodka was still drunk in free Kyrgyzstan, fermented mare's milk was the true national drink. This was proved by the fact that the nation's capital, Bishkek, was named for the churn in which mare's milk is fermented.

It was late afternoon before the tide of hospitality had subsided enough for business to be done. Zarah had not disappeared. She was simply hanging out with the rest of the females in the kitchen. Judging by the laughter in that room and the shiny smiling faces of the women who brought our food and drink, the ladies were enjoying her company.

When at last we were taken to the Saker falcon it became evident that Zarah's position as Lori's granddaughter was an asset. Lori—or Kerzira, as the Kyrgyz called her—had dealt with men on her own terms. Everyone seemed to expect Zarah to do the same. The Saker falcon was kept in a cave farther up the mountainside—actually in a sort of alcove deep inside the cave itself. Zarah insisted on going in alone with a candle. She remained inside for maybe fifteen minutes. It seemed longer to me, doubled up as I was beneath the low rock ceiling, and even longer than that to the falcon's keepers. Cousin or not, foreigner or not, Kerzira's granddaughter or not, Zarah was a woman. Women and falcons did not mix. Glances were exchanged, words muttered. Resentment simmered. Apprehension mounted. Who knew what harm this foreign female might be doing to a creature that was worth more in cash money than the combined life's income of everyone in the village? And who could be sure that she wasn't a spy for crazy foreigners who might show up with the police to rescue the bird, thus making the head policeman's fortune and getting everyone in this cave sent to jail?

At last Zarah emerged from the darkness into the smoky lantern light of the outer cave. The village headman, a fellow named Turdahun, lifted her hand and sniffed it. This was a strange liberty, I thought, but Zarah permitted it without complaint. Turdahun was just checking to see if she had touched the bird. Apparently she had not, because Turdahun made no complaint, either. I don't know whether this was Kyrgyz etiquette or the language barrier or some sort of tongue-tied reaction to this strange woman who had come out of nowhere like her grandmother, but in any case, mum was the word.

Fortunately, Askar was on the scene. Speaking pidgin Arabic to Zarah and rain-on-the-roof Kyrgyz to the other parties, he took over the negotiations. From his point of view and that of the villagers, this was the natural order of things. He was Zarah's male relative. Naturally he would speak for her, protect her, get her what she wanted at the fairest possible price. While most of the men in the village watched from the sidelines, Askar and Turdahun sat on a rug and drank tea and bargained, whispering to each other's ears when they came into important points. This went on for several hours. At some point the fermented mare's milk and the warmth of the dung fire put me to sleep. When I woke, the bargain had been struck. Askar had obtained the Saker falcon for three thousand grams of gold, or about $35,000, one-fourth the original asking price.

The gold was ceremoniously weighed in the presence of witnesses. To my surprise, Zarah had brought it with her in small ingots; like an indulgent father, I had assumed that I was going to pay for it. The bargain struck, the gold paid, we ate again (more mutton) and drank the excellent Russian vodka that David had brought. By now it was too late to leave, so we spent the night.

4

There was no question of oversleeping. Turdahun's entire household was up at dawn. Women rattled pans, men shouted, sheep bleated. I wandered outside and came upon two boys milking ewes. One of the lads offered me a saucer of milk straight from the udder. I was about as much interested in drinking it on top of fermented mare's milk and vodka as I would have been in eating the sheep's eyes. I drank it down anyway to be polite and said the Kyrgyz word for *thank-you.*

I wandered up to the hot spring and washed my face. The sulfurous water smelled faintly of rotten eggs, but it was truly hot, about the temperature of a Japanese bath. From the look and smell of the villagers, they did not often take advantage of the bubbling waters. After my ride in Askar's pickup and a night twisted into a pretzel on a very short sleeping pallet, I would have been glad to sink into the steaming spring and soak my weary bones, but at this moment my telephone vibrated. The instrument quivered three or four more times before I identified the source of the annoyance and dug beneath my parka and sweater to find it.

Playing the man who had nothing to hide, I barked, "Horace here!"

I was expecting to hear an Old Boy on the line—Charley with a bulletin from outer space or Jack or Ben or Harley with another kind of helpful hint. Instead I heard a voice I did not know. In my befuddled state I thought for a moment that someone had gotten a wrong number. But then I realized that the caller, who was speaking a kind of denatured English—grammatical but lacking any kind of emphasis—must be Chinese. His voice was reedy, faint, apprehensive, as if its owner had been hoping that he would get my voice mail instead of me. The sound of my name, spoken aloud into the ears of whoever was monitoring this call, had spooked him. I could understand why.

His silence was so complete that I thought for a moment that the line had gone dead. Then he said, "Ah! I have reached you."

In the background I could hear Chinese musical instruments, drums and reeds. Also the noise of a crowd. He must be having trouble hearing me. And why was he making a clandestine phone call from the middle of what sounded like a Chinese funeral?

Raising my voice, I said, "Yes, and I'm very glad, too. I'm interested in a backpacking trip into the mountains and I hope that your travel agency can help me with this."

It took the caller a long moment to understand this doubletalk. Then he caught on. His voice became a little stronger.

"Perhaps we can be of service," he said. "Though of course you must obtain the necessary permissions from the authorities."

"I understand. Let me ask you this. Can you offer references?"

My disused Outfit mind was beginning to work again, albeit sluggishly. It is no simple matter to beat around the bush in this way and still get your message across to someone who learned English from Chinese instructors in an academy in remotest Manchuria.

Ze said, "References?"

I said, "That's right, references. I'd like to speak to someone who has used your services. I have in mind one man in particular."

Another long silence as he processed this information. When at last he spoke, his volume went up another click. Maybe he was beginning to enjoy this game.

"Some time ago I had many conversations with an interesting man," he said. "Perhaps he would do."

"I see. And did you find him a good conversationalist?"

"I found him to be perfectly truthful."

The caller could be none other than Ze Keli, Paul's old interrogator. I was sure of it.

I said, "Have you kept in touch with this client?"

"I have seen him quite recently."

"Did you find him well?"

"He was happy to be with his mother and his brother."

"Can they come to the phone now?"

"Sorry. They are nearby but that is not possible at the moment."

"Then perhaps you and I can meet. I, too, am quite nearby."

There was a burst of noise on the line. It sounded like the burp of a submachine gun.

"What was that?" I asked.

"Firecrackers," the man said. "A wedding is taking place. Don't be apprehensive, please. How close are you, exactly?"

Ze had hidden himself in a wedding procession to make this phone call. Clever fellow—just another Chinese walking down the street in a merry procession with his cell phone pressed to his ear.

I said, "At the moment I am touring the Silk Road. I'm in the mountains, not far from Karakol."

"Ah," he said again. Another pause, more music and firecrackers. Then he said, "Listen carefully. The ots-hay pringsay near the edelbay asspay."

The *what?* I said, "Say that again, please."

He repeated the words, if that's what they were. I dug out a pen and scribbled them on the back of my hand.

"Got it."

Ze said, "At oon-nay in wotay aysday imetay. "

He broke the connection. I sat down on a rock and stared at the blue ballpoint squiggles the back of my hand.

I heard a commotion and stood up. Below me in the village several men appeared. The first two carried a box that was about the size and shape of an army footlocker turned on end. A dozen more surrounded them. They presented the box to Askar, who stood near his pickup truck, salt-and-pepper beard swept leftward by the breeze, a magnificent vista of mountain and fallow pasture behind him. Zarah stood just behind him, womanly and shy, hands clasped modestly at her waist.

One of the falcon handlers gave Askar something. They were several hundred meters away and I couldn't quite make out what it was with the naked eye. Askar turned and handed the thing to Zarah. He seemed to be helping her on with it somehow, buckling it to her arm, but his broad body was in the way so I could not make this out, either.

Suddenly Turdahun, the headman, stepped into the frame. He carried the Saker falcon on his right forearm. It really was white. He approached Zarah and transferred the bird to her arm. I understood, rather than saw, that what Askar had given to her was a gauntlet to protect her arm from the falcon's talons. Asker stepped back. So did all the rest. And there was Zarah, all alone, with the great feathered weapon she had purchased standing hooded and tethered on her arm. This bird was much larger than the peregrine falcons I had seen. I remembered Kalash's houbara bustard and its telltale shadow.

The "language" Ze had been speaking over the telephone was pig latin. "*The ots-hay pringsay earnay the edelbay asspay in wotay aysday imetay* translated to "the hot spring near the Bedel Pass in two days' time."

Who knows how he knew about this nursery patois? Maybe Paul had taught it to him in a light moment between hard questions. Everything else in this operation had begun with Paul, even my hangover, because if I had not set out to find him I certainly would not be standing by a hot spring where the

Mongol Horde might have soaked its feet, looking out over a lost world in which white falcons were worth a hundred times their weight in gold.

5

The Bedel Pass, lying at fourteen thousand feet, is the ancient gateway between northern Kyrgyzstan and Xianjing. From the Kyrgyz village it was a day's journey by car to the end of the road, then another two days by forced march to the pass. The trail followed a narrow river along the base of the Kakšaal Range, then went straight up the mountain to the pass. The river, running too fast to freeze, cascaded down a steep rocky bed, exuding frigid spray that coated everything along its banks with all but invisible black ice—the path we trod, rocks, trees, drifted snow. From time to time we saw an explosion of snow above us on the mountainside and seconds later heard the boom of an avalanche. Dead pack animals—a small wide-eyed shaggy pony with all four feet in the air, a two-humped Bactrian camel frozen into the scowling resentment that is the trademark of its breed—lay beside the trail. We saw no human corpses, but it was possible to wonder if Ze Keli was not luring us to our death by freezing.

Certainly Askar was reluctant to guide us. He was a wanted man in China, with a price on his head. We were going to be met, at least in theory, by a Han whom none of us knew and whose only recommendation was that he had been one of Paul Christopher's jailers. How many soldiers or People's Armed Police would this party man, this agent of the Guoanbu, have with him?

Askar had brought along four younger men, unsmiling Kyrgyz fighters swathed in felt and sheepskin. Ponies, slipping and sliding on the treacherous footing, carried our gear. The animals were at least as resentful as Askar's men. We weren't told the names of the men or what was in the packsaddles, but in the superclean upland air, the sharp smell of gun oil was almost as strong as the odor of lanolin.

As we climbed it grew colder. We made camp at a point where the river emerged from beneath a sheet of ice. A couple of Askar's men unsaddled the ponies and disappeared with two of them among huge ice-covered rocks. While they were gone, the remaining men tramped down a circle in the snow, holding onto a rope held by a fellow standing in the center and walking round and round in concentric circles, then spread carpets and lit a fire. The others returned with yurt poles, apparently cached nearby. They pulled thick sheets of felt off a couple of other ponies and in no time at all had erected a squat, round yurt. The dung fire and the heat radiated in close quarters by eight human bodies soon warmed the interior. Our guides had brought cooked meat and other food, carrying it under their clothes to keep it from freezing, and they shared this with us at body temperature. We were paying for all this in gold, of course. That didn't change the fact that nobody wanted to be here. There were no smiles and no conversation, not even with Askar, the usually affable bandit.

During the night it snowed heavily, and fat flakes of the stuff were still falling as we set off for the pass at first light. If you have never snowshoed up a twenty-degree slope for six or seven hours while swathed in felt and fleece I can assure you it is sweaty work. We arrived at the pass around noon. The hot spring Ze Keli had mentioned in pig latin lay off the trail beyond the summit, on the Xinjiang side of the frontier. Underfoot lay a fresh washboard trail left by a tracked machine. On seeing this, Askar and his men melted into the mountain.

A solitary figure, slender despite the quilted clothes he wore and tall for a Chinese, waited by the hot spring. He wore a high fur cap, like a Russian.

"That's our man," David said.

Ze Keli seemed to be alone. A sweep of the surroundings revealed no Han commandos, only the Honda snowmobile that had made the suspicious corrugated track, parked out of the wind behind a rock.

I said, "I hope you haven't been waiting long."

"Not at all," Ze Keli said. "Its quite warm here, near the spring. That's why I chose this meeting place."

Ze spoke David's name, nodding formally, and stared hard at Zarah from beneath luxuriant white eyebrows.

I said, "Allow me to present Miss Zarah Christopher."

Ze said, "Christopher?"

"She is Paul's daughter."

Remembering his own manners, Ze said, "A great pleasure, Miss Christopher."

I hadn't expected to meet the model of Confucian civility that Ze was turning out to be.

Zarah shook hands with him, looking him straight in the eye and saying how-do-you-do as no doubt she had been taught by her mother or whoever her mother had hired to teach her such things. Manners are designed, after all, to see one through awkward moments, and it is not every day that you meet the man who interrogated your imprisoned father for ten years, and in the end saved his life. When you do, formality is the best option.

Ze had brought with him a thermos of tea and another of hot soup. Also genuine Dixie cups that had somehow found their way from the heart of America to this far edge of China. He poured, and for the next few moments we stood in a circle, each with a steaming paper cup of sugared tea in one hand and a paper cup of noodle soup in the other. Both were delicious, and Ze's small talk—a learned discourse on the geology and history of the Bedel Pass—was pleasantly instructive. He had a Lowell Thomas delivery, mellow and low-key but breathless with the promise of what was coming next. If he knew, as he must have, that Kyrgyz fighters were pointing guns at him from several different directions, he gave no sign. There was no hurrying him. Whatever he had to tell us, he would tell us in due course. Meanwhile the rituals had to be observed. There is a lot to be said for this method of delivering news. It gives you a chance to prepare yourself for any possibility. At last Ze collected the Dixie cups, screwed the tops onto his thermos bottles, and stowed everything in the storage compartment of his snowmobile.

Then, smiling, he said, "Miss Christopher, I bring you greetings from your father and cousin, and also from your grandmother."

Zarah said, "They are alive, then."

"Oh, yes. But they are in custody."

"In prison, you mean."

"No, not exactly. In detention. An investigation is being conducted to determine if they have committed a crime."

"Have they?"

"In my opinion, no. But they were arrested in an area where no unauthorized persons are allowed, especially no foreigners. The local officials have certain suspicions."

"Suspicions of what?"

"Espionage, perhaps. At the very least, a very serious kind of trespassing. The area is forbidden to outsiders because it is a place where weapons research and other sensitive activities take place. Christopher and his mother were arrested quite close to one of those sites."

Ze produced an envelope. "I have brought you some pictures," he said in a bright new voice.

He handed them to us one by one—standard police ID black-and-white flashgun shots of Paul, full-face and profile, and similar photos of a woman who could only be Lori. In these pitiless snapshots she looked old, of course, but not so old as you might expect. What I saw was not only the old woman in the photograph but also the Lori of the legend. Several earlier faces had metamorphosed one after the other into the one she had now. She was not still beautiful, but the beauty that she had been was still visible. The resemblance to Paul and Zarah was not so obvious to me as it seemed to be to others, but then I was looking at a photograph, not flesh.

Zarah devoured the pictures, her face transformed by emotion. She was looking at pictures of ghosts. Ze watched her with deep interest but no sign of sympathy. He had a practiced eye and he was reading her reaction according to standards of his own. Was her reaction genuine? Ze seemed to think so. Zarah offered the pictures back to him. He waved them away.

"I have some others I took myself," he said.

He produced a digital camera. On the tiny screen at the back we could see color photos of Paul and Lori, together and separately. In all these shots they stood stiff and unsmiling in front of what looked like ramshackle military barracks.

Ze clicked the camera, replacing one image with another. Zarah saw something in the background of one of the photographs. She asked Ze to stop. He did so and handed her the camera.

"It's a man," she said. "But what's that he's wearing around his neck?"

Ze did not bother with the pretense of reexamining the picture.

"It's a collar, a square made of rough lumber, slightly longer than an arm's length on each side, with a hole in the center for the neck," he said. "It is built on the man. It is held together by bolts and screws. It cannot be removed by the man because the heads of the screws are on the top and he cannot reach them. The commandant of this camp is a student of the history of punishment. In Imperial China, habitual criminals were sometimes sentenced to wear this device. It was a death sentence, of course, because while you are wearing the thing you not only cannot unscrew the screws, you cannot reach your own mouth. Therefore you cannot eat or drink. You cannot lie down because you would strangle. You cannot go inside for shelter if it rains or snows because the collar is just too large to go through most doors. It is forbidden for others to help a person wearing such a collar in any way. Those who were sentenced to this punishment in ancient China were released from prison and permitted to wander about as they chose until they died. There was no need to confine them. They carried their prison with them."

Zarah said, "This practice has been revived?"

"Not officially," Ze replied, "but as I said, the present commandant of this particular camp believes in learning from the past."

So far Ze had done ninety percent of the talking, but it was mood music. What he actually said was getting us no nearer to our goal, which was the rescue of Paul and Lori. David Wong had taken no part in the conversation. Now he leaped in. Perhaps he was annoyed by my passivity. I was a little surprised by it myself. Maybe I thought Zarah had the right to ask the tough questions. Maybe it was the altitude. We were not standing on the roof of the world at fourteen thousand feet, but the air was not oxygen-rich and breathing had become to some degree conscious. I felt a bit queasy.

David asked the obvious question. "Why are you telling us all this?"

Ze took a deep breath and held it, then expelled it as speech. "I'm not quite sure you'll believe the truth," he said, "but the fact is, I consider myself in Christopher's debt. He was imprisoned in China once before when he was innocent of any crime against us. Now it has happened again. Because of his age, because of his mother, because he has bad luck, I think he should be released as soon as possible."

David said, "Do you think he's going to be released?"

"Not if the camp commandant makes the decision," Ze said.

"Have you recommended his release?"

"Of course. However, the commandant persists in his belief that Christopher has committed a crime."

"What crime?"

Ze answered David's question without hesitation. "Espionage," he said. "No formal charge has been laid, but in the commandant's opinion Christopher is guilty, and the commandant is the law in his own camp. The commandant points to the record. Christopher is a professional American spy. He spied on China before. Now he has come back to do it again."

I said, "In what, exactly, does this alleged espionage consist?"

It took Ze a moment to untangle this Victorian language. Finally he said, "That is an excellent question. The answer is, there is no espionage. Christopher's crime is far worse. He has embarrassed the commandant."

Zarah said, "Please explain."

"The camp is not a military installation," Ze said. "There are no military secrets to steal. It is a labor camp. The prisoners are political dissidents, also a few Christians and other such people who have been unhinged by religion. On the whole, however, it is an educated population. The prisoners, who are there for life although not all of them know that, make technical things—parts for computers, scientific instruments, and so on. These products are sold abroad, mainly in the United States. This commerce has made the commandant, not to mention certain high party functionaries, very rich. He and his bosses want to keep the camp secret."

This was serious. We all understood that, Ze best of all.

"Profits and justice cannot coexist," he said.

"In other words," Zarah said, "the commandant and his friends are capitalists?"

"Exactly," Ze replied.

His face was expressionless. All his life Ze had been an enemy of capitalists. China might be changing, the party's leaders might have become secret plutocrats, but Ze was the same Marxian idealist he had always been. If he had to commit treason to keep his ideals alive, he would do so. I have known many, many men like him, and all were good men who were capable of anything.

"I have brought you two things," he said. "A map and something that is made by the prisoners."

The map showed the exact location of the camp. It was two hundred miles away from the Bedel Pass, north of the Borohoro Shan in the vast, empty highland desert that took up most of the northwest quadrant of Xinjiang. On the back of the map, Ze had drawn a detailed sketch of the camp itself, with important build-ings marked.

The "something made by the prisoners" turned out to be a homing beacon, or rather a transponder that would pick up the beacon's signal and guide you to it. He placed this in my hand. It was quite small, about the size of a pound of butter, but lighter.

"You must come quickly for the Christophers," Ze said. "Within the week. After that I will be gone and you will have no one to help you."

Because Ze had been sent to the camp by the Guoanbu, he had certain powers independent of the commandant. He could, for example, summon the prisoners for interrogation at any hour. His plan was simple. When we were close, we would leave a message for him on the satellite phone David had given him. The phone would be turned off so that it did not ring at an inconvenient moment, but he would check it for messages at midnight every day. On the night he heard my voice or David's, he would sum-mon the prisoners at 2 AM and turn on the homing device. We could then come in at precisely 2 AM and carry out the rescue.

"There are guards on the perimeter but no fences," Ze said. "The guards look in, not out. No one has ever tried to escape *into* the camp, not even if they were dying of thirst in the desert."

Zarah said, "What if formal charges are made against my father and grandmother before then?"

Ze said, "That would complicate the matter, but I don't think it is likely to happen. As I've explained, the commandant prefers picturesque punishments."

Ze clicked to another picture and handed Zarah the camera. The new image was a close-up of the man in the lumber collar.

"That man is your uncle," Ze said. "I have been allowed to give him water because he would otherwise die of dehydration. The commandant has told Christopher and their mother that he will remove the collar if they confess. They don't believe this, of course."

Zarah stared at the image. So did David and I. Tarik was smil-ing, though stooped under the weight of the collar.

She said, "The commandant would do that to people their age?"

"With relish," Ze said. "It would expand his knowledge of the punishment, provide new data."

Zarah's face, like Ze's, was drained of all expression. She handed the camera back to Ze. He held up a hand in refusal.

"A gift," he said.

6

The descent from the pass was a slippery business. As dusk fell, it began to rain. The rain froze. Our clothing crackled as we moved across thin ice that crunched beneath our feet. Dark was falling. We couldn't see one another but kept in touch by sound. I was second from the last in the line of march. One of Askar's men brought up the rear, leading the single pony we had brought with us to the pass. Suddenly the man behind me shouted into the darkness. A curse, a warning? An instant later the pony went slithering by me, tobogganing down the slick ice-covered path, hooves thrashing. Into the darkness I shouted a pointless warning in English—pointless because the people below me could do nothing but stand still and hope that the pony somehow missed them. It was impossible to get out of its way without falling and skidding down the mountain yourself. Then, abruptly, the shouting stopped. Had the pony sailed over a precipice, hit something and broken its neck? There was no way of knowing. I shouted to Zarah and David. They answered, apparently still on their feet. We continued to inch our way downslope.

When we arrived at the yurt, four or five hours later, we humans were all present and accounted for. No one mentioned the pony, which was not present. We ate cold food and fell asleep. At dawn we broke camp. It was snowing again. Through falling snow we glimpsed lightning in the distance, and then heard thunder, as if we had somehow awakened on a planet with a weather system different from Earth's. Two of the Kyrgyz headed back up the mountain, presumably to find the pony and salvage whatever it had been carrying. The rest, including Askar, marched in silence and treated us as if we were invisible.

"They think we're bad luck," David said.

I was not surprised.

I waited until we were back in the village with full stomachs before discussing the situation with Askar. The conversation was strained. He listened impassively. I tried very hard to resuscitate the original happy warrior version of Askar. The rescue mission was not something David and Zarah and I could do without help. I didn't want Kevin's involvement at this point even if he and his team had been near enough to leap into action at a moment's notice. He had too many reasons of his own to want possession of the Amphora Scroll. What we required was someone who knew nothing about the scroll but knew the ground, had a reason to damage the Chinese, and could be induced to help.

I told Askar everything—everything—Ze had told us.

He listened impassively, then said, "You trust this Han?"

"Do I have a choice? If I assume he's lying and do nothing, Zarah's father and grandmother and uncle—your relatives just as much as they are hers and mine—are gone forever."

"You're sure you are their only hope?"

I handed Ze's digital camera it to Askar. He knew exactly how to work it—more than I could say—and he scrolled expertly through the stored images. When he saw the shot of Tarik wearing the lumber collar, his face darkened with family feeling—exactly what I had hoped to see.

I said, "Is that not Tarik?"

"Yes. And the old woman is Kerzira."

I showed Askar the map. He examined it carefully, measuring distances with his knuckles.

"This is close to the mountains, but more than one night's march from the frontier," he said. "The ground is flat, open. There are no trees, no cover of any kind. Even if we got them out we'd be found by helicopters as soon as the sun came up."

"There are no caves, nothing like that?"

"No big caves," Askar said. "Tombs. Sometimes they have mummies in them, people who look like us, not Han. The Han blow the tombs up whenever they find them because the mummies prove that our ancestors were in Xinjiang before theirs, so the land is ours, not theirs."

"These tombs are large?"

"Sometimes. But they're underground, hard to find. These mummies were entombed thousands of years ago."

"But you know where to find them, if I remember correctly."

"Perhaps. We used them in the old days, but the Han have surely destroyed many of the ones we knew, perhaps all. My men and I haven't been near them for years."

"But you could find them again."

"If they still exist."

If they did not still exist, we were out of luck. There was no time to scout them out before we started. We would have to find one on our way in.

We had quite a lot of gold left. Askar knew this, having handled the ingots during the negotiations for the Saker falcon. He did not ask for all the gold. Instead he suggested an honorarium of $2,500 for each of the four Kyrgyz fighters he thought he would need, plus a contribution of $5,000 to the treasury of the revolution, meaning Askar. Equipment and supplies would cost another $5,000.

I did not bargain. "Fine," I said. "When can we start?"

"On the night of the second day from now," Askar replied. "We will drive from Karokol into Kazakhstan and cross the border into Xinjiang beyond the mountains, south of the Dzungarian Gate. It's empty country on both sides of the frontier, with some hills for cover. There are Han patrols but they're not as alert as they used to be. We'll travel at night, hide during daylight. The Han won't see us."

I hoped he was right about that. "How long from the frontier to the camp?"

"We'll arrive at the camp on the second night."

Five days. This was cutting it fine.

7

While Askar was making his arrangements I got on the phone to Charley Hornblower and gave him a shopping list. Thirty-six hours later, a large package arrived in Karakol by FedEx. Inside, cushioned by several pecks of Styrofoam popcorn, were a notebook computer with a solar battery, a Global Positioning System locator and some other useful items. The most interesting of these were enlarged satellite photographs of the labor camp and the country surrounding it in a radius of fifty miles. The images were remarkably clear. Camp and desert looked as they might appear from the gondola of a balloon suspended at an altitude of fifty feet. You couldn't read license plates or recognize faces, but human figures were clearly visible to the unaided eye. Charley provided an Internet address in case we needed more images. By hooking up the computer to the satellite phone we could connect to NASA's Web site from wherever we happened to be, choose the images we wanted and pay for them with a credit card. It was all perfectly legal and proper, God bless America.

Two nights later we crossed the frontier into Xinjiang and, following Askar's instructions, walked straight east in blackness for an hour until we smelled horses. Eleven shaggy ponies awaited us—one for each rider plus three spare animals for Paul and Lori and Tarik. Askar's men—happily not the same moody fellows who had guided us to the Bedel Pass—quickly packed our gear onto the riderless mounts. Askar led the largest pony to me and gave me a leg up. If a horse can groan, this poor beast groaned when it felt my weight.

Although darkness was complete, it was only seven in the evening when we started off. We had twelve hours or a little less until sunrise. Askar, in the lead, kicked his mount into a trot. Up ahead I could make out the silhouettes of the other riders pistoning up and down in the saddle. Despite riding lessons in childhood, I had never gotten the hang of this. I bounced up and down on the horse's kidneys, jarred guts lingering behind as my pelvis hit leather, then sloshing about as gravity caught up with them. After an hour we began to canter, a much more comfortable way to travel. By now it was apparent that my horse hated me. It bucked, kicked and twisted its neck, trying to bite my leg. I sympathized. The animal, used to carrying lean, dashing Kyrgyz horsemen, almost certainly had never before been cursed with such a grossly incompetent rider, or such a heavy one.

After the canter we dismounted and walked for an hour. The stars came out. At our present rate of progress we should be at least fifty miles inside China by dawn, or halfway to the camp. The Kyrgyz did not stop to rest the horses or themselves. You could hear the horses making water and smell their manure. Once or twice I smelled carnivorous human urine; the Kyrgyz were emptying their bladders from the saddle. Remembering my Greek sniper, all this ordure worried me. An experienced tracker could follow it even in the dark. I wondered, too, if we were leaving tracks that could be seen after sunrise from the air. How could twelve horses fail to do so?

It was pointless to fret. I concentrated instead on the rescue, visualizing it as best I could on the basis of what Ze had told me about the camp, trying to foresee difficulties and avoid capture or untimely death. The biggest problem apart from the guards was Tarik's lumber collar. He could hardly run with a thing like that around his neck. I went over the plan to remove it. We'd have about ten minutes to do the job. Even though we had a couple of battery-operated screwdrivers, part of the care package Charley had sent, I didn't see how we could unscrew the thing in the time available. I should have asked for more power screwdrivers, for a saw, for divine guidance.

About an hour before dawn the horses' hooves began to ring on stony ground. By first light we could see mountains all around us. We dismounted and walked in single file down a narrow defile between low cliffs. The light strengthened. The horses, smelling of lather, drooped with fatigue. Mine was so tired it had given up trying to bite and kick me. I strained my eyes in the uncertain light and saw a horse disappear as if swallowed by the earth. Then another and another until I was at the head of the line, standing on the rim of a hole in the ground.

One of the Kyrgyz fighters clambered out of the hole, blindfolded my horse, took its reins, and whipped it into the pit. I followed and found myself in pitch darkness, walking down an earthen ramp. The horse whinnied in fear and balked and kicked and was lashed onward by its handler. After twists and turns I found myself in an inner chamber whose candlelit recumbent figures might have been painted by a Pre-Raphaelite on opium. They were mummies, still dressed in the shreds of the clothes in which they had been buried thousands of years before. Two men, a woman, a young girl. They were eyeless and lipless and shrunken and tanned by their long repose in the total absence of moisture. And yet they were lifelike. They seemed to slumber, even to dream. As in Ze's photograph of Lori, you saw the faces they used to have. Two of them had hair as golden as Zarah's. They seemed to be smiling, teeth gleaming in the candlelight. Oddly, there was no sense of having violated the mummies' privacy. Their smiles seemed to suggest they had been waiting for us to drop in. I smiled back at them quite affectionately, and looking around the circle of faces, saw that everyone else was doing the same.

While two of the Kyrgyz put the horses to bed, watering them from plastic jerricans and feeding them grain, the other two made a meal, heating tea over a camp stove and unpacking cold mutton and bread from cloth sacks. One of them spoke to us. David translated.

"He says there's a latrine bucket in the room with the horses. Don't go outside. Use the bucket, not the floor."

We had not been told the names of the Kyrgyz traveling with us. All were picturesque types with mustaches and bandoliers and submachine guns slung over their shoulders and pistols and knives thrust into their belts. They were perfectly at home in the tomb, respectful but unself-consciously certain they were welcome among these silent ancestors. It was cool in the tomb, stony and dry. The candles in the burial chamber had been moved so that the mummies now lay in darkness. The silence was deep. My eyelids drooped. I was dead tired and terminally saddle worn and would have traded all the gold we had left for a hot bath. That was my last thought before I fell asleep.

Andrew Marvell was right. The grave's a fine and private place. It is not, however, the ideal place to wake up. The blackness, the silence, the timeless smell of dust, the scalp-tingling realization of where you are and in what company add up to a moment of panic. Mummies by candlelight are one thing. Mummies in the dark are quite another. Their invisibility made their presence more noticeable, and as we all know, palpability is far more troubling to the mind than mere reality. I found my flashlight and switched it on. Zarah was sitting cross-legged on her sleeping rug, combing her hair in the dark. David was still asleep. There were no Kyrgyz to be seen.

Zarah said, "It's ten in the morning. I think the others are outside, standing watch."

"You're sure of that?"

"The horses are all present and accounted for."

As if to vouch for her, a horse snorted offstage. I was stiffer after a good night's sleep than when climbing off my unhappy horse the night before. I unfolded myself hinge by reluctant hinge into something like the full upright position and limped off to the bucket. Equine eyes rolled whitely in the beam of my flashlight, hooves flew. Evidently I didn't smell any better to the horses than they smelled to me.

By the time I returned, David was awake. Zarah had lit some of the candles, revealing the mummies. Our living shadows mingled with theirs. The scene was less beautiful, less composed somehow and less mysterious, than it had seemed the night before. Zarah produced granola bars and handed them out. We washed them down with water from big plastic bottles with garish labels. We were all careful not to scatter crumbs: the mummies again, silently teaching us etiquette.

I had packed Ze's maps, the Landsat images, the GPS thing-amabob and other navigational aids in an indestructible canvas briefcase with shoulder strap that I had bought thirty years before at Eddie Bauer. It also contained, in an outside compartment designed to hold books, a loaded Makarov pistol and a fearsome big commando knife. David had gone shopping in Karakol and bought these items, along with some Russian stun- and tear gas grenades. David was a crack shot and I assumed that Zarah was, too, but I hadn't fired a pistol in years or stabbed anybody since I got out of the Marine Corps. These skills, once learned, were like riding a bicycle, or so I hoped. They'd come back when and if I needed them.

With the briefcase slung over my shoulder and every muscle and joint protesting, I walked to the top of the ramp. The entrance was sealed with a large flat stone. I slid it aside. The sun exploded in my eyes, momentarily blinding me. Had hunters been waiting for me to stick my head out of my den I would have been dead. I saw no one—nor any trace of human passage. All sign of the horses' hooves and our own footsteps had been removed. The scalped landscape was empty. Even the sky was empty—not a cloud to be seen, not a bird, nothing but the blue-white sun directly overhead. I felt no heat from it. We were in a deep canyon, in deep shadow. The surrounding bluffs that I had sensed the night before were now fully visible. They were pock-marked with the mouths of caves, but only a human fly could have climbed into one of them. I stood up and beckoned to Zarah and David to follow me. There was no point in crawling or creeping. Anyone watching the ravine would already have seen us. I hoped that this included our Kyrgyz traveling companions, but looking around this sterile void and listening to the silence, I wondered.

Suddenly Askar's voice, issuing from the earth just behind me, said something in Kyrgyz. David, who was at my elbow, translated: "He says to be sure to replace the rock and sweep your footprints behind you."

Askar was lying under a sheet of burlap about five paces away. The burlap was the same color as the ground for the good reason that it was permeated with dirt. The dirt was pulverized and so loose, because so dehydrated, that the grains of it did not stick together. When you stepped in it, you kicked up a tiny sandstorm that took a long time to come back together. All of us were pow-dered with this flourlike grime from head to toe. Askar stood up and strode off toward the bluff. We followed. Zarah picked up the burlap and walking backward, obliterated our footprints.

We were soon inside a low cave, sitting in a circle. The other Kyrgyz were standing watch, presumably under burlaps of their own. Askar pointed vaguely up and down the ravine and to the tops of the bluffs. His submachine gun was wrapped in a plastic trash bag to protect it from the dust. I spread out the Landsat image of this area and took a GPS reading. I pointed to our exact position on the map. Askar made a polite face. He knew where he was and where he was going. No need for all this outlandish fuss and complication.

He began to talk. As Askar saw it, the rescue was a simple operation—walk in, find our friends, walk out with them in tow, evade pursuit, hide during daylight, run for the border by night. Make no noise, make no fuss, leave 'em snoozing. All this made good sense. Operations always sound tidy on the day before they happen.

Zarah said, "What about Tarik?"

"He comes with us."

"Wearing that collar? What if we have to run?"

"Then we leave him," Askar said.

"Impossible," Zarah said.

Askar shrugged. Zarah gave him a long cold look, then moved away and sat with her back turned.

8

We started out as soon as it was dark. To my great relief, Askar ordered us to lead the horses rather than ride them in order to keep the animals as fresh as possible for our getaway. We were in a labyrinth of ravines, gullies and escarpments. Askar, in the lead, turned left here, right there, or marched straight ahead with the confidence of a New Yorker walking to work in a geometric city. According to the radium dial of my old compass, we were headed east and north, right for the prison camp. Dust stirred up by the horses' hooves muffled the senses—taste, smell, touch, even hearing and sight. I counted footsteps, following the leader in a daze of dumb trust. Time did not fly.

By ten o'clock we could see the glow of the camp against the sky. Askar called a halt. One of his nameless men took my horse's reins from my hands and led it away. He and the other fighters hobbled the animals. Askar issued orders to his fighters and to us, who would do what on what signal. We would rest for an hour, then go in. At midnight, as arranged, David would call Ze's satellite phone and leave a message in Mandarin. Meanwhile we would sleep.

"Zarah will remain with the horses," Askar said.

Zarah said, "No."

"Someone must stay," Askar said. "Otherwise the horses will scatter."

"Then leave one of your people," Zarah said, looking him straight in the eye.

"All the men are needed," Askar said. "There's going to be a wind. The horses will be afraid. They'll scatter."

As if on signal, a breeze stirred up a few dust dervishes. Zarah walked away into the darkness. Askar shrugged. This woman preferred discovery and maybe death to obedience? So be it. He lay down on the ground and went to sleep. I was beginning to feel the excitement of the thing we were about to do. Nevertheless, I soon fell asleep, but twitchily, dreaming of bad moments in the past. When I roused I realized that Zarah was missing. This startled me so that I hardly noticed that the wind was stronger—so strong, in fact, that the glow of the camp had been obscured by a cloud of dust. The temperature had dropped many degrees. A cold front was arriving on the west wind. We were all masked now, scarves drawn across our faces against the wind and sand. Maybe Zarah was hidden by the blowing dust. I bumbled about looking for her but found no trace of her except for one very bad sign. The rucksack in which she carried her gear was missing. So was one of Charley's power screwdrivers. No one had seen her leave. There was only one place she could have gone—into the camp.

David made his phone call to Ze. Askar signaled his men to move out and led off, with David and me on either side of him. The wind blew harder every minute. We could hardly see the horses. Askar spoke a short sentence in Kyrgyz.

David translated: "Askar says it's a night within the night. Perfect for us."

Askar was in his element, happy and bloodthirsty. Allah was in charge. Despite the presence of unbelievers he had sent us these ideal weather conditions. We would be invisible to the guards at the camp. Our tracks would be blown away.

We seemed to be alone, just the three of us. Then Askar's men emerged from the whirlwind of dust, leading the horses. There was no reason, now, not to bring them. No one inside the camp would be able to see or smell them in this pall of dust or hear them over the howling wind. I'm no Bedouin, but it was obvious, too, that no one, not even Askar, would have been able to find the animals again if we left them behind. That meant that Zarah would not find them either if we missed her in the storm and she followed Kalash's rule for those lost in the desert and went back to the place where she had started.

Quite soon we were within sight of the camp. The weak perimeter lights were gauzy points of reference. Beyond these were other, even dimmer lights outside the buildings. Askar came close and shouted into my ear. Where, he wanted to know, was the homing device that Ze had given me? It was a good thing (Allah again?) we had brought the horses, because in my anxiety over Zarah I had completely forgotten the homing device. It was hanging from my saddle, inside my canvas briefcase. Without technological assistance in this night within the night, we wouldn't have had a prayer of finding the building where Ze and his prisoners awaited us. I retrieved the transponder and switched it on. It was equipped with earphones, like a Walkman. I clapped these on and followed the signal. It stuttered and faded if you strayed right or left but was loud and steady as long as you stayed on track. Askar and the others stumbled along behind me, blind and trusting. I dug the commando knife out of the briefcase and held it in my free hand, in case the homing beam walked us right into a guard. I liked the heft of the knife. My blood was up. Not for many years had I had this feeling. I was enjoying it more now, as my whole life passed before my eyes, than I remembered doing as a second lieutenant on night patrol with my whole life before me.

In the event, it was not a guard but an entire guardhouse I blundered into. Following the homing signal meant walking in a straight line. Obstacles did not register on the transponder, and it was a tribute to my lack of imagination that I nearly got us captured or shot or both by not realizing that before it was almost too late. The building in question was a shack, brightly lighted inside and out. Through the window, only inches from my nose by the time I halted, I could see uniformed men lounging about. They were listening to the radio, which was tuned very loud.

I skirted the building, picked up the homing beam again, then bobbed and weaved among structures, some lighted and some not. I hoped that Askar could find his way back through this maze, because there would be no homing signal on the way out and I knew that I would be lost without it. As I walked along the beam of sound, it increased in volume. The building dead ahead was outlined by a dim glow. I walked around the structure, looking for a window. When I reached the front, the noise in the earphones was so loud that I took them off. Immediately I heard a faint electrical whirring sound. It seemed to come from the front of the building. There was no need for concealment, obviously, but I dropped on all fours anyway and crawled to the corner of the building. Peeking around it, I saw something that I recognized. It was Cousin Tarik with the great wooden square of his collar around his neck. His head looked very small, jutting above the collar. He was kneeling, gripping his knees, the only things he could reach, in an attempt to hold himself upright despite the weight of the thing.

Zarah knelt in front of Tarik, her back to me. I realized what the whirring sound was. It was the power screwdriver. Zarah was using this tool to remove the screws and bolts from Tarik's collar. She had come on ahead of the rest of us to give herself more time to do this job. The collar was enormous, far bigger than it had seemed in Ze's snapshot. Just as Ze had suggested, its very size sent a nonstop message to the man who wore it. He was going to die wearing it and mummify or rot with it still around his neck afterward. Zarah worked methodically, without hurrying, unscrewing the screws and dropping them into the sand.

I was about to whisper hello when Askar and two of his men appeared beyond Zarah, submachine guns pointed at her head. Without pausing in her work, Zarah looked up at them and calmly pointed with her thumb at the door just behind her. Weapons at the ready, the Kyrgyz burst through the door like the half-crazy killers they were. I followed, knife in hand, adrenaline pumping. Askar and his men had come here to kill. They wouldn't hesitate for a moment to blow Ze's head off—or for that matter, Paul's or Lori's.

In English, a language these killers did not understand, I shouted, "Hold it!"

They ignored me. Lori, seated on a stool in the middle of the room, smiled at the desperadoes and said something in Kyrgyz. One of them knelt beside her and took her hand. A nephew? The look on his face, murderous just a moment before, can only be called tender.

Paul said, "Hello, Horace."

He was standing behind Lori, a hand on her shoulder. She reached up with her free hand—the fond young desperado was still holding onto the other one—and patted Paul's hand.

I said, "Hello yourself."

Lori smiled at me in grandmotherly silence, as if we did not speak a common language. After all these years perhaps we didn't. I smiled back—horribly, no doubt. Once again manners came to the rescue. I held out my hand and said, "Aunt Lori, I wonder if you know about me. I'm Horace Hubbard, Elliott's son."

Her expression was pleasant, detached, ladylike.

She gripped my hand and shook it like the Prussian she used to be, up, down, quick release. Her palm was callused, her grip firm, her skin warm.

Ze Keli said, "Perhaps someone should help Zarah. The guards make their rounds every half hour."

9

Outside, Zarah was still at work on Tarik's collar. He trembled with the effort of remaining still under its weight.

Zarah said, "I think we have about ten minutes before the guards come by. There's no way to hide him."

She had so far removed two rows of screws and bolts. Many remained, set an inch or two apart. She had been working along a seam in the structure, so now the boards were loosened.

Askar had followed me outside. He dropped to his knees, rolled over onto his back, and examined the underside of the collar.

I tried to pry the boards apart with the commando knife and broke the blade.

Askar said something to Tarik in Kyrgyz. Tarik nodded his head.

In Mandarin Askar said, "We're going to break this thing without breaking Tarik's neck. Pull straight toward yourself. Do not twist it. Understand?"

I nodded.

Askar said, "Take hold of your side."

I did as he ordered. Askar seized the other side.

Askar said, "On the count of three. Use all your strength, cousin."

He counted off in Mandarin. When he got to three, the two of us pulled in opposite directions. The collar resisted, Tarik made a strangling noise. The boards groaned, budged, then screeched and splintered and came apart in our hands. Tarik shouted loudly in pain.

At this moment two guards, wearing the padded uniforms and floppy caps I remembered from days gone by, dashed out of the storm. They stopped in dumb-show astonishment when they saw us. They began to level their rifles. One of them opened his mouth to shout. Then, wondrously, their feet left the ground and their rifles fell from their hands. They made gurgling sounds. The two Kyrgyz fighters who had cut their throats lowered their twitching bodies to the ground and wiped their bloody knives on the dead men's clothes.

10

———

Inside the hut, Paul and Lori were on their feet, dressed for travel in Kyrgyz garments.

Ze said, "You should go now. The guards will be missed when they don't relieve the men at the next post."

"We're on our way," I said. "What can we do for you before we go?"

"Shoot me," Ze said. He pointed to his left shoulder, just below the collar bone. "Please don't hit the bone or the lung. The medical facilities here are primitive."

Ze might have just asked me for a cigarette for all the concern he was showing.

"Are you sure?" I asked, producing the Makarov.

Ze gazed thoughtfully at the large blue pistol in my hand and from his waistband produced a smaller caliber handgun of his own, a genuine made-in-Germany Walther PPK.

"Use this one, then," he said, jacking a round into the chamber and handing it to me butt-first. "But take it with you when you go."

I took Ze's gun but I still didn't trust myself. What if I hit an artery?

Ze said, "Wait. Take this, too."

He handed me the transmitter for the homing beacon. It was

surprisingly small. I put it in my pocket and pointed the pistol at Ze. I really did not want to do this. My hand didn't shake but I had no confidence that I could hit a spot smaller than a twenty-five cent piece, even from a range of six inches.

Zarah came in from outdoors. I lowered the pistol. She took in the scene at a glance.

Ze explained the situation to her.

"Why me?" she said.

"Better you than the Kyrgyz," he replied. "And as you see, Horace is not enthusiastic."

Expressionless, Zarah held out her hand for the pistol. I gave it to her. Without further question or hesitation she lifted it and fired. The report was deafening. The round exited from the back of Ze's shoulder, pulling a skein of blood behind it, and kept right on going through the matchwood wall of the shack.

Askar, who hadn't understood a word of this conversation conducted entirely in English, must have thought that Zarah had missed. He lifted his submachine gun as if to finish Ze off. Lori stopped him with one sharp word in Kyrgyz.

Ze looked surprised, as people who have just been shot almost always do. He swayed, as if to faint. Paul was beside him instantly. He put his arms around Ze and lowered him to the floor. Zarah crouched beside Ze, lifted his bloody shirt at the collar, and peered inside. She touched the bruised flesh around the neat circular wound with a fingertip and examined the collarbone.

"Nothing broken," she said to Ze. "It's a clean wound."

Ze nodded politely. He was in shock, conscious but speechless and unmoving, as if his entire nervous system had been disconnected. He was pale anyway for a Chinese, but now his skin was utterly drained of color. Paul said nothing, but I knew as well as I knew that the sun was shining on the other side of the planet that he would have stayed behind to take care of Ze if he thought that his friend was in danger of his life.

Ze, who knew better than most people what made Paul tick,

sensed this, too. He said, "Christopher, go." His voice was surprisingly strong.

Paul stood up. The whole family, Tarik included, headed for the open door. Lori went down the steps on tiptoe like a girl of seventeen, and it was she who led us out of the camp, familiar ground to her.

As soon as the horses were unhobbled and everyone was in the saddle, Askar took off at the gallop. Lori and Zarah followed, riding like Kyrgyz. I held on as best I could, and I assure you there is nothing, absolutely nothing, like clinging to the back of a galloping horse in a raging sandstorm over broken country knowing that you are apt to ride over a precipice at any moment.

This time Askar's destination was not a tomb but an empty cave inside a glacier. We reached it just before dawn, or so my watch said. The storm was still in progress, though the wind was not quite so strong. The sunrise, refracting from billions of dust particles, created a strange shimmering pastel rainbow in this bone-dry desert. As soon as we were inside the cave Zarah tended to Tarik's neck. It was raw. Dozens of splinters were embedded in his oozing flesh. While Lori held a flashlight, Zarah removed the slivers. Then the two women bathed his wounds with vodka from David Wong's portable minibar.

The cave was cool and quiet. Lori built a dung fire—apparently the Kyrgyz carried an emergency supply of dried dung when they traveled. Zarah chipped ice from the wall and melted it in a pot over the flames to make tea. Zarah worked with her grandmother just as Lori had worked with her on the first aid, as if they were old familiars who knew each other's every move and thought in advance. Anyone could see that they were happy to be together— beyond happy. Attuned.

The cave, really just a long narrow passage through a huge deposit of compressed ice, was very chilly and except for the feeble glow of a candle or two, black as pitch. A dung fire leaves no embers, only a lingering scent, so it lacked even the dull light of a dying campfire. The Kyrgyz, lying on sheepskins and wrapped in felt, slept soundly. One of them talked in his sleep, spitting out what sounded like peremptory orders in a clear tenor voice. After several sleepless hours I switched on my flashlight to look at my watch. Eleven o'clock. Hours to go before the others woke. I shone the flashlight's beam on the walls and ceilings of the cave. The ice was dirty blue.

Paul's voice said, "Looks like rock salt, doesn't it?"

"Does it? I've never been in a salt mine."

"Don't give up hope."

Paul, joking? I shone the light on him. He was sitting upright with a felt blanket wrapped around his shoulders. The flashlight beam shook. I was shivering.

He said, "Let's go outside."

We picked our way among the Kyrgyz, each one of whom woke up with wild eyes and a weapon in his hands as we stepped over or around their supine bodies.

The wind had slackened to a strong breeze, but dust still blew. Visibility might have been ten feet, not more. Paul had brought a bottle of water with him. We had a drink, then gazed into the roiling dust, backlit by the invisible sun, as if it were some unearthly new art form. In a sense it was: eddying colors and pinholes of blue light. Paul had never been prone to break a silence unnecessarily. For the moment I myself was not disposed to chatter. Nothing makes talking less useful than achieving your heart's desire, and I had done that by finding the lost Christophers. To my surprise my chief emotion was disappointment. Not that I wasn't glad to see Paul or wasn't filled with curiosity over what he'd been up to. The problem was, how to begin again with someone freshly back from the dead.

I said, "You're officially dead, you know. Buried at Arlington."

"So Zarah said."

Paul seemed to find nothing remarkable in this. After all, this wasn't the first time he'd been given up for dead. Nevertheless I filled him in on the details of his funeral and interment. He listened with his usual concentration, wryly smiling now and then, but made no comment.

Finally he said, "I wonder whose ashes those were."

I told him about the stranger in his grave in Ulugqat and began to fill him in on the rest of my odyssey. We were not yet in Paris when Paul held up a hand for silence. The dust had thinned somewhat, enough so that you could see into it as if into a wispy fog. Something was moving inside it. Neither of us was armed, not that either of us would have been likely to start shooting.

The figure became more distinct as it came nearer and when it was five or six paces away, turned into Askar. He was accompanied by one of his men and by two exhausted horses, and he carried a package wrapped in a green plastic trash bag. This he handed to Paul.

Speaking Mandarin, Paul said, "You found it without trouble?"

"It was where your mother left it," Askar said. "If you're going to stay out here you should have weapons."

"You've seen Han?"

"Heard them," Askar said. "They're in vehicles, shouting to each other, crashing into rocks. They're lost but they might find us by accident. Take these."

Askar handed Paul his submachine gun and gestured for the other Kyrgyz to give me his, along with a sack of spare ammunition. Both weapons were also wrapped in plastic garbage bags as protection against the sand.

"You're the lookouts," Askar said. "Use your ears. Don't fire unless you absolutely have to. We need sleep."

Askar and his man—probably another nephew or cousin or son—went into the cave.

Paul laid his weapon across his lap and carefully unwrapped the package Askar had delivered. He drew the Amphora Scroll from the bag and handed it to me. It was still in its glass tube, and through the glass I could see Septimus Arcanus's handwriting—or more likely, the handwriting of the slave who had been his clerk. The scroll was smaller, lighter and more ordinary than I had pictured it. I half-expected a voice to issue from it, speaking in Aramaic. Some of this must have shown on my face.

"Bizarre, isn't it?" Paul said.

"In what way?"

"The way it makes you wonder if you're a believer after all."

I laughed out loud. If the supremely rational Paul Christopher, of all people, was as spooked as I was by this relic, agnosticism had no future whatsoever.

Just then we heard diesel engines and the whine of gearboxes and rough voices shouting in a dialect I did not understand except to recognize it as Chinese. These sounds seemed to be quite far away, but maybe the dust had the same effect on sound as on light, bending and transforming it.

Paul said, "I'll wake Askar."

He disappeared into the cave, taking the Amphora Scroll with him but leaving the green plastic garbage bag on the ground. A gust of wind took it; it skittered away into the dust cloud. I almost dashed after it but I knew I had a better chance of finding a squad of troops than of retrieving it.

11

The wind rose and with it, the dust. I couldn't see a thing. If I could trust my hearing, and in these conditions I wasn't sure that I could, the Han vehicles were headed straight for the mouth of the cave. I thought it might be useful to take up a flanking position, so I picked up one of Askar's submachine guns and the ammo bag and ran about a hundred paces to the right and took shelter behind a large rock. The Han were driving blind and would have to fire blind, but a lucky shot is always a possibility. I could hear our visitors quite clearly now, not just their noisy vehicles but the men too as they shouted to each other.

The noise seemed to be headed straight for me. I glimpsed the first vehicle when an errant breeze opened a peephole. The car was a Chinese version of the Soviet Jeep, painted in sand-colored camouflage. The driver wore goggles and a white surgical mask. So did the man standing upright in the front seat beside him and two or three riflemen deployed in front of the vehicle in a skirmish line. I ran another hundred paces to my right and took up a new position behind another rock. This time I lay down to make a smaller target of myself. My intention was to keep moving to the right until I was behind the Han and then, if I heard firing, to close in until I could see them and open fire.

More shouting. The whiny sound of vehicles in reverse, then

advancing in low gear. The crash of metal against a rock. Another gust of wind cleared away another patch of dust. To my immediate front, perhaps ten meters away, I glimpsed a second vehicle and more skirmishers. How were all these different people finding me? Was it dumb luck? Were they searching in all directions in spokes-of-a-wheel fashion or what? I moved again. I had no idea where I was in relation to the cave. I half expected to find myself at any moment running in mid-air after having stepped off a cliff. My nose was full of dust. I had an overwhelming desire to sneeze. Before I could drop my gun and squeeze my nose shut, I emitted a loud honking *ah-choo*.

Almost immediately a grenade exploded on the other side of the rock I was hiding behind. It made a terrific flash and bang, shrapnel flying all over the place, and its concussion sucked a hole in the dust. For an instant I could see again. Three skirmishers, one of them fitting another rifle grenade to the launcher on his weapon, were spread out before me. All were in the kneeling position, Kalashnikovs pointed straight at me. If I could see them, they could see me. I opened fire with the submachine gun and saw one of them knocked backward. Many others, seen and unseen, returned fire, sparks flying from the muzzles of automatic weapons and bullets flying every which way. I dug a grenade out of Askar's bag, pulled the pin, and threw it in the general direction of the gunfire. As soon as the grenade went off I ran back the way I had come. This time bullets followed me as I ran, ricochets whining off rocks, as if I were a visible target. When I stopped and flopped down behind another rock, the fire seemed to be concentrated on that point.

What was going on here? How did they know where I was in this haze? How could they know? And then *I* knew. The transmitter for the homing beacon. It was in the pocket of my parka, where I had put it after Ze had handed it over to me the night before. They were reading its signal. That is what had guided them straight to the mouth of the cave. That was the reason that Askar and his friend had ridden right by them in the storm without being detected. But how could it be on? I hadn't touched the switch. Ze must have handed it to me with the switch on. This was a suspicion I was loath to entertain.

I got out the transmitter. Sure enough, it was switched on. At this discovery I felt, of all things, deep embarrassment. Why had I not checked the thing out before dropping it trustingly into my pocket? I switched it off. After a moment the firing stopped. How gratifying to know what had been causing it. I was about to tiptoe away when I realized that I had been presented with the opportunity of a lifetime to perform a useful action—the opportunity of a very short lifetime perhaps, given my present circumstances, but an opportunity nevertheless. I picked up the transmitter—it was turned off now, remember—and walked straight toward the enemy. It was easy enough to avoid bumping into them because they were still shouting to one another through the fog and one of them was screaming in agony.

I walked until I could hear voices all around me to my left and right and to my front and rear. I was right in the middle of the attacking force, or near enough. I found a tall rock, placed the transmitter on top of it, and switched it on. I then hit the dirt as enthusiastically as if I were once again a young Marine being shot at by these kids' grandfathers. Fire erupted from all points of the compass. Grenades exploded. Cries of pain broke out, a choir of the wounded, as the Han, firing blindly into the dust, shot at the transmitter signal, missed me, and killed and wounded one another. Someone with a good set of lungs bellowed the order to cease fire. I recovered the transmitter and switched it off.

Moans, curses, the acrid smell of cordite. Owing to my own cleverness, I was surrounded, with enemies between me and every possible exit. It was imperative that I move before these people recovered their wits and started closing in. I did so, gingerly. The Han were still making a lot of noise—recriminations, no doubt— but all it would take to undo me was one alert soldier keeping his mouth shut. Naturally I ran into him in a matter of seconds. He was crouched, rifle at the ready, with his back to me. He must have sensed my movement because he sprang to his feet, firing his Kalashnikov wildly as he spun on his heel. There was no time to aim and shoot or run away, which was the option I wanted with all my heart to exercise, so without thought I launched myself sidewise into the poor frightened fellow. All two hundred-forty pounds of me clipped him at the knees. His assault rifle, still firing, flew from his grasp and he collapsed, shrieking in pain. I must have torn every tendon in both his knees. I wish I could tell you that I slipped away into the rosy murk that enveloped us both and left him shrieking. But I did not. I kneeled on his back, seized his chin and jerked his head sharply backwards.

I heard his neck break, then heard hoofbeats. A Kyrgyz on horseback plunged out of the dust, then back into it again, missing me by inches. Invisible now, he fired his submachine gun. Someone fired back. Others were shooting, too. Muzzle blasts embroidered the dust all around me. Hooves pounded, gears clashed, ricochets sang, men shouted and grunted and screamed. Grenades exploded. The Kyrgyz were attacking the Chinese vehicles on horseback. I flattened myself onto the dead man's body. This put me cheek to cheek with him. He was an underfed, smallish fellow, probably not yet out of his teens, with a backcountry face pitted by acne, a flattened nose. I still held his head in my hands. It was quite heavy. This was the second human neck I had wrung on this trip. The first, in Moscow, was an accident, but it was a strange specialty to acquire so late in life.

Suddenly the firing ceased—at least the automatic gunfire did. I still heard single shots, sandwiched between moments of silence. The fight was over and the winners were hunting down and killing the wounded. Both sides were using Russian weapons or Chinese copies thereof, so it was impossible to tell who was doing the shooting.

I heard another horse nearby. In a piercing stage whisper, Someone said, "Horace!"

I said, "Here."

I realized that I was whispering, too. I cleared my throat and shouted the same word. Zarah, on horseback, emerged from the cloud. She led a second horse. "Climb up," she said. "We should get out of here."

I couldn't have agreed more. But which way was the way out? Zarah seemed to be in no doubt about this. I mounted the horse, the same irascible hammerhead I had been riding all along. As soon as the beast felt my weight it kicked, reared, bucked. Somehow I held on. Zarah tossed me a rope.

"Hold onto that," she said. "I'll lead."

That was fine with me. I suspected that this was not the first time Zarah had ridden a horse through a sandstorm. I grasped the rope, let go of the reins, and let my horse follow the others.

We rode at the trot for a couple of hours. This was excruciating because I had cracked a rib or two when I threw the illegal cross-body block on the young soldier. We were headed west and the storm was blowing eastward, so the visibility got steadily better. By the time we stopped to rest the exhausted horses, the sky was almost blue again, and in the distance, far below, we could see a very large lake.

Lori pointed to it. "Kyrgyzstan," she said.

TEN

1
―――――

A week after this, I met the rest of the Old Boys and the Christophers near a small lake at the foot of the Žetimtov Hills, at the northern edge of the Jomon-Kŭm sands. If I tell you that this spot was approximately 250 miles northwest of Tashkent, not far from Učkuduk and fifty miles from the nearest unpaved road, you'll know precisely where we were: in the middle of nowhere. The Christophers arrived first. I caught a glimpse of their camp from the top of a rise about half a mile away. It was late afternoon. This was a wrinkled khaki landscape, more barren than Xinjiang, so the azure lake filled with snowmelt was a startling punctuation mark— especially since Zarah's Saker falcon hung above it, looking whiter than it really was in the diagonal light of the descending sun.

By the time I drove down into the valley and parked beside the yurt, all four of the Christophers were on hand to greet me. Zarah kissed me on the cheek, Paul gripped my hand, Lori and Tarik stood apart and watched me with matching blue-gray eyes as if they had never seen me before. In a way they hadn't. We had traveled together in a sandstorm, barely speaking, and we had parted and gone our separate ways as soon as we crossed the frontier. Lori and Tarik were as much strangers to me as I was to them. For all intents and purposes so was the resurrected Paul. I knew no more about how he happened to be alive or about his recent adventures with Lori and Tarik than I had known when we were reunited in the labor camp in Xinjiang. There had been no chance for a family pow-wow then or while we were moving through the dust storm or shooting and being shot at during the firefight by the ice cave or riding blindly for the frontier.

Inside the yurt, with the last light of the winter day falling through the smoke hole, I got out the vodka and food I had brought from Tashkent. Tarik drank the vodka Russian style, bottoms up, and showed not the slightest effect from three quick glasses of the stuff. He was a taciturn, watchful fellow. Apart from skin tone and Tarik's handsome curved nose, he and Paul resembled each other—gesture, posture, timbre of the voice, their athletic way of moving. During supper we conversed as politely, as lightheartedly as if we had been seated around a mahogany table in evening clothes instead of crouching in a circle on a dirt floor while eating with our fingers. The Christophers told me about their long drive from Kyrgyzstan to this place. They had crossed the frontier at night, with Tarik and Lori on foot, because Tarik had no passport and Lori had done such a good job of disappearing that it was impossible to prove that she even existed. I was handling the vodka less well than Tarik, and after an hour of civilized generalities I was ready to turn the conversation in a more useful direction by asking a rude question or two. Of all the faces in the circle, only Paul's was turned my way. He had picked up on my mood. I knew the signs—the smallest of smiles, a hint of amusement deep in the eyes. Paul was reading my thoughts as if they were subtitles. Knowing me as he did, he guessed what might be coming next. Or so I was convinced. At any rate, he saved me from myself before I could even clear my throat.

"Horace," he said in a surprisingly audible voice, "How about a breath of fresh air, a look at our little lake?"

Zarah had been silent throughout the meal. Now she stood up. "Wait a minute," she said. "Lori and Tarik and I will come, too."

Lori said, "We will?"

"Yes," Zarah said. "This is the first time the whole family has ever been together."

Lori shook her head. "Not tonight," she said.

"Ah, my dear, especially tonight," Zarah said.

"Why especially tonight?"

""There are questions I want to ask.""

The two women locked eyes. They were not smiling at each other now, but my, they were alike. The moment stretched to a breaking point.

Then Lori said, "All right."

She adjusted her shawl, took Zarah's hand and followed her out of the yurt. It was a short walk to the lake. The water, when you stood close to it, smelled of snow and gave off waves of cold. Paul had said nothing, had scarcely moved except to walk alongside me. Now he picked up a flat stone and skipped it along the thread of light laid down on the glassy water by the new moon. Four skips. We had played this game in the Berkshires when I was a child. My stone bounced five times before sinking. Paul spun another stone across the water. This time all was as it always had been and should be: he won with a near-impossible six skips.

Tarik had brought a rug. While Paul and I skipped stones, he spread it on the ground and helped his mother to sit down. Zarah, legs crossed, sat down facing her grandmother and very close to her. We three men sat down, too, Tarik taking his mother's hand. He did this as if it were the most natural thing in the world. Paul watched, and even in this uncertain light I could see that this was a gesture that he felt he had no right to make.

Zarah said, "Now tell us what happened."

"When?"

"Begin in 1940."

Lori nodded, then began to speak with absolute directness, as if she had long been rehearsing these words. She had a rather hoarse voice and I wondered if she had sounded this way as a young woman. If so, it must certainly have added to her allure.

One sunny day in the late summer of 1940, Heydrich came for

Lori when she was riding in the park. "He usually sent his men to do this, but on this day he came in person. He was in full uniform."

One of his men led her horse back to the stable. Lori got into Heydrich's parked car, a long Gestapo-black Daimler.

"There were lots of people about," Lori said. "Men walking to work, women holding small children by the hand, Gestapo men who worked as lookouts and eavesdroppers for Heydrich."

Heydrich was excited. In the backseat of the car, Heydrich peeled off one of Lori's riding gloves and kissed her hand.

"He said, 'Today we do something different. I want you to select a passerby. A man. A youngish healthy man, about your husband's age. He must be tall. Anyone will do as long as he is tall.' Heydrich loved to play games; you never knew what might be next, and he was capable of anything. I tried to pull my hand away, but he held on. I said, 'No.'"

" 'As you wish, my dear,' Heydrich said. 'I already have under arrest a tall man who fits the type.' He meant my husband. On days when he abducted me he always had Hubbard, and very often Paul, too, brought to Gestapo headquarters for questioning. This gave him hostages as well as the assurance that my husband would never burst in upon us. I didn't know what he had in mind, apart from the fact that I knew it would be something barbaric, but I made the choice Heydrich knew I must make. I pointed to the first tall man who came along. He was a thin fellow, well dressed, a lawyer, perhaps. He wore a gold watch chain and a gold signet ring, but no wedding ring. He read a folded newspaper as he walked. Heydrich raised his hand; the gesture was enough to send anyone in Germany to his death. Two of Heydrich's men, waiting on the sidewalk, seized the tall thin man and hustled him into the back of another black car. His watch fell out of his waistcoat pocket and swung on its chain, knocking against the metal of the car. Dozens of people watched this happen. They all looked away."

Heydrich's car took him and Lori to his hunting lodge.

"It was a lovely day, unusually bright and balmy for Berlin,"

Lori said. "Lunch was served in the garden and then Heydrich asked me to play the piano—he adored good music, but in the middle of the day he liked operetta tunes, pretty Lehár melodies; he loved 'Dein ist mein ganzes Herz.'"

After she finished playing, Heydrich said, "Come, dear lady. We have some special music today."

They descended into the cellar of the hunting lodge and walked along a corridor so long and low that Lori realized it must be a tunnel. One of Heydrich's men went ahead and opened a series of doors for them while another followed behind and closed them. Lori found herself looking through a one-way mirror into a brightly lighted room next door. The tall thin man was strapped naked to a table. He was being tortured. His screams were very loud.

"I turned my back and put my hands over my ears—a foolish thing to do because it showed Heydrich his power over me. He said, 'Does the outcry offend you? I'm very sorry.'

"Heydrich imagined that he had beautiful manners. He rapped on the glass and on the other side of the window one of the torturers injected something into the man's tongue from a large hypodermic syringe.

"'Novocain,' Heydrich said. 'He won't disturb you much longer with his noise.' The torturers went back to work.

"Heydrich watched through the glass as though he was showing me a delightful sight, fit for the eyes of innocent children. What he was telling me, obviously, was that the man writhing on the table could just as easily be my husband or my son. In a tender voice, he then said, 'And now for my news. I have found a way for us to be happy together.'

"And then he gave me my instructions. That very evening, after my husband and my son came home from Gestapo headquarters, I must tell them that we must all three of us escape from Germany at the earliest possible moment. Two days from now, Hubbard, Paul and I would take a certain train to the French frontier. Our seats had already been reserved, the tickets had already been purchased. At the frontier I would be arrested by the Gestapo—or so it would appear to Hubbard and Paul. I would be escorted back to Berlin. Hubbard and Paul would be sent on across the border into France. This was Heydrich's gift to me. There they would be safe, but also quarantined. Neither would ever be permitted to reenter the Reich. Nor would I ever be permitted to leave.

"'My men will make certain that the arrest looks authentic,' Heydrich said. 'Your husband will never suspect the truth of our little plan, and you and I will be together forever.'

"So it was pretty much as you may already have imagined it," she said. "I made a deal with Reinhard Heydrich. A simple swap. Myself for my family. Not just Paul and Hubbard. My entire family. Everyone."

Zarah said, "Even so, how could you do it?"

"It was already too late to do anything else," Lori said. "I was like Germany. Nothing that I had ever been before this experience and nothing that I could ever be after it was over counted for anything."

"I don't understand."

"You must be the only person in the world who doesn't. In twelve short years the Nazis lobotomized Goethe, Beethoven, Luther, Kant, Kepler and several hundred other Germans who were inventors of civilization from the mind of mankind. All that remained was the horror. The same transformation happened to me, and to others. So I made the choice I made."

"I would have killed myself," Zarah said.

"Me, too," Lori said. "But first I had to kill Heydrich."

2

The opportunity did not present itself until two years later, after Heydrich had taken her to Prague.

Lori said, "The contact was a child, a girl of nine or ten, who befriended me in a park in the Lesser City. I was allowed to walk and take the air for an hour or two every other day. Heydrich said he was worried about my safety, so I was always accompanied by one of the Gestapo women who passed as my maids but were really my keepers. The little girl wasn't always in the park, but when she was, she and I played with dolls together on a bench—the usual tea parties and dress-up games. Her name was Liesl. She called me by my name, Hannelore. I enjoyed it; it diverted the mind. Everywhere you looked everything was in ashes, but little girls still played with dolls. Then the child began to pass messages to me. At first I didn't understand. She did it as part of the I-say-then-you-say make-believe conversation between the dolls. Nothing was ever in writing. The dolls were called Liesl and Hannelore. At the second meeting the child began delivering messages: 'Liesl says, Hannelore, we want to kill the evil man. Hannelore says, I will help you, Liesl.'

"But I would not say it. It was so diabolical, using a child as an agent provocateur, that I thought that Heydrich must surely be behind it. The child spoke German as if she had learned it from educated parents and she had a German nanny, a tall, athletic, handsome woman with a Viennese accent. My Gestapo maid talked to the nanny while I played dolls with the little girl. This child was the only person I knew in Prague apart from Heydrich and my keepers. It was plain to see that the maid and the nanny enjoyed each other's company even more than the child and I liked being with each other, but for quite different reasons."

At first Lori pretended not to understand what the child was saying to her. She regarded the episode as some sort of demented test of what Heydrich called their love, especially since her maid always led her straight to the nanny and child, as if to an assignation. By now the maid and the nanny were holding hands, whispering, giggling. The child continued to deliver messages: "Liesl says, Please tell me you understand my messages; Hannelore says, I do understand and I want to help."

"Gradually I began to regard what was happening as an opportunity for escape," Lori said. "If I betrayed Heydrich and he found out about it, he would either kill me outright or, far more likely, send me to a camp to die. Both alternatives were acceptable. In either case I would be free of him, so I decided to play the game. One afternoon when Liesl and I were playing dolls and the maid and the nanny were walking back and forth in front of the bench arm in arm, heads close together as they whispered to each other, I made a move. I said, 'Hannelore says, I will help you. But Liesl must tell me how.' The child said, 'Liesl says, Hannelore must say where he is going to be outdoors and at what time.'

"It was some time before I had the necessary information. Heydrich was close-mouthed about his public appearances, but I overheard a lot because he visited me almost every day and talked over the telephone to his aides. By eavesdropping I learned that he was going to be in a certain place at a certain time two days hence. The next day, I met the child and gave her the information. The child said, 'Thank you. Liesl says, We will come for you at that same hour. Be ready.'

"On stroke of the hour at which Heydrich was assassinated by gunmen while riding in his car, the nanny turned up, alone, at my apartment," Lori said. "She said it was her day off. She was a big, strapping girl with a very sweet face. The maid was delighted to see her. They kissed—I was watching through a crack in the door—and immediately went into a bedroom together."

Moments later the nanny emerged from the bedroom with a silenced pistol in her hand and shot the other maid through the forehead. She then opened a book in Heydrich's study, found a key inside, and opened a trunk-size strongbox filled with jewels, gold coins, and reichsmarks. She loaded some of the jewels and gold coins into the pockets of her coat, the rest into two handbags. She handed one of these to Lori: "Carry this." The Amphora Scroll was also in the trunk. Lori took it. Holding a forefinger to her lips for silence, the nanny opened the door into the outer hall. When the Gestapo man on duty in the hallway turned around with a smile, the nanny shot him dead also, caught his dead body as it fell, and dragged it inside the apartment.

"Not a word had been spoken," Lori said. "But now, in a whisper, the nanny said, 'Liesl says, Put on your coat and follow me.'"

The nanny led Lori to a streetcar stop. They got on the next streetcar. There were German soldiers in uniform on board. They stared at Lori and the nanny, but got off without making an approach. Two stops later, the nanny said, "I leave you here. Get off at the next stop. Follow a man wearing a green scarf. You will need this."

Lori said, "*This* was the handbag she had told me to carry, weighed down with gold coins and paper reichsmarks."

At the next stop Lori got off and followed the man as instructed into an apartment building. He left her alone in an empty flat.

"Like the nanny, he was silent," Lori said. "Inside the apartment he said, 'I will come for you in a few days. Don't leave fingerprints. Don't go near the windows. Don't make noise. There is food in the kitchen.' He left and locked me inside. It seemed quite possible that I had exchanged one prison for another, one madman for another. But a week later, after dark, the man in the green scarf let himself in with the key."

He took her to another empty apartment at the edge of the city. After that she was passed from empty safe house to empty safe house until she was close enough to the Hungarian frontier to walk across.

"And the rest you have found out for yourself," Lori said. "Or so Zarah tells me. Hungary, Palestine, Norman Schwarz, my life in the mountains."

"Not everything," I said. "Why Kyrgyzstan?"

It was too dark to see Lori's face, but when she answered her voice was as faint as Paul's; I had to strain to hear her. Tarik gave her a sip of vodka and her voice came back, but even hoarser than before.

"Heydrich may have been dead," she said. "But his men lived on. I had done something to be punished for no matter how long this took, and besides, I had the Amphora Scroll; I had stolen their gold. If I went back to Hubbard—and how could I?—they would hunt me down eventually and kill him and everybody else I loved. In the library at the country house in Hungary I found an old journal written by a dead member of the Bathory family. It described a trip he had made to Kyrgyzstan, described the people and the language. There were maps. He had gone in through Afghanistan. I memorized the list of Kyrgyz words in the diary, copied the maps, waited for the war to end."

I said, "You realized that Kyrgyzstan was part of the Soviet Union and what that meant, especially to a German in 1945?"

"Of course, but that was its charm." Lori said. "It was the most inaccessible place in the world for a Nazi, the last place even Heydrich's men would or could go."

Nevertheless Lori had never believed that she was safe. Not while Heydrich's men lived, not while she had the Amphora Scroll and they knew she had it, because who else but Lori would have known enough about it to steal it?

"That was why she ran to Xinjiang when she heard that an elderly foreigner who claimed to be her son was looking for her," Paul said. "She thought it must be one of Heydrich's men. She had never imagined me as an old man."

"But you followed her."

"With Tarik's help, yes," Paul said.

I said, "What made you trust him, Tarik?"

I spoke English. Tarik replied in the same language. "I knew all about him, Mother had told me about her other son," he said. "Besides, he looks like our mother. I knew that. Now I saw it. We went back for her together. We knew where to look. She thought the scroll would be safe in the labor camp."

"And you were caught by the Chinese?"

"No."

I said, "You just walked through the gates of a labor camp of your own free will?"

Paul shrugged. "I'd come a long way to find her. I felt as she did, that a Chinese labor camp was as good a place as any to end my days, and no worse than the camp she and my father and I would have been sent to in 1940 if she hadn't saved our lives on the train at Aachen. And then, I'd been looking for her all my life."

At this point I thought that I had heard all that I had any business to know. Why the Chinese had sent fake ashes to Washington when they knew that Paul Christopher was alive and well in Xinjiang was simply beyond my power to understand. I left the Christophers together, seated in a circle in the center of a vast empty quarter of the Earth. They murmured to one another. Soon I couldn't hear their faint voices. A few steps after that I could not see them by the light of stars.

3

To my mild surprise, all of the Christophers were still with me in the morning. Kevin appeared just after first light, right on schedule. He arrived on horseback. This time he was wearing Uzbek dress, assault rifle slung across his back, knife in his belt, pistol in a shoulder holster, grenades, binoculars, satellite telephone—everything but war paint. He and some of his men had set up camp about thirty miles away in the hills near the Jomon-Kŭm Sands. Another team was posted at the airstrip in Turkmenistan. Each team had a satellite phone and a backup radio.

"The guys in Turkmenistan are waiting for Ibn Awad's party to arrive and set up camp," Kevin said. "When that happens, our guys will study the target, watch the pattern of activity, count heads, identify weaknesses."

"And hope they're not discovered."

"Not much chance of that because no one expects them to be there and they'll stay hidden and study Ibn Awad's security routine. The idea is to get the information that will make the job of capturing the old man feasible instead of merely possible. And in the end, overcome the security, extract the target, and get everybody out alive and all in one piece."

"How many people will you need to carry out this extraction?"

"A minimum of eight," Kevin said.

"Ibn Awad has at least fifty bodyguards."

"Eight will be enough," Kevin said.

"I hope you're right," I said. "However, let's say you make the snatch and somehow kill or immobilize all of Ibn Awad's holy warriors. You'll still be in the middle of a desert with hundreds of miles of empty country between you and the nearest town and thousands of miles between that town and safety. Not to mention that everybody in the town in question will be a Muslim eager to save Ibn Awad from the infidels. How exactly are you going to extract your prisoner?"

"Improvise," Kevin said.

"Improvise? You're an interesting fellow."

Kevin smiled his inimitable smile. "We'll be in touch," he said.

He mounted his horse and rode away.

4

That afternoon, the rest of the Old Boys arrived. We sat in a circle on Lori's rug, drinking tea and watching as Tarik worked the Saker falcon against the cloudless sky. And then Charley Hornblower reminded us that life is full of surprises. While the rest of us had been watching the falcon, he had been emptying one of his large manila envelopes and arranging its contents onto the rug before him—text, maps, photographs, each held down by a small rock. A photocopy of Kalash's map was spread out as the centerpiece. The map was much annotated with yellow Post-its and highlighter inks in various colors.

"I think I've found something interesting," Charley said. "The migratory path of the houbara bustard passes right over every airstrip on Kalash's map. Except one."

Charley's blunt forefinger traced the flyway, marked on the map as a thick line of pale blue ink. Just as Charley had said, the birds flew right over the airstrips in Sudan, Balochistan, Iran and Turkmenistan, where Kevin's scouts were at this moment keeping watch over Ibn Awad's advance party.

After Turkmenistan, the bustards' migratory path turned east, missing the airstrip in the Jomon-Kŭm Sands by a couple of hundred miles. This was unsettling news. Kevin had concentrated his forces at the Jomon-Kŭm Sands airstrip, less than fifty miles from where the Old Boys were now sipping tea. Kevin believed—I believed, we had all believed—that the Jomon-Kŭm Sands airstrip was the best place to make our move on Ibn Awad. I didn't ask if Charley was sure of his facts. Of course he was.

I said, "I'm somewhat surprised."

"It surprised me, too," Charley said. "But every bit of data I could find and all the expert opinion suggests that the airstrip in Uzbekistan is no place to find the houbara bustard at this time of the year. Or any other time."

"So where is the bird's next stop?" Jack asked.

"The Sardara Steppe in Kazakhstan," Charley said.

Jack said, "Can Kevin fall back to that location?"

"I'd have to ask Kevin," I said. "He and I talked about the Jomon-Kŭm Sands and only about the Jomon-Kŭm Sands as the point of attack."

Jack nodded amiably, suddenly calm and agreeable, as if this problem was perfectly manageable. But the message in his voice, his gaze, his body language was written in a personal Braille that everyone present could read: *Kiss the operation good-bye, boys.*

I said, "Any thoughts?"

Silence. Then Paul said, "If there are no houbara bustards at the Uzbekistan airstrip, then why is it on the map?"

That was the question, all right. One possible answer was that there was no such airstrip. Except that Kevin said there was. Another was that it was a trap. I looked around the circle of faces and saw no sign that anyone wanted to make a guess. The question remained. Why would Ibn Awad build an airstrip to hunt the houbara bustard in the Jomon-Kŭm Sands if there are no houbara bustards there?

It was Paul who broke the lengthy silence. "Maybe Ibn Awad stops in the Jomon-Kŭm Sands for some other reason," he said.

"Such as?"

"Such as paying a visit to his bombs."

"Now that," Harley said, "is what I'd call an interestin' idea."

We ate a cold supper and went to bed early. I tossed and turned until shortly before dawn, then went outside. There was better visibility in this desert than there had been in Xinjiang. Even as a sliver, the moon produced a sort of warped daylight. Distant objects, such as the Žetimtov Hills, wrapped in blue shadow, were quite visible.

"It all looks primeval, doesn't it?" Zarah said. Her voice was hoarse, another trait she shared with her grandmother, but strong and distinct.

I jumped. I hadn't seen her and despite everything I've just said about the revealing light of the moon, I couldn't locate her. Then she sat up and I saw that she had been sleeping on the rug where we had taken tea earlier in the day.

"However, it is not so untouched as it seems," Lori said. "Tarik and I were talking about it during the night. He was here as a child with his father, and one night while everybody was sleeping the earth moved."

"An earthquake?"

"That's what they thought at the time even though it didn't feel exactly like an earthquake."

I said, "Did it happen on this spot, where we're camped?"

"Further west and north," Lori replied. "They were camped near the well at Sarim, about two days' journey from here on foot. The well at Sarim is miles and miles from anything else, which is interesting, because according to the map it lies between two highways that seem to go nowhere, and it's only twenty miles or so from the end of a railroad that begins in Samarkand and also goes nowhere."

That *was* funny. I said, "Anything else?"

"Tarik says the railroad and the roads were brand-new back then. The Russians built them after the war with Gulag labor. They were always doing things like that. Nobody paid attention, just steered clear."

"So there was this shaking of the earth," I said. "Then what?"

"After the shock they saw headlights, lots of them, converging on a single point. In the morning, there were many, many Russians in uniform running hither and yon."

At long last we had our stroke of luck.

After breakfast Tarik and Charley and I piled into a vehicle and headed for the well at Sarim. It was a wild ride. Only Tarik knew exactly where we were going, so he drove. His Kyrgyz genes were in full command of him and he was in command of the bucking, rattling machine. Charley, notebook computer open in his lap, bounced around in the back seat. How he could type under these conditions was a mystery but somehow he managed. The computer was hooked up to the satellite phone.

At last he shouted, "I think I've got something. Stop the car."

Standing on solid ground, Charley showered us with facts. There had been 596 underground nuclear tests in the Soviet Union between 1949 and 1985. Nearly all were conducted in Kazakhstan or on the island of Novaya Zemlya in the Soviet Arctic.

"However," Charley said. "There were two underground tests in Uzbekistan. One of these occurred around the time Tarik is talking about."

"Where?"

"Here, if Tarik's recollection is correct."

I said, "For what purpose?"

"It was classified as 'peaceful,' meaning not for military purposes," Charley said. "A lot of these peaceful underground tests were designed to study seismic waves. The Russians also mined for oil and gas with nuclear explosions. Or created underground storage chambers for liquefied natural gas."

"Underground storage chambers?"

"Yep," said Charley.

We got back into the car. When we reached the site, or what Tarik believed was the site of the underground explosion, Charley was first out of the car. Naturally he had brought along a Geiger counter—essential equipment, after all, if you're looking for stolen

A-bombs—and he whipped this out. When he switched it on, it chattered. Charley read the gauge and whistled.

"You think it's an underground chamber?"

"If Tarik saw what he thinks he saw," Charley replied, "it's likely to be, isn't it?"

For the next couple of hours, we drove in concentric circles while Charley took readings with his clattering Geiger counter and I noted the numbers on the odometer. In the end, this gave us a rough idea of the size of the cavity in the earth. It was many acres in extent. We had no idea how deep it was. One thing was sure: It was an ideal place to store a dozen small nuclear bombs. The background radiation would mask the radiation leaking from the bombs themselves. They could be dispersed underground, so that a thief or a spy might find one bomb but would have no idea where in the darkness the others might be hidden.

The frontier with Turkmenistan, home of Darvaza-76, the secret Soviet installation from which Mikhail had told us the bombs had been stolen, was a short distance away, and the country in between was virtually empty. We had no time left for skepticism. If luck had brought us here, then we'd better trust our luck.

The sun was falling. This was not the best place to spend the night. A mile or two away stood a range of bald mountains, higher and more rugged than the Žetimtov Hills. Horizontal rays of the sun blistered the mountainside with intense light, banishing shadows. I saw something move, squinted my eyes, saw something else move—soar, actually.

"Eagles," Tarik said.

If Kalash was right about the eyesight of birds, these saw us eight times better than we saw them.

We drove toward the hills.

5

I went to sleep on a hilltop that night thinking that I still had time to mull things over, work things out, make plans. The next thing I knew I was lying on my back looking straight up at the belly of a jet airplane. It passed directly overhead, landing lights ablaze, wheels down, spewing the stink of burnt kerosene. It was headed for the landing strip in the Jomon-Kŭm Sands, and though the sky was black, its aluminum skin flashed like a heliograph in the rays of the rising sun, which stood just below the horizon.

Ibn Awad's advance party had arrived early.

The sun popped up in the east. As if a switch had been thrown, its stinging light flooded the hilltop and I saw something else I had not expected to see—Kevin. Still dressed as an Uzbek, he sat cross-legged in the sand beside me, his assault rifle in his lap. He whispered in some sort of military gibberish into the mouthpiece of the miniaturized headset that he wore. I was still half-deafened by the noise of the airplane and I could not hear Kevin well enough to make out his words. Half a dozen previously invisible men suddenly rose out of the ground. All wore headsets just like his and all were costumed and armed and accoutered like him. Charley Hornblower was propped up on one elbow, befuddled, looking like somebody else without his glasses. Tarik was a study in stillness as he gazed upward toward the crest of the mountain.

I followed his gaze and saw two more of Kevin's men, posted as lookouts on high ground.

Kevin said, "Sorry about the rude awakening."

"You knew they were coming today?"

"I hoped so," he said. "Our guys in Turkmenistan radioed that they had loaded up and taken off. I left a heads-up on your voice mail. You didn't get it?"

"I haven't checked for messages lately."

"Ah."

Kevin was completely at ease, in his element, in command of all the necessary facts and of the means to deal with them. Military procedure had the situation in hand. Except for the lookouts, his men were crouched now, weapons slung, fussing with foil packets that I recognized as U.S. military field rations. I got to my feet, not quite so nimbly as I might have wished in the presence of all these supple young witnesses, and gave Charley a hand up. We stumbled together behind a convenient rock to relieve ourselves. Charley said nothing about the airplane that had just shocked him awake, nothing about finding himself surrounded by commandos when he opened his eyes. He took his several morning pills.

Charley looked over his shoulder. "How much are you going to tell this fellow?" he whispered.

The habit of a lifetime dies hard. Charley was a Headquarters man. An airplane full of killers had just flown over our heads and their leader, a homicidal maniac we had been chasing for months, would be on the next flight, but the important thing to Charley was keeping secrets.

I said, "What parts would you leave out, Charley?"

"What we found out yesterday, for starters," he replied.

"That might be difficult."

I pointed to the desert floor, a few hundred feet below. The tracks we had left while driving in circles had left a huge target-like pattern at least a mile in diameter. It could have been seen from outer space.

I said, "Charley, this thing is almost over. Kevin knows what we're after; he's always known. What do we have to hide?"

"Nothing, if Kevin really is on our side. But what if he isn't?"

"In that case," I said, "he's got us surrounded, hasn't he?"

"My point exactly," Charley said.

Tarik was conversing with one of Kevin's men in what seemed to be Kyrgyz. None of the men said a word to Charley or me. They were crouched in their baggy native dress like genuine men of the desert, breakfasting on U. S. Army Meals-Ready-to-Eat. Kevin handed each of us a steaming foil envelope full of food and a plastic spoon. I got beef stew, Charley macaroni and cheese. Charley ate pickily and in silence, his usual good fellowship buttoned down. Holding his spoon in his fist instead of his fingers, Kevin gulped down his utilitarian meal with utilitarian speed. He then produced a toothbrush and toothpaste and brushed his teeth, rinsing from a canteen and spitting on the ground, then rubbing the white streaks into the dirt.

From where we stood we could see the pattern left by our wheel tracks. Kevin pointed to it and said, "By the way, what was all that about? We saw the dust cloud from ten miles away."

I told him. At first Kevin was politely skeptical, like a farmer listening to a city fellow predict the weather. A cavern dug by a nuclear explosion? An underground lake of liquefied gas?

"*Radioactive* natural gas."

"Isn't that hazardous to the gonads?" Kevin said. "We've been walking across that ground for a week."

"According to Charley it's not quite Chernobyl, but it's hot."

Kevin said, "And you think the bombs are hidden somewhere in this cubic mile of nuclear soup?"

"I think it's possible," I said. "It would make sense to hide them in a radioactive site. The background radiation would mask their presence, and nobody would go near the place."

"Mikhail said he checked every such site in the Soviet Union."

"Except maybe the one he didn't tell us about."

Kevin said, "Poor Mikhail, nobody trusts him. Suppose you're right and this is the mother lode. How do we get the bombs out without melting ourselves down?"

That was the problem, all right. Unless you were a suicide bomber.

6

At noon the plane took off and disappeared to the south. An hour or so after that, three of Ibn Awad's men, robes and head cloths billowing, Kalashnikovs slung across their backs, arrived on motor-bikes. They rode right across the bull's-eye of tire tracks that Charley and Tarik and I had left without seeing them. Meanwhile Kevin's advance scouts, posted on yet another hilltop overlooking the airstrip thirty miles away, reported in by radio. The plane had been offloaded. Tents were going up, water pipe was being laid from a spring, the generator was up and running, sentries had been posted, and as we had just seen, patrols sent out. It was a pious camp. Everyone had rushed off the plane as soon as it landed, spread prayer rugs on the runway, faced Mecca, and said the dawn prayer. At noon they had done the same—even the sentries.

Presumably they would pray three more times before they went to bed. Kevin liked this picture. Everybody in Ibn Awad's camp would be down on elbows and knees and vulnerable five times a day, providing five opportunities for infiltration or attack. I found it difficult to share his enthusiasm. I knew that I should be smelling blood, eager for the kill, happy to be in position to fin-ish the job my aging friends and I, all alone in the world, had set out to do. But I was tired. Also exasperated. Although I devoted most of my life to them, secret operations always exasperated

me—the wasted motion, the misspent energy, the pointless anxiety, the trivial results that remind you how little good you've done
for all your trouble and how foolishly you are wasting your life. It's
a young man's game, of course, and by the time you realize all of
the foregoing you're too old to change careers. Not to mention
having a résumé that would frighten any personnel director in the
world out of his wits. I was tempted to walk off the hilltop and let
Kevin do the rest. I had mixed feelings about saving the world, or
whatever portion of it Ibn Awad was threatening to consume by
fire. In the great scheme of things, what was the point of stopping
him? Maybe Ibn Awad was some sort of Tarot card that was fated
to be turned over. Who was I to trifle with destiny? Besides, I had
already killed the old maniac once, only to discover that he was
only pretending to be dead, so was it also in the cards that I should
murder him, or fail to murder him again? So much depended on
chance, on luck, on the adversary making the necessary mistakes,
on everything falling into place, on the happenstance of being in
the right place at the right moment. I had spent six months getting into position on this hilltop in a far corner of Uzbekistan and
now all I could do was wait.

But not for long. Just before sunset the airplane returned and
landed again on the airstrip in the Jomon-Kŭm Sands. Ibn Awad
stepped off. I did not see this with my own eyes, of course, but listened over a headset as one of Kevin's scouts reported the landing.
In a sort of play-by-play commentary, the lookout described Ibn
Awad's every move. The old man was upright, moving under his
own power. He wore his usual white robes. He was weaponless,
not even a ceremonial dagger in his belt. He wore an oxygen mask,
his male nurse following along behind bearing the tank. The sun
was touching the western horizon and as soon as Ibn Awad
reached the bottom of the ramp he fell onto a prayer rug that had
been spread for him and performed the sunset prayer. After that
he walked unassisted to his tent with firm step, but slowly. He was
surrounded by the bodyguards who had arrived with him—a
dozen fighters, armed to the teeth. Added to the ones already on

hand, these new arrivals brought the number of battle-ready holy warriors to about twenty. Kevin took this head count as good news. He had been expecting fifty, but now he was only outnumbered three to one, a ratio he seemed to regard as ideal odds.

As soon as darkness fell Kevin and his men moved out. Their destination was the hills overlooking the airstrip. They had gone so thoroughly native in matters of dress—even Tarik had taken them for Uzbeks on first sight—that I half expected them to produce a string of camels and climb aboard. However, they traveled on foot.

We watched through binoculars as they moved across the moonlit plain, double-timing for a few hundred yards, then walking, then double-timing again. At this pace they should reach Ibn Awad's camp in the small hours of the morning, about the time the moon set.

While Kevin's men were still in sight, David and Harley and Jack arrived in another car. They brought with them food and water and a collection of equipment that would have been astonishing if anyone besides David had put it together—assault rifles, grenades, blocks of explosive, and of all things, a heavy mortar with a crate of shells. All of these weapons were Russian.

"The market's flooded with this stuff since they stopped paying the Russian army," David said. "Army officers sell it for peanuts."

I said, "What are we going to do with it?"

"You never know," David said, "but it's better to have it and not need it than need it and not have it. I don't know about you, but I felt a little naked in Xinjiang."

Harley gazed pensively at the scars we had left on the desert floor. He said, "Correct me if I'm wrong, Charley, but the way I remember it, the Soviets made three of these underground reservoirs that we know about, all north of the Caspian Sea. Drilled a shaft, dropped an H-bomb down it, plugged the shaft, and let 'er rip. When it went off it made this great big cavern. The idea was to store oil and gas as a strategic reserve, like we do back home in salt domes."

This much I had already figured out for myself, but it was nice to have confirmation from Harley, who in his palmy days as a master spy was usually the first to know about such things.

"Other thing is, there's no natural gas around here, so they must have liquefied it elsewhere and hauled it in tank cars," Harley said. "That's what the railroad was for."

"So what does that mean?" Jack said.

"It means, Jack, that all we have to do is find the place where they dumped the gas in," Harley said. "There must have been some kind of pumpin' station, maybe more than one, and pipelines. That means steel and concrete hidin' places. Find that and you've found the bombs."

"If they're here," Jack said. "And if we can locate them without a whole lot of equipment we don't have."

"When it comes to lookin' underground there's more than one way to skin a cat," Harley said.

"Do you have a method in mind?"

"Well," Harley said, "usually you use a forked stick you cut off an apple tree. They call it a witchin' stick. There're no apple orchards around here, so maybe a coat hanger will do."

He just happened to have one. He produced it, untwisted it, straightened it out, and then retwisted it into the shape of a Y. I may have been a summer kid but I had spent enough time around Yankee farmers to know what Harley had in mind. None of the city boys present had the faintest notion, as the look on Jack Philindros's face testified.

Harley said, "David, you've got a lot of scrap metal available. Why don't you go off in the dark and bury somethin'?"

"Why?"

"Want to test this out. Not sure it'll work. Bury the stuff about two foot deep."

I went along with David and helped with the shoveling. We buried the base plate of the mortar, an AK-47, and a couple of hand grenades in separate holes. The ground was stony, so this took a while. We didn't mark the holes and the moonlight was not strong enough to reveal signs of digging.

"We can kiss this stuff good-bye," David said. "We'll never find it again."

I wasn't so sure of that.

"Now blindfold me," Harley said, when we got back to him. "Don't want to be accused of cheatin'."

Jack handled this chore. We led Harley to the vicinity of the buried metal, but not too close. He gripped his coat hanger by the arms of the Y.

"Point me in the right direction, boys," he said, and stepped off.

He walked about twenty paces. When he was on top of the hole in which the mortar base plate was buried, the coat hanger dipped.

"Right here," he said. "Good-sized chunk of somethin'."

"There are more," David said.

"Don't tell me how many," Harley said. "Just tell me when I'm done."

He missed the AK-47, which was off to the right, but found the grenades a few paces further on.

"Small," he said.

"One more behind you," David said.

Harley turned around and began pacing back and forth in straight lines. Finally he was close enough to the AK-47 to pick up its emanations, or whatever they were, and the coat hanger dipped.

"Medium-sized," he said. "Long piece of iron. Any more?"

"That's it."

Harley removed the blindfold. We uncovered his finds. As a boy I'd watched one of our neighbors in the Berkshires find a spring with a forked branch cut from an apple tree. He'd done it in broad daylight without a blindfold, but his stick had bobbed just like Harley's, as if tugged by an invisible troll pulling on a string. The spring he found (fee: $2) was still providing icy cold water to anyone who wanted to dip a tin cup into it and take a drink.

I said, "Harley, I never knew you were a dowser."

"Half forgot it myself until earlier today when Charley told me what the problem was over the telephone," Harley said.

"I thought you could only find water by this method."

"Not true," Harley said, "you can find anything. "A hundred years ago my grandfather found oil in Pennsylvania with a cherry switch. *Thought* it was water till he dug down a ways."

"How does it work?"

"Dunno. It's a mystery, but it works. Runs in the family. Skips a generation usually."

Jack was nonplussed, wondering perhaps why, when it had had Harley, the Outfit had spent all that money on space satellites that peered down on the Evil Empire. But more likely not believing what his own eyes had just seen. Harley was smiling, eyes only, head turned away to hide this sign of the sin of pride. All of a sudden I felt much better about our prospects. Optimistic, even.

7

Tarik was not a babbler. He spoke Kyrgyz and English and Mandarin, and considering the time his energetic mother must have had on her hands while he was growing up, he may have been taught German and classical Greek and who knows what other tongues. For a while I thought his reticence had something to do with that half-door the Chinese had hung around his neck. Maybe it had given him a sore throat or an unsettled mind. But no. Like his half brother Paul, he just wasn't talkative. Somehow silence fit his character, even his appearance. With his coppery complexion, high cheekbones, steady eyes and silent deeps he resembled another Central Asian, James Fenimore's Cooper's Chingachgook, stalwart and silent and no longer young (Tarik must have been about fifty), but still a warrior.

Tarik had observed Harley's demonstration of witching with close interest. After it was over, while we were still standing in an admiring circle around Harley, skeptics and believers together, Tarik startled us by speaking.

"You can see what the Russians tried to hide quite plainly in the moonlight," he said.

I said, "What do you mean by that, Tarik?"

"Come," he said. "I'll show you."

He led us uphill for a few meters to a spot where we could overlook the valley. He pointed a finger.

"I don't see it," I said.

"I only saw it myself for the first time tonight," Tarik said. "You're looking for traces of an old highway and a railroad roadbed."

Now that Tarik had told me what to look for they leaped to the eye. Two long parallel cuts were visible on the desert floor below. The fainter of the two must have been the highway. The railway roadbed was easier to detect because it had once been a raised embankment and now it was scattered over a much wider strip of land. It was obvious that the highway and the railroad had been bulldozed. And it was just as obvious why this had been done. The Russians had wanted to hide what they had done here—not because they were ashamed of themselves for having despoiled yet another untouched natural fastness, but because it was one of their innumerable Cold War secrets.

Just before the end of the line, the railroad had made a sweeping left turn, buttonhooking in that direction for a mile or so before it curved right again. From where we stood on the hilltop, the traces of this unusual track looked like a backward question mark.

"That must've been where they offloaded the gas from the tank cars," Harley said. "That buttonhook must be two, three miles long. They could move up their tank cars in a half circle, park 'em on the track, and pump 'em out one by one as slick as you please. Wish I'd known about that when they were doin' it. Where were you when I needed you, Tarik?"

It was obvious where the pumping station was likely to be— at the tip of the hook of the question mark. The moon, now waxing toward the half, provided all the light we need. We drove down the hill and paced off the distance to the center. This was rough measurement indeed but the best we could do without a surveyor's transit. Harley commenced pacing back and forth, his coat hanger held before him. Meanwhile Charley, feeling no doubt like the forgotten man, went prospecting with his Geiger counter—ancient wisdom versus twentieth-century science. It was surprising how far the Geiger counter's clicking, or any mechanical noise, carried in a place so lifeless that there were no natural sounds except when the wind blew.

A couple of hours before dawn, Harley's coat hanger dipped. "Pretty strong dip," he said. "Must be somethin' down there."

He stood where he was, marking the spot, until the rest of us got there with shovels. The dirt here was far looser than it had been on the hilltop and with Tarik and David and me taking turns with the shovel, we made steady progress. When the hole was about hip deep, we struck concrete.

"Problem is, it's just concrete," Harley said. "Now we know there's somethin' there. But what we got to do is find the way in."

We dug again. Despite the nip in the air—at four in the morning it couldn't have been more than forty degrees Fahrenheit—we were all sweating. I had always imagined that ditch-digging left the mind free for long trains of poetic thought, as it had for Paul Christopher during his first prison term in China. However, I found that I had to concentrate every minute on what my body was doing. Also I was beginning to get blisters on my hands and if I thought at all, it was about them.

Fortunately, Tarik had lived in a world of toil and sweat all his life, so he could wield a shovel and keep his wits about him at the same time. It was he who spotted the headlights approaching from the south, the direction in which Ibn Awad's camp lay. I counted fifteen, moving slowly, and so did Tarik. Nobody else could see well enough to run a total.

"Fifteen's an odd number," Harley said. "Guess that means there's at least one motorcycle. Or a one-eyed car."

Charley's Geiger counter chattered. He said, "Very hot spot here."

We all knew what the headlights meant: we'd better get out of there as quickly as possible. On the other hand we could all hear Charley's Geiger counter and we knew what that very possibly meant: We'd found Ibn Awad's bombs minutes before Ibn Awad's men were going to arrive, shoot us all dead, and take possession of them.

I said, "Tarik, how long before they get here?"

"Half an hour, maybe less."

David said, "Dig we must, don't you think?"

Jack said, "I have a question. Suppose we've found the bombs. What are we going to do with them even if we dig them up? If we take them with us, we die of radiation poisoning. If we leave them here, a lot of people may die in other places."

"That pretty well sums up the choices, Jack," Harley said. "So why don't we just dig the durn things up now and think about what to do with 'em later?"

He grabbed the shovel and attacked the ground, making dirt fly. After thirty seconds of all-out effort he handed the shovel off to me and staggered away, clutching his chest and gasping for breath. The hole was three feet deep when Tarik took over from me. Soon the shovel rang as it struck an obstruction. Tarik bent over and touched it.

"Metal," he said. "I think it's a hatch."

Five minutes more and he uncovered the wheel that unlocked the hatch. Charley handed him the Geiger counter. It went wild.

Charley said, "I don't think you should open that thing. Radiation will come out like smoke up a chimney."

This was wise counsel, but if we did not open the hatch how would we know what we had found? Tarik apparently had the same thought. He spun the wheel until we heard the latches click, then tugged. The hatch did not open. I got down on my stomach, reached into the hole, and took hold of the wheel. David did the same. We heaved. The hatch came open with a whoosh. Charley's Geiger counter chattered again, more rapidly than before.

Someone handed me a flashlight. I shone it inside and there in their tomb were the Uncle Joes, all twelve of them side by side. They seemed to be in mint condition. According to my watch, digging down to the hatch and opening it had taken about fifteen minutes. The headlights, though still distant, were about the size of baseballs now. We had maybe another fifteen minutes.

David had backed his vehicle up to the hole. The cargo area was a jumble of gear—vodka, food, guns, ammunition. I assumed he meant to load the bombs aboard and try to make a getaway, but then I saw that he had another idea. While Tarik and I were shoveling, he had kneaded together several blocks of Red Army surplus explosive and was screwing a fuse into the putty-gray blob that resulted. The blob was about the size of a soccer ball—big enough to destroy almost anything in an enclosed space.

By now insect intelligence had taken over. We were all thinking the same thought in the same moment—even Jack. This thought was, *Blow the damn things up*. Nobody asked if we had time to get clear, or what the effect would be on the atmosphere or the people downwind from this site. The headlights were closer.

"We drop the explosive down the hatch and cover the hole," David said. "We set up a remote detonator, jump in the cars, and drive fast. When we're a couple of miles away, we throw the switch on the transmitter and up it goes."

Jack said, "This is a *Russian* radio detonator we're talking about?"

"What can I say?" David asked. "It's what we have and it's all we have. We can use two, in case one fails."

David handed me the blob. I lowered it through the hatch. It was attached by wires to an antenna and a radio receiver. David set this up some distance away. The approaching vehicles were so close now that we could make out the sound of their engines, though we could not yet see anything but yellow headlights. They were traveling abreast. I squinted, trying to make out more details. One by one our own vehicles departed, all except the one driven by David Wong. He stood beside it, shouting at me to hurry up.

He jumped out of the car and ran back to me.

"What's the matter?" he shouted.

"What if it's Kevin?"

"Then he should have told us he was coming. Come on, Horace, we've got to go."

Three men on motorbikes shot out of the dust cloud and accelerated toward us. I felt wind on my cheek and heard the snap of bullets passing by. We sprinted to the vehicle and jumped inside. David put it into motion before the door closed and drove at breakneck speed across the desert. I stuck my head out of the window and looked back. Within the dust cloud I could see muzzle flashes as the motorcyclists fired at us with automatic weapons. The back window of our vehicle was shattered by a round that zipped between David's head and mine and blew out the windshield.

When you stopped to think about it, as I now had the leisure to do, this was strange behavior. Why were these people shooting at us? So far we had done them no harm. We had found the bombs, yes, but how could they know that for sure? How could they even know who we were? Did the answers to all these thoughtful questions really matter? These guys were trying to kill us no matter who we were or what our intentions.

David had grasped this reality right away. He opened the roof and handed me a loaded Kalashnikov. It was no easy trick to fit myself and the weapon through the small opening in the roof, but I managed to do so just in time to see the motorcyclists pulling abreast of our car. They wore wind-filled burnooses and, incongruously, bulbous, shiny white crash helmets with black face shields. The one on the left was leveling his rifle at David's head from a range of about ten feet. A split second later his weapon flew out of his hand and he shot off his bike, propelled backward as if lassoed. I smelled gunsmoke, saw a flash, looked behind me, and saw a gun barrel protruding from the rear side window. Tarik had shot the man. Up to that point I had not even noticed that Tarik was with us.

The motorcyclist on the left, either oblivious to the fate of his friend or in love with death, was now aiming his weapon at me. Before I could raise my own rifle—knowing all the while that I hadn't time to do so before the other man fired—David swerved the vehicle and sideswiped the motorcycle.

A hundred meters or so to our rear the dust was thinning, settling. I could see no more pursuers. Maybe we had gotten away. Then I looked to the left and right of our tail of boiling dust and saw headlights. Up ahead, quite close, was the steep ochre mountain where we had camped. David was pounding on my leg. I put one arm inside the vehicle, intending to fold my whole body back inside, joint by joint and appendage by appendage. David put something in my hand. It was the transmitter for the remote detonator.

"I'm going to speed up now," he said.

Speed up? The landscape was already a blur. I expected the bucking vehicle to start tumbling end over end at any moment.

"As soon as we're parallel to the mountain, but just before we get behind it, push the button," David yelled. "Can you hear me?"

We had no idea what was going to happen if the bomb went off. David saw this in my face.

He shouted, "Horace, just do it. Please!"

David was right. This was not the moment for second thoughts. I understood his plan. He wanted to be on the other side of the mountain, shielded from the blast, when the bomb went off. If we were killed before the button was pushed it would never go off. Not only were a couple of dozen gunmen trying to murder us, but their friends were almost certainly trying to disarm our bomb at this very second.

The sun came up. David began to turn hard right—car rocking, motor racing—for his run behind the mountain. I pressed the button on the transmitter. For an interminable moment I heard and saw nothing. Then I heard the explosion, distorted and louder than seemed possible, rolling over us as if it was being amplified through a very old loudspeaker. The ground, the whole landscape, shook itself like a wet dog. A chunk of the mountain the size of a church fell off and bounced across the desert. Then another, then an avalanche. The sky filled with a flickering glow, yellow and blue like a gas burner, which was then enveloped by a huge black cloud.

David fought the wheel. I expected the car to turn over at any moment and in spite of all that was going on, I still had a thought for myself because my head and shoulders were sticking out of the roof.

Like Dr. Oppenheimer in Nevada, I thought, "What have we done?"

That is a question you ask yourself only if you already know the answer and wish that you didn't.

8

No, we hadn't touched off a nuclear explosion. We had ignited the underground reservoir of liquefied gas, and of course this released a large amount of radiation. The pumping station where Ibn Awad's bombs had been stored was connected to a pipeline running into the lake. When our explosive went off, it sent a blast of flame and heat down the pipeline. This triggered an underground explosion that very nearly brought the mountain down. Common sense should have told us this would happen, but in the heat of the moment we had not been listening to our more judicious selves. Somehow the cavern contained the explosion, but a huge jet of burning gas vented into the sky through what used to be the pumping station. The ground above the lake writhed with tongues of blue flame escaping through cracks in the underlying rock.

From the hilltop we saw no sign of human beings living or dead, and the fact of the matter was, we didn't know for certain whom we had killed. Terrorists? Kevin's men? Was there a difference? We assumed that the dead and missing were Ibn Awad's men, but as you have seen as this report unfolded, our assumptions were not always correct.

"Nice work," Harley said.

Jack said, "We're going to have half of Kazakhstan on our necks before we know it."

"Not to mention the Sierra Club," Charley said.

Ah, liberal guilt. We had just accomplished one of the two impossible things we set out to do and instead of being wildly elated, we were overcome by shamefaced embarrassment. Lighting eternal flames fueled by radioactive gas was politically incorrect. We were old enough to know better. We had violated the sacred Outfit creed: Do Good by Stealth. We had accomplished the mission, yes, but nobody could say we had tiptoed in and tiptoed out.

"Well," said Harley. "At least we'll get no thanks for this and that's somethin' to be thankful for."

Meanwhile Ibn Awad was probably among the privileged few who were watching the fireworks from afar. Unless Kevin had used the distraction we had provided to take the old man prisoner, Ibn Awad would be thinking about getting on his airplane. If he was permitted to do that, the whole cycle would begin again. He would find someone else to sell him more bombs and this time he would use them before we or anyone else could catch up to him. It took me a moment to find my satellite phone and punch in Kevin's number. It rang several times. I got Kevin's voice mail.

The airstrip was thirty miles away. There was no road. We could not get from here to there in less than an hour and a half. I wasn't sure if we had enough gasoline to get there. We siphoned the fuel from two of the three vehicles and poured it into the tank of the one that seemed least likely to break down. David handed out weapons and ammunition to everybody and all six of us piled into the one car, Tarik at the wheel. We skirted the site of the explosion. The earth crawled with worms of flame. The fumes were suffocating, the heat intense. Again I looked for corpses but saw none. I don't know why I expected to. Anyone who was anywhere near the pumping station—the likeliest place to be if you were trying to prevent David's blob from going off—would have been vaporized by the explosion of burning gas from underground.

9

Tarik got us within sight of the airstrip in a little over an hour. We saw no lookouts on our way in. There was no point in caution, no time to reconnoiter. Tarik drove right onto the runway and parked our car in front of the airplane. We jumped out. In addition to assault rifles, we had two rocket-propelled grenade launchers. Charley and Harley, our two least agile commandos, were issued these weapons with instructions to fire on the aircraft if it attempted to take off.

The rest of us—Jack, Tarik, David, Ben and I—headed into camp, rifles at the ready, expecting to be cut in half at any moment by a chainsaw of AK-47 rounds. We could smell coffee, hear goats bleating behind the cookhouse, see windblown clothes drying on a line. Nothing happened. The camp was deserted. Not a soul could be seen, not a sound could be heard, not a trace of life could be detected except for six magnificent peregrine falcons, wearing hoods, that sat on perches at the back of Ibn Awad's dining tent. They were absolutely motionless, apparently asleep. Had Ibn Awad and everyone else in camp rushed to the fire that burned beyond the horizon? This seemed unlikely to me and apparently Tarik has his doubts also, because he turned on his heel and ran from the tent. By the time I got outside he was dog-trotting toward the edge of camp, his eyes fixed on the ground beneath his feet. He was following the wheel tracks that led northward, in the direction of the fire. After a few moments he stopped and ran off to the right, his eyes still on the ground. Then he stopped and pointed east.

I joined him. Tire tracks told the story. A large number of vehicles had left the camp together. After about two hundred meters a car and five motorcycles had split off from the main convoy, made a sharp right turn, and driven due east. The yurt was due east of Ibn Awad's camp. This made perfect sense. Ibn Awad was interested in gaining possession of two things—the bombs and the Amphora Scroll. He had sent messengers to pick up the bombs and gone himself to collect the scroll. Lori had the scroll. Lori was in the yurt.

Tarik said, "We should go. Now."

Tarik followed the tracks left by Ibn Awad's convoy, or what we assumed was Ibn Awad's convoy. We hadn't used the GPS to locate our position since Tarik joined us. He seemed to know exactly where he was at any given moment. After an hour he stopped the car and got out to listen. The Žetimtov Hills were framed in the windshield. The yurt was quite close now. I dismounted also. In the distance I heard the pop-pop of gunfire. The sound was too far away to tell if two different sets of weapons were being fired, so we couldn't tell which was in progress, a firefight or a massacre. There seemed to be too much shooting for it to be the latter, considering that there were only three people in the yurt.

Tarik and I armed ourselves from David's bomb and gun shop in the back of the vehicle and set off on foot. The idea was that David and the others would wait by the car and follow on foot if I called on the satellite phone and told them they were needed. Tarik had spent his life climbing up and down mountains and he seemed to have unlimited breath and endurance. He moved too fast for me, but I only had to take two steps to his three, so I managed to keep up after a fashion. By the time the yurt came in sight I was gasping. My hands shook violently. Had an enemy popped up out of the ground, as I was expecting one to do at any second,

I probably would not have been able to hit him with a shotgun, and I didn't have a shotgun.

The yurt had been burned. Only its charred poles were still standing. Apart from this dismal sight it was impossible to guess what had already happened or see what was happening now. A lot of shooting was still going on but the shooters all seemed to be in the prone position. The ground where we lay was so flat and so utterly lacking in cover that they couldn't stand up or even crawl without being shot. Each side was sending out fire inches above the ground to keep the other flat on its collective face. At the rate at which ammunition was being expended I didn't see how the fight could go on much longer, but who knew? If we were spotted, either side would fire on us as a precaution.

So far we hadn't been seen, but this could change at any moment. Tarik took charge. He pointed to the hills and set off at a run without bothering to see if I followed. By now I had gotten my breath back, or enough of it at least to keep him in sight. I had not had a stitch in my side since school days, but I had one now. After a few more minutes I was reminded of another thing that every teenage runner knows about—the second wind. The stitch went away. I breathed easier, I stopped hearing the hammering of my own heart. My hands steadied, my knees stopped trembling.

A few hundred feet up the flank of the hill, Tarik found a vantage point. I flopped down beside him. We saw men in robes and red-checkered Arab head scarves on one side, men in Uzbek dress on the other. There were many more Arabs than Uzbeks, so many more that I wondered where they had all come from. They couldn't possibly have fitted aboard the small executive jet parked on the tarmac at Ibn Awad's camp. In the distance, sun flashed on glass. Through binoculars I counted ten pickup trucks parked in the distance. Ibn Awad had brought in reinforcements overland.

There were seven Uzbeks, one of whom was dead or soon would be, judging by the splotch of blood on the back of his shirt and the disjointed way in which he was sprawled on the ground.

I could see their weapons—the Belgian assault rifles Kevin and his men carried. But where were the Christophers? There was no sign of Lori or Paul or Zarah.

The impulse not to interfere was strong. As long as the two sides were firing at each other, we had relative freedom of movement. Freedom of movement was exactly what we needed if we were to have a prayer of finding the missing Christophers. On the other hand, Kevin's team was on our side at least in theory, whereas Ibn Awad's men were irrevocably our deadly enemies. If they won this skirmish, our life expectancy would shrink dramatically. But how to help the good guys? Tarik and I could hardly open fire from our aerie. We were at least half a mile from the battlefield. We could move off to the side and open enfilading fire, except that we'd have to stand up or at least kneel to do this and we'd almost certainly be filled with lead by both sides before we squeezed off a shot. I called David on the satellite phone and told him what was going on and what I thought he could do about it.

He said, "You'll be the observer?"

"That's right. Just stay on the phone. Do you remember how to do this?"

"I've got a vague recollection. And no doubt I'll have a lot of advice."

Minutes later the Old Boys' vehicle came into view. Through the glasses I saw David jump out, run around to the rear, and start rummaging in the cargo compartment. Moments after that our lads were hustling forward, carrying heavy objects. They fitted these together as if they were an infantry squad that practiced this sort of thing every day instead of once every fifty years. Before I knew it they were ready to fire the Soviet mortar that I had ridiculed when David showed up with it the day before.

David's voice came over the phone. He was panting. "What's the range?"

"Call it four hundred meters," I said. "Fire for effect."

Seconds later a mortar round exploded a few yards behind Ibn Awad's men. David adjusted his fire a couple of degrees to the right. The next shell landed between two sprawled Arab fighters, putting them both out of action.

"You're right on them," I said. "Now walk your fire forward. They're lying abreast about a meter apart."

Through the binoculars I could see Ben—who else?—sighting the mortar while David dropped shells down the tube and Charley and Jack fed them ammunition. Harley cheered. So did the others; I could hear their voices in the silence after each mortar round detonated. They sounded like the sideline at a prep school football game in which the players are the only spectators. The effect may have owed more to good luck than good planning, but the bombardment devastated the terrorists. After the fourth or fifth explosion the fellows in red-checkered kaiffiyehs jumped to their feet and retreated, firing wildly as they ran backward. One or two of them were shot or tripped on the hems of their robes. Kevin's men cut them down with rifle fire. In seconds the field was scattered with the bodies of Arabs wrapped in white robes that now looked like blood-soaked shrouds.

I spoke into the phone. "Cease firing."

"Roger," said David.

This military jargon fell strangely from my tongue and into my ear, but it was a language we all understood even though none of us had spoken it for a long, long time.

I said, "Get out of there before they come looking for you." Tarik and I watched as the Old Boys departed, jouncing north at a speed that made Tarik's driving style look tentative. Meanwhile on the dusty plain below, Kevin's team continued its mopping-up operation. The fleeing Arabs did not have a chance. The team moved with the speed and certainty of highly trained men who were in peak physical condition and, having found themselves alive against all expectation, were glad to have this opportunity to kill their enemies without mercy. Little did they know that they had just been extricated from the mess they had gotten themselves

443

into by a bunch of arthritic, pill-taking old men who last saw combat before these kids' fathers were born. This was not, perhaps, the moment for such thoughts, but as I have mentioned, life is fraught with irony. We had ended up rescuing the people we'd hired to rescue us.

10

Now that they were standing up I could see the faces of the men in Kevin's team. Kevin was not among them. The headset he had loaned me was still hanging around my neck. I adjusted it and switched it on. The instrument immediately picked up radio chatter among the team. They were speaking Russian to each other. The reason why was as obvious as if they had all smiled at once, revealing mouthfuls of the finest aluminum teeth Soviet dentistry could provide. Kevin's men in Budapest had been silent and most of his people in Russia had been as mute as statues, too. Until this moment I had never asked myself the reason why. First impressions are the best, as we all find out when it is too late, and it was now obvious I should have paid more attention to my initial feeling that Kevin was too good to be true.

I made another phone call. This time Harley answered. I told him what I had just heard over the headset.

"We'll be comin' round the mountain," he said.

Tarik and I scrambled to the summit. He moved just as fast uphill as on the level, so keeping up to him was out of the question. When I got to the ridge he was waiting for me. We could see for miles. We saw nothing that moved except the Old Boys' vehicle, approaching from the west, dragging the usual wake of dust behind it. I stood up so that they could see me. Their headlights blinked.

Tarik plunged down the other side of the mountain and ran with long strides straight down the treacherous crumbling slope. His idea, I guessed, was to intercept the Old Boys' vehicle at the bottom, with the mountain between it and Kevin's men. I followed as best I could, legs trembling, blood pounding, balance somewhere between lost and gone forever, inner voice telling me what a fool I was to be taking such chances. If I broke a bone—*a hip!* I thought, suddenly remembering my age—I was a goner. Self-taught stuntman though he appeared to be, Tarik would never be able to carry a hulk like me down the mountain. Not that he was likely to try. His mind was on his mother and half brother and niece. So was mine, for that matter, but for the moment I had all I could do to keep my bones unbroken.

The Old Boys awaited us at the bottom. I was too winded—and too surprised to be all in one piece—to take much part in the ensuing conversation.

Harley said, "Can you talk yet?"

The best I could do was to lift a hand and point at Tarik. He knew everything I knew. More, probably.

Harley said, "Sorry to ask this, Tarik. But you didn't see any sign of their dead bodies, did you?"

Tarik said, "No. But Horace had the binoculars."

I shook my head No.

"That could mean they've been carried away," Harley said, "and the only reason that would happen is they didn't have the Amphora Scroll. If they'd had it with 'em, the bandits would've killed 'em and taken it. Ibn Awad or Kevin or whoever wants to talk to 'em at leisure."

For once Ben could think of no better explanation of the Christophers' absence. "Let's assume they got away," he said. "When and which way did they go are the questions."

"Anybody's guess," Harley said.

My own guess, informed by blood and many years of disappearance and reunion, was that our lost sheep were not lost at all,
but had done what Christophers do in a case like this one, i.e., the
opposite of whatever conventional wisdom dictates.

By now I had recovered enough of my voice to say, "They
wouldn't run away. They'd run toward us."

Jack said, "But the sky was on fire in that direction."

"They'd run to it *because* it was on fire."

"But why?"

I shrugged. This was not the moment to compose a psychological profile of the Christophers even if such a thing were possible. Their plan and their whereabouts, as usual, were anybody's
guess. If there was an expert among us on Lori and on this countryside, it was Tarik. Naturally no one asked his opinion. He sat
silent in the front seat between David and me while the words and
theories flew over his head.

It was David, who had also kept his peace, who asked the question. "Tarik, what do you think?"

"If they're alive," Tarik said, "they will give us a sign. We have
to get close enough to see it."

And with that he closed his eyes and seemed to go to sleep. I
didn't understand how such a thing could be possible until my
own eyes closed. Despite the bone-rattling progress of the car,
despite the dust blowing in all four windows, despite the heat,
despite my old friend nausea, I fell asleep too.

The whine of the transmission woke me. David had shifted
into low gear. The tilted vehicle was climbing a steep hill, its
gearbox shrieking in protest. I stuck my head out of the window
and looked back. In the distance I saw plumes of dust moving
toward us across the desert floor—Kevin's men, I assumed, driving fast in their commandeered pickup trucks, or maybe on
captured motorbikes. David parked in the lee of the hill, just
below the top. Tarik immediately headed for the summit. I
followed him as if the two of us were joined by a cord. From the
hilltop we had a clear view of the airstrip and Ibn Awad's camp

a thousand feet below. The airplane was still parked on the tarmac, the empty tents filled with wind and expelled it. There was absolutely no sign of life except for a pair of eagles soaring in the distance.

"They will come," Tarik said.

But where were they now? The sun was already sinking. I looked behind us. The distant vehicles were closer now but could not reach these hills before the sun set. This was comforting in a way, but the prospect of being hunted in the dark by Kevin and his men or even by what remained of Ibn Awad's bodyguard was not a happy one. About two miles to the west, beyond the airstrip, was another set of hills, slightly higher than these.

I got out my satellite phone and punched in Zarah's number. It rang once, the receiver clicked. It went dead. I tried again. Same result. Zarah's phone had caller ID like all other satellite phones I had ever seen, so if she was the one who was answering and immediately hanging up she knew who was calling but had some reason not to speak. Unless somebody else had taken possession of her phone. Tarik's eyes were fixed on the hills opposite. The eagles still circled, no doubt looking for a place to spend the night now that their old aerie was bathed in the poisonous fumes of the burning gas.

And then, seeming even whiter and swifter than usual in contrast to the bruised hues of the discolored sky, the Saker falcon was flying. Its great wings propelled it upward in a near vertical climb and soon it was hundreds of feet above the eagles. Then it dove. I had seen this before, of course, but the speed and verticality of the descent took my breath away. It hit one of the eagles. The eagle seemed to explode, dark feathers and blood flying. The eagle shrieked, or I imagined that it did, as the two great birds, striking at each other, tumbling toward earth.

"That's the signal," Tarik said. "They're in those hills."

As he spoke the Saker falcon labored upward, the eagle's limp carcass gripped in its talons. With a slow beating of wings it rose to a great height and then, unable to keep its grip, dropped the eagle. The Saker falcon circled a few times as if contemplating an attack on the second eagle, then swept down to the hilltop where we now knew the Christophers were waiting for us.

Ah, the symmetry. Zarah had conceived the Saker falcon as a signal to Ibn Awad, something that would intrigue him and draw him to us. No doubt that is exactly what would now happen. We had intended to capture him. Now we were the ones in danger of capture.

The others had seen the Saker falcon's kill and knew what it meant. There was no need for an elaborate plan. Tarik and I would try to find the Christophers in the dark and bring them back. The others would stay behind and look out for themselves as best they could. If we made it through the night we'd call each other up in the morning and decide what to do next. David's cornucopia of lethal devices—AK-47s, grenades, what little remained of his supply of plastic explosive—were spread out on a blanket. Tarik helped himself to a formidable knife, pulling a hair from his head and slicing it in half to test its sharpness.

As soon as it was dark Tarik and I set off. I half-expected Tarik to make another devil-may-care run down the mountain, this time in the dark, but he proceeded with caution. Once down, we walked boldly across the airstrip. There was no cover of any kind on the desert floor, so it was pointless to behave as if there were. Besides, our friends were watching from the ridgeline behind us, satellite telephone in hand. If they saw anyone stalking us, they would call. The incongruity of the thing was enough to make you laugh— Tarik and I plodding in moonlight across this wasteland like a couple of bloodthirsty hunter-gatherers while keeping in touch with the home cave, just a mile or so away, via earth satellite.

We reached the other hills and began to climb. Big rocks cast pools of shadow. We paused in one of these. I was breathing hard. Tarik had been moving uphill at a rapid pace. Now he crawled to the edge of the shadow and for a long while looked upward, studying the ridge. He came back, sat down beside me, and took my hand. I was oddly pleased by this brotherly gesture.

He said, "If there are enemies here, they'll head for the place where they saw the falcon come down."

"You think Paul and the others will still be there?"

"No, but with luck I will be, so he'll know where to find me. We should split up, you and I. Try to get behind them."

"And when I'm behind them, then what?"

Still holding my hand as if he might never see me again—a distinct possibility, it seemed to me—Tarik just smiled and then was gone. Truly gone, invisible as a ghost. I stared into the darkness for some sign of him, knowing that he was there. But this time all my birder's tricks availed me nothing. He had blended into the sand and rocks, not making a sound or even casting a shadow.

In my own climb up the mountain, accomplished mostly on all fours, I created considerably more disturbance, stirring up miniature avalanches, grunting loudly when I fell. However, luck was with me. No one leaped out from behind a rock with weapon in hand. As far as I could tell, I had attracted no attention whatsoever.

On the valley floor, the aluminum skin of Ibn Awad's airplane glinted in the moonlight. The camp was dark, apparently still deserted. Across the way in the other range of hills, the Old Boys were watching, or so I hoped. Though not quite sure where I was going, I stumbled off in the direction of the place where the Saker falcon had come to earth. Two meters farther on I stumbled across a corpse. It was still warm. The man lay on his back, eyes staring, white shirtfront soaked with blood. He had thick black eyebrows and a flowing black beard. There was no visible wound. I kneeled, lifted the beard, and saw that his throat had been cut. How, I wondered, had Tarik managed this without slicing off part of the beard?

For all he noice I heard I might as well have been inside a soundproof room. I crept from shadow to shadow. The question was, What lurked in the shadows? As far as I could tell, nothing, even though the evidence suggested that this could not be the case. I reached the place where I thought the Saker falcon had landed. I found footprints, just visible by moonglow, and followed them for a time, concentrating so deeply as I stared at the ground that I could have walked into the arms of an assassin and never known it until I felt the blade or the bullet.

The tracks dwindled, then disappeared. I stood on the backbone of the mountain, gazing at the pillar of fire on the horizon, alone.

My vibrating telephone woke me from a sound sleep. As soon as I opened my eyes I knew that something was seriously amiss.

It was David Wong on the line. He said, "Do you see what we see?"

I did indeed. Ibn Awad's camp had come to life. Lights burned, men bustled about, trucks and motorcycles moved through the darkness, headlights blazed. All of this was happening in dumb show and in Tinkertoy scale because I was a couple of miles away from and a thousand feet above the scene. One of the scale-model trucks was a tanker. It pulled up beside the parked airplane. Men leaped out and ran hoses to the plane's fuel tank. There wasn't enough light to use my binoculars. What I saw with the naked eye were silhouettes—men darting through the beams of headlights or briefly framed in light from within as they lifted the flap of a tent.

David was closer to this scene than I was. I said, "Who are these guys?"

"Reinforcements, maybe. Everybody here is asleep except me. Any sign of the others where you are?"

"No."

David went on whispering into my ear. I was disoriented and despite the excitement of the moment, still half asleep. Because my mind was so thoroughly elsewhere, his words did not immediately register, but one of his phrases rattled around in some part of my head even though I had not really heard it on the conscious level.

"What did you just say?" I asked.

David said, "'Somebody just went into Ibn Awad's tent carrying the Saker falcon.'"

This brought me fully awake. If they had the falcon they must have the Christophers, either dead or alive. And if they had the Christophers they must have the Amphora Scroll. This realization touched off an emotion that was new to me—rage: uncontrollable, overwhelming physical rage that seized control of my mind and body as though some Stone Age Horace had leaped out of his cave and into my skin. My brain—in the state I was in I could hardly call it my intelligence—began to race. About two hours of darkness remained. That gave me just enough time to get off this mountain, cross the open ground below, penetrate the enemy camp, and kill someone. Anyone.

I did not even say good-bye to David. Before I knew it I was halfway down the mountain. Likely I wouldn't have remembered even this much of the descent but I stumbled over a punctuation mark—another dead fedayee. His throat had been cut, too. I paused to take his AK-47 ammunition and pluck two eggshell-smooth Russian hand grenades from his shirt. They were sticky with the blood from the gash in his throat. Down below, assault rifles were being fired. The shooters were not aiming at me but into the air. Apparently they had something to celebrate. Another bad sign.

Nearer to camp, scouts on motorcycles buzzed around like insects. I passed among them as if invisible. I was in the dark, looking into a lighted world. The enemy were in the light, looking into the dark. It was almost dawn. I had to strike before the sun came up and made us all equal in terms of eyesight. The tanker truck's crew were winding their hoses onto drums. I crept closer. Ground crew swarmed around the plane, inspecting surfaces, checking whatever such people check, peering into engines.

A man approached from the camp. He limped slightly. Light fell momentarily on his face. I recognized him—it was Captain Khaldun, Kalash el Khatar's pilot who had flown me in and out of Cairo in Kalash's Learjet. I contemplated this funny coincidence without surprise. What was one more example of betrayal? Captain Khaldun walked around the airplane, clipboard in hand, and carried out his own inspection. One side of the fuselage was awash in the headlights of a rank of parked trucks, apparently as an aid to the refueling. The other side lay in darkness that seemed all the deeper by contrast. I was standing upright about a hundred feet from the plane. Captain Khaldun, still the humorless single-minded fellow who had dropped me off near Jef Jef el Kébir, was so absorbed in what he was doing that he did not see me. I wait-ed until he disappeared around the tail of the plane, then walked without concealment to the wing, jumped lightly into the air like an eighteen-year-old going in for a lay-up, and without pulling the pins, tossed the grenades I had taken from the dead man into the jet engine. If all this seems recklessly showy, I should explain that I was not so spacey that I forgot my tradecraft altogether. When it comes to penetration operations the key to success is not subtlety and maneuver but brazening it out. A skulker is more likely to be nailed than a lunatic who behaves as though he is in no danger, has no fear. As soon as I stepped into the light, I broke into a run and headed straight for Ibn Awad's tent. Before any of the many guards could shoot me, I was inside.

There Ibn Awad sat on a rug, dressed like a pilgrim in rough-spun garments, eating his curds and whey. Behind him on a perch sat the snow-white Saker falcon along with half a dozen pere-grines. Ibn Awad looked up and squinted—his eyesight had always been dim—and actually said, "You!" In Arabic, of course.

The two bodyguards who stood behind him had made the mis-take of slinging their assault rifles around their necks instead of holding them at the ready. While they struggled to unlimber their weapons I shot them both dead with the Kalashnikov. This made a lot of noise inside the tent. The gunfire startled the falcons—out of the corner of my eye I saw wings flapping—but escaped the notice of the people outside because they themselves were still firing merrily into the air.

Before my ears stopped ringing, Ibn Awad was scrabbling on hands and knees toward the back of the tent, bony backside in the air, uttering choking sounds. Naturally I thought that I had shot him by mistake. I was wrong. It was not Ibn Awad I had shot but two of his falcons, which had been knocked off their perches by stray rounds from the full magazine I had fired at the bodyguards. Ibn Awad was now gazing tearfully at the broken bodies of his pets. He paid no attention whatever to the two men who had just laid down their lives for him.

I said, "Old man, turn around and look at me, please."

Ibn Awad heard me, but his mind was on more important things. He was grieving for his birds, holding one in each of his outstretched hands so that I might see their bloodstained plumage, behold their lolling heads and opaque yellow eyes that glittered no more, and understand exactly what I had done.

I said, "The owners of the Saker falcon. Where are they?"

Ibn Awad shrugged. His indifference was so obvious that it practically gave off an odor. Clearly he did not fear me. He knew perfectly well that I had every reason in the world not to shoot him and probably he also believed, oh so wrongly, that I was the fully rational person he used to know and trust.

I said, "What orders have you given about my cousins?"

He shrugged again. This infuriated me. I became the raving caveman again. I seized Ibn Awad, threw him over my shoulder, and dashed out the back of the tent into the darkness. Probably the old man had never before in his life been touched by infidel hands, let alone treated like a rolled-up rug being carried off by a thief. He offered no resistance; he could not have done so even if he wished; his starved bony body felt as if it had no strength in it at all. Fortunately for me, Ibn Awad was an ascetic. Years of eating only enough food to keep himself alive had reduced his weight to what felt like around ninety pounds, so I was able to move quite swiftly through the night. Each time one of my feet hit the ground Ibn Awad uttered a sound, half grunt, half moan, as if every shock came as a total surprise.

After I had run flat-out for about a quarter of a mile (who knows where I got such energy?) I came upon a good-sized altar-style rock and dumped Ibn Awad on top of it. There was no one behind us. I could scarcely believe this, but it appeared to be true. The folks who were supposed to guard Ibn Awad had been so busy readying his airplane for escape that they had not noticed what had gone on in his tent. They were in for a surprise when they went inside and found the martyrs and the falcons lying about, but no madman.

12

The sun came up at last. At the exact moment that the first thread of dawn appeared in the eastern sky Ibn Awad fell to all fours atop his flat rock, wheezing and keening and gesturing in fervent prayer. I am not usually moved by demonstrations of religious feeling, but I was oddly touched by his behavior. For a fleeting instant I was almost fond of him again, as I had been in the past before my orders changed. It's amazing how touching the enemy softens the heart. For months I had been demonizing Ibn Awad from afar. Now I was close enough to hear him gasp for enough breath to talk to Allah; I had not brought along his oxygen tank and his emphysema was clearly all too real. He smelled faintly of cloves; I wondered why. His hands, moving in the gestures prescribed for Muslim prayer, were so brown that the falcon blood on them was barely visible. It must have troubled him to pray without washing himself first, but I suppose that unwashed hands were permitted to the devout in the extreme circumstances in which he now found himself. His gesticulating figure, perched on top of that rock, must have been clearly visible from the camp, but no one seemed to notice. This was not surprising. Most of the people in the camp were praying, too.

To all appearances his absence had not been noted. Men in robes were busy striking the camp and loading it onto trucks. One after the other the tents collapsed until only two were left—Ibn Awad's big tent where the dead fedayeen and falcons awaited discovery, and another smaller one. It was not difficult to guess what was hidden inside the second tent. It could only be the Christophers. I pictured them bound and gagged, all four of them—Tarik, too if he still lived—sitting in a row, awaiting whatever fate their captors had in mind for them. Whatever that fate was, it probably did not in the mind of their captors involve salvation, for they were unbelievers and if they died they would die like dogs with no hope of heaven. Ibn Awad finished his prayers and sank onto his haunches. He stared serenely at me, turning blue for lack of breath, no hint of fear or ill feeling in his eyes. I thought I still knew him well enough to read his mind. He seemed to be waiting for someone to come and kill me. As far as he was concerned it was all in the hands of God. Everything was, including me as the bizarre nemesis who kept showing up in his life and ruining all his plans. He was Job, I was Satan, wandering about the Earth and administering tests of his love for the Almighty who had given him so many reasons to love him—oil wells, a mission to destroy evil on Earth, even a resurrection of a kind after the assassination failed and Claus Bücher healed his wounds. You could feel his submission to the divine will. He knew his present situation was nothing but a test, that he was being teased by the Author of the Universe who would never let him come to real harm, that in the end he would kill the enemies of the faith on Earth as he was born to do, and enter paradise.

Suddenly his eyes lit up and shifted and I whirled, weapon at the ready, expecting to see his thugs behind me. What I saw instead—you've guessed it—was Kevin, rising up out of the dust with a tremendous minstrel smile splitting his face, which was smeared with camouflage grease. I was in no way surprised. Kevin gazed at Ibn Awad, who gazed back at him with unruffled serenity, as though a jolly commando from Ohio was exactly what he, too, had been expecting to see.

Kevin said, "We watched your run for the roses just now. Nice fireman's carry, Horace."

We? I looked beyond him and sure enough, there were his men lounging on the sand. Evidently they had been there all the time. But why? What had they been waiting for? What was the point of sneaking up on an objective under cover of darkness if you were going to wait until daylight to attack it? I asked no questions. There was no point in that, either.

Urbane as ever, Kevin said, "I don't know why you thought you needed us, Horace." He waved a hand at the pillar of fire, the pall of smoke to the north, then indicated the captive on the rock. "You're a one-man action movie."

He was standing upright now as if all need for concealment had vanished and he had nothing to fear from the swarm of armed desperadoes who were buzzing around the camp. He was carrying Ibn Awad's oxygen tank. Gently, even tenderly, he adjusted the mask over the old man's nose and mouth, then turned the valve. Ibn Awad inhaled convulsively for a full minute, then began to breath normally again. Kevin patted him on the arm.

The air stirred. A quarter of a mile away Ibn Awad's tent inhaled the breeze then blew it out and hung slack. Still no one had gone inside to check on Ibn Awad. Suddenly something clicked, the pieces came together, and it dawned on me that there was a reason for this. Ibn Awad *didn't* have anything to fear. He had been a captive. The men I had killed had been his captors, not his bodyguards—Kevin's men, not his. The old schizo had been gazing on me so benignly because he thought I had rescued him.

I said, "Kevin, what exactly are you up to?"

"Fulfilling my mission," he said.

"I see. Do you have my cousins in your custody?"

"Not exactly. But they're alive and well and I have no interest in them. Others do."

"Others? What others?"

He nodded toward the camp. "Those fellows over there. They're Turkmen and I think they're going to expect to be paid a ransom."

"A ransom?"

"I'm afraid so. And compensation for their two friends whose throats Tarik cut before we got to him and saved him from Turkoman revenge, which is not, I assure you, a pretty sight."

"These Turkomen are with you?"

"I wouldn't go that far," Kevin said. "Let's say we're working together. It's our policy to work with the locals. That's primarily what our fellows were doing in Turkmenistan, finding locals to work with. They cleaned out the camp and took Ibn Awad prisoner. I think they'll want payment for the two Turkmen you zapped."

"What sort of ransom did *you* pay them?"

"They get everything but the airplane and Ibn Awad," Kevin said. "That's why they're so happy, firing into the air and so forth."

Ecstatic might have been a better word, judging by the amount of ammunition that was still being fired into the wild blue yonder.

I said, "Frankly, Kevin, I'm at sixes and sevens. If your Turkmen friends get everything but Ibn Awad, who gets Ibn Awad?"

Kevin's smile turned apologetic. "We do."

"'We' is not you and me, I gather."

He shook his head.

"Then you and who?"

"I'm not allowed to say. But the old fellow will have a good home."

My gorge was rising. It was late in the day for games. The beast I had been the night before was awakening again and I was mightily tempted just to shoot Ibn Awad and put an end to his story. However, I had other people to think about and I knew that I'd be dead myself before I took my finger off the trigger if I actually did what my reptile brain was now instructing me to do.

Nevertheless I pressed the muzzle of my Kalashnikov against Ibn Awad's heart. In the most pleasant tone of voice I could muster, I said, "I noticed that Captain Khaldun has joined the party."

Kevin seemed surprised. "You've met?"

"Is Captain Khaldun on loan from Kalash el Khatar?"

"Gosh, what a lot of little details you know, Horace. The answer is yes. Ibn Awad's pilot wasn't deemed reliable as a getaway driver."

"Is this another example of working with the locals, or do you and Kalash go back farther than that?"

Kevin had stopped looking me straight in the eyes and was now smiling upward as though waiting for advice he knew could never come. He sighed audibly.

"Look," he said. "The objectives of this operation were to destroy Ibn Awad's bombs and eliminate him as a threat to mankind. Thanks mainly to you and your pals, these things have been accomplished. What difference does it make what the auspices are or who gets Ibn Awad?"

"So you're going to give me the credit and take Ibn Awad as your share?"

Kevin said, "Something like that. Horace, will you please stop poking your weapon into the prisoner's body?"

"You want him alive."

"Of course I do. What good is he to anyone dead?"

"What good is he alive? What are you going to do with him? All questions about him have been answered. There'd be no point in hooking him up to a battery and making him talk because he'd just thank Allah for the agony."

"Nothing like that is going to happen. Now please, Horace, it's time for all of us to get out of here. I can't believe the Uzbek army isn't here already."

"If interrogation isn't part of the plan," I said, "what is? Are you going to sell him to Kalash, or what?"

Kevin ignored these impassioned questions. His eyes were fixed on Ibn Awad, who could not have been more serene or more disinterested in his own situation if he had just taken a whole bottle of Valium.

Kevin said, "He really is insane, isn't he?"

"Either that or he's achieved union with the ineffable and God and his angels really do talk to him," I replied. "In either case, sweet and harmless as he seems, I'm not prepared to turn him loose on the world again unless I know the details. To whom are you planning to deliver him?"

Actually I had no intention of turning the old man loose no matter what Kevin said. He had too much money, too much hatred for the Great Satan, too much faith in the idea that life on Earth was transitory and without value except as an opportunity to wipe out false religions. However, I was beginning to see a pattern. This whole thing had started with Kalash. Was it now ending with Kalash?

The muzzle of my gun was still pressed against Ibn Awad's chest. Kevin was beginning to look positively unfriendly. He said, "You know, they always warned us about getting mixed up with formers."

"Getting mixed up with what?"

"Former operatives. Old Boys. People like you. Now I know why. You geezers are dangerous."

I got out my telephone and speed-dialed Kalash's number. If he was as closely involved in this as I suspected, he would be waiting for a call.

And so he was. He answered the phone himself. And recognized my voice.

"Ah, Horace. The weather is filthy in Paris. How is it in Uzbekistan?"

"Overcast."

"So I've heard. What a fellow you are, Horace."

"I'm standing here with our mutual friend Kevin and your cousin."

"Is anyone pointing a gun at you?"

"Not yet. But I am pointing a gun at Ibn Awad."

"Then you're in an ambiguous position and so am I. May I speak to Kevin?"

"No."

"I see. Then why are you calling? What do you want?"

"Reassurance. What exactly are your plans for your relative?"

"I told you. An island in the sun where he can pray in peace. Somehow I've gotten the idea from past events that that's not a solution that would appeal to you."

"I don't have the resources to keep him happy and healthy in that kind of assisted living facility."

"Of course you don't. On the other hand I have a family obligation, you know. Don't want to flunk the orals on Judgment Day."

I had one more question, the only one that mattered. I expected a truthful answer. Kalash was unlikely to lie to someone as lowly as me. It was beneath him. Not only was I his profound inferior in every way that mattered—even my scrap-metal soul, if I had one, was worth far less than his golden one—but he also must have expected that I would be dead in a matter of seconds. I was almost as certain of this outcome as he was, but I was dying of curiosity. Years of my life had been crossed out by my connection to Ibn Awad. What was left of it was hardly worth worrying about.

I said, "Once you have your cousin, you have control of his wealth, correct?"

"I suppose I would have some sort of fiduciary responsibility, yes."

He was talking about billions of dollars. Ibn Awad still controlled the wealth of his entire country with its huge oil reserves. Although I was a good one to talk, the idea of placing such wealth in the hands of a man who seemed to be a complete cynic made the blood run cold. Not because Kalash actually cared about nothing but because in some hidden part of himself he must care about something very much indeed to keep it such a secret. And in the age of terror, in an age when two versions of the same god were wrestling with each other in the minds of the zealots of two civilizations, what else could he care about but the same mission that obsessed Ibn Awad? This wasn't a simple case of swapping one bad risk for another. Kalash was more dangerous than Ibn Awad because he was five times as intelligent and absolutely sane. He would get the job done, and quickly, efficiently, remorselessly.

I could never let him get his hands on the money.

I said, "Hold on a moment, will you? I want to ask Kevin a question." To Kevin I said, "Will you give me the Christophers, all four of them, if I let Ibn Awad live?"

Kevin shrugged. "That's fine by me."

"No. You have to guarantee it. I'll walk Ibn Awad to the plane. Paul and Zarah and Lori and Tarik must be on the tarmac, waiting for us. You must get us away from the Turkmen and get us across the frontier into Kazakhstan."

Kevin nodded. "That's a lot of 'musts,'" he said. "But okay."

I spoke into the telephone. "Did you hear all that?"

"Every word," Kalash said. "Of course you can have the Christophers. Wouldn't want anything to happen to old Paul. But I must have the Amphora Scroll."

"That's the price?"

"That and my poor cousin, safe and sound, yes."

"I must have your promise."

"You trust me to keep it? I'm touched."

I said, "Do we have a deal or not?"

"Done," Kalash said. "Go in peace."

13

It was a short walk to the airstrip, but Kevin had been muttering into his headset and by the time we got there the Christophers awaited. They looked the same, except for Tarik, who had one arm in a sling. To my surprise Zarah held the hooded Saker falcon on her arm. When Ibn Awad saw her uncovered face and unbound hair he turned his head away and spat, eyes glittering with righteous anger and disgust. Kevin, too, noticed Zarah, but reacted in a more Christian manner. I thought that his eyes might drop out of his head, and it must be said that she made a striking composition with the wind blowing her hair across her face and the huge alabaster bird gripping her slim forearm with its talons and the whirling demons and noise and smoke of chaos all about.

Captain Khaldun was already in the cockpit. The door of the plane was open, the ramp in place. Ibn Awad's outraged reaction to Zarah's harlotry had lasted only a moment. He shrank back into the passive old duffer he had been all morning. It was strange how utterly harmless he looked in his muslin robes and black turban and bare feet. His head was slightly cocked, as if he could hear things that the rest of us could not. He wore a slight smile. If it was voices he heard they must have been soothing ones.

Kevin said, "Shall we get him aboard?"

"Are you going with him?"

"Nope. I'm leaving with the fellow that brung me. Wasn't that the deal?"

"What about Ibn Awad?"

"Minders have been provided. A doctor and a male nurse. Ibn Awad seems to know them."

"The doctor's name?"

"Mubarak."

I laughed. Kevin gave me a sharp look. What else did I know now that I wasn't supposed to know? It was time to load Ibn Awad onto the plane. At this last minute I was loath to do so. Thirty bearded Turkmen fingered their weapons and watched my every move, looking theatrically grim. There was no way to be sure of what might happen to the Christophers and me after I let Ibn Awad go, especially after my grenades did their work on the left engine of the jet. Whatever they might do, it was unlikely to be friendly and pleasant. Kevin's men, who were making a point of standing well apart from me and my friends, were our best if not our only hope of getting out of this alive and with all our body parts still attached. Yet I still didn't even know what the native language of Kevin's men might be—or Kevin's either, if it came right down to it.

"Time to load him aboard," Kevin said. "But first, you and I have some unfinished business."

His tone was heavy with meaning. Paul gave me a look. So did Zarah. I saw no sign of the Amphora Scroll, but then Lori had never carried it in plain sight.

I beckoned to Paul and handed him my Kalashnikov. While he covered Ibn Awad, I walked over to Lori, who was standing somewhat apart from the others. Tarik moved closer as if to protect her even from me. I did not blame him. The air quivered with tension, Turkmen stood in a ring around us, Kevin's intentions could not be guessed, confusion reigned. Lori seemed almost as oblivious to it all as Ibn Awad.

Talking to Lori was an echoless experience at the best of times. She simply absorbed whatever you said into the deep silence that seemed to be at the center of her being. I explained about the Amphora Scroll, that Kalash wanted it and that we had to put it on the plane or probably die, in which case it would be taken from her dead body.

She said, "What will he do with it?"

"That's not going to be a concern."

"What are you saying to me?"

"That the scroll will be out of your life. Out of Zarah's life. It will cease to exist right in front of your eyes. Do you understand?"

"You're certain of that?"

"On my honor."

Lori looked at Zarah, a long look, which must have been like gazing at herself in another time and place, and perhaps she remembered Heydrich and who knows what else. And then this woman who had guarded the Amphora Scroll, who had carried it next to her skin for more than sixty years and given up everything for it, reached under her voluminous Kyrgyz skirts, brought it out and handed it to me. Tarik gasped. She laid a motherly hand on his cheek, and for a brief moment when she smiled at her son, the one that she loved, she looked as she must have looked when she still looked like Zarah.

I handed the scroll over to Kevin. Solemnly we marched Ibn Awad to the plane. A hostile young man in a white coat whom I knew must be Mubarak and a male nurse met us at the bottom of the ramp. They helped him up the stairs. Kevin and I followed, Kevin carrying the portable oxygen tank as well as the Amphora Scroll. On board the aircraft, he handed the oxygen tank to the nurse and the Amphora Scroll to the doctor, who snatched it from his hand and tossed it into an overhead compartment.

Ibn Awad was being strapped into a large seat like a dentist's chair, more suitable for an execution than a journey. The male nurse strapped his oxygen tank into the seat next to him. I tried to catch Ibn Awad's eye; this would be the last time I would ever see him and to my surprise I found myself wishing to exchange some sort of good-bye. The old man breathed easily through his nose tube, eyes seeing afar, a little smile on his face, his head cocked. He seemed to be listening to something pleasant. There would be no good-byes. God had sent messengers for him. He had forgotten me already.

Mubarak said, "Get out."

He looked as if he might plunge a syringe full of cyanide or plague into my arm if I did not depart immediately and take my revolting kaffir germs with me. I disembarked.

On the tarmac, while Captain Khaldun taxied the plane toward its takeoff point, I gave the impatient Turkmen the Saker falcon and what gold we had left in payment for their dead. They were not happy with the price. Kevin helped with the negotiations, speaking to the Turkmen in their own language, shouting above the whine of the jet engines as the plane taxied, pivoted, then hurtled down the runway for its takeoff.

It rose from the runway and climbed steeply, almost vertically, to avoid the hills in front of it, then banked sharply to avoid the pillar of flame dead ahead. And then, just as I was beginning to fear that the things had been discovered and removed, the grenades I had tossed into the left-hand engine detonated. The engine disappeared in a gout of flame and smoke. The plane shuddered and kept flying. I looked at Kevin, who had taken such an interest in Ibn Awad's oxygen tank. He was looking at his watch, as if timing something. A second later there was a second explosion, this one inside the cabin. Flames shot from the portholes. A wing fell off. Like a flaming checkmark, the plane cartwheeled, spewed parts, then disintegrated.

Kevin smiled a brilliant smile. "Oxygen," he said. "You really can depend on it."

The Turkmen were all looking upward and pointing to the shower of debris.

Kevin said, "Get ready."

One of his men pulled up beside us in a brand-new SUV.

Kevin said, "Go. Fast."

I jumped into the driver's seat and took the wheel. Tarik swept his mother into his arms and leaped in after me. Zarah and Paul took the back seat. Courtesy of Kevin, there was a loaded Kalashnikov for every passenger. We drove away. Kevin and his men made no attempt to interfere with the Turkmen who started to pursue us. It was the Old Boys on the hilltop who got us away. They dropped half a dozen mortar shells on the Turkmen, over-turning a couple of their vehicles. The survivors turned around and fled.

It was only my imagination, of course, but I thought I heard schoolboy cheering from the hilltop.

EPILOGUE

Paul Christopher decided to remain dead to everyone except his mother and Tarik and Zarah. The four of them went off together, where I do not know and will not follow. It is my hope that I will see Paul and Zarah again, but if this doesn't work out we will always have Uzbekistan, not to mention Xinjiang and the several other places where it would be unwise of their little family to settle down.

After we returned to the United States, we Old Boys saw little of each other. We had not really been friends before our search for the grail, just a bunch of fellows who had lived the same life and had more or less the same scores to settle. We did not so much drift apart, as soldiers do after a war, as doze back into ennui. On the whole, I think, we were happier than we might have been if we had not committed this one last folly. Everyday life is a cover identity for operational types. Inside the golfer, the backyard chef, the fond grandfather, the cutthroat remembers what is hidden and listens for the phone to ring at midnight and the muffled voice he knew so well to say, "You're needed in Berlin." Most of us had never really expected the phone to ring again, so Jack and Charley and Harley and David and Ben, and I most of all, had reason to be grateful to Paul Christopher for one last trip on the expense account.

With the proceeds of the sale of my house in Georgetown, I lived a comfortable life. Washington did not seem the place to do this. I moved to the Harbor, the family homestead in the Berkshires and rattled around in the company of ghosts whose measured tread across the squeaky attic floor I had known since childhood. Living alone, I limited myself to two vodkas per day, sometimes dared to eat a peach, and cast my mind entirely in the future, which was a tuneful Ruritania in relation to the scorched continents of my several pasts.

It was Harley, naturally, who decided that a reunion was in order. He handled all the arrangements and one November day, the anniversary of the memorial service for the vermilion urn that supposedly contained Paul's ashes, the Old Boys arrived. They seemed older, smaller, quieter, less opinionated. Conversation lagged. There was no reason to tell one another what we already knew, which was that whatever we had done did not really matter. Our work did not exist, had never existed, not in the annals of history or in the memory of those who had asked us to do it. All of it, going back to our dewy youth, was a laugh, a prank, a game, and like any other game, the one we had just played, our last, had not really changed a thing. There was no *remember the day Horace and Kevin blew up the same airplane*, no mention of the album of odd new friends we'd made on our travels, then lost forever. Or so we hoped, although we knew there would always be another bomb, another believer, another game of blindman's buff, and one day a different outcome.

During dinner, Christopherian in its undercooked simplicity—smoked fish, cold soup, rare meat, and the inevitable asparagus—we drank several bottles of Montrachet and Romanée Contis from the well-stocked cellar that Paul had bequeathed to me. We talked about his taste for the pinot grape and his luck with women. At sunset we walked up the hill to the family burial ground, a bottle of Perrier-Jouët in an ice bucket, to drink a toast on Christopher's grave.

What, Horace? You actually went so far as to mark a fake grave with his name?

Not me—Stephanie, for whom one burial at Arlington had not been enough. She had saved a cupful of what she insisted were his ashes and planted them here and raised a handsome polished stone with Paul's name and dates carved upon it. I found the thing when I came back from Kazakhstan, and I guess you could say that in a way, for Stephanie at least, Paul had been fastened to the earth at last. In two places, with a third yet to be designated—and if I knew Paul, unmarked.

I poured the bubbly. Memories moved in the circle of dimming eyes that gazed down on Paul's monument, a last disguise written in stone.

"Old times, old friends, old everything," said Harley.

We drank. Plastic glasses bounced off the mock headstone. The champagne, as it should, left its half-sweet lingering aftertaste on the tongue.

TO THE READER

Old Boys is a work of fiction in which no reference is intended to anyone who ever lived or anything that ever happened. This disclaimer applies in particular to Ibn Awad, who appeared in two of my earlier novels, *The Better Angels* (1979) and *Shelley's Heart* (1997). In the earlier works, he sponsored a wave of suicide bombings, a flight of the imagination so bizarre thirty-five years ago that it was regarded by many an obstacle to the reader's ability to suspend disbelief. Conversely, some of the events described in the Amphora Scroll are based closely on the Gospel According to John. Where mere information is concerned I have, as usual, attempted to stick to the facts. For details of life, landscape and archeology in Xinjiang province, I drew on the recollections of Robert M. Poole and the writings of Tom Allen. Some details of life on a country estate in Hungary were suggested by András Nagy's review in the autumn 1999 issue of the *Hungarian Quarterly* of *The Memoirs of a "Proud Hungarian"* by Tibor Scitovsky. The material on falconry is drawn largely from the eleventh edition of *Encyclopedia Britannica* but also from memories of a long-ago friendship with a falconer who presented my children with a fully trained golden eagle from the Atlas mountains. (Their mother declined the gift.) For data on satellite tracking of the migration of the houbara bustard, I am indebted to an article in *Arabian Wildlife* by Thery Bailey and Dr. Fred Launay. The material on Soviet Naukograds was mined from the Web site globalsecurity.org. Details of "peaceful" underground nuclear tests in the USSR were drawn from nuclearweaponarchive.org. Everything else came from thin air.

C. McC.